About the Authors

City loving, book addict, peony obsessive, **Katrina Cudmore** lives in Cork, Ireland with her husband, four active children and a very daft dog. A psychology graduate, with a M.Sc. in Human Resources Katrina spent many years working in multinational companies and can't believe she is lucky enough now to have a job that involves daydreaming about love and handsome men! You can visit Katrina at www.katrinacudmore.com

USA Today bestselling author **Michelle Major** loves stories of new beginnings, second chances and always a happily ever after. An avid hiker and avoider of housework, she lives in the shadow of the Rocky Mountains with her husband, two teenagers and a menagerie of spoiled furbabies. Connect with her at www.michellemajor.com

USA Today bestselling author **Lynne Marshall** used to worry she had a serious problem with daydreaming, then she discovered she was supposed to write those stories! A late bloomer, she came to fiction writing after her children were nearly grown. Now she battles the empty nest by writing romantic stories about life, love, and happy endings. She's a proud mother and grandmother who loves babies, dogs, books, music, and travelling.

Wedding Belles

Wedding Belles: The Wedding Date

KATRINA CUDMORE

MICHELLE MAJOR

LYNNE MARSHALL

MILLS & BOON

First Published in Great Britain 2021
By Mills & Boon, an imprint of HarperCollins*Publishers,* Ltd
1 London Bridge Street, London, SE1 9GF

www.harpercollins.co.uk

HarperCollins*Publishers*
1st Floor, Watermarque Building,
Ringsend Road, Dublin 4, Ireland

WEDDING BELLES: THE WEDDING DATE © 2021 Harlequin Books S.A.

Second Chance with the Best Man © 2019 Katrina Cudmore
Always the Best Man © 2016 Michelle Major
Wedding Date with the Army Doc © 2016 Janet Maarschalk

ISBN: 978-0-263-30061-1

MIX
Paper from
responsible sources

FSC
www.fsc.org

FSC™ C007454

This book is produced from independently certified FSC™ paper to ensure responsible forest management.

For more information visit: www.harpercollins.co.uk/green

Printed and bound in Spain
by CPI, Barcelona

SECOND CHANCE WITH THE BEST MAN

KATRINA CUDMORE

To Majella, the best little sister in the world!

CHAPTER ONE

THE BEAST PRESSED his snout against Hannah McGinley's car window, the glass instantly fogging up. 'Good doggy, off you go, now,' Hannah called out, trying to sound in control but also cheerful—the last thing she wanted to do was anger this beast any further. Her arrival on the driveway of Château Bonneval had already caused him to run alongside her car like an entry at the Grand National, his incessant barking almost causing her to drive into one of the hornbeam trees lining the long avenue.

As a farmer's daughter from Shropshire, she'd been told time and time again she'd no cause to be so scared, but no amount of cajoling from her family had ever rid her of her terror of even the smallest of dogs, never mind the donkey-sized version staring at her right now as though he couldn't wait to sink his teeth into her.

Looking in the direction of the front door of the château, Hannah willed someone to come out and rescue her. Surely they had heard the beast's hound-from-hell baying?

Not for the first time, Hannah wondered at her decision to agree to travel to France to act as the celebrant at her best friend Lara's wedding blessing. An easy, joyful decision in most circumstances, but not when you had dated and fallen in love with the best man and brother to the groom, Laurent Bonneval, only for him to end it all. And the worst part of it all was that the wedding was taking place in his home—Château Bonneval. Why couldn't it at least be at a neutral venue? Her only hope was that they would be surrounded by others all weekend and she would manage to project the air of calm professionalism she'd been rehearsing ever since Lara and François had travelled to London from Manchester, where they lived, just to ask her to be their wedding celebrant.

Though moved beyond words that they trusted her to perform their wedding blessing, especially given the fact that she was so new to being a celebrant—this would only be her fourth wedding—she'd asked if they were really, *really* sure it was she they wanted to be the one to perform the ceremony. Lara and François had exchanged a tentative glance before Lara had leant across the table of Hannah's local Richmond coffee shop, and touched her arm. 'You've been my best friend since we were seven.' Pausing, Lara had given her a half-smile, one that had asked Hannah to understand, to trust her. 'It would make our day even more magical to have you bless our marriage.'

Tears had blinded Hannah for a moment as she'd remembered how Lara had waded in on her first day at Meadlead Primary School and told Ellie Marshall and her gang to mind their own business when they had interrogated Hannah during the break with endless questions as to who she was, why she was joining the school in the middle of term, why she was so skinny. Frozen inside, confused by everything in her life, Hannah had been taken aback at just how grateful she was to Lara when she'd led her away from her interrogators. For weeks after, she'd remained silent. And while that had garnered her endless suspicious glances and whispered words behind cupped hands from the rest of class, Lara had cheerfully chatted away, her quirky humour and buoyant outlook on life thawing Hannah's numb heart.

That day in the café in Richmond, Hannah had turned to François, her heart as usual jolting in remembrance— some of François's features were so like Laurent's: the thick dark wavy hair, the strong and proud Gallic jawline, the wide, high cheekbones, the clean blade of a nose. 'Will…?' She tried to form the word Laurent, but it stuck in her throat and refused to budge. Eventually she managed to mutter, through a false smile, 'Will having me as the celebrant be okay with all of your family?'

François's eyes were different, a softer, more forgiving blue, none of the striking, pain-inducing brilliance of Laurent's. The care in his eyes had matched his gentle tone when he had answered, 'Laurent is to be my best man,' but Hannah had still felt it like a whip to her heart.

She'd looked away from the discomfort in both Lara's and François's expressions, hating that they had been put in this position. Their wedding should be a carefree celebration, not tainted by the fact that she'd foolishly fallen in love with Laurent, confusing his Gallic charm and romantic gestures for a sign that he'd felt what she did, that he too had wanted more.

In the months after he'd left London to return to the family business and château in Cognac, telling her before he left that he didn't want to continue their relationship, she'd puzzled over the overwhelming effect he'd had on her. The pain, the disappointment, the humiliation had been so engulfing she'd struggled to comprehend it all. Was it the fact that he was the first man she'd ever truly fallen in love with? Which admittedly was pretty tragic at the age of twenty-nine. But up until then, she'd never met anyone who had quickened her heart, who had communicated so much with a glance, who intrigued her.

At first she'd resisted the chemistry between them, her age-old need to protect herself holding him at arm's length. But in truth she'd been changing and had been more receptive to allowing someone into her life. She'd chased security and stability throughout her early twenties, desperately needing the safety of establishing her career in finance and buying her own apartment. But as she neared thirty, she'd realised she wanted more. A more free life, a more optimistic life. One of taking chances and not being so afraid. And into this new way of thinking and daring to dream had walked Laurent Bonneval. The brother of her best friend's new boyfriend. And he'd swept her off her feet. But ten months later he'd left her with a broken heart.

But that heart was now mended and firmly closed to Laurent Bonneval's charms.

Hannah jumped as the beast's tail hit against her door panel as he turned and bounded away, disappearing around one of the château's fairy-tale turrets that sat at each corner of the four-storey building.

She breathed out a sigh of relief. But then her heart plummeted to the car floor. From around the corner, sprinting at first, slowing to a jog when he took in her car, came Laurent, the beast at his side.

Stopping, he raised a hand to shield his eyes from the low evening sun. Behind him his shadow spilt across the gravelled drive, his tall, broad frame exaggerated.

She waited for him to move. Tried not to stare at the fact that he was wearing only running shorts that revealed the long length of his powerful legs and a lightweight vest top that showcased the taut, muscular power of his broad shoulders and gym-honed arms. His skin glistened with perspiration.

Heat formed in her belly.

He moved towards her car.

Her heart somersaulted.

She grasped for the window control and buzzed down her window a couple of inches, only then realising how stifling the car had become as she'd been held hostage by the beast. She longed to run a hand through her hair, check her make-up in the mirror. But she resisted giving him any sign that she cared how she looked in his eyes.

He came to a stop a few feet away from the car. The beast came to heel at his command. 'Hannah...' Her heart pinged at the concern in his eyes. 'Are you okay?'

The low, intimate sound of his voice almost undid her. Memory after memory rushed through her brain—how he used to leave her voicemails that had her blush and giggle. His mouth against her ear when they would be out with others, whispering a compliment, a promise. The Saturday mornings when they used to cycle to their favourite French bakery in Putney Heath and eat breakfast while playfully flirting, her legs trembling when his fingers would stroke her hand, her arm, her cheek, before he would suggest that they head home. His murmured words when they made love afterwards that had swelled in her heart and burst like joyful bubbles in her bloodstream.

Hannah breathed in deeply. She was over him. She had to remember that fact. Her focus now was on deciding which direction her life should take. Stay in her career in finance either in London or Singapore or take the risk of becoming a full-time wedding celebrant in Spain. Her old cautious side told her to hold on to her regular income and secure career but deep inside of her she wanted to be free to make her own decisions away from the confines of corporate life, to make a difference by being an integral part of one of the most important days in any person's life.

She was here to support Lara. To celebrate with her and François. Laurent Bonneval was just a minor aggravation in what should be a gloriously happy weekend.

Now was the time to enact the calm professionalism she'd sworn she would adopt for the weekend. Unfortunately her trembling hands and somersaulting stomach didn't appear to have received that particular memo.

She buzzed down her window a fraction more. Nodded in the direction of the beast. 'I'd appreciate it if you'd lock him away.'

Something unyielding kicked in Laurent's chest at the coolness of Hannah's tone and stony expression. He pointed in the direction of the stables; at his command Bleu ambled away to where he slept alongside the horses.

Hannah's gaze followed Bleu's every step and even when he disappeared from view, her gaze remained fixed in that direction. 'Will he come back?'

He edged closer to her door, crouched over to speak to her in the small gap of the window. 'I heard him barking—I'm sorry if he scared you.'

She shook her head as though to deny any suggestion she'd been scared. 'Is he yours?'

'Yes.'

She grimaced at that. He knew that she was scared of dogs. He cursed himself for not having locked Bleu away. Lara had told him Hannah was due to arrive around this time but Bleu had looked so despondent when he'd led him to his kennel earlier, Laurent had relented and allowed him to accompany him as usual on his evening run. 'Despite appearances, he's as soft as a marshmallow. He just wanted to say hello to you.'

Hannah shook her head, clearly not believing him. 'He's terrifying—I've never seen anything like him.'

'He's a Grand Bleu de Gascogne. He has a very affectionate temperament.' Moving to the car door, he opened it. Hannah's gaze shot back to the corner of the château where Bleu had disappeared and then back to him. He gave her a smile of encouragement. 'He won't come back, I promise. You can trust me on that.'

Her forehead bunched and her mouth dropped into an even deeper scowl.

For long seconds she stared at him unhappily, heat appearing on her high cheekbones, but then with a toss of her head she yanked her handbag off the passenger seat and stepped out of the car.

In the silence that followed he cursed François. When François had told him that Hannah was to be their wedding celebrant he'd been incredulous. François knew of their history, how uncomfortable it would be for them both, but François, usually so sanguine, had refused to change his mind in the face of Laurent's demand that someone else take on the role. His only compromise was his pledge that he and Lara would be present in the château at all times over the weekend to smooth any awkwardness between him and Hannah.

'Your journey—was it okay?'

Hannah shrugged at his question and moved to the boot of her car. 'I'd like to go inside and see Lara.'

By her tone, he knew she was as keen as he was for the others to be present in the château. But once again, his father had decided to make life difficult for everyone around him. He followed her to the boot of the car and lifted out her suitcase. 'François and Lara called me earlier—there's been a change of plans. They're now staying in the family apartment in Bordeaux overnight. Lara tried calling you but she couldn't get through.'

Her expression appalled, Hannah pulled her phone from her handbag, 'I'm having problems connecting to the French network.' Then with an exasperated breath she asked, 'Why are they staying in Bordeaux?'

'Apparently my father had already made a restaurant booking for them and refuses to cancel. He wants to show Lara and her parents some of the city's nightlife.'

Her head turning in the direction of the château, she asked uneasily, 'So who's staying here tonight?'

'Just you and me.'

Her eyes widened with horror.

Irritation flared inside him. He'd known she wouldn't be keen for his company, but did she have to make it so obvious?

But then his indignation sank into guilt. He and he alone was the cause of all this tension. The least he could do was try to make this weekend somewhat tolerable for them both.

Leading her in the direction of the main entrance, he said, 'Let me show you to your room. All of the château staff have this evening off as they will be working long hours in the coming days with the wedding.' Inside the coolness of the double-height hallway of the château, his desperation to take a shower and have something cool to drink abated a fraction. The heatwave hitting most of south-west France for the past week was becoming unbearable. He kicked the front door shut with his heel, knowing he was only trying to kid himself—the weather had little to do with how he was overheating.

This always happened when Hannah was nearby.

Pale pink sleeveless blouse tucked into mid-thigh-length lemon shorts, plain white plimsolls on her feet, thick and glossy brown hair tied back into a high ponytail, she was all delicious curves and sweetness.

He uttered a low curse to himself. He knew he'd hurt her. She deserved better than him remembering how incredible it was to hold her, to feel her soft curves. But in truth, their relationship had been built on a bed of intoxicating mutual attraction.

He'd seen it flare in her eyes in the moments after they had first met, their handshake lasting a few seconds longer than necessary, neither trying to pull away.

That first day, as they'd sailed on his yacht, *Sirocco,* which had then been moored out of Port Solent but was now moored out of Royan, Hannah had been friendly but he could tell that she was avoiding being alone with him. He'd wanted to shrug off her indifference but in truth her reticence had intrigued him and the intelligence in her eyes and her close friendship with Lara had had him wanting to know her better.

She had turned down his invitation to meet for a drink later in the week.

So he'd orchestrated it for her to attend a dinner party he'd thrown in his Kensington town house. He'd hoped to impress her with his cooking but she'd left early, saying she had an early flight to Paris in the morning. As he'd walked her out to her awaiting taxi, for the first time ever, he'd felt tongue-tied. All night he'd been unable to stop staring across the table at her, her natural warmth that was evident behind her initially reserved nature, her genuineness, her authenticity lighting something inside him. On the few occasions she had looked in his direction, he'd seen that spark of attraction again, but she'd always snatched her gaze away. That night of the dinner party, he'd let her go, without pressing his lips to her cheek as he'd ached to, something deep inside him telling him he had to wait until she was ready to accept the spark between them.

Their paths had crossed several times in the months that had followed. He'd used to playfully remind her that his offer of meeting for a drink was still on the table but she would smile and turn away.

And then, one day, when they had all gone swimming in the Solent after another day sailing on his yacht, *Sirocco*, she'd watched him dive from the rail. When he'd emerged from the water deliberately close to her, her initial frown that had spoken of some deep internal turmoil had transformed into a gentle smile and she'd softly said, 'I think I'm ready for that drink.'

He'd trod the cold English Channel water, grinning widely, not caring that everyone else in the party could see his delight. He'd wanted to stay there for ever, staring into Hannah's soulful brown eyes, his heart beating wildly in delight and anticipation that had been more than about the desire to tug her gorgeous bikini-clad body towards him.

Now he led her up the main marble staircase of the château to the second floor where, at the end of the corridor, he opened the door to her bedroom. Hannah walked inside, her gaze widening as she took in the antique jade hand-painted wallpaper, the Louis XV furniture.

He stayed at the doorway. They had dated for over ten months. The chemistry and intense attraction never waning, escalating in fact. But as they'd grown closer, as his heart had begun to need her, panic had set in. Laurent didn't believe in love and commitment. When he'd been twelve, François ten, his father had left the family home to conduct an affair. The following year his mother had done the same. And in the years that had followed his father had disappeared from the family home at least once a year to continue his affairs. The affairs, the hurt they had inflicted on everyone around them, had poisoned Laurent for ever against any thought of commitment in his own life.

His panic had soared when he'd visited Hannah's family one weekend and seen their love and devotion to one another. How could he ever bring her into the toxic mix of his own family, which was so full of unspoken anger and accusations? And his panic had soared even more when Hannah had told him of her plans to become a wedding celebrant. At first he'd laughed, thinking she was joking. But she'd been serious. The woman he'd thought of as being as career-minded and as focused on success as he was, who had never given any indication that she was looking for commitment, wanted to be the officiator of the institution he'd no regard for—marriage.

Increasingly he'd realised just how incompatible they were despite their attraction and laughter and warmth for one another. And then he'd learnt of his father's stroke and his need to return to Cognac to head up the family business. For years he'd waited on the sidelines to be given the role of CEO, beyond frustrated at the decline in the Cognac House's market share under his father's neglectful leadership. Bonneval Cognac had been in existence since the seventeenth century. It was Laurent's legacy and one he was determined to restore to its rightful place as the most exclusive cognac house in the world. It was a promise he'd made to his beloved grandfather before he died, a man who had despaired at his own son's disloyalty and irresponsibility, not only with the business, but with his own family.

Knowing that there was no future for him and Hannah, Laurent had ended their relationship when he'd returned to France. It had been a gut-wrenching conversation, and he'd seen the pain and confusion in her eyes, but it was not a conversation he regretted. Hannah deserved someone who actually believed in love and commitment. Someone who reflected the love and devotion and stability of her own background.

This weekend would be awkward. But they needed to somehow build a new relationship as their paths would cross time and time again in the future. Maybe having to spend time together this evening was an opportune time to begin that process. He was the one who had messed up by allowing their relationship to become too intense—the least he could do was ensure that the next few days were as painless as possible. For both of their sakes.

'I had planned on eating out tonight—I need to go and check on my wedding present to François and Lara first, but there's a restaurant nearby. Will you join me?'

CHAPTER TWO

HANNAH STUDIED LAURENT and marvelled at his ability to forget the past. It hurt her, angered her, but part of her envied him for it. Wasn't it what she was striving to achieve herself, after all? For a moment she was about to say no to his invite. The last thing she wanted to do was spend time alone with him.

Standing in the doorway, a shoulder propped against the frame, his arms crossed on his chest, his expression untroubled, he waited for her response. He was still the best-looking man she'd ever met. And damn it, she was still attracted to him. As her mum would say, *figgity, figgity, fig.* Well, if he could shrug off the past then so could she. She popped her suitcase on the luggage rack. Flipped the lid open, pulled out her laptop and placed it on the desk by the window, determined to have some control.

Opening up the laptop, she asked him for the Wi-Fi password and, logging in, she said, 'I'm doing an online thirty-day yoga challenge and I want to do today's session now. I'll need a shower afterwards.' She glanced behind her in his direction. 'I won't be ready for at least an hour so don't wait for me if that doesn't suit you.'

'I didn't know you practised yoga.'

She shrugged. 'It helps me to let go of all those small things that irritate me in life.'

He made a grunting sound low in his throat before saying, 'I'll see you downstairs in an hour,' and then walked away.

She closed the door and leant heavily against it. This room, the entire château, was beyond incredible. She'd stolen glances into the endless rooms they had passed downstairs, her breath catching at their delicate elegance.

It was hard to comprehend that Laurent lived here. All alone. She knew from Lara that his parents had moved to a lodge on the thousand-acre estate after he'd returned from England to take up the role of CEO. She'd heard Lara's description of this magnificent château, had known of the world-famous cognac brand, but until now she hadn't fully grasped his family's wealth and standing.

This was not her world. It brought out all the inadequacies she so desperately tried to keep hidden.

Now, more than ever, she was glad that she'd never told Laurent about her early childhood. How could someone who came from this background ever understand her? Not believe she was tainted by it?

She was even more grateful that she'd never fully opened her heart to him, dared to tell him she loved him. She'd felt too vulnerable, too unsure of what his response would be—which should have told her everything she needed to know about their relationship. Though deeply charismatic, Laurent somehow managed to never fully reveal himself or show any vulnerability. For most of their whirlwind relationship she'd been blind to that, too excited by the fact that this gorgeous man wanted her in his life. He'd been attentive and fun with a determined and self-possessed streak she'd found utterly compelling. But he'd never really answered her questions about his background, what he wanted in the future. And in their last conversation he'd told her that he couldn't give her commitment, a permanent relationship.

Thankfully she'd managed to stop herself from pleading that she was happy to keep things casual, knowing that in truth she only wanted to buy more time to persuade him that he could commit. At least she hadn't followed that particular deluded path of trying to change another person.

After her yoga and shower, she changed into a knee-length white shift dress, a narrow gold belt cinching in the waist. Brushing out her hair, she let it hang loose and applied some make-up. About to leave, she paused to stare out of one of the four windows in the room. Below her room, set amidst a wide purple border of lavender, sat a huge swimming pool. Beyond the pool an immaculate lawn ran down to a tree-lined river. Laurent used to talk about that river, the Charente, when he spoke about home, which admittedly was a rare occurrence. In London, his whole focus had seemed to be on his career as a fund manager and the busy social life he'd created in his adopted city. He'd lived life with abandon, hungry to experience new places, new things—she'd travelled more in her short time with him than she'd ever previously done.

Downstairs she busied herself with staring at the landscape paintings of country scenes hanging in abundance in the hallway as she waited for him, and when his footsteps tapped, tapped, tapped on the marble stairs as he jogged downwards, she realised how much she missed his endless energy and enthusiasm for life. She gave him the briefest of smiles when he came alongside her, tried to ignore how good he looked with his damp hair, his pale blue shirt open at the neck worn over lightweight navy trousers, tried to ignore how his freshly applied aftershave flipped her heart with the memory of waking to find him crouched beside her, dressed for work, a cup of tea in one hand, a plate with toast in the other, his brilliant smile turning her weak with happiness.

'Ready to go?'

She nodded to his question and followed him to the front door. As he was about to pull the ancient handle that opened one side of the heavy double oak doors she could not help but ask, 'Will he be out there?'

He turned, confused at first by her question, but then reached out as though to touch her forearm. Hannah jerked back, unable to bear the thought of him touching her. Afraid for how she would react. For the briefest of moments he looked thrown by her reaction before he dropped his hand. Opening the door, he answered, 'No. Bleu knows to stay in his kennel when I send him there.'

Tentatively she followed him out onto the gravelled driveway. 'Did you inherit him from your parents?'

He walked to the side of the château, past a parked four-by-four, and opened the doors of one of the five stone-crafted single-storey outbuildings that were set back from the château. Daylight flooded the building to reveal a silver sports car. Hannah swallowed the temptation to exclaim at its beauty.

'I didn't inherit Bleu but this car I did inherit. My father is an avid vintage-car collector. He moved most of his collection to an outbuilding at the lodge but left this car here as there wasn't enough room for it. He wanted to sell it but my mother persuaded him to keep it within the family. I don't get to use it as much as I'd like to…' he paused and glanced out at the blue, cloudless evening sky '…but this evening is the perfect night to take it for a run.'

Hannah watched him manually lower the soft top of the car, the pit of disappointment in her stomach at his answer having her eventually ask, 'So where did you get Bleu?'

In the initial days and weeks after Laurent had returned to France she'd held out vain hope that he might call, change his mind, her heart slowly splintering apart, but after a month of silence, her heart a void, she'd accepted that it was truly over between them. But somehow, the thought of Laurent choosing Bleu, knowing her fear of dogs, spoke more than a year of silence of him moving on from her.

After he'd left she'd been numb, but eventually, when she'd grown exhausted by the emptiness inside herself, she'd insisted that her heart mend. She'd worked harder at fixing her heart than at anything she'd ever tackled before. She had thrown herself into her work and her training course to become a wedding celebrant. She'd filled every minute of every day with work and exercise and reading and meeting up with friends and family.

Only once had she slipped up and shown just how deeply devastated she was. She'd taken her newly acquired wedding celebrant certificate to show to her parents on the day she graduated from her course. Her dad had been out at the weekly livestock market in their local town, but her mum had made a fuss of her achievement, even opening a celebratory bottle of champagne. In the comforting cocoon of her childhood home, once the euphoria of achieving the qualification had worn off, she'd realised how tired and lonely she really was. And when her mum, with her usual gentle perceptiveness, had asked how she was, the tears had come. Hannah had fought their spilling onto her cheek, not wanting to upset her mum. She'd just nodded instead at what her mum said in response to her hiccupped short explanation before quickly changing the subject to a much happier topic—

her sister Cora's pregnancy and the much-anticipated arrival of the first grandchild into the family.

Later, back in London and alone in her apartment, she'd reflected on what her mum had said and taken some solace from her observation that at least she was risking her heart now and living life as she should be, with its invariable ups and downs, joy and disappointments. Hannah had been taken aback; she hadn't realised that her mum saw through how much she was protecting herself. Which was silly really—her parents were the most empathetic people she knew. Of course they understood why she struggled so much to trust others.

She'd met her parents when she was seven. She hadn't wanted to be in their house; she hadn't wanted their smiles, their kind voices. Their encouragement to eat her food, to play with their daughters, Cora and Emily. She had wanted to be back in her old house. With her birth parents. But the police had taken her away and now she had to live with new people. She'd been so scared. Above all else she'd hated change. Because it meant things might get even worse. She'd known how her birth parents operated, but not these strangers.

Now opening the passenger door for her, Laurent moved to the other side of the car. It was only when they were both seated inside the car that he turned and answered her question. 'I found Bleu one night when out running in the woods of the estate. I heard his whimpering first—the vet believes he ate some poison a local farmer may have put down. He was already an undernourished stray. We didn't think he'd pull through. But he did. He's a gentle giant. But I'll make sure he's locked away while you're here.'

Hannah swallowed at the tenderness of his tone, at the emotion in his eyes. Torn between her deep fear of dogs and the guilt of locking away this poor animal who had been through so much already, she answered, 'No, don't, that's not fair on him. I'll keep out of his way.'

Turning on the engine, which started with a low throb, he turned and regarded her. 'I can introduce him to you if you want.'

She jerked in her seat, instantly terrified. 'No, don't.'

He gave her a concerned look before backing the car out of the garage. When he'd turned it in the direction of the drive he said, 'You never really explained to me why you're so scared of dogs.'

She shrugged. 'I've always been petrified of them, it's just one of those things.' Which wasn't true. She could remember a time when she wasn't scared. But like so much of her early childhood, the story of why she feared dogs was one she'd locked away inside herself years ago.

Laurent's gaze narrowed. For a moment he looked as though he was going to probe further but then, putting the car in gear, he sped off down the drive and out onto the narrow lanes of the Cognac countryside.

The wind whipped against her hair. She tied it back with an elastic band from her handbag. Despite her anxiousness about the entire weekend, for a moment she felt exhilarated as they zipped along and she smiled to herself as the force of the warm air blasted against her skin. The car was small. Laurent's thigh was only inches away from hers. She tried to focus on the low hedges they sped by, the endless bright fields of smiling sunflowers, the gorgeous order of vineyards with their row upon row of vines, and not the way Laurent's large hands clasped the wheel, the assured way he handled the car. They slowed behind a tractor. Hannah felt a jolt of nostalgia for her Shropshire childhood. The rides with her dad out on his tractor. The carefree days filled with her dad's laughter,

the late evenings of drawing in bales of hay. But even
then a part of her could not help wonder how she'd managed to escape from what came before, wondering if one
day she'd have to go back to it.

Laurent slowed as they approached a village. The road
narrowed even further to wind its way past pale stone
houses with light blue shutters, then a *boulangerie* shut
for the evening, a bar with some locals sitting outside
who waved to Laurent as he passed by. At the other end
of the village he pulled into a narrow driveway, a plaque
with the name Villa Marchand on the entrance pillar,
the viburnum hedging dense with white delicate flowers
brushing lightly against the sides of the car. And then a
two-storey house appeared, its blue shutters tied back.
Jasmine and wild roses threaded their way up the outer
walls, curling around the Juliet balconies on the upper
floor. To the side of the house stood an ancient weeping
willow tree on the banks of a river.

Laurent parked the car and got out. Hannah followed
him to the front door. He opened it to reveal a stone-
flagged sitting room, large white sofas surrounding a
heavy teak chest that acted as a coffee table. The walls
were painted in a soft white; a large grey painted mirror
hung over the open fireplace.

'Why are we here?'

He frowned at her question as though he'd expected
her to already know the answer. And then, stepping into
the room, he said, 'This is my present to François and
Lara. A summer home. It's where François proposed to
Lara. I'm hoping it will tempt them to visit more often.'

She followed him into the room, leaving the front door
ajar. 'You miss François?'

He turned at her question. Her heart lodged in her

throat as his blue eyes twinkled and his wide generous mouth lifted in a smile. 'Don't tell him.'

Before she could stop herself she heard herself say, 'You could always move back to England to be closer to him.'

She turned away from how his expression fell, winced when he said, 'My life is here now. I'll never leave Cognac again.'

Picking up a small bronze figurine of a cat from the side table, she said, 'That's quite a turnaround from before.' She lifted her gaze to study him. 'You used to say that there was nothing here for you.'

'Things change.'

'But not people. They just reveal their true selves to you.'

'I never—'

Regretting instantly the bitterness of her voice, that she'd revealed her upset with him, Hannah interrupted with a forced laugh, 'You're certainly putting my wedding present of a set of organic cotton bath towels into the shade with this villa.'

Laurent shook his head. 'The infamous wedding list.' Pausing, he gave a smile. 'It has caused a lot of amusement amongst my parents' friends.'

Hannah swallowed a giggle, imagining the other guests' bewilderment at some of the items Lara and François had listed. 'I think water filters, recycled furniture and garden equipment for their allotment are very practical gifts to ask for.'

Laurent's eyebrow lifted. 'My father had to explain to a friend of his who's a guest at the wedding what a wormery is. Trust me, it was a very long telephone conversation.'

Hannah smiled, trying so hard to pretend that she was

finding all this easy, a bittersweet thickness forming in her throat at how easily they fell back into their shared humour and banter.

Silence fell between them. Laurent's smile receded. The room closed in around them. She looked away from him. But even then she felt the force of his gaze. Heat grew on her cheeks, a rumble of attraction stirred in her stomach and, when she glanced back at him, it exploded at the rigidity of his expression—his square jawline fixed, his dark thick brows drawn downwards, his mouth stern. She'd at first been drawn to his easy charm but it was this more private, serious-minded side of him—the responsible older brother who was so protective of his only sibling—this self-assured and professionally astute man she'd fallen in love with.

His jaw moved a fraction. The chemistry that had always been so strong, so potent between them was at work again.

She willed herself to walk away, to break the silence, regretting having come here.

His mouth tightened. The knot of fear and anticipation twisted even tighter in her stomach.

'How have things been for you?'

She jolted in surprise at his question. His voice, as always, like warm honey trickling through her insides. For a moment she was about to answer in a similarly low intimate tone, but caught herself in time and instead, with a flourish of bonhomie that took even her by surprise, she walked away, pretending to inspect the books in the bookcase. 'Great. I've been busy. Emily married late last autumn in Granada in Spain. We had a great week there—it really is a beautiful city and it was so nice for all of my family to have spent the time together.' Her forced smile was replaced by a genuine one when she added, 'And Cora had a little girl. She's called Diana. She's gorgeous. I'm totally smitten by her.'

Laurent smiled at her description. For the briefest moment, the old ease that had existed between them flared. Hannah was thrown; her smile faded, and disappeared altogether when she thought of her sisters' happiness. She loved her sisters with all her heart and would never begrudge them anything...but faced with how content they were, how successfully they managed their personal lives, Hannah not only felt lonely but also doubted she would ever manage to achieve a similar happiness.

Laurent winced as the wistfulness in Hannah's expression was replaced with an unsettling sadness. She wanted what her sisters had. Marriage, children, a united family. The things he could never give to her.

He gestured for her to follow him into the kitchen, a sudden urge to keep moving, to be distracted by doing things, taking hold. 'Let me show you around. I had an interior designer manage the renovations and furnish the rooms but I could use your advice as to whether there are additional items Lara would like.'

Hannah walked around the island unit of the hand-painted kitchen, her gaze shifting out onto the garden and the river beyond. 'Have they seen the villa since you redecorated?'

Earlier, when she'd asked why they were here, for a moment he'd been thrown by the fact that she didn't know. Somehow it felt as though she should know everything that was happening in his life. 'Not since their last visit. They had wanted to stay here before the wedding day but I told François that there was a problem with the electricity.'

'When are you going to tell them?'

'I'll give them the key on their wedding day. They can spend their first night here together.'

The weariness in her expression faded and the warmth he'd so adored about her in London appeared. She gestured around her, towards the kitchen and then the garden outside. 'Lara is going to be so happy. She has always wanted a garden of her own. Right now they only have their allotment and that's miles away from their apartment.' In this enthusiasm, her happiness for her friend, he realised how much he'd missed her. He missed this warmth, her laughter, her sheer presence.

Pointing towards a notebook hanging from the kitchen's noticeboard, he said, 'Take a look upstairs and note down anything you think I should get the interior designer to add.' Then, backing towards the garden door that led out onto the newly laid patio, he added, 'I need to check out some work that was carried out in the garden today.'

Outside, he walked across the stone patio—as he'd guessed, the contractor had done a good job—hating his need to get away from Hannah. From her smile. Hating the reality of what he'd walked away from.

He was standing on the riverside steps when she came out and joined him ten minutes later, handing him a bullet-point list in her neat and precise handwriting. She'd listed bathrobes, champagne, Belgian chocolates, decaffeinated coffee and a double hammock. He lifted an eyebrow at that last item.

Hannah laughed and gestured towards the giant willow. 'It'd be fun for them if it was hung from the willow across to the boundary trees. I can see them lying there on their wedding night staring up at the stars before going to bed.' Her voice trailed off and her gaze dropped down to the new wooden rowing boat that he'd asked his interior designer to organise.

Heat radiated from the stone of the river steps. There was a vague creaking noise as the overheated house and earth shifted in expansion. But the heat on Hannah's cheeks, the heat in his belly, had nothing to do with the weather and everything to do with her mention of bed. In London, they would meet after work sometimes in the city, other times he would meet Hannah off her train in Richmond if he'd been travelling that day, with the intention of having a drink or a meal, a visit to the theatre, but more often than not they would head directly home and into bed and only surface hours later to eat before tumbling back into bed until the following morning.

Hannah had always craved chocolate after they had made love. She had a particular love for dark chocolate straight from the fridge. 'Do you still have an addiction to chocolate?'

Her head whipped around at his question, a spark of anger in her eyes. 'I try to stay away from things that aren't good for me these days.'

He forced himself to smile, knowing he deserved that comment.

She folded her arms, stared across the river towards the bank of poplars growing there. She bit her lip for a moment and paused in deep thought before saying, 'Now I know what's missing in the house—I couldn't put my finger on it for a while—family photographs. You should get some framed and placed around the house to add a personal touch. I can send you some of Lara and her family.' She paused and considered him. 'You don't think it's a good idea?'

He rubbed the back of his neck and admitted, 'I can't remember the last time my family had a photo taken together.'

She grimaced. 'Not with your dad being ill and everything.'

He didn't bother to tell her that it was probably close to a decade since they'd had a family photograph taken. In the years after he'd left home, Laurent had rarely returned to Château Bonneval, and when he had his visits had always been brief. Some briefer than others when he would leave almost immediately, completely frustrated when his father would refuse to listen to his advice on saving the business.

He walked down the steps and, pulling the boat towards himself, stepped into its hull and turned to Hannah. 'Let's go for dinner. The restaurant is a ten-minute row down the river.'

Hannah stepped back on the grassy verge and considered him. As she tilted her head to the side her ponytail swept against her shoulder, exposing the arched curve of her neck, and a memory of her giggling when he used to press his body to her back, place his lips on the tender skin of her neck, left him momentarily dizzy. The boat rocked beneath him. He jerked, almost losing his balance.

Hannah laughed. He shook his head at her amusement at his predicament and almost lost his balance again.

When she joined him on board she sat down as clumsily as possible, obviously in the hope of tipping him into the river.

Laurent effortlessly rowed against the light flow of the water and Hannah studied the neighbouring gardens they passed by, seeing in the long and narrow plots the unfurling of family life. A woman on a recliner reading a newspaper while her husband clipped a bay tree. A family of five sitting at the edge of the river eating dinner beneath a huge oak tree and stopping to wave hello as they passed by. Hannah wanted this domesticity but would it ever happen for her?

A surge of anger towards Laurent caught her by surprise. Why had he come into her life? Why, when she'd lowered her defences for the first time ever, thereby allowing herself to fall for a man, had he broken her heart? And as she watched him pull on the oars, his shirtsleeves rolled up, his forearm muscles bunching with each pull, her anger soared even more. She didn't want to be so aware of him, so giddy around him, so vulnerable, and her resolve that she would never let him get to her again hardened.

She needed to remember his faults. He liked to eat strong-smelling cheeses that had made her gag whenever she'd opened his fridge. He took work even more seriously than she did—how often had he cancelled dates or forgotten about them, to her annoyance? And despite his gregarious personality, in truth he was a closed book. She knew so little about his background, his family. And he had a birthmark on his bottom. Okay, so she'd admit that that was actually cute.

'You're starting to scare me.'

She jumped at his voice. 'What do you mean?'

'You look like you're trying to figure out the most effective way of murdering me. In fact, it reminds me of the evening your work colleagues came to a party in my house.'

Their first fight. 'You were over an hour late for your own party. My colleagues were wondering if you were a figment of my imagination.'

His eyes glinted. 'Ah, so, despite your denials to the contrary, you had been talking to them about me as I had suspected.'

I couldn't stop talking about you. I could see my col-

leagues' amusement as I recounted things you had said and done, day after day, but I was too giddy with amazement over you to stop. 'They wanted to see for themselves if your wine collection was as impressive as I said it was.' She smiled when she admitted, 'My senior partner especially. He was rather put out when he saw it was a much more extensive collection than his.'

And then she remembered what had happened that night after the others had left, how Laurent had made love to her in the moonlight that had streamed through the window and onto the floor of his bedroom, his eyes ablaze with passion and emotion.

She dropped her head. Inhaled against the disturbing mix of desire and pain that was grabbing her heart.

'How's work?'

She looked up at his softly spoken question. Had he guessed she was remembering that night on his bedroom floor? Her anger resurged. 'I've been offered a promotion which would involve a transfer to the Singapore office.'

Up ahead on a bend in the river, below a string of lights threaded through trees, a wooden sign on the riverbank announced that they had arrived at La Belle Epoque.

Laurent guided the boat towards the restaurant's river steps, nodding approvingly to her news. 'That's fantastic. When are you moving?'

He shifted the oars inside the boat, wood upon wood making a solid thump, a sound just like the thud her heart gave to his enthusiastic congratulations.

She gritted her teeth and eyed him, not caring at the hurt heat flaming in her cheeks. Did he not even feel a single pang that she would be moving so far away? How could he not realise how torn she was about leaving her family behind?

The move to Singapore was an incredible opportunity, but in truth, deep down, she was scared of being lonely... forgotten by her family.

'Are you going to accept?'

She shrugged at his question. 'Do you think I should?'

He considered her for a moment and then those blue eyes blazed with an ominous energy. 'Is something or somebody keeping you in London?'

She folded her arms. 'Perhaps.'

The blaze in his eyes intensified. 'Are you dating someone?'

She'd been on some dates during the past few months; wasn't getting back on the figurative horse the best way to get over a fall? By dating other guys she'd hoped that maybe she could rekindle the hope and optimism and openness that had been growing in her before she'd met Laurent, but her dates hadn't been a success. She'd felt too wary, had struggled to connect with them. Now she clung to the hope that maybe it was just a case that she'd tried dating too quickly and that with time she would be more open to a relationship...but she feared that maybe she would never find it inside herself to trust a man again. 'How about you? Are you seeing someone?' she countered.

Laurent stood and jumped onto the landing steps, jealousy coiling in his stomach. For the past year he'd immersed himself in work, driven by the need to prove himself as a worthy CEO, but now as he turned to find Hannah's eyes sparking with anger he realised it was also to distract himself from the pain he'd caused her. He held out his hand and Hannah reluctantly took it. When she leaped, her hand tightened for a split second on his but the moment her foot touched the step she snatched it away.

They stood facing each other, the air between them dense with tension.

Hannah's jawline tightened. 'So, are you dating someone?'

'I'm too busy with work.'

'You worked crazy hours in London—it didn't stop you dating then.'

'It's different now.'

'In what way?'

She was testing him, pushing him for an answer and he wasn't sure what her question really was.

'Running a family business is complicated.'

Her nose wrinkled at that.

He pulled in a breath and admitted, 'After what happened between us, I don't feel like dating.'

'Yet?'

Would he ever want to date again? Right now, he couldn't see himself wanting to ask another woman out. But he couldn't admit that to her so instead he simply shrugged.

She looked at him with a puzzled expression. 'You're the one who ended it.'

When he'd ended their relationship, he'd used the excuse of needing to focus on his new life in France. And the fact that they wanted different things in life, namely that he wasn't interested in marriage. He'd kept from her the actual reasons why he would never marry, how his trust in others had been destroyed as a teenager, because to do so would have meant revealing his true self to her, a self he spent most of the time trying to avoid.

They shifted apart at the sound of footsteps behind them. Gabriel, the owner of La Belle Epoque, greeted them warmly and guided them to an outdoor table with views of a weir and an old mill.

Local teenagers were playing in the river, laughing and calling to one another in the evening sunshine.

After Gabriel had taken their order and poured them a glass of white wine each, Hannah smiled as one of the teenagers swung over the river, whooping loudly before landing with an enormous splash in the water, which earned her applause from her gang. 'When we were teenagers and the weather was fine, I used to go down to the river that ran through our land with Cora and Emily to swim and hang out. Did you and François do the same?'

'We spent our summers with my grandparents in Paris.'

She placed her elbow on the table and balanced her chin in the cup of her hand. 'I thought Parisians left the city for the summer. Why didn't they come here?'

'My grandparents moved to Paris after my father took over the family business.' He stopped with the intention of saying no more, but thanks to Hannah's expectant silence he found himself eventually admitting, 'There were arguments. My grandfather didn't approve of how my father was running the business, so they moved away. When we were old enough I asked my grandfather if François and I could spend the summers with them in Paris.'

'Did your parents not mind?'

He couldn't help but give a rueful laugh. 'They were too busy to even notice we weren't around.'

She grimaced but then, ever the optimist, asked with excitement, 'Did you like Paris?'

'We both loved it. François even stayed and finished his final years of school there.'

Her brows shot up. 'Wow, I couldn't see my parents agreeing to that—they even struggled when we left for university. Your parents obviously encouraged you to be independent.'

She was reading the situation all wrong. Not surprising given her background. Once again this evening he felt torn between changing the subject and telling her about his family. Before, he'd never felt that compulsion. In London, he'd been able to block out his past, but being back in Cognac for the past year had stirred up all the memories and emotions of how betrayed he'd felt by his parents' affairs.

'Is everything okay? You seem upset.'

He started at Hannah's words. She'd always been so good at reading his moods.

'Our family life was rather chaotic. I persuaded François he would do better in a calmer environment.'

'Have you always been the protective older brother?'

He grinned at the playfulness of her question. 'Probably.'

Hannah grinned back and then in a flash memories and attraction danced between them.

His throat tightened.

Hannah twisted her wine glass around and around. 'It was a shame you couldn't make Lara and François's civil ceremony in London last week. I know François was disappointed but at least your father was well enough to travel with your mother.'

'I was travelling in Asia—promoting the House.'

She snorted, clearly not buying his answer. 'I reckon, given your views on marriage, that you were simply avoiding the ceremony.'

'That's possibly true too.' Seeing her smile of satisfaction that she'd called it right, he added, 'But before you accuse me of disloyalty or not playing my part, can I point out that there is no tradition here in France of there being a best man at weddings? But as Lara is keen to have her sister as her bridesmaid, to keep some British traditions, I have agreed to be the best man.'

She laughed at that. 'You make it sound as though you have agreed to take a place on a battlefield.'

Was marriage, commitment, trusting in others, so easy for her? 'Did you mind being asked to be the wedding celebrant?'

'I was honoured. What else did you expect?'

He wanted to say that he thought she should have said no to François and Lara. But instead he said, 'Are you actually enjoying the work? It can't be easy combining it with your day job.'

'You still don't understand why I want to be a celebrant, do you?'

'It's not the career direction a young and successful finance director usually takes.'

Their conversation was interrupted by one of the waiting staff arriving with their orders: *salade au saumon et l'avocat* for Hannah, double *carpaccio de boeuf* for himself.

After they had eaten for a few minutes in silence, Hannah placed her cutlery on her plate and said, 'I love being a wedding celebrant because I want to contribute something meaningful to people's lives.' She paused and looked at him with a determined pride. 'I need something positive and uplifting in my life.'

He lowered his own cutlery. 'I'm sorry that I hurt you.'

She sat back in her chair, folded her arms and stared towards the teenagers who were walking home through the meadow on the other side of the river. 'It's in the past.'

'We'll see each other in the future. I don't want to cause you any further hurt.' For reasons he didn't under-

stand he felt compelled to add, 'Nothing has changed…
there can be no future for us.'

Her gaze flew back to him. Anger now sparked in her
eyes. She stood. 'It's been a year. I'm over it… I'm over
you, Laurent. I've moved on. Don't overinflate your importance in my life.'

CHAPTER THREE

THE FOLLOWING DAY, leaving his Sales and Marketing director to wrap up a meeting with the buyers from an international airline in the tasting room, Laurent rushed back to his office located in the recently opened modern extension he'd commissioned last year. Designed by world-renowned architect, Max Lovato, the acclaimed building was his signal to the world that Bonneval Cognac was about to retake its positon as the most exclusive cognac brand in the marketplace.

A wide walkway joined the second floor of the old cognac warehouse to the executive floor of the new building. Max's vision of the walkway resembling a floating garden had been realised thanks to an extensive and lush planting scheme of mature trees and plants that had produced an eye-watering bill.

Laurent rolled his shoulders against the financial pressures that perched there permanently these days like an overloud and insistent chatterbox parrot. Only time would tell if his ambitious and costly expansion and marketing strategy would pay off. If they didn't make the projected sales figures he'd forecast for this year, things could get very difficult. He would even have to seriously consider selling a share of the business. Which in his eyes would be nothing less than abject failure.

His assistant, Mila, rose from her chair when he entered her outer office and gave him an apologetic smile. He shook his head as if to say that he understood why she'd called him out of his meeting—they both knew of old how obstinate his father was.

When he entered his office he gritted his teeth at the sight that welcomed him—his father sitting behind his desk flicking through his paperwork. When was he going to accept his retirement, that Laurent and not he was now the CEO of Bonneval Cognac?

'Ah, Laurent.' His father gave him a smile, the left side of his mouth not rising quite as high as the right. Laurent felt his frustration ease at this reminder of his father's stroke, but it flourished again when his father added, 'You took your time.'

Laurent breathed down his irritation. 'I was meeting with AML Airlines. We're trying to persuade them to carry our XO Exclusif in their first-class cabins.' Seeing his father's sceptical expression, he added, 'Unfortunately we have a lot of ground to make up for the way their contract was managed in the past.'

'It was not our fault that our competitors undercut us.'

He bit back the temptation to laugh bitterly at his father's poor defence and said instead, 'We didn't negotiate the contract renewal properly. We backed them into a corner where they had no choice but to go with the competition.' He paused, about to say that living off past glories and perceived status had no place in today's business world.

For long seconds he and his father glared at one another. But then a discreet cough from behind him had him spin around to find Hannah.

He nodded in acknowledgement of her presence and received a lukewarm smile in response. She was still angry with him for reiterating last night that they had no future together. But he'd needed to say it, for his sake as much as hers—there was too much lingering physical attraction between them, which, thrown into the mix of the crazy emotions that came with a wedding and their forced proximity over the weekend, could lead them to doing something that they both regretted. After their dinner last night they had travelled back to the château in silence and he'd left for work this morning before dawn, leaving a note to say that he'd taken Bleu to stay with his friend Phillippe for the duration of her visit.

'This morning I gave Hannah a tour of the House.' Laurent turned his attention to his father, who added, 'Hannah was all alone in the château when your mother and I returned from Bordeaux. François and Lara were delayed in the city.' His father shook his head in reprimand. 'We can't have our house guests not entertained, Laurent. It's your duty as a host to ensure they're well cared for. I had planned on taking Hannah to lunch now but your mother is insistent that I return to the château— she's getting much too stressed about this wedding. I want you to take Hannah to lunch instead.'

Laurent was about to say no. He'd a string of meetings this afternoon he'd yet to prepare for. But he could tell his father was waiting for him to object. His father relished arguing with him. And he certainly wasn't going to embarrass Hannah by having an argument over who would take her to lunch.

Before he could say anything, though, Hannah stood. 'Antoine, I'll drive you home.' She gestured to his paper-strewn desk. 'I'm sure Laurent is busy.' Giving him a brief smile, she turned towards the door.

His father walked after her. 'I don't need you to drive me. I called François and told him to collect me on his way back from Bordeaux. He and Lara are downstairs waiting for me. You should see more of the town. You can accompany me downstairs on the way. I need to rush, though—apparently François and Lara are late for a meeting with their wedding planner.'

Hannah looked at him helplessly. Obviously waiting for him to argue against taking her. His father, meanwhile, looked all set to have an argument with him. 'It'd be my pleasure to take you to lunch.'

Hannah regarded him curiously. 'You never liked to take lunch in London.'

She was right. In London he'd worked at a furious pace; he still did so here, but he somehow also managed to fit in lunch and regular runs. He regarded Hannah, only now realising how well his new life suited him despite the pressures of his role. Aware of his father's keen gaze on them both, Laurent shrugged. 'I guess Cognac and the way of life here has changed me.'

For a moment he thought Hannah was going to ask what he meant but instead she held out her arm for his father to take.

Laurent grimaced and waited for his father to bat Hannah's arm away, as he did any other offer of help—he'd even thrown the walking stick his physio had given him out of one of the château's windows one day, and had grumbled like crazy when Bleu had gone and fetched it back.

But instead of rejecting Hannah's offer of assistance, his father placed his hand on her arm and Laurent followed them as they moved in the direction of the elevator, his father's limp slowing their progress.

Downstairs, his father chuckled when they walked outside to find François and Lara propped against the fountain in the entrance courtyard, arms wrapped around one another, Lara giggling as François whispered into her ear.

'*Le jeune amour est si puissant*...young love is so powerful,' his father said quietly.

Laurent rolled his eyes. His father certainly knew about love, or, in his case, lust and ego. Had he ever loved all those other women? In his teenage years, Laurent had been certain that his parents didn't love one another. How could they when they'd had those affairs? Yet they'd kept coming back to one another. And now, since his father's stroke, they were closer than ever. His head ached from trying to understand them. *Young love*—his gaze shifted to Hannah. She was the only woman he'd ever come close to loving.

His jaw tightened to see how she was watching Lara and François's playful flirting.

With a shriek, Lara broke away from François and ran to Hannah. The two women embraced, laughing and chatting over one another. Laurent looked away from the delight shining in Hannah's eyes, at the relief lightening her whole expression. It was as though in Lara she'd found a safe and secure harbour. Had she ever reacted like that with him? On occasion, but now, with the distance of time, he could see that even in the depths of their relationship Hannah had held herself back, as though uncertain of him. Why was that? Had she rightly sensed in him a man damaged by his past, a man who would bring her no happiness?

The Bonneval Cognac House was located on the outskirts of the town, its high greystone perimeter wall surrounded by pretty tree-lined roads and the Charente River to the south. When Hannah had driven the ten miles from the château to the House with Laurent's father, Antoine, this morning, for the first time since arriving in France she'd managed to relax, thanks to Antoine's easy company.

He'd surprised her by his quietness. When he and Laurent's mother, Mélissa, had arrived at the château he'd been like a whirlwind of charm and activity. But in the car after five minutes of idle chatter, he'd closed his eyes. She'd assumed he'd fallen asleep but as she'd slowed for a red traffic light as they'd neared the town, he'd said with his eyes still closed, 'I'm sorry for being such poor company. I get so tired at times.'

Hannah had been tempted to reach out and touch him, to respond to the bewilderment in his voice.

'It's okay. I enjoy silence, having time to think,' she'd said instead.

It was a while before he'd responded, 'You're sad.'

Hannah hadn't known how to answer, feeling completely undone by the simplicity of his statement. 'I was before.'

He'd opened his eyes at that, the intensity of the Bonneval blue-eyed gaze faded with him, but still more than capable of seeing through her pretence.

His quiet calm in the car, his attentiveness as he'd guided her around the distillery and the visitor centre had been so in contrast to his combative encounter with Laurent just now that she'd been thrown by the unexpectedness of it all.

Now as she watched Laurent open the rear door of François's car and his father's refusal to accept his offer of assistance to sit into the low seat, she wondered at their relationship.

Then, having waved the others off, Laurent asked her to wait a moment before he disappeared down a cobbled laneway at the side of the reception area.

A few minutes later he was back, now riding a sleek black Italian scooter. He handed her a white helmet to wear and then pulled on a black one himself. 'I have a meeting at two. Travelling by bike will save us from having to look for parking and we'll also be able to bypass the summer tourist traffic.'

This was not how she'd planned for this weekend to work out. At worst she'd thought she'd have to observe Laurent from a distance; now she was about to ride on a scooter with him. She yanked on her helmet, trying not to stare as he pulled off his silver tie and bunched it into his trouser pocket, releasing the top buttons of his white shirt, before pulling on a pair of mirrored aviators. Did he seriously have to look so hot all of the time? Did this man have any down days? Maybe this could be a form of aversion therapy? By spending all this time with him and how it reminded her of her previous heartache, then maybe she would develop an aversion to him.

She swung her leg over the scooter seat, glad she'd opted to wear her navy Bermuda shorts instead of the new white and blue summer dress she'd bought for the weekend. For the past month as the wedding weekend had loomed ever closer she'd found herself constantly drawn to the boutiques near her work at lunchtime. She'd go out with the intention of picking up a sandwich from her local favourite deli, only to find herself in a changing room trying to convince herself that she was only there to buy new things because her existing wardrobe was dated. When in truth this weekend had been the real reason. Her trips to the beautician and hairdresser had also ostensibly been about looking professional for the wedding, but whenever she looked into the mirror, she'd wondered what Laurent would think.

She edged herself back in the seat. As far away from

him as possible, with the intention of holding on to the side of the seat, but Laurent's sharp right turn as they exited out onto the street soon had her clinging to his waist.

From the low-rise modern outskirts of the town they soon entered the old town, Laurent buzzing down narrow cobbled streets, past imposing centuries-old sandstone houses, many with ornate carvings around their doorways, past outside diners sheltering beneath sun umbrellas. They passed tourists staring into the windows of the specialist Cognac and Bordeaux wine sellers and elegantly dressed locals walking with purpose towards lunch dates.

Laurent came to a stop at a *fromagerie*.

From outside she watched him purchase some items while talking animatedly with the young blonde woman who served him. She looked away when the young woman waved out to her, annoyed with herself for feeling jealous.

Afterwards they drove along a maze of deserted alleyways, the restaurants and shops giving way to old stone warehouses, ancient pulley systems hinting at their previous use.

They came to a stop on a grassy bank by the river. Under the shade of a lime tree, he spread out their lunch of cheese, crackers, quince and a bottle of sparkling water each. She smiled and sat a distance away from him, trying not to show how thrown she felt that he'd chosen a picnic for them to share.

Laurent broke off a piece of *reblochon*, placed it on a cracker and handed it to her. At first they ate in silence, the only sound the roll of the river and birdsong from the trees lining the riverbank.

'It's so pretty here.'

Laurent grinned. 'Given your love of picnics, I thought you'd appreciate it.'

She bit into the cheese, trying to focus on the creamy texture and the nutty taste and not how her heart was melting at his warm smile, at the fondness in his voice. For want of a distraction she tentatively prodded the parchment paper of the other cheeses.

Laurent chuckled. 'I promise I haven't bought anything offensive.'

'I'm still terrified to open my fridge door.'

'Even a year later?' he asked, turning, his knee touching her thigh. Despite herself she jerked away.

She caught the disquiet that flashed in his eyes and said, 'Some fears are deeply ingrained.'

He picked up another cracker, placed a thin slice of quince paste and then some creamy Brie on top. She shook her head when he offered it to her, feeling undone by the intimacy of this picnic, the act of him preparing and offering her food.

'Dogs, pungent cheeses and hair down the plughole, I already know you fear all those…anything else you'd like to confess to?'

Reaching for a cracker and loading it with some more of the *reblochon* even though she really wanted to taste the Brie, she admitted, 'After my flight here, you can add turbulence—we were thrown around for a good ten minutes.'

Laurent's expression grew concerned. 'Were you hurt?'

'Luckily I had my seat belt fastened.' She shrugged, trying not to make a big deal of it, but in truth when the plane had been tossed around the sky she'd longed with every fibre of her being for his calm reassurance. And, tragically, seeing him again brought home the sad truth that every night for the past year when she'd come home from work to her empty apartment, she'd longed for his company. It was him she'd wanted when she'd read, heard or seen something that had fired her imagination and had been bursting to share it with someone. But he hadn't wanted her. She had to remember that. She rolled her eyes, forcing a light-hearted tone to her voice. 'I was okay until the guy next to me panicked and grabbed my hand. His grip was incredible. I had to ask him to let go after a while. He'd already told me that he was a fireman from York on the way to see his sister in Bordeaux. You'd think after five years of service turbulence wouldn't worry him.'

Laurent leaned back and threw her a sceptical look. 'That sounds to me like a perfect excuse to flirt with you.'

She was still smarting from what he'd said last night at the restaurant about them not having a future. She hated his assumption that she might even think that that was a possibility, hated that he'd no understanding that there was no way she'd ever allow herself to fall in love with him again, hated that he must have been alarmed enough by her obviously poor attempt to disguise her attraction to him to even say it… Had she given him some unconscious sign? Had she stared at him too much in the boat, been too jumpy around him? So she said, 'He did ask for my number when we landed.'

He leaned towards her, his expression a mixture of incredulous and irritated. 'I hope you didn't give it to him.'

Deciding not to answer his question, just to rile him, she said instead, 'I loved my tour of the Cognac House earlier. Your father was a great host, fun and full of great stories.'

He picked up a cracker and snapped it in two. 'He's always had an eye for a pretty woman.'

Hannah couldn't help but laugh at his disgruntled tone.

'I think we both know that I was a convenient way for him to escape the château and your mother's long list of things she wanted him to do.'

Throwing his head back, Laurent took long annoyed gulps of his water. Confused by how agitated he was at her mention of his father, she felt a desire to try to understand their relationship. She knew from their time together that he didn't have an easy relationship with his parents, his father in particular, but he'd never gone into specifics; instead he'd shrugged and said that his parents were different from him.

When he'd learned of his father's stroke, however, he'd been visibly upset. He had called her in her office, told her what had happened, and that he needed to leave for France immediately. Hannah had gone to his house, wanting to comfort and support him, but he'd rushed about packing, shutting down any attempts she'd made to discuss how he was feeling. He'd barely hugged her before he'd run out to the awaiting taxi. After that day, things had changed between them. He'd grown distant from her. Constantly preoccupied, he'd flown home to Cognac at every possible opportunity.

'He said he's probably never going to be able to drive again.'

Laurent let out a sigh. 'It's what frustrates him most.'

'Losing that freedom must be hard.'

Arching his head back, he stared up at the canopy of the tree for a few moments before saying, 'He's certainly making life hard for those around him.'

After his father's stroke, she'd once suggested to Laurent that she travel with him to Cognac but he'd said it wasn't a good idea. She'd tried to hide how hurt she was, tried to remain supportive, but increasingly she'd known that he was excluding her from his life. Now, having seen his home here, the vastness of the Cognac House, his place as CEO of such a prestigious brand, she understood why he'd seen no place for her here. She cleared her throat, trying to focus on their conversation, and asked, 'In what way?'

Propping himself back on his elbows, Laurent stretched his legs out on the grass. 'For a start he doesn't accept that he's no longer CEO of the House.'

Distracted by the sight of his long legs, the narrowness of his hips and waist in his grey trousers, the gleam of light shining from the silver buckle of his belt, remembering all the times she'd clumsily, desperately, unbuckled his belts in the past, she asked weakly, 'Can he take on another role?'

'And give him a legitimate reason to come in and interfere? I don't think so.'

His shirt was pulled tight across his chest, revealing the outline of taut skin and defined muscle beneath. She shifted on the grass, and against her better judgement angled herself a fraction closer to him, a thrilling sensation flourishing in her limbs. 'All of his experience could be a valuable asset to the business.'

His gaze lingered on her silver ankle bracelet. His blue gaze was darker than usual when he looked back up. 'I don't remember you ever wearing an ankle bracelet before.'

There was a low and seductive timbre to his voice. Her heart turned over. 'I spent the New Year in India. I bought it there as a memento.'

He sat up, leaning back on one arm. 'Did you go alone?'

'The yoga teacher I follow online, Kim Ackerman, was running a week-long course there, so I signed up for it.' She was tempted to add that it was the online videos from Kim, a London-based online yoga superstar, that had kept her sane for the past year—chasing away the memories of him that had threatened to subsume her, replacing her regrets with a more productive mindset of being grateful for what she had in life and the opportunities out there waiting for her to grab hold of. 'It was a spur-of-the-moment decision. I decided I couldn't take any more of the wet weather we were having.' She shifted away from him again, the chemistry between them making her way too jumpy. 'There must be a role in the company your father could take on with all of his experience.'

He ran a hand tiredly against his jawline and for a moment she thought he wasn't going to answer her, but then he said quietly, 'My father almost brought the business to ruin.'

'I didn't realise...'

He shook his head. 'You had no reason to.'

'Am I right in guessing that you have a strained relationship with him?'

He laughed at her question. 'That must be hard for you to comprehend, given how well you get on with your parents.'

Despite his laughter, his voice contained an edge, a disappointment, a hurt that stabbed at her heart. 'It's a shame you don't get along—is it the fact that you've taken over as CEO? In my work I often deal with family businesses. It's not unusual for there to be conflict between generations, especially when the younger one takes over. It's hard for the older generation to let go and for the younger people to listen to advice.'

He eyed her with exasperation. 'Trust me, it has nothing to do with me not listening. The issues between us go back decades.' A tic appeared on the ridge of his jawline. 'Both of my parents had affairs when I was a teenager and left each other. When the affairs petered out they would eventually return.'

Hannah startled at the raw hurt in his voice. 'Seriously?'

Laurent's eyes widened. She flinched at the crassness of her response.

'Would I joke about something like that?'

She shook her head, seeing the hurt in his eyes, her heart pulling, her mind racing to understand what it would do to a teenager to experience such turmoil. Emotion clumped in her throat—anger and sadness and compassion for a teenage Laurent trying to deal with his parents' affairs; upset and regret that he'd never felt able to tell her any of this before now. She leaned towards him, her fingers brushing against his thigh. His eyes met hers. Softly she whispered, 'That must have been so painful for you.'

Bewildered, Laurent felt the electric charge of Hannah's touch, trying to reconcile it with the empathy in her eyes. He never spoke about his past. Why then was he telling this woman whom he knew he needed to keep his distance from? His mind reeling, he knew he had to somehow downplay it all. 'It was chaotic. Escaping to Paris to stay with our grandparents helped to bring back some normality. That's why I encouraged François to stay there.'

'Why didn't you?'

'I came back to Cognac in the hope of persuading my father to hand over the business to me.' He began to fold up the cheeses in their parchment paper, placing them back into the paper bag, thrown by the realisation that it was more than just that. He'd returned because he'd feared for his mother, who had always become withdrawn and silent whenever his father left the family home. 'From the age of sixteen I worked in every operation in the business from the distillery to the warehouses and Admin. I wanted to know every facet of the business inside out. When I turned twenty my grandfather and I made one final attempt to persuade my father to hand the business over to me but he refused. I left for Paris after that and then London. Staying in Cognac was pointless. The only reason I'm CEO now is because of his stroke. It was a decision forced upon him.'

'That annoys you?'

He blinked at her question. He'd assumed his issues with his father were because of the past, but with Hannah's question he realised it was also about his father's lack of acknowledgement and recognition of everything he was doing to turn the business around. 'He doesn't trust me and questions every decision I make.'

He stood and went to a nearby bin, throwing the bag of half-eaten cheeses into it.

Hannah was waiting at the scooter when he turned around. She handed him his helmet and asked gently, 'Are you enjoying the role of CEO?'

That was the first time anyone had asked him that question, the first time he'd stopped to consider it himself. 'Yes, I am. We're slowly turning the business around. I've appointed some new talent who are as keen as I am to see the business thrive. We've a great team with a world-class product.' He paused as a sense of ease, almost the freedom of self-determination, swept over him in acknowledging to himself the job satisfaction the role was giving him. Then his heart lurched at Hannah's smile at his words, at her obvious pleasure that he was enjoying the role. For some reason he wanted to include her in the conversation, to, in a small way, let her know that he still thought about her. 'I travel a lot with the role. I try to incorporate some downtime in the places I visit, especially to go and see any alternative museums.'

A glint sparked in her eye. 'I bet none have been as exciting as the lawnmower museum we visited in Finland.'

He grinned. 'Well, I did visit a museum of bad art in Berlin and a balloon museum in Perth.'

She gave him a teasing smile. 'And to think how you used to complain when I dragged you to museums in the past.'

'What can I say? You converted me to the more quirky places.' He was tempted to tell her that when he'd visited the museums he had missed her laughter, the serious way she would read out the exhibition notes, loving the peculiar facts.

'I'm jealous. They sound really cool.' Her hand coming to rest on the gear shift of the scooter, she gave him a tentative smile. 'Why did you never tell me about your childhood when we were together?'

'There was never any real cause to.' Which was the truth. But not the full story. How could he tell a woman who had grown up in a textbook happy family the truth of his dysfunctional one? What would have been the point?

'But you have now,' she said.

'In London, I didn't handle our split well. I was distracted by my father's illness, taking over as CEO, wrapping up my affairs in London. I should have explained myself better. I saw how unhappy and chaotic my parents' lives were, growing up. I don't want any of that… I can't give you what you want in life—marriage, commitment.'

'Trust me, Laurent, I'm more than aware of that fact. Anyway, I don't recall ever asking you for those things.' With an angry tilt of her chin, she asked, 'So, are you enjoying being back in Cognac? Do you miss London at all?'

Mixed with the irritation of her question was a hint of wistful hope. Softly, not wanting to hurt her, he answered the truth. 'I feel completely at home here. I hadn't realised just how much I missed Cognac when I was away. It's where I belong. Bonneval Cognac is my legacy. I passionately want to make it a success.' He rubbed a hand at the tension in his neck rather than give into the temptation of reaching over and touching the soft skin of her cheek in a bid to wipe away the frustration in her expression. 'There are aspects of London that I miss greatly, but the decisions I took when coming back to Cognac were the right ones.'

She worked her jaw, unhappy with his answer. 'You say Bonneval Cognac is your legacy but who will inherit the business if you don't believe in love, in marriage? Or will you have children regardless of all that?'

'Look, up until my father became ill, it was never certain I would inherit the business in the first place. I think for now I should concentrate on having a business to pass on. Who actually inherits it is a far-off issue that doesn't concern me right now.'

She stepped back from the scooter. 'François is so eager and happy to marry... How can two brothers be so different in their views on relationships?'

He grimaced at her question. 'When something is wrong in your life, it can make you reject it even more fiercely or the exact opposite—crave it with all your being.' She frowned in confusion so he added, 'Our teenage years were extremely volatile. My guess is that François is looking for security.'

She shook her head and laughed. 'I'm sure François has more reasons to marry than just looking for security.' She paused before adding, 'You really are cynical about love, aren't you?'

He raised a sceptical eyebrow. 'What other reasons would he have to marry?'

She blinked at his question. 'Shared dreams, friendship, companionship, loyalty, commitment…love. Will that do, or do you want me to list even more?'

'And what happens when it all goes wrong?'

'It doesn't have to.'

'More than a third of marriages here in France end in divorce.'

Hannah stared at him, the anger in her expression shifting to frustration and then sad resignation. Pulling on her helmet, she said, 'I need to get back to the Château to prepare for the wedding rehearsal later this evening.'

In no mood to prolong this conversation he jumped onto the bike and fired the engine. They were driving back towards the old town centre, her warm palms disturbingly placed on his waist, when he heard her say, 'Maybe someday you'll meet the right person who'll change your mind.'

CHAPTER FOUR

OUT BEYOND THE dining room, the softly lit swimming pool beckoned Hannah. She shifted in her seat, the silk skirt of her halter-neck dress welding to her legs. What she wouldn't give to stand and run across the lawn, unzipping her dress and tossing it aside, before diving into the water. The cool water would wash away the unbearable heat of the night. Wash away her exhaustion from trying to converse in French. The seating plan for the rehearsal dinner taking place in the formal dining room of the château had placed her at the centre of the long dining table, Nicolas Couilloud, a business associate of the Bonneval family, on her right, a school friend of François's from Paris on her left. Both men had spoken of sport and politics all night and Hannah had struggled to keep up, with her schoolgirl French.

The blissful pool water might also wash away her ever-growing anxiety about tomorrow. The earlier rehearsal hadn't gone to plan. To start with they hadn't been able to locate Antoine and Lara's dad. When the errant fathers had eventually returned to the château Lara's dad had sheepishly admitted that they had gone to visit a friend of Antoine's who owned a nearby vineyard and had stopped to taste some of his cellar. Lara and François had been decidedly tetchy and the whole rehearsal had been conducted with a frostiness in the air. Hannah had tried to lighten the mood but no one else had been inclined to follow her lead. And Laurent's silent and brooding presence hadn't helped matters either. Having him standing beside François and continually stare at her had caused her to stumble over her words.

What if the same happened tomorrow? What if she failed to capture the magic of the event? The wedding celebrant was like the conductor of an orchestra; it was she who would set the tone of the wedding. What if she messed up? Messed up in front of her best friend and the two hundred and fifty influential guests. Messed up in front of Laurent.

She cast her eye around the rest of the table. No one else seemed inclined to leave even though the meal had ended over an hour ago. Would they notice if she slipped away to work on her blessing speech? She still wasn't certain it fully captured the essence of Lara and François's relationship.

The seating plan had placed the younger generation to her left—the tension of earlier forgotten, Lara and François were chatting with their close friends who had travelled from around the world to celebrate with them. And to her right were Lara's and François's parents along with old family friends and associates, all busily chatting.

It was only she and Laurent who seemed like lone islands cast aside from the noisy anticipation that came before a big life event. Laurent was seated at the head of the table. At the pre-dinner drinks on the terrace he'd easily moved between the guests, being his usual charming self. It was only when Nicolas Couilloud had taken him aside and spoken to him that Hannah had seen him tense. He and Nicolas had ended their conversation with much shaking of heads. Instinctively she'd moved towards Laurent wanting to ask if everything was okay but, on see-ing her approach, he'd turned away and spoken instead to Lara's sister and bridesmaid, Stella.

Already halfway across the terrace, suddenly without purpose, Hannah had faltered before she'd forced her-self to continue, skirting past Laurent and Stella with-out a glance in their direction, hoping it looked to the other guests as if it had been her intention to step inside the château all along. She'd washed her trembling hands in the downstairs cloakroom, trying not to think about how beautiful twenty-four-year-old Stella looked in her red silk sheath dress with its daring slash to the thigh.

She had to give Laurent his due. He was doing an excellent job at avoiding her this evening. Which she should welcome. Wasn't that what she wanted after all—for them to keep their distance from one another? But it was so at odds with the intimacy of their conversation at lunchtime. Was he regretting having been so open with her?

She closed her eyes for a moment. Suddenly ex-hausted by this whole weekend. Exhausted by the wealth and culture of Laurent's life now. The opulence of the dining room, the sophistication oozing from the other guests, all reminders of the contrasting squalor of her early years. This wasn't her world. Even after she'd been rescued she'd been brought up in the warm simplicity of country life. Her dad wouldn't know a derivative, a Chagall, the difference between a Saint-Émilion and a Médoc, even if they all bit him on the bottom. And she loved him for that. Love, loyalty, family and his animals were all that mattered to him.

She was also exhausted from being so physically close to Laurent. Not only was she struggling to contain her at-traction to him, but after what he'd told her today, opening himself up to her, she stupidly, crazily, felt more connected to him. The very opposite of what she'd hoped to achieve this weekend.

Why was this weekend turning out so different from how she'd imagined it would? Only this evening, Lara had decided, with the encouragement of her parents and in a nod to tradition, that she should spend tonight away from François. So now Lara, Stella and their parents were spending the night with Laurent's parents in their lodge but there weren't enough beds for Hannah to move too. It shouldn't matter but she felt excluded by this change of plans. The vulnerability, that deep fear of disconnection that sat at the core of her being, was being stirred back into life by this weekend and she hated how out of control it made her feel.

She opened her eyes. Blinked at the brightness of the room and then was dazzled by the opulent diamonds hanging from the ears and throat of Nicolas Couilloud's wife sitting opposite her.

Her gaze unconsciously moved up the table, past the other guests, her heart performing an impressive leap to find Laurent staring towards her with concern. She twisted away, trying to tune back into the conversation between Nicolas and a glamorous French movie star seated across the table from him about redevelopment plans in Cannes, where they both owned summer houses, which they were vehemently opposed to, grumbling about the effect on the already chaotic traffic.

Laurent stood. Immediately all of the chatter around the table died as all heads turned in his direction. Was it his height, his powerful build, his ridiculously masculine features that were so exaggerated and beautiful that when people first met him they were often silenced by the need to study him, or was it simply his aura of command that so effortlessly had people respond to his movement?

He gave them a smile. A closed-mouth smile. The smile he gave when being polite. 'Thank you for coming to dinner tonight. I hope you've had an enjoyable evening.' He paused and nodded in the direction of François and Lara, his smile widening in affection. 'But as we have an important and busy day ahead of us tomorrow we need to draw this night to a close.'

The guests nodded, chairs moved backwards, some of the women picked up their evening purses, but all came to a stop when from the opposite end of the table Antoine called out, 'One more drink out on the terrace.'

For the briefest moment a pulse twitched at the side of Laurent's jawline. 'We can party tomorrow. For now, we all need to rest.'

Antoine stood. The entire table swivelled in his direction. 'One more won't do us any harm.'

Now everyone turned back towards Laurent and waited for his response. His eyes narrowed.

Without thinking Hannah stood. 'As wedding celebrant I agree with Laurent. I don't want any of you tired tomorrow.' She smiled at a frowning Antoine. 'I'm expecting you to dance with me, Antoine.'

Antoine's blue eyes twinkled. 'It will be my pleasure.'

Hannah said her goodbyes to her dinner companions and then, after a quick hug with Lara, encouraging her to try and get some sleep, she slipped out of the dining room before everyone else, averting her gaze when she saw Laurent unhappily follow her hasty departure.

Laurent went to knock on Hannah's bedroom door but at the last second pulled his hand away. In the aftermath of their lunch, as the hours had passed by in a blur of work meetings and telephone calls, a chasm had opened up in him as to the wisdom of having been so frank with Hannah. Would she think less of him, knowing his background? Now, after deliberately keeping his distance from her all evening, was he really about to throw all of that good work away? It was an easy question to answer. The tension that had been etched on her face earlier when she'd sat with her eyes closed at the dining table was too profound to ignore.

He knocked on the door. Swallowed when the consideration that Hannah might answer the door in her nightwear dawned on him. Despite himself he smiled at that thought.

The door swung open. Hannah eyed him, her gaze narrowing when it honed in on his smile. She folded her arms. He mirrored the action, propping himself against the doorframe, unbalanced not for the first time at how striking she looked in her figure-hugging knee-length purple halterneck dress that accentuated every glorious curve of her body. The urge to step forward and release her hair from its tight bun had him tense every muscle in his body. 'I had the situation downstairs under control.'

She raised an eyebrow. 'Have you come all the way to my room to tell me that?'

Despite himself he laughed at her deadpan expression. Then, taking in the paperwork in her hand, he said, 'Come outside, there's something I want to show you.'

She shook her head. 'I need to prepare for tomorrow's ceremony.'

'You're nervous about tomorrow.'

She stepped back. 'No, I'm not.'

He pushed away from the doorframe. 'Come outside— what I have to show you might help you relax.'

Shoving a hand onto her hip, she answered, 'For the last time, I don't need to relax.'

Something about the tilt of her hip got to him. Shrugging off his tuxedo jacket, he stepped into the room and threw it onto the back of a bedroom chair. His bow tie soon followed.

She looked at the jacket and his bow tie with dismay. 'What the hell are you doing?'

Her horrified expression only fuelled his need to push her to be honest. 'This damn heat. Prove to me that you're okay about tomorrow by coming with me.'

She gave him a disbelieving look before slamming her paperwork down on the bedroom console table next to her open laptop and then storming out of the door. He walked behind, his eyes taking in the angry sway of her hips as she hurried along the corridor and down the stairs in her high heels.

The château was silent. Earlier, François and he had waved all the guests goodbye, but no sooner had the tailgate lights of Lara's parents' car disappeared in the direction of his parents' lodge when François had raced to his car, shouting that he needed to see Lara one more time.

Laurent had stood watching the trail of François's tail lights, envying his brother's ability to throw himself into love so wholeheartedly. But then he'd shivered despite the heat of the night and prayed that life would be good to François and Lara, that time, and the dimming of passion, the reality of committing yourself to another person for eternity, the lure of others, the selfishness that was at the core of every human being, would not destroy their marriage.

Outside he led Hannah in the direction of the estate's farm. The farm's single and double stone outbuildings were built around a cobbled courtyard, a water pump in the centre. Opening the door of one of the smaller buildings, he stepped inside, to a chorus of chirping, inhaling the scent of the heavy blanket of fresh straw on the floor.

She paused at the entrance and gave him a dubious look. Then as she peered through the doorway her expression lit up. 'Oh, wow, they're so beautiful,' she whispered, taking small tentative steps towards the hen and her seven yellow fluffy chicks.

Stopping a distance away from them, she crouched down and watched the chicks stumble around their mother, chirp, chirp, chirping away. 'When did they hatch?'

The knuckled wave of Hannah's spine was exposed by a gap in the back of her dress. He swallowed against the memories of running his fingers along her back when she lay beside him, a slow sexy smile forming on her lips when it was a prelude to sex, a sated smile when it was in the aftermath. He stuffed his hands in his pockets and walked to stand next to her. 'Earlier today.'

She stood. 'They're adorable, but why did you bring me to see them?'

'Remember the endless photos of newborn animals that your mum sent to you, which you then forwarded on to me? I thought seeing these little guys might help you forget about tomorrow.'

She eyed him curiously. 'Do you think I *should* be nervous?'

'You'll ace tomorrow.' He paused and watched the chicks stumble away from their mother and then with a jolt of alarm race back to her as though terrified they were about to lose her. Then turning to Hannah, the unease in her brown eyes slamming into his heart, he added, 'You're amazing. Always remember that.'

Reddening, Hannah gave a faint smile and backed

towards the door. Outside she looked around the near-empty courtyard, a single tractor the only sign of any farming activity. 'I'm guessing there isn't a working farm here any more?'

'There was in my grandfather's time. My father let it go. I've recently employed a farm manager. He's reintroducing some livestock. I want the château to be self-sufficient.'

She nodded to this. 'Good idea.' The night sky was clear, a fat moon shedding bright light down on their surroundings. Into the quiet of the night she said in an almost whisper, as though she was telling him something very intimate, 'The option of moving to Singapore isn't the only one I'm considering. I'm also thinking about moving to Granada in Spain to become a full-time wedding consultant.'

'Really? Your career is in the city. Why would you give up everything you've achieved?'

She shrugged, the long delicate lines of her exposed collarbone lifting and falling. 'I fell in love with Granada when I was there for Emily's wedding. It would be an exciting option, a new start for me.'

He'd always thought of her as being ambitious in the corporate world only. These new ambitions made him uneasy. Unfairly and irrationally, he hated the idea that she was forging a new and unexpected life. 'What about your promotion? Your transfer to Singapore?'

'Granada is only a short flight away and Emily and her husband are planning on buying a holiday home there. Singapore is so far away from everyone I love.' Wounded eyes met his for a moment. Guilt and regret slammed into his chest. Then with a brief grimace she added, 'Do you want to talk about your conversation with Nicolas Couilloud earlier?'

When they had dated, they had been a sounding board for one another over work issues. Hannah's advice had always been solid. For a moment he considered telling her, realising how much he missed having someone to talk to about issues that were troubling him. But talking about work would feel as though they were dropping back into their old relationship. 'It's just a business issue.'

'A sizeable business issue, I'm guessing.'

He gestured for them to walk back through the lightly wooded copse that separated the farm buildings from the château. He tried to resist talking but Hannah's patient silence, the worry, the frustration of his discussion with Nicolas had him eventually blurt out, 'Nicolas is one of my father's oldest friends but he also owns the company who distributes our cognacs. He's vital in our supply chain. He has the whole market sewn up—he has no competitors with the same market reach. He told me tonight that he's going to increase his fees when our contract with him is up for renewal next month.'

They emerged from the shade of the copse. Hannah came to a stop and asked, 'Why?'

'He's citing increased transportation costs.'

'You don't believe him?'

He inhaled a deep breath, frustration clogging his lungs. 'I can't help but think that it has something to do with my father.'

Hannah's eyes widened. 'Surely not. Why would Antoine have anything to do with Nicolas's decision?'

He could not help but smile at Hannah's innocence, part of him deeply envying her for never having experienced the soul-destroying destructiveness of a dysfunctional family.

'Why are you smiling?'

He jolted at the anger in Hannah's voice. Then, shrugging, he walked away, answering, 'Not all families are sweetness and light.'

She caught up with him on the terrace. 'Do you think that I'm that naïve, that I don't understand how people hurt others driven by their ego, by fear, by insecurity? I've seen it time and time again in my work, partnerships falling apart, family businesses not surviving. And do you know what the common denominator in all of it is? A lack of communication, a lack of connection and honesty.'

He sat on the arm of an outdoor sofa and crossed his arms. 'Being an outsider is easy. Try getting mangled up in the politics and personalities and history of a family business—then such logical analysis goes right out of the door. My family aren't like yours...so bloody normal.'

Hannah eyed him angrily before shifting her gaze towards the pool and the river beyond. She folded her arms, her delicate chin jutting out furiously. 'There's nothing normal about my family.' She paused and then added softly, 'My real family.'

Laurent stood. Confused by her words. 'Real family?'

She bit her lip, her gaze refusing to meet his. Silence descended between them. He waited, thrown by the emotion playing out in her expression as she made several attempts to answer his question. Eventually she answered in a faint whisper, 'I'm adopted.'

His brain tried to process what she'd said. 'Adopted?'

Her gaze met his, a flicker of disappointment soon being replaced by anger. 'Yes. Adopted. It happens.'

'You never said before...why not? *Dieu!* Why not?' He knew he was saying the wrong things but frustration, the awful feeling he hadn't known Hannah at all, drove him on, 'Why tell me now?'

She blinked at his questions. 'After what you told me today about your parents… I guess it seemed right that you know.'

He cringed at the now calm softness of her voice, which only emphasised his own angry torrent of questions. He breathed in and out to the count of four, trying to focus on Hannah rather than his hurt that she'd never told him before. He sat on the sofa properly, gestured that she should sit on a chair opposite.

Reluctantly she did so.

'What age were you?'

She raised a hand and kneaded her collarbone. 'Seven.'

For a moment he flailed for the right way to talk about it all. He'd been an insensitive sod up until now and he desperately wanted to get this right. He gritted his teeth against the ball of failure that was rapidly growing in his gut—what type of boyfriend had he been that Hannah had never felt inclined or able to tell him this before? 'What happened?'

For a moment her concentration seemed to be on running her fingertips against the interwoven rattan reeds of her chair. But then she tilted her head in his direction, pride burning from her eyes. 'My birth parents were both drug users. My memories are hazy, as you can imagine, but I remember a lot of parties and being left alone in the house on many occasions.' She stopped and swallowed. Her bottom lip gave a quiver. 'One night the police came and took me away.'

'You were scared.'

She gave a humourless laugh. 'Terrified.'

He fell back into his chair and stared up at the night sky for a brief moment. Then with a sigh he sat forward. 'I'm so sorry, Hannah. I wish you had told me before now.'

'What difference would it have made?'

Her question was a challenge. She wasn't hiding that fact in her direct gaze as she waited for his response, in the tension of her body, one leg wrapping around the other tightly at the calf. Would knowing about her adoption have changed anything? He swallowed and admitted, 'Maybe I would have been kinder...maybe I would have taken better care not to hurt you.'

Hannah's heart crumbled at the softness of Laurent's tone, at the sincerity of his expression. But at the same time her brain stirred in indignation and demanded that she show some pride. 'For crying out loud, Laurent, I don't need your pity just because I was adopted.' She sat forward in her seat, keen to change the subject, keen to bury the past once again, and the vulnerability and emptiness and confusion that arose in her any time she unearthed it all. 'If Nicolas ups the cost of distribution, what will be the impact on the business?'

Laurent eyed her with bewilderment. 'That's not of importance right now.'

She forged on. 'Will you speak to your father about it?'

He paused for a moment, clearly toying with whether to allow her to change the subject, but then with a sigh admitted, 'For all I know my father could be behind this price increase.'

Her mouth dropped open. Was he being serious? 'Why would he do that?'

His expression darkened at her disbelief. Tensely he answered, 'My father didn't want me to take over as CEO. It was my mother who insisted upon it. He would love to see me fail.'

Hannah shook her head. 'Are you sure? Maybe your father knows nothing about it. Why not at least talk to him? Maybe he has some advice he can pass on to you. Surely he doesn't want to see the business struggle… which I'm guessing it will, based on how anxious you looked all night.'

'I did?'

She could not help but smile at his annoyance that she'd spotted his tension. 'Don't worry, no one else would have noticed. But I know the signs—your right eye twitches.'

He crossed his arms. 'It does not.'

She laughed. 'Yes, it does.'

He shook his head but his bright blue eyes gave away his amusement. Then softly he said, 'We did have some fun times together, didn't we?'

Her smile faded. She swallowed at the fondness in his eyes. Despite herself she heard herself admit, 'Yes, we did.'

He gave her one of his wide-mouthed smiles that always reduced her to putty. 'Do you remember the night we went kayaking on Lake Saimaa?'

Hannah smiled in remembrance of the stunning beauty of the crystal-clear Finnish lake and exploring it under the summer midnight sun. 'How could I forget? It was magical.'

'And the time we went snowboarding in Ještěd?'

Hannah grimaced. 'I reckon the locals are still deaf from my screaming.' She paused and threw him an accusatory glare. 'And you were all Mr Cool, zipping around the place, showing off.' She could see that he was about to object, so she interjected, 'Never mind the travel, what I miss is having a gorgeous meal cooked for me in the evenings. You've ruined me to the pleasure of a ready meal for ever.' Only when she'd said those words did she cringe and wonder why she did.

She sighed in relief when he laughed and added, 'And I miss having you there in the mornings to pick out my ties.'

She shook her head. 'I'm still convinced that you're colour-blind.'

He stood and held out a hand to her, to help her rise. She took it, every cell in her body responding to its familiar strength. She went to take her hand away, but Laurent tightened his grip and stepped even closer. For long seconds he studied her, his blue gaze quickening her heart, sending fire into her belly. The scent of lavender hung heavily in the air, almost drugging in its density. In a low voice he eventually said, 'You never answered my question as to whether you're seeing anyone.'

Heat formed on her cheeks. Her throat grew dry. He always had this effect when he stood this close, when he spoke, when his eyes played games with her heart. She lowered her gaze to his mouth. She wanted to kiss him. She wanted to kiss him hard and remind him of everything he walked away from. But instead she whispered, 'Stella is young—don't break her heart.'

He let out a low disbelieving sigh and said in a grumble, 'She's at least ten years younger than me.'

'Eight actually, which is nothing.'

He inched forward, forcing her to tilt her head to meet his stare. 'I'm not interested in Stella.' Heat and chemistry and emotion whirled and twisted around them.

Hannah blinked, trying to shake off the hot need burning through her veins, the cloud of desire that was fogging her brain to everything but the desire to feel his lips, to touch the hard muscle of his body. Just for one more time. What was the harm?

She leant forwards and then up onto her tippy-toes. His eyes darkened. She angled her head, shifted an inch away from his mouth. Her head swam with his nearness, with his familiar scent and heat. With a whimper of annoyance she placed her mouth on his.

It took a few seconds for her to realise that he wasn't responding to her kiss.

He didn't want this.

Shame exploding in her chest, she went to pull away.

But at her movement his arms wrapped around her waist, stopping her, and he kissed her with an urgency that had her instantly on fire. Her breasts, pushed hard against his chest, immediately felt tender and desire trickled through her body like an illicit pleasure. His kiss grew ever more hot and demanding and she met that demand, wanting to punish him. One hand wrapped around his neck, holding him closer, the other ran over the heat of his chest, past the soft leather of his belt and then lightly over his trousers, euphoria spreading through her when he groaned. She wanted to make love with him.

At that thought she broke away.

Panting hard, they stared at one another. What self-destructive part of her would sleep with him? Her ridiculous pride that wanted him to regret ending their relationship?

She flailed for something to say. Eventually she realised she could find a safe harbour in his business concerns. 'What's the worst-case scenario if Nicolas increases his fees?'

Laurent gave a disbelieving laugh. 'You kiss me and then ask a question like that.'

She decided to try to brazen this all out. 'To answer your earlier question, yes, I've been on dates, but none recently. I'm a young woman with desires.' She stopped as she inwardly cringed, before adding, 'I guess this wedding is bringing them out more than usual.'

Laurent's mouth dropped open. 'Are you proposition-ing me?'

'Are you kidding? It was a kiss. Nothing more. A moment of physical weakness from me. Don't get ahead of yourself.'

Laurent frowned. 'Hannah, you know—'

'Yes, yes.' Hannah interjected. 'Trust me, you were more than clear about our future in London, just as clear last night and again today at lunchtime.' She winced at the bitterness in her voice and decided to change tack. 'Now, putting my professional hat on, can I advise that you speak to your dad? I know how difficult it is to put the past behind you, but surely the future is more important?'

With a look of exasperation he sighed. And then, his expression sobering, he considered her for much too long before asking gently, 'Are you in contact with your birth parents?'

Hannah eyed the main doorway into the château and the softly lit hallway beyond. She swallowed before she admitted, 'They both died. Soon after I was taken away my dad overdosed. My mum died ten years ago.'

'Dieu!'

Her gaze shot back to his, disappointment barrelling through her at the disgust in his voice. 'Not very pretty, is it?'

Laurent grimaced. 'I wish you had told me.'

Hannah edged towards the doorway, suddenly feeling beyond exhausted. 'Just as I wish you had told me about your childhood.' She gestured inside. 'I need to go and check over my paperwork for tomorrow.'

She'd stepped onto the marble floor of the hallway when he called out, 'I thought we had known one an-other.'

She tried not to wince at the tired bewilderment in his voice. Turning, she nodded in agreement, her heart once again tumbling on seeing him. She forced herself to give him a smile of encouragement. 'Speak to your dad.'

He shook his head. 'I'll find a solution…by myself.'

Her exhaustion washed over her like a fresh wave. 'Do you let anyone into your life, Laurent?'

A deep frown bisected his forehead. 'Maybe it's safer not to let others in.'

She understood why he thought that way. She too carried hurt and pain and ghosts from the past. 'Perhaps it's safer, but I'm guessing it's an unhappier life for doing so.'

CHAPTER FIVE

THE FOLLOWING AFTERNOON, at the entrance to the walled garden, Laurent pulled François to a stop. François eyed him restlessly, keen to keep moving. Placing a hand on François's shoulder, Laurent looked him straight in the eye. 'Relax. Everything is going to be okay.'

François let out a frustrated breath. '*Dieu!* I feel sick with nerves.'

Laurent rolled his eyes, deliberately being obtuse. 'I still don't understand why you're insisting on marrying, but if you are going to do it at least try to relax and enjoy it.'

François shook his head and laughed. 'You're not fooling me, Laurent. I know how much you love Lara. Deep down I know you're happy to see us marry.'

Laurent held his hands up in defeat. 'Okay, I'll admit you two might actually make it work.'

François smiled triumphantly. 'I can't believe you've actually admitted that. You've made my day!' Then, looking down, he scuffed his shoe off the brickwork of the garden path before saying, 'It's good to have you by my side, you know.'

Laurent swallowed, taken aback by the affection in François's gaze. As brothers, they weren't given to displays of emotion. He lifted an eyebrow. 'I'm going to make you pay for it somehow.'

François laughed. 'I appreciate the supreme sacrifice you're making by being my best man.'

Laurent grinned at his brother but then, sobering, he said, 'Whatever my views on marriage, I do wish you and Lara every happiness.' Then taking a key from his tux jacket, he handed it to François. 'My wedding gift to you both: Villa Marchand. I've had it renovated for you.'

His eyes wide in surprise, François weighed the key in the palm of his hands and shook his head. It was a considerable time before he managed to say, in a voice choked with emotion, 'I'm lost for words... I've loved that house ever since I was a boy and Lara fell in love with it too when we visited there last summer.'

Laurent shrugged, trying to pretend not to be choked up at François's delight. 'I know. That's why I'm giving it to you. You can stay there tonight if you wish, rather than here in the château.' He gave François a grin. 'I thought you might like the privacy. Hannah visited the house with me Thursday night and suggested some items that Lara might enjoy, so the house is honeymoon ready.'

François grimaced. 'How are things between you two?'

'Awkward.'

'I saw you out on the terrace last night when I returned to the château.' François paused and threw him a questioning look. 'You seemed very close.'

Dieu! Did François see them kissing? 'What do you mean "close"?'

François stepped back from his growled question. 'You were chatting, oblivious to the fact that I'd walked out to say hello—what did you think I meant?'

Guilt and relief washed over Laurent. 'You should have interrupted us. It would have been nice to chat with you over a drink. And nothing is going to happen between myself and Hannah. Relax.'

'You were so good together—' François shook his head '—but I'm not going to lecture you again on all of that.' His expression hardening, François added, 'Don't hurt her.'

Memories of their kiss last night slammed into Laurent. Turning in the direction of the garden, he said, 'I have no intention of doing so.'

He walked away but when François did not follow he turned at the doorway to the garden to find his brother eyeing him sceptically. When François eventually decided to join him, he said, 'Lara needs Hannah in her life. Promise me that you won't make things any more awkward than they already are. Stay away from her, Laurent.'

Laurent tried to make an acquiescing noise. François raised an eyebrow.

With a sigh, Laurent relented and said, 'I promise.'

Seating had been arranged on the lawns either side of the central cobbled pathway. Bows had been tied onto the rose bushes dense with blowsy blooms that were planted at regular intervals along the herbaceous border, their heavy scent filling the air. At the wisteria-covered archway that led out to the lawns of the château, a pedestal and two gilt chairs had been placed for the blessing ceremony to take place.

Laurent's heart took a sizeable wallop when he spotted Hannah breaking away from a conversation with a friend of Lara's and walking towards the pedestal. Dressed in a knee-length pale pink dress, the fitted bodice emphasising her curves, the skirt flaring over her hips, her hair tied back into a sleek ponytail, she looked both professional and as sexy as hell.

Dieu! Their kiss last night had been unbelievable. Hot, sultry, beautiful. But it'd been too much of a reminder of how much he missed her. And not just physically. It had brought home how much he missed her warmth, her gentleness, her easy presence.

Moving towards the archway, François and he nodded hello to the already assembled and seated guests. But all the while, an invisible force was pulling him towards Hannah, who was checking through her paperwork.

Her gaze shifted upwards as their footsteps neared. She smiled warmly at François and, walking towards him, hugged him tightly. 'Gosh, you look incredibly handsome, François.'

Laurent blinked at the affection in Hannah's voice, at her calm enthusiasm.

François fiddled with the collar of his tux jacket, casting a critical eye down over his suit. 'Is everything looking okay?'

Hannah adjusted his bow tie a fraction. 'There, now you're perfect.'

Then, with an unenthusiastic glance in Laurent's direction, she returned to her paperwork.

He cursed under his breath. Today was going to be as awkward as he'd feared.

The arrival of his parents kept him busy for the next few minutes as he had to encourage his father along the path as he insisted on stopping and chatting to the guests, despite the fact that the ceremony was about to start at any minute. When he then tried to assist his father to sit, his father pushed his arm away, muttering that he wasn't an invalid.

Taking his seat beside François, he tried to tune into the chamber orchestra playing to the side, tried to find some reassuring words to say to François, whose legs were jigging like crazy. But time and time again his attention was drawn back to Hannah, who was going through a constant ritual of thumbing through her paperwork and then looking expectantly towards the entranceway before glancing back to her paperwork again.

Circulate. Mingle. Do his best man and host duties. And stay the hell away from Hannah. That was the plan of action for today he'd formulated in the middle of last night when unable to sleep, thanks to the after-effects of their kiss.

But it hadn't just been their kiss that had kept him awake. It was also the haunted look in Hannah's eyes when she'd spoken about her adoption. He'd caused her enough hurt as it was. He wasn't going to add to that tally by spending time with her, which would only be asking for trouble given the chemistry that whipped between them like a live coil.

His plan of action, which had made sense in the middle of last night, had one major flaw, however. It hadn't taken into account how alone and nervous Hannah would look as she stood waiting for Lara's arrival. He moved restlessly in his chair. Telling himself to stay put. The last thing they needed were wagging tongues from those who knew of their previous relationship.

Once again Hannah's gaze shifted down over the crowd, towards the entrance. A bumblebee flew close to her. She leapt backwards, flapping her hands wildly. The bee got the message and buzzed away. With a grimace Hannah glanced nervously out towards all the assembled guests before her hands gripped the wooden sides of the pedestal, her skin flushing.

Standing, he approached her, deliberately blocking her from everyone else's view. 'I know you are going to do an incredible job...' He paused, knowing he should step away now but Hannah's brown wide-eyed expression, and the way her dress gave a faint glimpse of the valley between her breasts, pierced through all his resolve to keep his distance. 'You're looking beautiful today.'

Hannah's hand shot from the side of the pedestal to switch off the microphone.

Dieu!

Hannah glared at him.

For a moment all he could hear was the orchestra's light playing. Maybe the guests didn't hear him. That brief glimmer of hope was soon dispelled, however, when sudden whoops and claps of approval thundered behind him.

He grimaced in apology. Hannah gave him one last glare before painting a calm professional smile on her face and looking beyond his shoulder as though waiting for a stage curtain to rise. He turned from her. Shrugged at the assembled guests, many of whom they had socialised with when they had visited François and Lara in Manchester and who had let it be known of their disappointment when their relationship had ended, trying to pretend that what he'd said wasn't of significance.

He retook his seat.

Leaning in towards him, François hit him with an exasperated stare. 'So much for promises.'

Hannah knew that it was a bride's prerogative to be late. But she wished with every fibre of her being that Lara would hurry up and arrive. She was already ten minutes late. Which under normal circumstances Hannah wouldn't even notice in the special hum and excited anticipation that came with the waiting for the bride.

Why did Laurent have to come up and speak to her? She'd just about been coping up until then. For a brief few seconds when he'd looked at her with that reassuring smile of his that had her heart turn over, his eyes soft and tender, she'd felt weak with relief that he was there to support her. But then he'd spoken and the dark edge in his voice when he'd said she looked beautiful had unsteadied her. And then the echo of his voice fading out over the sound system had registered. God, she couldn't bear the thought of people speculating incorrectly that their relationship might be back on. And now, there he was, sitting in front of her, looking all gorgeous and brooding in his tux, his black dress shoes shining brilliantly, his long legs spread out in front of him, his blue gaze continually glancing in her direction, making her already frayed nerves unravel even further.

She looked out over the guests and tried to maintain her professional smile. While inside she was a churning mess of emotions. Not only was she thrown by having Laurent so close by, but she still wasn't certain that her speech was any good. Was it just rambling thoughts? Would it have any meaningfulness for Lara and François?

Why did she feel so damn lonely, so vulnerable today? It felt as though a hole were opening up inside her. Would her relationship with Lara be the same once she was married? Had she been wrong in telling Laurent about her adoption? Had it really served any purpose? She'd wanted him to understand that she too knew of broken families. That it didn't have to define you. But she'd failed to explain all of that last night. Maybe her speech today might convey some of what she was trying to say.

Of course, the irony was that even though she believed your past didn't have to define your future, she knew only too well that putting that belief into practice was easier said than done. Some fears seemed to tether you to the past by their force.

Laurent turned in his chair and, looking towards the entrance, said something to François. Hannah smiled at François's nervousness. Laurent shifted around in his seat and for a moment their eyes met. Unaccountably, tears threatened at the backs of Hannah's eyes at the light smile he gave her. The loneliness inside her deepened.

She looked away. She was *not* going to think about how she used to sit in work meetings daydreaming of one day walking towards him, becoming his wife. She used to fantasise about her dress, what her bridesmaids would wear, marrying on her parents' farm and, God help her, making love to her new husband.

Now she pulled back from the impulse to roll her eyes at her own naivety.

A movement at the entranceway had her pause and then she was smiling crazily, tears once again forming in her eyes as first Stella, dressed in a primrose-yellow midi-dress, walked down the path, soon followed by a beaming Lara on her father's arm. Her lace, full-skirted midi-dress was perfect for a summer wedding, as were the rosebuds threaded lightly through her blonde hair tied up in a loose chignon.

When Lara reached François, Hannah's heart swelled to bursting point at the love that shone in both of their eyes, at how they smiled at one another shyly. How glorious to know that you were going to spend the rest of your life with the person you so deeply loved.

Hannah gestured to them to take their seats before her. She returned Lara's excited smile. Hannah gave her ear a quick tug. Lara giggled. Ear tugging used to be their secret way of communicating to one another when in school. One tug indicated a positive reaction, two tugs a negative response.

On François's and Lara's behalf she welcomed all the guests and expressed how honoured she was to be their wedding celebrant. Then, pausing for a moment, she stared down at her speech, praying her love and hope and wishes for them would be adequately reflected in what she was about to say.

'When I was training to be a wedding celebrant I spoke to many friends, colleagues and family about what they felt was the key to a successful marriage. Many people cited love, respect, honesty, trust and kindness as being key. But another word was sometimes used as well, a word that intrigued me, because up until that point I hadn't thought of it as being important. And that word was hope.'

She paused and looked first at Lara and then François, swallowing against a catch in her voice. 'I was lucky enough to be present on the first night that you met. Immediately I could see how suited you were to one another, and the hope that immediately sprang between you. At first came the hope that the other person was feeling the same way, that they would call again. And as the weeks passed, the hope was that the obstacles you faced would not stand in your way—François living in Paris, Lara in the middle of exams.'

Hannah looked out towards the guests. 'What is life without hope? What is love without hope? We need hope to know and believe that everything in life passes. Hope allows us to work together through tough times, knowing there will be a brighter future. Hope makes us more resilient. Hope allows us to dream, to share a vision for the future. Hope is also vital in forgiveness. We all make mistakes in life and hope is central to us learning from that experience and allowing ourselves to move on.'

From the corner of her eye she saw Laurent shift restlessly in his seat. She willed herself not to look in his direction, but as she continued her gaze slowly drifted towards him. 'Hope is integral to daring to dream, daring to believe that the person you have fallen in love with will love you back for ever, will understand and support you, will respect your marriage, will be your partner and friend and confidant.'

She pulled her gaze away from Laurent's tight-mouthed grimace, loneliness swamping her heart like a lead weight. She focused instead on Lara and François. 'Hold tight to your love and hope in one another. With hope you'll conquer whatever troubles life will invariably throw at you. Hope will allow you to share a life that is optimistic and ambitious and fun. They say that marriage is a huge leap of faith, but I actually think marriage is the ultimate song of hope. The hope of believing in the magic of love, in trusting the other person with your heart, in daring to dream of a future together. With all of my heart I wish you a joyful future together.'

She paused. A fat tear rolled down Lara's cheek. Hannah smiled through the heavy emotion clutching at her heart when Lara tugged her earlobe once. Then, pulling herself together, she looked towards Stella. 'And now, before I conduct the exchanging of vows, Lara's sister, Stella, will read a poem that Lara and François have chosen to be part of today's celebration.'

Moving down the lawn towards the river where the wedding photographs were to be taken, Laurent smiled when his mother held back from the rest of the wedding party to wait for him.

'It was a beautiful ceremony.'

He nodded in agreement when she took his arm, trying to mask how much Hannah's speech had unsettled him. Hope. It was a concept he'd never considered before. He was an achiever, ambitious for his career. But the hope Hannah had spoken about during the ceremony, the hope of shared dreams, of trusting in others, did he possess any of that?

He and his mother walked in silence until his mother finally said, 'It's nice to finally get to meet Hannah.'

He studied his mother, wondering where this conversation was going.

'I'd like you to meet someone, marry one day too.'

Laurent stared at his mother. This chat was not following the normal pattern of their conversations, which usually revolved around business and social events and the practicalities of everyday life. They *never* spoke about anything personal. He was about to give a glib reply but the emotion of the day, seeing François so happy, recalling his conversation with Hannah last night had him ask instead, 'Why did you and Papa stay married? Why were you both so unhappy that you had affairs?'

His mother came to a stop. Stared at him with consternation. 'I'm not sure that's really a question for today.'

'Did you ever really love one another?'

His mother winced, but then, rolling her shoulders back, she answered, 'We married too young. We allowed our selfishness, our restlessness, our own insecurities and frustrations to get out of control—your father should never have taken over as CEO of the House. It didn't play to his strengths. From the first day, he struggled in the role and was deeply unhappy and overwhelmed, but he wouldn't admit to any of that. For me, it was hard to accept that the man I married wasn't the person I thought he was. I thought I was marrying an ambitious CEO when in truth I'd married a man more interested in buying and selling cars. But neither he nor I could accept that fact. We were too proud and we also felt the weight of family history and expectations. It soon became a vicious circle of us taking our disappointments, our frustration and hurt, out on one another. And on you two boys.'

Hard, confused anger rose up from deep inside him. 'When you and Papa walked out on us we never knew when you would return, or indeed if you ever intended to.'

His mother looked at him helplessly. 'I thought having one parent at home would be enough.'

He bit back a bitter laugh and shook his head in disbelief. 'And that was supposed to make up for the fact that I knew one of you was away with other people, enjoying life. At least you had the decency to only do it the once, whereas Papa must hold a world record for infidelity. Was it the same woman all of the time or do you even know?'

His mother blanched and then, looking down towards the lake where his father was talking with Lara's parents, said in a barely audible voice, 'You need to speak to your father. There are things he needs to explain to you.'

In the distance, walking in their direction from the lake, François called out, 'Mama, you are needed for the photos. You too, Laurent. And has anyone seen Hannah?'

His mother looked at him expectantly. As though waiting for a response. His gaze moved back towards the walled garden. Hannah was standing at the archway talking to an old university friend of François's from Paris. He heard her laughter and then she was waving him goodbye. She turned in Laurent's direction and even from this distance he could see her hesitate in coming down the path to join the rest of the wedding party.

He turned to his mother. His anger dimming at the plea in her eyes, at the age spots on her cheeks he was only noticing for the first time. 'You and Papa seem happy together now. Why is that?'

She gave him a regretful smile. 'With experience we have learnt not to hurt one another. Your father's pride and need to be in control is less of an issue and I've adjusted my expectations of him. He's a good man. I wish we both had been less worried about status in the past and focused on what was important—our family.'

Laurent ran a hand against the tautness in his neck. Studied his father giving directions to the photographer as to where he should position the waiting bride and groom. 'Are you certain being in control isn't still an issue for him?'

His mother laughed lightly, observing what was unfolding between his father and the harassed-looking photographer too. 'He can slip back into old habits like the rest of us sometimes.' She paused and grimaced. 'Speak to him, Laurent. Let him explain himself. He struggles knowing you have such a poor opinion of him.'

Taken aback, he stared down at his father, who was now slowly limping towards Lara's parents. He swallowed against a lump in his throat. Then, turning in Hannah's direction, he saw that she'd turned away and was walking back through the walled garden. 'I should go and tell Hannah that she's needed.'

He could tell his mother wanted to say more. But he needed to get away; he needed breathing space. And to his alarm he realised he wanted to be in Hannah's company right now. He needed her calmness, her ability to distract him from even the worst of his thoughts with her smile, her quick-witted humour.

He bolted up the path, close to breaking into a jog. Hannah was heading along the path towards the pre-dinner drinks reception on the terrace when he caught up with her. 'You're wanted for some photographs.'

She looked at him as though she didn't believe him. 'I am?'

For a moment he wondered if the small pearl earrings

she was wearing would feel as smooth to his touch as her skin. And suddenly the need for lightness, to hear her reassuring laughter, grabbed him. 'You're one of the stars of today's celebrations, of course you're wanted for the photos. Especially when you are looking so beautiful.'

She eyed him suspiciously but then, with a look of curiosity, asked, 'Is everything okay? You don't seem yourself.'

She was right. But he didn't want to talk about how unsettled he felt by his conversation with his mother. 'You have that effect on me.'

She stared at him wide-eyed for a moment but then, throwing her head back in laughter, she threw her hands up. 'That's the cheesiest line I've heard in a very long time.'

She walked away from him in the direction of the river. He watched her for a moment, cursing his inability to think straight, his pulse upping a notch when he took in the sway of her hips and those much too sexy strappy sandals in the same shade as her dress that had distracted him throughout the wedding ceremony. When he caught up with her he said, 'Well done on a great job. The ceremony was excellent.'

'Even to a wedding cynic like you?'

He smiled at the scepticism in her voice. 'You don't have to personally believe in something to be able to identify brilliance.'

A hint of a smile flashed on her mouth. 'Just don't try broadcasting that to the other guests, will you?'

He swallowed a chuckle. 'Sorry about that. I hadn't realised the microphone was on.'

For a moment her gaze met his and they shared a moment of private amusement that flowed over him like calming balm.

In the distance, they could see the wedding party.

François and Lara were leaning against a tree barely taking notice of the photographer, who was circling them, snapping them from every possible angle. Lara's parents and Stella were watching them, nibbling on canapés.

And then he spotted his mother and father, a distance away from the rest of the wedding party, talking intently, their bowed heads almost touching.

He came to a stop. And stared towards them.

'Something is definitely up.'

He started at Hannah's words. And was about to deny that anything was wrong, but then his mother ran a hand against his father's cheek, the tenderness of the movement catching Laurent by surprise, and without thinking he admitted, 'My mother believes that I should speak to my father about his affairs, that he needs to explain things to me.'

'You don't want to?'

'Who in their right mind would want that conversation with a parent?'

'It might ease the tension between you. It might help you understand what happened back then. It could be your opportunity to explain how it affected you.'

She was right, but the anger inside him didn't want a rational explanation. Waving in response to the photographer's beckoning for them to join the others, he said, 'They're waiting for us.'

Shading her eyes from the glare of the sun, Hannah nodded and then, her gaze shifting towards his parents, who were now accepting glasses of champagne from a waiter, said quietly, 'They seem so close now, it's hard to believe that they both had affairs and that their relationship survived it.'

Hannah swivelled around to study him when he gave a dry laugh. With a disbelieving shake of his head, he explained, 'I was thinking that exact same thought.'

Hannah rolled her eyes. 'The synchronicity of our thinking strikes again.'

The pearly white eyeshadow on her eyelids glittered when she blinked and his heart quickened at her soft smile, at the amusement sparkling in her eyes. They used to joke when they were together about their frequent simultaneous thoughts. From wanting a glass of wine all the way to ideas in the bedroom. He breathed in at that thought, remembering that dark winter's night he'd answered his intercom close to midnight to Hannah, and as he'd gone to open the door had fantasied about her wearing nothing but her overcoat. He'd opened the door to find her wearing her killer black heels and knee-length white woollen coat. She'd walked past him, dropping her coat onto the floor, and he'd watched her walk naked up the stairs, turning once with a flirtatious smile.

With the photographer's beckoning becoming ever more frantic, he reluctantly led Hannah down towards the river.

'So, what did your mum say?'

'That their affairs stemmed from their unhappiness, primarily due to my father not coping in his role as CEO.'

'You don't sound convinced.'

He shrugged, not knowing what to think.

'Put yourself in his position. You've wanted to be CEO from a young age—how would you feel if you were now failing, realising that you weren't capable of the role?'

He let out an angry breath. 'I certainly wouldn't go and have an affair as a way of coping.'

Hannah nodded. 'No, I don't think you would either. But I think you'd struggle to accept it—just as anyone else would. I'm not saying you should forgive your father. But maybe you should try to understand him.'

He was about to argue why he should do anything of

the kind, but Hannah interrupted and said, with empathy shining in her eyes, 'Not for his sake, but for yours. Don't let your parents' mistakes hold you hostage to the past.' As they neared the others Hannah said softly, 'If you want to talk later I'll be here for you.'

Aware of François's narrowed and unhappy gaze as he watched them on the path he said, 'François told me to stay away from you.'

'And Lara warned me to keep well away from you,' Hannah admitted with a grimace.

Coming to a stop, he said quietly, 'We should really listen to them.'

For a moment she looked as though she was about to agree with him, but after some consideration said, 'I think what we had between us deserves better than that. I know it's over between us and I accept that fact, but avoiding each other...' She paused and shrugged. 'It seems childish but also a disservice to how close we once were.' Reddening, she looked back down to the river. 'I don't know if that makes any sense to you.' Then nodding towards François, who was now beckoning for them to join them, she added, 'Why don't you ensure that the photographer takes a photo of your family and Lara? You can get it printed and place it in Villa Marchand for when they come back from honeymoon.'

Nodding, he placed his hand lightly on the small of her back and together they joined the others, his plan of action to stay away from Hannah crumbling in the face of her softly spoken truth—what they had in the past, the friendship and fondness, the connection between them even now, deserved better than easy avoidance. Spending time with Hannah might be dangerous and an emotional minefield but it *was* the right thing to do.

CHAPTER SIX

WITH A DEEP SIGH, Lara stepped out of her high heels and leaned against the wall of the château. 'Do you know what this reminds me of?'

Having similarly divested herself of her own shoes, Hannah closed her eyes and lifted her face to catch the last rays of the setting sun. 'When we used to hide at the back of the school in year seven during break?'

'Exactly! Mrs Wilson was certain that we were up to no good.' With a chuckle Lara added, 'Remember how she used to try to smell our breaths to check if we'd been smoking?'

'When in reality we hid there to make up stories and games about an imaginary zoo.'

Hannah opened her eyes in time to see Lara roll hers. 'All of the other girls thought we were so dorky. I guess we were really.'

Shifting closer to Lara, Hannah rearranged some of the rosebuds that were working their way loose from Lara's fine hair and said, 'I'm guessing you refused to allow the hairdresser to use any hairspray to fix these in place?'

Lara gave Hannah a teasing smile. 'We all have to do our bit for the environment.' Both Lara and François worked for environmental agencies. They had met when

François had visited Manchester to spend the weekend with an ex-colleague who now worked with Lara. In both their professional and personal lives, they were passionate about protecting the planet.

'François told me about Laurent's gift.'

Hannah's heart tightened at the emotion in Lara's voice, the tears shining in her eyes. 'Are you pleased?'

Lara gave her a beam of a smile. 'Thrilled and stunned. It has made today even more incredible. Buying our own house was always going to be a challenge on our salaries. Villa Marchand is everything I ever dreamed of in a home, even before it was renovated. I can't wait to see it later. And of course it has such special memories of our engagement. François is already thinking that we should move here permanently. I suppose we could look into the possibility of working remotely for our current employers or apply for positions in Bordeaux.'

Hannah took a step back. 'Leave England?' She tried not to show her disappointment but then blurted out, 'I'll miss you so much.'

'And me you…but flying to Bordeaux from London would almost be as quick as getting the train to Manchester.'

Lara was right, but, still feeling unsettled at losing her best friend to France, Hannah asked, 'But what's the rush. Why move now?'

'We need more room. We're only able to afford a one-bedroom apartment in Manchester at the moment.'

Hannah was about to ask why that was a problem when up until now she and François had loved their apartment in Didsbury, but then Lara gently laid her hand on her stomach.

'Oh, my God! Are you pregnant?'

Lara nodded, her cheeks flushing, her eyes sparkling

with tears. 'You're the first to know. I'm only seven weeks pregnant. We've agreed to wait a little while longer before we tell others but I wanted you to know. I could never keep a secret from you, could I?'

Hannah pulled Lara in for a hug and whispered, 'I'm so, so happy for you.'

Lara, so much smaller than Hannah, dropped her forehead against Hannah's collarbone. 'Promise you'll come and visit me if we move here.'

Hannah pulled back at the doubt in Lara's voice. 'Wild horses couldn't keep me away.'

Lara grimaced. 'With Laurent being so close by... I wasn't sure how you'd feel about visiting here.'

Hannah wasn't certain how she would feel about visiting either. The stirrings of panic shifted in her stomach as she imagined having to pretend not to be affected by Laurent time and time again. But she couldn't let Lara know any of that. Slipping back into her shoes, she indicated that they should go back to the reception. Earlier when Lara had pulled her away from the ballroom after the marathon celebration dinner, muttering that she needed some air, François had warned them to be back within ten minutes for the slideshow that Stella and their Manchester friends had compiled and which was about to show against the side wall of the château, next to the walled garden. Hannah had been as keen to escape; a three-hour meal seated at the same table as Laurent had made her decidedly jumpy and exhausted from the constant adrenaline rush that came from observing him and the moments when their gazes would meet, a pointless harpoon of desire and connection piercing her heart.

Heading down the path in the direction of the walled garden, Hannah said, 'We'd better get back to the slideshow before François sends out a search party.'

'You're spending a lot of time with Laurent today.'

Hannah felt a brief but intense burst of annoyance and then guilt at the worry in Lara's voice. 'No more so than with anyone else.'

Lara raised a disbelieving eyebrow to that.

After the official photos had been taken they had walked up to the drinks reception together and had stayed chatting, talking about work and travel. And over the long dinner, when many at their table had swapped seats to chat to others, Laurent had invited her to come over to his side of the circular table to join his conversation with Lara's mother.

'There's nothing behind it other than the fact that we still get on. I have dreams of my own to follow—you know that.'

'The move to Singapore I understand but your idea of moving to Spain doesn't make any sense. What's in Spain for you?'

Hannah laughed. 'Spanish men!'

Lara shook her head, a ghost of a smile on her lips.

'I have dreams, Lara, ones that don't contain Laurent. I'll always be fond of him. I can't switch off completely the friendship we had. Yes, he hurt me, but I have good memories too. I want to remember those, learn to have a new type of relationship with him now. I'll need to, you know that. We have years ahead of us of seeing each other, especially if you move here.' She paused and gave Lara a reassuring smile. 'But I have moved on.'

For long seconds Lara eyed her, clearly weighing up whether she should believe her or not. Hannah forced herself to maintain her reassuring smile, but it hurt her cheeks and her heart to do so; it was hard to smile when doubt was mocking what you were trying to convince yourself and others of.

* * *

Laurent chuckled when a baby photo of Lara popped up on the wall of the château. Her fine, wispy blonde hair was standing on end, and the writing on her mud-stained jumper—TROUBLE—was an apt description for the mischievous glint in her eyes as she lunged towards a wary sheepdog with muddy hands. And then he groaned when an unfamiliar picture of himself and François in the bath appeared. He looked about three, François, a year old. Both of them were smiling wildly at the camera oblivious to the crowns of bath foam on their heads, which Laurent guessed, given the grin on their father's mouth as he knelt beside them supporting François with a hand against his back, he'd placed on his sons' heads.

His father looked so young, so carefree in the photo. It was hard to reconcile him with the man who had become so irritable and secretive in later years. Hannah's question as to how he would react if he wasn't capable of running the business came back to him. He stared at a new photo, this one of him pushing François in his pram, his hands barely able to reach the handles. Five previous generations of Bonneval sons had successfully run Bonneval Cognac; it undoubtedly would be hard for anyone to accept that they were the first inheritor not to be up to the role. But that didn't in any way excuse his affairs, his betrayal, his abandonment of his family.

Another photo flashed up, this time a family photo of the four of them all linking arms in front of his father's beloved Citroën Traction Avant. He glanced in the direction of his parents, who, like all of the other guests, were standing in the darkness on the lawn to watch the projection show. His mother smiled at something his father said and then they both looked in his direction. Thrown by the affection in their expressions, he studied them, his brain trying to process the easy love in the pictures being displayed on the wall and this new, calmer and contented version of his parents in comparison to the chaotic and angry people they had been when he was a teenager. His mother's smile faded.

He became aware of someone moving beside him. 'You were a beautiful family.'

He jerked at Hannah's softly spoken comment. Her attention remained on the wall, her head tilting when a video played of himself and François running through a forest, shouting to one another and then disappearing. Then there was the sound of his father's voice, playfully calling out to them, but then Laurent could hear the panic growing as he called and searched for them to no avail. The crowd tensed, as his father's panic grew. His voice became more desperate. The dense forest took on a sinister air. Laurent held his breath. Unease rippled through the guests. And then, as one, the entire crowd started when Laurent and François burst out of a heavy growth of ferns and then relieved laughter ran around the startled guests.

The video cut to one of Lara and Stella playing in the snow as toddlers.

Hannah shifted closer to him. She glanced at him, her eyes twinkling. 'Of course, you're still a beautiful family.'

He smiled at that, but then, glancing in his parents' direction, he said, 'I'm not sure you could call us a family.'

Hannah came even closer, spoke softly so only he could hear. 'I saw how upset you were when your dad was ill. How keen you were to get back here to support your mother. I know they hurt you in the past, but I also know that in your own way you love them greatly.'

Laurent gazed past Hannah to the wall, smiling automatically when Lara fell against the snowman she and Stella had been building, demolishing it completely. Stella's crying rang out while Lara lay in the snow, looking horrified at first but then rolling around in the snow chuckling to herself.

He glanced in his father's direction. Then back at Hannah. She was waiting for him to respond. He shrugged but did not look away from her. Her gaze held such a tenderness, an understanding, that he felt his heart crack open. He wanted to place his arm around her shoulders, pull her to him. Take refuge in the warmth of her body, for even a minute feel the full force of how grounded, how real he felt in her presence.

New sounds had them both look towards the château wall. Lara, aged seven or eight, dressed in pink shorts and a rainbow-coloured tee shirt, was chatting to the camera, excitedly exclaiming that they were panning for gold. The camera moved beyond Lara towards the small stream behind her, to a girl standing in the water. Hidden behind a mass of dark hair, the girl lifted a household colander out of the water. Her arms were thin, her denim shorts hanging loose on her waist. Her quietness was in stark contrast to the excitement of Lara, who was now wading into the stream with her yellow wellington boots, oblivious to the fact that she was splashing the other girl, who didn't even flinch. From behind the camera, Lara's father called, 'Any luck yet?'

The dark-haired child turned to the camera. With a start Laurent realised it was Hannah. Solemn brown eyes, much too pronounced cheekbones faced the camera and with a single shake of her head she returned to her job of sifting through the gravel in the colander.

He leant down and whispered against her ear, 'Did you find any gold?'

Her gaze held a distant haunted expression and for a moment she looked at him blankly before finally answering, 'A fake gold ring, but I saw Lara's mum plant it in the water.' She stopped and gave a faint smile. 'To this day Lara thinks we unearthed it.'

Dieu! He so badly wanted to pull her into a hug, to comfort her. A desire that became even more intense when photos of Lara and Hannah a few years older flashed on the wall, Hannah's gaze more open, her thinness no more, then them as teenagers, dressed for a night out, their make-up too extreme, their skirts much too short, but the happiness and joy in their expressions quickening his heart.

His respect, pride, admiration for her soared. She'd survived her childhood, moved beyond it, to become a warm and loving and compassionate person with a huge strength of character.

Next, photos of Lara's and then François's graduation appeared. In Lara's she was surrounded by her family and friends, including Hannah. In François's photo, however, it was just him and François. At the time, neither of them were in contact with their parents. A few years later, François had begun to have regular contact with them again, but Laurent had kept up minimal contact with them until his father's stroke.

He glanced over at his parents. Was Hannah right? Should he talk to his father? Would it backfire on him? He swallowed. The slow realisation hitting him that he was scared. Was that even the right word...? Scared seemed wrong for a grown man to use, but, yes, he was scared of once again confronting his father's disapproval and dismissive attitude to his ability to run the business. An attitude he'd been facing since the age of sixteen. He could never do well enough in his father's eyes and it tore strips off his heart.

The slideshow came to an end with a selfie picture of Lara and François on the evening François had spontaneously asked her to marry him, sitting together in the gardens of Villa Marchand, Lara flashing her makeshift engagement ring of bound grass as proudly as she would a diamond.

Around them the guests began to move back towards the terrace and ballroom. For long seconds his and Hannah's gazes met. Something fundamental passed between them. A silent understanding. He touched his hand against hers. Skin against skin. A brief connection. He smiled at her and was rewarded with a tender smile in response.

Then he spotted François and Lara unhappily looking in their direction. Guiding Hannah towards them, he excused himself, saying he needed to play host, intending to go and speak to an old friend from Paris but instead finding himself move towards his father, who was walking back towards the ballroom alone.

The band had long stopped playing and Lara and François had left for Villa Marchand hours earlier, but Laurent and Hannah still had to encourage the small but determined group of guests intent on partying through the night into their awaiting taxis as the sun slowly rose in the August sky.

Hannah laughed when one of Lara's friends leant out of the window as his taxi pulled away and shouted merrily, '*À bientôt*, we'll see you later... I want a rematch, Laurent, and my ten euro back.'

'Remind me to lock the gates when we go inside,' Laurent said wryly.

Hannah folded her arms and gave him a pretend look of chastisement. 'That'll teach you for taking on drunk opponents when you're completely sober.'

Laurent raised his hands in exasperation. 'For the last time, I didn't take his money. Anyway, it was his idea to challenge me to a game.'

As she remembered the sight of Laurent, jacket removed, shirtsleeves rolled up with a table tennis bat in his hand, taking on opponent after opponent, his reflexes lightning sharp as he cleared the ball easily time and time again over the net, then his quiet pride at winning that was so infectious, a slow warmth spread throughout Hannah.

Arching his back as though to stretch the long night out of his spine, Laurent said, 'Time for bed, I think.'

Hannah nodded, trying not to react to the tenderness in his voice, how it added to the giddy sense of anticipation that had been slowly building inside her all night.

The dancing had taken place in the ballroom, but the wedding guests had also partied out on the terrace, where the impromptu table tennis tournament had sprung up, Laurent being crowned the overall winner as the caterers had finally taken their leave at four in the morning. It had been at that point, when she and Laurent had thought that the party was finally coming to a close, that some of the younger guests had dive-bombed into the swimming pool. She and Laurent had stood by the pool and tried to encourage them to get out, laughing between themselves at their good-natured high jinks.

Inside the hallway, Laurent closed the main door, turning the key in the lock.

'It was a great night, really fun,' she said.

He turned and studied her for a moment, his eyes holding hers fondly. 'Thanks for your help. I'm not sure how I'd have managed if you weren't here.'

It would have been so easy for Laurent to have ended the party hours ago, but seeing what fun everyone was having, François and Lara in particular, he'd asked for Hannah's assistance in extending the celebrations.

'I didn't do much.'

'You arranged for the caterers to remain here after their planned finish time to look after the guests, drove my parents home and on your return had to act as a lifeguard and fish out some guests from the swimming pool and organise for them to dry off inside.'

All night they had easily fallen into a way of managing and communicating over everything that had needed to be taken care of as the party had evolved, and for a moment Hannah was on the verge of pointing out what a good team they made, but thankfully good sense kicked in and instead she said, 'Your mum looked exhausted. I was happy to drop them both home.' Pausing, she asked, 'I saw you talking to your dad earlier. Did it go okay?'

He grinned and Hannah almost melted at the playfulness sparkling in his eyes. 'I asked him why he accepts your help and not mine.'

'And what did he say?'

Laurent crossed his arms on his chest, the teasing smile intensifying. 'That you're a whole lot prettier.'

Hannah could not help but giggle. 'I guess it was a start at least in you two talking.'

Pointing down the corridor, Laurent moved away. 'Come on, I think we both deserve a drink.'

He led her in the direction of the kitchen. Daylight was starting to flood the downstairs rooms, light birdsong filtering in from outside. As she walked by his side, lazy, happy tiredness washed over her.

'I mentioned Nicolas Couilloud's threatened price increase to him.'

Entering the kitchen, she asked, 'What did he say?'

'At first he asked me what I had done to cause the increase.'

Hannah winced. 'Oh.'

'Precisely.' He moved away from her and opened a cupboard teeming with drinking glasses. 'What would you like to drink—wine, spirits or a soda?'

Hannah shifted towards the countertop and, lifting the electric kettle, popped it under the tap to fill it. 'This time of the morning I can only face tea.'

Laurent closed the cupboard door. 'I'll join you.' Taking some teacups from a cupboard, he placed them on the countertop before leaning back against it. 'My father eventually accepted that Nicolas's increases were unwarranted. He's pretty incensed about it all.'

'So you don't think he was involved?'

'No.'

Pouring hot water into the white china teapot Laurent had placed on the countertop, Hannah asked, 'Had he any ideas on how to resolve it all?'

'He offered to talk to Nicolas. I was tempted to say no but, seeing how important it was to him to take it on, against my better judgement I agreed.'

'And his affairs, did you speak to him about those?'

'No. I'm not sure what there is to be gained.'

'I think you deserve to have your father understand what impact those years had on you.'

He just shrugged at her comment and brought the teacups over to stand beside the teapot. Hannah expected him to back away but instead he stood looking down at her. 'I never got to dance with you tonight.'

Heat exploded in her belly at his nearness and shot

all the way up onto her cheeks. She looked towards the kitchen door. 'I should really go to bed. I have a busy week ahead. I need to fly to Edinburgh first thing Monday morning.'

He backed away a fraction, studied her for a moment, then, reaching for the teapot, he poured tea into the cups before passing one of them to her. 'Before you do go to bed, tell me something—the hope you spoke about yesterday during the ceremony, was that what got you through your early years?'

Thrown by his question, Hannah ran a finger around the rim of her cup before answering. 'I guess. I was very young, my memories are hazy, but I remember hoping for small things, that they wouldn't leave me alone in the house, that one day I'd be able to bring my friends from school home with me...but then I stopped going to school.'

'It kills me to hear what you went through.'

By the anguish reflected in his eyes, Hannah could see that he really meant what he'd said. She reached out, touched his forearm, her breath catching at the warmth of his skin. 'Those years were tough but then I was taken in by the most amazing parents anyone could ever wish for. I'm so grateful I had them and Cora and Emily. They taught me so much about love, about trusting in others, about being honest about my feelings and owning them.' She paused, the sudden realisation that she'd never been honest about how she felt about Laurent mocking her. But that was an act of self-preservation; surely she was right to keep those feelings to herself.

She looked out of the window over the sink and nodded towards the ceremony chairs that were stacked by the walled garden and ready to be collected later today. 'You'll be glad to get back to normal after the chaos of the past few days.' The thought of leaving pinched her heart. 'And poor Bleu must want to get home. I still feel so guilty that you had to send him away.'

'Bleu regularly stays with Phillippe when I'm travelling and he loves spending time with Phillippe's spaniels. You have no reason to feel guilty.' Pausing, he considered her for a moment before asking, 'Your fear of dogs— did something happen when you were with your birth parents?'

Her head snapped up at the perceptiveness of his question. She arched her neck and lifted her shoulders to ease out a kink, only now realising that her whole body was aching with tiredness. She wanted to go to bed. She glanced out again at the ever increasingly bright morning sky, grimacing at the realisation that she wanted to go to bed with Laurent. She wanted to lie next to him. Have him hold her. Hear his breath as he slept. She shook herself. That type of thinking was crazy.

'I don't remember exactly what happened. I just vaguely remember a man and a woman coming to the house with a dog. He was huge, dark coated. I must have gone to bed because the next thing I remember is waking to find him next to my bed growling. Every time I went to move, he growled even more, baring his teeth.' She brought her cup to the sink and rinsed it, thrown by how upset she felt. 'I have no idea how long it took for my mum to come in and find him. I tried calling but there was music playing too loudly downstairs. I tried not to cry. I thought that would only make him angrier. I remember pushing myself against the wall and pulling my duvet against myself, hoping that would protect me if he attacked.'

When Laurent came to stand beside her she gestured that she would wash his cup too. But, shaking his head, he placed the cup out of her reach and, laying his hands on her shoulders, he gently turned her around to face him.

'I wish I'd been there to protect you.'

Her heart tumbled at the intense care in his voice, emotion welled in her throat, and she blinked rapidly, trying to hold back the threatening tears. He pulled her into him, his long arms tightly wrapping around her. His body enclosed hers as though he were trying to protect her from shellfire, his shoulder tilting to form a sheltering hollow for her forehead to rest on. His hand ran along her spine, light movements that had her fall even harder against the strength and shelter of his body. She didn't fight him. Her need to have his care right now was far greater than her need to protect herself.

Fully aware of what she was doing, she pulled back, and even though her heart was racing, her voice was surprisingly calm and assured. 'I don't want to be on my own when we go upstairs.'

He studied her for a moment, as though trying to decide if he'd heard right. Then in a tender voice that had her want to cry all over again, he said, 'You know why that's not a good idea.'

'Just hold me. I want to be with you.' There was so much more she was desperate to say, to explain why she wanted to be with him—her confusing mix of elation and loneliness at seeing Lara so happy, her dread at leaving later today, all the bittersweet memories this weekend had unearthed. But she couldn't tell him any of that because to do so would expose what he meant to her.

Laurent took a step back. Dizzying disappointment crashed over her.

But then his fingers trailed softly against her cheek, his gaze moving from concern to understanding acceptance. Taking her hand in his, he led her upstairs to his bedroom. He left her staring at his king-sized antique bed, the imposing headboard and curved footboard made of wood and cane, ornate roses carved into the pale painted wood, the crisp white linen and mountain of pillows making her sway with tiredness…and the dizzying anticipation of lying there with him.

Her gaze shot to the adjoining bathroom. What if he was about to change his mind? She heard the sound of running water and then he was back out in the room with her, opening a drawer in the three-door armoire that matched his bed with the same carved roses along the woodwork and garlands on the cane. Lifting out a grey tee shirt, he handed it to her. 'The shower is running for you.'

For a moment she hesitated. Suddenly having second thoughts.

'I'm going to hold you, Hannah, be there for you. No more. I'll keep you safe, but if you want to go back to your bedroom then I'll walk you there.'

No. That was not what she wanted. She shook her head firmly and on a shaky breath turned for the bathroom. Knotting her hair up into a bun, she allowed the warm water to ease the tension in her body and wash away her racing thoughts.

When she emerged from the bathroom, he was standing in front of the bed wearing only bed shorts, running a towel through his damp hair.

'I didn't mean to throw you out of your own bathroom.'

Walking past her, he threw his towel into a linen basket. 'I used the bathroom in the guest room next door.'

She tugged unconsciously on his tee shirt she was wearing, wishing it smelled of him rather than some unfamiliar fabric conditioner. His expression tense, he went and closed the shutters of the room, plunging them into darkness. It took a few moments for her eyes to adjust enough to be able to see him remove some pillows from the bed before he came and released her hair from the band holding it up and, leading her to the bed, gestured for her to lie down. When she curled on her side, he curled in behind her, his thighs skimming against the backs of hers, his arm lying on her waist.

He whispered, 'Dors bien. Sleep now. I'll be here.' His hand shifted up, first to skim over her arm, and then over her hair, the soft reassuring pressure, the comfort of his huge body lying next to her having her eyes droop with tiredness.

CHAPTER SEVEN

LAURENT SIGHED, DROWNING in a sea of happy confusion. He shifted his body, an unwelcome ray of awareness intruding on his dreams, telling him to fight against the bone-tired contentment that was dragging him back towards sleep and oblivion.

A deep shiver ran the length of his body as a warm weight passed over his chest. His abs contracted as the weight continued moving downwards over the band of his shorts. Adrenaline surged through his body. And then he was awake, leaping up in the bed and pulling away from Hannah.

She was awake. Just about. She considered him through drowsy eyes, her sensual smile slowly fading away.

Had she even been conscious of what she'd been doing? Of where her hand had been travelling towards? He closed his eyes for a second, trying to control the need drumming through him, trying to get his body under control. Which was nigh on impossible with Hannah lying there, looking sexy and cute and irresistible, with her huge soft brown eyes holding the same need that was pulsing through him. He tried not to stare at her pale pink lace underwear where her tee shirt had ridden up, or at the outline of her breast, a hardened nipple visible beneath the grey cotton.

He collapsed back down onto the bed, keeping a safe distance between them. He knew he should get out of the bed. But it felt as if he'd had only an hour's sleep, and in truth he wanted to lie here with her.

For long minutes they stared at one another, the quietness of the early morning, the low light in the room casting an intimate, dreamlike air to the moment.

He longed to reach out and touch his finger to her lips, plump with sleep, touch the warm silkiness of her flushed cheeks. She shifted her hips to turn fully onto her side, the tee shirt riding even further up so that the inch of lace on her hip was exposed along with the soft wave of her hip bone.

He pulled in a long deep breath as blood pounded in his ears. A year of sleeping alone, of dreaming about her, was catching up with him.

Her hand moved out, rested on the expanse of sheet between them. Her gaze met his. 'I want to be with you.'

He sucked in some air at the soft surety of her voice. 'We can't.'

She tipped her head, her skin flushing even more. 'Are you saying you don't want me?'

He gave a disbelieving laugh, shifting fully onto his back, running a hand through his hair as he stared at the ceiling before turning his gaze back to her. He'd known when he'd taken her to his bedroom that this was the most likely outcome, but he also had wanted to lie down with her and simply hold her, have her forget all the things that she'd told him about her past. 'Nothing has changed, Hannah. I don't want to hurt you again.'

'I know all of that. But last night, when I told you that my parents taught me to be honest, I realised that I'm not being truthful with you.' She paused, bit her lip, her hand pulling down the tee shirt over her hip, covering the deli-

cious curve of her bottom. 'I'm deeply attracted to you…
I need you physically. I have no expectations or wishes
or hopes other than to have sex with you.' She smiled, a
beguiling smile that was both sexy and shy all at once.
'We were always great in bed together.'

He could not help but smile back. 'On that point I can't
argue with you.' Taking hold of her hand, he threaded
his fingers through hers. 'Are you certain this is what
you want?'

'I want sex with you. Is that clear enough?'

He laughed at her teasing tone that also held a hint
of frustration. 'You were never patient when it came to
sex, were you?'

Her eyes lit with mischief. 'I never thought I'd complain about having too much foreplay.'

He lifted her hand and one by one kissed each finger
before flipping her hand over to kiss the palm. 'You need
to slow down when lovemaking, cherish every single
moment.' His tongue ran a circular path around the soft
skin of her palm.

With a groan she shifted onto her back, her hips wriggling against the mattress. 'But it feels like torture.'

He trailed kisses up the inside of her arm, his cheek
brushing against the side of her breast, and then his
mouth found her neck, her back arching as his tongue
licked against the soft skin behind her ear. He moved
along her jawbone and at her mouth he hovered over her
parted lips, his heart tripping over at the wonder and
passion and need in her gaze. 'Are you certain this is
what you want?'

She made a noise of annoyance. 'Will you quit asking
me that?' And then to cement her answer she wrapped her
arms around his neck and pulled him down to her mouth.

His pulse rocketed, his body tightened, all thought left

him as her mouth explored his with a frenzy he understood and responded to, her legs wrapping around his, her entire body moving upwards to press into his.

For a brief intoxicating moment, as he moved towards where she lay in his bed asleep, Laurent saw the long seductive length of Hannah's back, but then, as though she'd sensed his approach, she twisted from her side onto her back, pulling the sheet up. For a moment he considered giving in to the temptation of lying back down beside her and losing himself again in the cocoon of her warmth and musky scent.

He placed a teacup and a plate with a freshly baked croissant and an apple on the nightstand, smiling when she gave a faint snore. He'd never told her that she snored. For some reason he'd wanted to keep that a secret to himself. Just as he'd never told her how he'd watched her every morning before he'd left for work as she'd slept, her contented form grounding him for the day ahead, her warmth and beauty making the world a whole lot brighter before he'd even stepped out into the day.

He sat on the side of the bed, his eyes trailing over her dark arched eyebrows, her nose twitching ever so slightly in her sleep, her cheeks still flushed from their lovemaking. He buried his head into his hands. How was he going to manage the next few hours before she left for London? When she woke, despite her insistence that she'd wanted to be with him, would she be upset, angry, regretful over their lovemaking? Would she look at him with the same hurt and bewilderment as she had in London before he'd left for France?

He inhaled a deep breath. Feeling more rattled than he'd ever been in his life. Their lovemaking earlier had been intense—a year of absence and regrets and affection all spilling out into a confusing but beautiful act of passion, connection and tenderness.

Making love with her, having spent the weekend together, the intimacy of what they had shared with one another about their pasts, all added up to the inescapable fact that today was going to be even harder than London. He needed to tread carefully, make saying goodbye as painless as possible for them both. His gaze moved back to her. Tonight he would lie here in this bed without her. He closed his eyes. Hannah leaving for London was for the best. But somehow, and he was still not sure how, he wanted to show her before she left that he cared for her even though he would never be able to give her the love and commitment she deserved.

He bowed his head for a moment, recalling his mother's shouting, his father's silence. Recalling the night he'd watched his father dump suitcase after suitcase into his car and drive away. The awkward telephone conversations in the months that had followed when he'd been at first too confused and then too angry to speak to his father, who had demanded to know if his mother was poisoning Laurent against him. And then, months later, when his father had returned to the château, his foolish, excited, naïve relief that it was all over. Only to have to endure it all again when his mother had left the following year. And then his father's frequent absences in the years that had followed when he'd left to continue his affairs. He'd stopped trusting in others, stopped allowing himself to be vulnerable by loving them. He cared for Hannah. But he could never love her.

He laid his hand on the warmth of her shoulder, his thumb stroking the oval birthmark below her collarbone. The first time they had gone sailing together, he'd seen it when she'd changed into her red swimsuit. Dumbstruck by the gorgeousness of her curvy body, he'd wanted to maraud his way down the boat to where she was sitting chatting with Lara, and throw all the other males on board who had also been staring in her direction overboard. Instead he'd bided his time, waited for Lara to invariably be drawn back to François, before he'd gone and spoken to her. Spotting her birthmark, he'd told her that it was a kiss from the gods. She'd folded her arms and looked at him suspiciously, rightly knowing that he was trying to charm her, but as she'd turned away to stare out to sea, he'd seen a smile lift on her mouth.

'Hannah, it's time to wake up.'

Her eyes drowsily opened. For a moment she gave him a contented smile, her eyes sparkling with a sexy affection that had him lower his hand from her shoulder for fear of lowering his mouth to her soft lips.

Her smile faded at his movement and she bolted upright in the bed, clasping the sheet to herself. 'What time is it?'

'It's close to ten o'clock.'

Her eyes widened. 'I didn't mean to sleep in for so long.'

'Yesterday was a long day.' He paused, cleared his throat, the remembrance of their disturbed sleep adding a husky note to his voice. 'You needed to rest.'

She dipped her head for a moment, biting her lip, and then looked back at him, the heat in her eyes having him shift on the mattress as desire surged through him.

In need of a distraction, he lifted the teacup and handed it to her. She yanked the sheet even higher against her chest and considered the cup of tea before her gaze shifted back to him. He winced at the sadness in her eyes.

But then her expression hardened. He cursed himself for wincing. He was about to make an excuse but, with a firm shake of her head, Hannah refused the tea and, yanking the sheet further up against herself, she said, 'I should go for a shower and get dressed.'

Placing the teacup back on the nightstand, thrown by the coolness in her voice, her desire to get away, he cleared his throat and said, 'About earlier—'

She interrupted him with a shove against his back, forcing him to stand. Swinging herself out of the bed, she wrapped the sheet around herself. Waddling awkwardly across the room, she said, 'There's really no need for us to talk about earlier, is there?' and gathered up her dress and shoes from where she'd placed them on a bedroom chair last night.

He watched her shuffle towards the door, yanking up the falling sheet time and time again. Her urgency, her insistence on acting all cool and calm, irrationally irritated him. And then that irritation disappeared to be replaced with an uneasy thought that maybe their lovemaking really didn't mean as much to her as he'd thought it did. Her words on Thursday night sounded in his brain. *I'm over you, Laurent. I've moved on. Don't overinflate your importance in my life.*

Following her, he called out, 'You forgot these.'

He tried to hide his amusement at her horrified expression when she spotted her lace knickers hanging from his index finger. She grabbed them from him and in the process the sheet dropped to expose a gorgeously erect dusky pink nipple. She tugged up the sheet furiously.

Dieu! He wanted to pull that bloody sheet away. Make love to her. Thick, dangerous desire was pumping through him. He stepped back. 'Wait, I'll give you my bathrobe to wear.' Seeing her reach for the door handle, he added, 'I don't want you giving my housekeeper,

Marion, a heart attack by having your sheet fall down as you walk back to your room. Her heart gives her enough trouble as it is.'

In the bathroom he removed his bathrobe from the hook. Back out in the bedroom he held it out for her to put on. She dumped the items in her hands onto the floor, turning her back to him as she placed her hands into the robe sleeves. The sheet fell slowly and seductively to the floor. She tied the belt of the robe with a yank and, turning around, she lifted her own items and the sheet, which she threw in his direction. 'Yours, I believe.'

He caught the sheet, feeling more in control now that her initial icy coolness had been replaced by an air of defiance. Gesturing to the bathrobe, the arms hanging well below her fingertips, the white material swamping her frame, he shook his head. 'It's much too big for you, and I'm detecting a certain lack of gratitude in me gifting it to you.'

She eyed him cautiously. In London, they used to tease each other this way. Spring surprises on one another.

He stepped closer. 'In fact I'm having second thoughts about letting you wear it.'

Her eyebrows shot upwards. And then she was making a dash for the door.

He chased after her and wrapped his arm around her waist and lifted her off the ground.

'Laurent Bonneval, you put me down, you brute.'

He laughed and could feel her body jerk with silent laughter too.

And then rather primly she said, 'Yesterday you said you needed to work today. Please don't delay heading into the office on my account.'

He lowered her down and turned her around to face

him. 'My father was right when he said as your host I should ensure that you are looked after. I've decided not to go into work today.'

She looked at him with surprise. 'Oh.'

He opened the bedroom door. 'Downstairs is in chaos thanks to the clean-up after yesterday. I have a beach house in Royan—we can go there to escape the noise. Marion is packing a picnic for us to take.'

'But my flight is at seven this evening. Do we have time?'

He nodded. 'I'll drop you straight to the airport from Royan. So bring your suitcase.'

She eyed him curiously for a moment and then with a shrug she went to pass him, but out in the corridor she turned to him. 'I want to go and see Lara before we leave for Royan. I'd like to say goodbye to her.'

'I'll ring ahead and let them know we'll call in.'

'You said yesterday that you were going to collect Bleu from Phillippe today on your way into work.'

'I'll also ring Phillippe and ask him to keep Bleu until this evening.'

She shook her head. 'No. He has been away from you for too long already. Let's collect him on the way to Royan. We can take him for a walk on the beach.'

Bleu adored the beach. And Laurent couldn't wait to see him again. But despite the determined tilt of Hannah's chin as she waited for his response the quiver in her voice told him how much of an effort it would all take. 'I'll collect him later this evening.'

Tugging the belt of the robe tighter, she grimaced and said quietly, 'I need to get over my fear of dogs. It's gone on for far too long.' Her bare feet on the marble floor of the hallway shifted and her gaze moved to a point beyond his shoulder. 'I'd like to try to spend time with Bleu... knowing that you are there.'

Without stopping to think, Laurent moved to her. Touched his hand against the soft white cotton of her bathrobe. 'In his size Bleu is intimidating, but he really is a marshmallow. My vet believes he was mistreated by his previous owner. Bleu and I have spent a lot of time with a dog trainer, training him to respond to my commands. All he wants is love and affection.'

She gave a wry chuckle. 'That sounds familiar.'

An awkward silence settled between them. Hannah's cheeks reddened. She cleared her throat, gave him a hesitant but teasing smile. 'I'll blame you, though, if Bleu tries to eat me.'

Walking back to the nightstand, he picked up the teacup and plate of food and handed them to her. 'Have something to eat and drink. We'll leave to collect Bleu as soon as you are ready so that we can make the most of the day at Royan.' He laughed lightly and added, 'And don't worry, if Bleu strays too close to you, I'll do my best musketeer impression and will protect you.'

She laughed at that. 'I'd give anything to see you wearing tights and a floppy hat while wielding a sword.' Then, sobering, she looked him directly in the eye. 'But I can protect myself. I don't need you.'

And walked away.

CHAPTER EIGHT

SHUTTING THE DOOR to her bedroom, Lara leant against it with a sigh and asked, 'What's up?'

Taking in Lara's wedding gown, hanging perfectly on a white satin clothes hanger on the door of the wardrobe, Hannah said, 'I'm guessing that you didn't drag me upstairs after all in order to hang your dress properly.'

Dropping down onto the bed, Lara answered, 'Obviously. You're jumpy and clearly upset. What's up?'

Running her hand over the delicate lace of Lara's wedding dress, Hannah shrugged, swallowing down the temptation to tell Lara the awful truth that in sleeping with Laurent she'd realised that she was still in love with him. 'I guess it's post-wedding blues. I hate the thought of going back to work tomorrow.' Turning, she gave Lara a smile. 'And I'm going to miss you while you are away on honeymoon.'

Lara shook her head and sighed. 'Guess what? I'm not buying any of that.'

Hannah rolled her eyes, trying to act nonplussed when in truth an ache was gripping her throat. Why did Lara have to be so perceptive?

For a moment she considered changing the subject but knew that Lara deserved the truth, even if she was going to go crazy about it. 'I spent the night with Laurent.'

'Hannah!'

Hannah held her hands up in admission. 'I know. But don't freak out about it. We both know that it was straightforward, uncomplicated sex.'

Lara covered her face with her hands, shaking her head in despair before saying, 'Oh, Hannah, why? Why allow yourself to get hurt again?'

Hating Lara's disappointment in her, hating just how vulnerable she felt, Hannah bit back. 'Why don't you believe me when I say I'm over him? That I have my own plans and dreams to follow?'

Anger flared in Lara's eyes. 'Because I see the way that you look at him.'

Trying not to blush or give in to the frustrated tears threatening at the backs of her eyes, Hannah snorted. 'He's a good-looking man. Of course I look at him.'

Lara stood. For long seconds she looked at Hannah sadly. 'You're still in love with him, aren't you?'

'Do we really need to talk about this now? We should be talking about yesterday.' Forcing herself to give Lara a cheeky smile, she asked, 'So how's married life, Mrs Bonneval?'

Lara inhaled an impatient breath. 'Are you going to tell him about how you feel?'

'He doesn't want a relationship. I'm cool with that.'

Moving to the bedroom window, Lara looked out of it. Joining her, Hannah saw that she was studying Laurent and François, who were sitting at the garden table next to the river. Lara shook her head. 'I want to go down and throttle him. He shouldn't have slept with you.'

'Don't blame him. It was me who initiated it—you could say that I slept with him.'

Eyes wide, Lara turned and asked in an appalled voice, 'Why on earth did you do that?'

Hannah searched for some glib reply, but as she began to speak her voice cracked and to her horror a fat tear spilled down her cheek. Knowing her pretence was now of no use, she answered, 'Because I'm lonely…because I miss him.'

With a sigh, Lara pulled her into a hug. Then, grabbing a tissue from the dressing table, she wiped Hannah's tears and asked quietly, 'What are you going to do?'

With a wry laugh, Hannah answered, 'Get through today. Continue to pretend I have no feelings for him other than that he's a friend of sorts. And after today, go and forge a new life for myself.'

Later that morning, above the hum of the air conditioning, Bleu's snoring reverberated around Laurent's four-by-four like low rumbling thunder.

'Does he always snore like that?'

Slowing at a junction, Laurent glanced over at her. 'I think snoring is cute.'

Hannah stared at him, confused by the amusement playing out in his expression as he signalled to the right and pulled out into the heavy traffic when a gap became available. Conscious that Lara had so easily seen through her pretence, and determined not to allow Laurent to see that her heart was a mangled mess, she attempted to adopt a congenial tone. 'He certainly was happy to see you.' Folding her arms, she added, 'But I thought you said that he was well trained.'

Laurent gave a guilty chuckle. 'Usually he follows my commands.'

Reaching forward to lower the air conditioning, Hannah threw him a teasing look. 'I was just glad I was in the safety of the car when he bounded towards you. I was certain he was going to knock you over.'

He grimaced at that. 'He'll be calmer when we get to the beach house, I promise.' Then, his gaze meeting hers for a moment, he added, 'You seem to be coping with having him in the car. That's an incredible step forward for you.'

Her heart melted at the admiration and care in his voice. But she knew that she needed to maintain the nonchalance and teasing banter she had been hiding behind all day in a bid to harden herself against his effect, his ability to tear out her heart and leave her confused and vulnerable and so incredibly lonely for him even though he was sitting right next to her. How could they be so close, both physically and on a surface emotional level, but yet be so distant from one another? She hated all of this pretence and dishonesty. It wasn't who she was. Or at least trying to be. But what other option did she have? She could hardly casually drop into their conversation that she was in love with him.

Instead she turned and eyed the rear of the car where Bleu was lying in the back compartment and, thanks to her frayed nerves, gave an almost hysterical laugh. 'Coping. Are you kidding me? I'm a bag of nerves. The only reason I'm not tempted to jump out of the car is because there's a metal grid separating him from me.'

She jumped when Laurent's hand came to rest on the side of the seat, his fingers almost touching her thigh. His gaze remaining fixed on the heavy flow of traffic ahead of them, he said quietly, 'We're almost at the beach house. When we get there I'll show you into the house and then take Bleu out. You don't have to spend time with him.'

A lump formed in her throat at the understanding in his voice. She swallowed hard, knowing that she needed to toughen up, not only with Bleu but also in how she allowed his master to get to her. 'No, I meant it when I said I wanted to spend time with him.'

Laurent glanced at her. 'Are you sure?'

'I'm tired of having mini panic attacks every time I jog through Richmond Park and a dog comes near me. Last week, I actually screamed when I almost tripped over a dog no bigger than a hamster who came flying out of the high grass. He was being walked by two teenage girls who clearly thought I was crazy and ended up doubled over laughing at me.'

Laurent cleared his throat, clearly trying not to laugh at the image she'd painted. 'Okay, I can see why you want to deal with your fear.'

Turning her attention back to the passing scenery, she smiled when a golden beach and glistening sea appeared on the horizon. 'What an incredible beach. How long is it?'

'About two kilometres. *Sirocco* is moored here in Royan.' Pointing towards the far end of the beach, he added, 'You can see the marina in the distance.'

Hannah blinked away all the threatening memories that came at the mention of his yacht and the days they had spent on the Solent. 'Do you get out on *Sirocco* often?'

'Not as often as I'd like to. Work has been crazy since I got back here.'

'What about the beach house?'

He glanced at her and shrugged. 'Even less.'

'Maybe if your dad had a role in the business, even for a few hours every week, it might take the pressure off you.' Thinking about Lara's pregnancy, she added, 'Perhaps in time François might be interested in joining the business too. I'm guessing his environmental background could be of huge benefit.'

Laurent slowed and pulled off the main road into a residential street. Halfway down the street he pulled into a driveway and used a remote control to open grey panelled wooden gates. 'It's a possibility…about François. Up until now he hasn't been interested in working in the company, but his circumstances are changing.' Driving through the gates, he added wryly, 'However, I'm really not convinced about my father permanently getting involved in the business again.'

A tall cypress tree towered over the front lawn of the Malibu-style, single-storey beach house. Beyond the house Hannah caught a glimpse of the vast expanse of the beach. 'What a location.' Turning as Laurent switched off the engine, she asked, 'Did you inherit this house too?'

'No. I bought it a few years back.'

She tried to hide her surprise and hurt and said with a forced smile, 'You never mentioned that you owned a property here when we were together.'

From the rear of the vehicle, Bleu stirred, his movements rocking the car. Hannah glanced back to see him looking with adoration in Laurent's direction.

Opening the door of the car, Laurent answered, 'It didn't seem important at the time.'

'No, I don't suppose it did.'

About to get out of the car, he paused and turned back in her direction. 'This is my first time visiting the house in over five years. Only the second time since I bought it.'

Her mouth dropped open. 'Seriously?'

'It was once my family's summer home. My parents sold it over fifteen years ago. I bought it back from the family who bought it from them.'

'But why have you never used it?'

'We spent our summers here as children. Both I and François were disappointed when my parents sold it.

They said at the time that they sold it because we were insisting on spending our summers in Paris. I always felt guilty about that. Five years ago, when I told my mother that I had purchased the beach house, she told me the truth about why they had sold it.'

Given the anger and pain in his expression, Hannah asked quietly, 'Which was?'

'Apparently it was here that my father lived with his mistress when he left home.'

Hannah winced. 'Oh.'

'Exactly.'

Following Laurent's lead, Hannah climbed out of the vehicle. The white walls of the house sparkled in the midday sun, the lush, well-maintained planting in the garden swaying in the light breeze. 'It doesn't look like you haven't been here in years,' she said, joining him as he walked up the gravelled path to the front door, glass panels at the side showing an open-plan living space with a huge sea-blue sofa and an off-white painted kitchen to the side, enormous windows running the length of the back wall with views over the bay.

'I've paid for it to be maintained.'

As Laurent placed a key in the lock she asked, 'Weren't you tempted to sell it?'

Laurent ran a hand against the base of his neck. She longed to reach there as she'd done countless times in London, laughing when he groaned in pleasure, the tight knot which he frequently arrived home from work with loosening under her touch. 'I thought about selling several times over the past few years but couldn't bring myself to. But if business doesn't improve I might be forced to.'

'I didn't realise things were that serious.'

He shrugged and gestured for her to enter the house

and said, 'I'll let Bleu out of the car. You can wait inside here or come out and join us if you decide it's what you want to do.'

As he walked away she asked, 'Why did you decide we should come here today?'

Stopping, he turned. His dark skin glowed in contrast to the whiteness of his button-down shirt. His hair caught in the breeze and he had to smooth it down. 'I thought visiting here might be easier with you at my side.'

She stared after him when he turned away, wondering if she'd heard his gently spoken answer correctly.

For a few seconds indecision rooted her to the spot but then, seeing Laurent about to open the back door of the car, she called out and ran towards him.

Coming to a stop, she smiled at him, her heart lifting as he returned her smile even though his held an element of puzzlement. 'Thanks.'

Despite her promises to harden herself to him, the power of their earlier lovemaking, the connection, the synchronicity between them that felt so instinctive and right made what followed inevitable.

He reached for her, one hand on her waist, the other touching her cheek. He kissed her with an aching tenderness and her heart kicked both in fear and delight.

Even with his blood pounding in his ears Laurent could not ignore Bleu's barking. With a groan he pulled away from Hannah and gave her a regretful smile.

Her lips were swollen from their kiss, a deep blush on her skin.

He backed away, away from the temptation of resuming their kiss, his need for Hannah more intense now than it had ever been before.

Placing a hand on the rear door, he asked, 'Are you certain you don't want to stay inside?'

Hannah shook her head. But then stepped to the side of the vehicle as though searching for cover.

Opening the door, Laurent patted Bleu and spoke to him in a low comforting voice. Bleu's barking ceased, to be replaced with a delighted wagging of his tail.

Turning to Hannah, he gave her a triumphant smile. 'See. I told you he responds to me. You have nothing to be concerned about.'

But no sooner had he said those words than Bleu bounded out of the car, ran down the driveway and, turning in a wide arc, leapt over low hedging, before racing back towards them. Hannah yelped and ran behind him, her forehead digging into his back, her fingers coiling around the belt loops of his waistband.

A wave of protectiveness for Hannah had him shout at Bleu as he neared them. *'Non! Couche.'*

At his command Bleu came to an immediate stop, his head tilting to the side at his master's never-before-heard yell.

Reaching behind him, he took hold of Hannah's hand and, pulling her around to stand at his side, he gave Bleu a further command. *'Assieds.'*

Immediately Bleu sat.

Hannah was shaking. Placing his arm around her, he pulled her into a hug. 'Are you okay?' She nodded yes, but still she shook. He ran a hand against her hair. His own heart was pounding, the strength of his instinctive need to protect her taking him aback. Against the lemon scent of her hair he whispered, 'Wait here. I'll lead Bleu inside.'

She backed away from his hug, gave him a grateful

smile that liquefied his heart and, glancing in Bleu's direction, said, 'No. I want to get closer to him.'

Admiration swelled in his chest at the determination in her voice. And then the image of Hannah as a young child curled up in bed, shaking and terrified by the snarls of a dog, had him clasp his hands tightly in rage.

He gulped down that rage and went to Bleu, whose tail swept across the driveway in large arcs of happiness when he approached, his head falling back in adoration, anticipating a rub, his brown eyes tracking every movement as though it were precious.

The rage inside him flowed away as he rubbed Bleu, his love for this animal, who had been so weak and accepting of his fate when he had found him starved and dying in the woods, rooting him to the spot. Sudden, unexpected emotion stuffed the backs of his eyes. A vulnerability, a loneliness, a bewilderment that he couldn't comprehend. Disconcerted, he tried to blink it away.

Behind him, surprisingly close, he heard Hannah's soft laugh. 'Bleu reminds me of François when he looks at Lara—complete infatuation.'

Turning, he grinned up at her. 'And I adore him.' Rubbing Bleu along the long length of his spine, he added, 'Don't I, boy? Aren't you the bravest, most lovely dog ever?'

Panting hard with happiness, Bleu rolled over onto his back, wanting his belly rubbed. Four giant legs and paws reached skywards like mini skyscrapers.

Once again Hannah giggled. 'That is the most ridiculous thing I've ever seen. You're right. He is a complete marshmallow…albeit a donkey-sized marshmallow.'

He held out his hand to her. 'Come and crouch beside me. Rub him too if you feel like it.'

With a worried look in Bleu's direction, she tentatively took Laurent's hand. She was still trembling. He gave it a little squeeze. For a moment she paused in her tentative steps towards Bleu. He inhaled a breath at the question in her gaze—can I trust in you? Instinctively he wanted to pull his hand away, tell her not to trust in him, not to invest any emotion in him, but shame and annoyance at that reaction had him smile and nod encouragingly instead.

When she was crouched at his side, she reached slowly for Bleu's belly and rubbed him with short jerky movements. Taking her hand once again in his, Laurent guided her to make longer, more soothing movements. He heard her gasp in, but then as her hand moved against Bleu time and time again and Bleu gave a comical yawn of contentment, she exhaled a long breath of relief.

'Good job.'

She smiled proudly at his praise. His heart tumbled at how her eyes were sparkling with relief and joy.

'It's hot out here.' He stood and added, 'Let's go inside. Bleu should be in the shade.'

Positioning Hannah to one side and Bleu to his other, he led them into the house. Taking Bleu immediately into the storage room to the rear of the kitchen, he plucked some beach towels out of a cupboard and made a temporary bed for Bleu while asking Hannah to find a suitable bowl in the kitchen for him to drink from.

When she appeared at the door with the bowl he nodded for her to place it by Bleu's bed. Lowering it down, she tentatively moved her hand towards Bleu's head, placing it a short distance away from where he was lying on his side curled up, ready for yet another sleep. Bleu slowly, instinctively, as though sensing Hannah's fear, nudged his nose towards her hand and sniffed it. Then withdrawing, he tucked his head down towards his chest and closed his eyes.

Hannah stood and smiled down at Bleu. 'I think I could actually fall in love with him.'

Laurent could understand the wonder in her voice. 'There's something special about him, isn't there?'

Hannah nodded and then gave him a teasing smile. 'I thought Bleu was lucky that you found him when he was so ill, but maybe you're the lucky one to find him.'

Laurent gave a low disbelieving laugh. 'I was just thinking that. These simultaneous thoughts are getting out of control.'

Hannah placed her fingertips to her temples. 'Okay, let me guess what you're now thinking.' She scrunched her face, as though deep in thought. 'You're going to suggest we go for a swim.'

'How did you know that?'

'It could be telepathy…or the fact that you're standing there holding beach towels.' Grinning, she walked out of the room. 'I'll go and fetch my bikini from my suitcase.'

Laurent knew Bleu would be comfortable in the shade of the room and, with one final pat for him, closed the door to the room gently.

After showing Hannah to a guest bedroom where she could change, he threw on swimming trunks he'd brought to the house five years ago, fetched the picnic basket from the car and then, going back into the living room, he opened the doors that led out onto the decked terrace. Stepping out, he inhaled a deep breath of sea air and turned and regarded the house. The previous owners had modernised both the interior and exterior, but the overall house structure and the sweeping views had remained the same.

The last time he'd visited the house, five years ago,

he'd only stayed long enough to unpack. Unable to handle the sickening thought of his father spending all those months here when he should have been at home.

He'd driven back to the airport, not bothering to even pack his luggage, and taken the first flight back to London.

He walked to the pool, stared down at the tiled dolphin at the base, which he and François had spent endless hours racing to.

At the sound of footsteps behind him, he turned and smiled as Hannah tugged down her blue-and-white striped dress, the yellow straps of her bikini visible. She came and stood beside him. 'This view is amazing.' Then with concern she asked, 'What are you thinking about?'

He led her towards the steps down to the beach. 'I thought you were telepathic.'

From behind him, her flip-flops slapping on the concrete steps, she asked gently, 'Are you remembering your childhood here?'

He waited until they reached the beach, his bare feet sinking into the soft sand, to answer. 'Our time here was idyllic. I lost all of that when I found out about my father… He had always refused to answer my question as to where he was staying when he called home. For the past few years I've been incredibly angry with him for sullying my memories, but maybe it's time that I create new ones for this place.'

She nodded but there was a sadness to her expression that punched him in the gut. He smiled, wanting to lighten the mood, and headed in the direction of the sea. 'Starting today.'

He went further down the beach, dropped the picnic basket and blanket onto the sand.

She was still at the steps eyeing him dubiously but then

walked towards him with a mischievous expression. 'So what memories will you have of today?'

He waited until she came to a stop in front of him before he answered. 'You rubbing Bleu's belly, being brave and determined.'

Something low and carnal throbbed in him when she pulled off her dress to reveal her yellow bikini. An inch of the soft flesh of her high breasts was exposed, the strings of the bottoms tied into a bow on the swell of her hips. He tucked her hair that was lifting in the breeze behind her ear. 'I'll remember also how incredibly beautiful you looked.' He lowered his head, whispered against her ear, 'I'll remember how I was woken this morning... and what followed.'

She leant into him, her breasts skimming against his chest for a much too brief second. And then she was stepping back from him, giving him a look full of bravado that didn't match the heat in her cheeks. She called to him when she was well out of his reach, pointing towards the sea. 'You can also remember how I beat you in a race to the swimming platform.'

Enjoying the sight of her running to the breaking surf, he allowed her to gain a considerable lead on him. Then, breaking into a light jog, he followed her, diving into the sea, gasping at the coldness. Out on the sea platform, he waited for her by the ladder.

When she arrived, she looked dumbfounded when he reached down to help her out. 'How on earth did you get here before me?'

He laughed and pulled her up. 'You really need to learn to swim in a straight line.'

For a while they lay in silence on the platform, staring up at the wisps of clouds that were passing overhead.

Then with a loud exhalation, Hannah admitted with a laugh, 'I'm so out of breath.'

Her chest heaved up and down and he fought the temptation to place his hand on her wet skin. 'I'll have to teach you how to sea-swim properly some time.'

'You've promised me that numerous times.' Her gaze darted away from his but he saw the disquiet that flickered there. Shielding her eyes, she added, 'Anyway, my sea-swimming is better than your tennis.'

'You beat me once.'

She grinned. 'Just saying. What height advantage do you have over me?'

'You well know that it's eight inches.'

Her eyes twinkled. 'A whole eight inches.'

And suddenly their conversation was taking on a whole different meaning. He leaned over her, deliberately being provocative, his mouth close to hers, his gaze playing with hers. 'It's what you do with those eight inches that counts.'

Her eyelids fluttered. 'Care to remind me again?'

He raised an eyebrow. 'I'm not sure that I do.'

She wriggled, her hip bumping against his belly. Her fingertips trailed over the valley between her breasts. 'Are you really certain about that?'

'I've never been able to resist you, have I?' And then his mouth was on hers, elation spreading through him at her softness, at her warmth, at her groan. His hand ran over her ribs, down over her stomach and over her hips. Her hands gripped his neck, her thumbs stroking the indent at the top of his spine.

Her body pressed upwards against his. Knowing he was about to lose control, he broke away from her mouth, groaned against her ear. 'If we don't stop we'll be arrested.'

Lying down next to her, he took hold of her hand. He could suggest that they go back to the house. Finish this off in private. But the need to do right by Hannah had him lie there beside her instead.

'Lara's so happy with Villa Marchand. It was such a thoughtful and generous present.'

He turned his head, considered her. 'I would almost swear that Lara deliberately pinched me when I hugged her goodbye earlier. Does she know about us?'

Hannah gave him a panicked and guilty look but then, with a shrug, she regained some of her composure and said, 'I told her I seduced you.'

He laughed at that. And then realised she was being serious. 'Please tell me that you didn't.'

Her answer was a smug smile.

He shook his head and something lodged in his throat when he remembered François's earlier delight whenever he looked at Lara, his buoyant mood and excitement for their honeymoon in the Galapagos Islands, how at home they both had seemed in their new house. 'Villa Marchand will be a great family home.'

Taking her hand from his, Hannah propped herself up onto her elbow. 'François told you?'

He feigned confusion. 'Told me what?'

Clearly thrown, she shrugged. 'Nothing. Forget about it.'

He frowned and asked, 'Is there something I should know?' but then, unable to stop himself, he laughed and added, 'You're so atrocious at lying.'

She gave him a playful slap on his arm. 'My parents brought me up to be honest.'

He was sorely tempted to kiss her again, run his hands over her body, but instead he admitted, 'I didn't realise how excited I'd be at the prospect of being an uncle.'

CHAPTER NINE

HANNAH COULD FEEL her pretence that she was in control and wasn't about to spew out all the thoughts and emotions crowding her brain and making her heart crumble at Laurent's words. She wanted to say that based on his love for Bleu he would make for a brilliant uncle. She wanted to point out to him that, not only would he be an incredible uncle, but, if he allowed himself, he would be an amazing father too. She turned onto her back. Closed her eyes.

She couldn't look at him today without her pulse soaring. But as her pulse soared, her heart felt as though it were slowly melting into nothing. It felt as though two beings were inhabiting her body: a physical self who was hyperaware of the chemistry spinning between them, and an emotional self, whose soul was aching with the need to connect fully with him.

Opening her eyes to the brilliant blue sky overhead, she said, 'I spoke to my parents before we left the château. They were asking about you.'

'In a good or bad way?'

'Good, of course. Why would you think otherwise?'

'I thought your parents, your family in general, might not be too happy with me.'

Despite her having invited him to visit her parents on

several occasions, Laurent had always had an excuse as to why he couldn't. But six months into their relationship she'd finally persuaded him to go with her. The weekend had been a disaster. Laurent had been disengaged, his reluctance and caution around her parents totally throwing her. 'They liked you but would admit that they never really got to know you.' Pausing, she added, 'The weekend you visited them with me, you seemed uncomfortable.' She swallowed and added, 'Didn't you like them?'

He sat up and stared at her. '*Dieu!* Of course I liked them.'

Hurt and bewilderment surged inside her, some of it months old, some fresh from the past twenty-four hours. Sitting too, she asked, 'Did you think I was trying to put pressure on you by inviting you to visit my parents? Because that wasn't the case. I wanted you to get to know them because they're fantastic people…and I love them to bits.'

Closing his eyes, Laurent inhaled a breath while running his hand tiredly down over his face. 'Being with your family, seeing how you all love one another, reminded me of how fractured my own family are. Your parents are wonderful, Hannah. I just didn't want to raise their expectations in terms of where our relationship was going.'

A swell of emotion grabbed her heart. He would never really know her parents, her sisters. She breathed against the loneliness that was threatening to drown her. 'They're good people.' She shot him a meaningful look. 'They deserved better from you.'

He grimaced and then with a nod said, 'You're right. Will you pass on my apologies?'

She wanted to say that he could do so himself. But,

of course, he would never see them again. Instead she asked, 'Have things improved with your family at all?'

He looked back towards the beach house. 'Not really.'

'Do you want a good relationship with them?'

'I'm not sure.'

'I think you do. I think you love them despite everything that happened.'

At that Laurent gave a disbelieving laugh. He glanced in her direction and then away. 'I don't understand love.'

Despite the heat of the day, Hannah shivered at the quiet certainty in his voice. 'You show love all of the time with your family. You've cared for and protected François since you were both teenagers. And when your parents were in crisis last year, you responded. Caring, protecting, responding to the other person, that's all love.'

He shook his head. 'You're forgetting that it was my opportunity to take over Bonneval Cognac.'

'I saw how upset you were the night your mother called to say how ill your father was. Getting to him and your mother was your priority. I bet the business didn't even enter your mind. Am I right?'

He gave a non-committal shrug. 'Perhaps.'

It felt as if an invisible wall had suddenly sprung up between them; she could feel Laurent distancing himself from her. Panic was curling inside her. She shifted around to face him directly, desperate to try to connect with him. 'There's time for you to develop a good relationship with them again.' She paused, trying to gather her breath against the hard thumping of her heart. It felt as though her body was sensing something that was about to come.

Frowning, he studied her for a long while, as though trying to understand her. An intense pain squeezed her heart at the coolness of his gaze. 'How do you manage to be so trusting of others despite everything you have gone through?' he asked.

'It's not easy. But my parents always told me that I need to be honest, to respect and own my feelings.' She stopped and gave an involuntary smile as his expression softened, but inside she was increasingly feeling vulnerable and desperate. She wanted him to understand her fully. She was so tired of pretence and hiding her true self. 'It was an important part of me coping with everything that had happened.'

His hand reached for her bent knee, his fingertip running over the faint scar there she got when she tripped over a tractor tyre in the barn one day. 'Your parents are very wise.'

'Yes, they are. But unfortunately I don't always follow their advice. Before you I was very cautious around guys. I was worried about getting things wrong. With my family, with friendships, I was okay...' she paused, not sure if she should continue, but something deep inside her was telling her to be honest with him '...but I've always been afraid of falling in love.'

A guarded expression formed in his eyes. She knew she should stop. She was only going to embarrass herself. She had worked so hard to get over him and was now about to throw all of that away. She was about to compromise all the plans she had made for an independent future. She was going to make herself vulnerable all over again. But she couldn't put a brake on the words that insisted on being spoken, how her heart wanted to have its say after months of being kept in check. 'I really, really care for you, Laurent.'

She smiled at him in hope, in embarrassment. Waited for him to say something. But instead he looked away from her, frowning. She wanted to cry. She wanted to yell at him. She twisted away from him. Willing him to say something. But they sat in silence, the happy cries from children on the beach washing over them; a swirl of embarrassed anger rose up from her very core and her heart shattered with the pain of feeling so utterly alone and disconnected from the man she was in love with.

Trying to quell the panic growing inside him, Laurent pulled in one long breath after another. He bunched his hands, self-loathing vying with his panic. 'This morning was a mistake.'

Hannah's gaze shot to his. 'That's wonderful to hear.'

He exhaled a breath at the sarcasm in her voice, his stomach churning to know he was to blame for all of this. He caught her gaze, gave her a smile of appeasement. 'You know I didn't mean it that way.'

She folded her arms. 'Do I?'

'After yesterday, we were both feeling emotional. Weddings do that type of thing to people.'

She shifted away from him, towards the edge of the platform, and gave a bitter chuckle. 'You make it sound like it was sympathy sex.'

He shook his head furiously. 'When did I say that?'

'Well, you're clearly regretting it.'

Taking in the defiant tilt of her head, the heavy emotion in her voice, the hurt in her eyes, he asked gently, his heart heavy with fear, 'Aren't you?'

For a moment her expression softened, and her gaze caught his as though pleading with him to understand. But to respond to her, to take her in his arms as he wanted to, would be cruel. He knew what Hannah was trying to say to him. She wanted more from him, from their relationship, than he could ever give.

Her expression hardened again. 'Well, I'm certainly regretting it now.'

He flinched at her hurt, her anger.

He tried to think straight, to find something to say, but his heart was pounding too hard, his brain a too-confused mess of panicked thoughts. He'd numbed his heart, his expectations, his need for love, for closeness, for trust, for comfort, so long ago, he didn't know how to open himself up to it all again…or if he ever wanted to.

'Things are never going to be right between us, are they?'

He barely heard her question, she'd spoken it so quietly. He grimaced and shook his head. Standing, she threw him an infuriated look before diving into the sea.

Hannah flicked off the shower. Towelled herself dry furiously. Yanked on her underwear and dress. She knew she needed to calm down. The anger inside her frightened her. But as hard as she tried she couldn't hold it back. It felt as though years and years of repressing herself were spilling out in Laurent's cold indifference to her telling him what he meant to her. Had he any idea how exposed, how hurt, how embarrassed she felt? Couldn't he have at least tried to meet her halfway, say something of comfort?

He was out in the living room, showered and changed, when she went there on the way out of the house.

She pulled her suitcase even closer to herself, tightening her grip on the handle. 'I've called a taxi to take me back to my car at the château. There's no need for you to take me to the airport.'

He gave her a disappointed, almost impatient look.

She gritted her teeth, telling herself to leave here with some dignity, but that pledge lasted all of five seconds because suddenly words were tumbling out of her, words that made her cringe at their neediness and bitterness, words that reminded her that she was her birth parents' child. She gestured around the room, out towards the beach. 'Why the hell did you bring me here? What was the point of all this?'

She didn't wait for him to respond but instead she paced the marble floor and continued, her hands rising to hold her head in disbelief. 'You know, you make me want to pull my hair out. You're...you're the most infuriating man.'

She came to a stop, suddenly breathless, her anger gone in those sharp words to be replaced by a tiredness, a confusion that physically hurt in her chest. 'What we have is good. Isn't it? Or is it just me being delusional?' She waited for him to respond. When he didn't she considered walking out of the door, but something was pushing her to speak from her heart, to explain her feelings and not be ashamed of them. For so long she'd been ashamed of her background, had felt sullied by it, ashamed that her classmates had known her when she had been withdrawn and terrified, ashamed of loving her parents more than her birth parents, ashamed that she was so terrified of so many things in life: dogs, loud knocks on the door, unexplained noises during the night. 'This morning, when we had sex... I saw how you looked at me. And anyway, it wasn't sex, was it? We made love, Laurent. I don't know why I'm saying all of this. I know I'm humiliating myself but I can't go around pretending that my heart isn't breaking.'

He buried his head in his hands, rubbing at his skin. When he looked back at her his expression was bewildered. 'What do you want from me, Hannah?'

Her throat closed over, her legs suddenly weak. 'For you to be honest with me.'

He walked across the room, came to a stop a few feet away. 'I'm happy with my life as it is. I can't offer you any commitment, a long-term relationship. I've always told you that.'

His voice was pained, his eyes brimming with confusion. Stupidly she wanted to cry at how alone he seemed. 'Yes, but why?'

'I don't seem to have the capacity for it.'

She laughed at that. 'That's such rubbish.'

'Okay, so we stay together. Maybe even marry, have kids. And then one day one of us grows bored, becomes disappointed in the other person. And we hurt one another.'

'Not necessarily.'

He turned from her, walked to the doors out to the terrace, stared out towards the beach before turning and asked, 'Doesn't it worry you that *both* of my parents had affairs?'

'Have you ever been unfaithful before?'

'No.'

She moved towards him, stepping onto the sea-green rug at the centre of the room, her bare calf touching against the wooden coffee table. 'Then why do you think that you'll be unfaithful in the future?'

He threw his head back and inhaled deeply. 'I've never been tested in a relationship, have I? I never dated anyone as long as I dated you. I always ended other relationships within a few months, before they got too serious.'

Thrown, she said, 'I never knew that.' Then with another disbelieving laugh she added, 'You're even more messed up than me.'

'Exactly.'

She moved towards him again and asked, 'Why are you so scared of love? What are you scared of, Laurent?'

He moved away from her, towards the kitchen counter. He opened up the picnic basket and answered, 'Nothing.'

She followed him and stood beside him. 'Not being able to love, how cynical you are over marriage because of what your parents did…it all feels like a front for something else you're hiding.'

He turned and looked at her, bewildered. 'I'm not hiding anything.'

'Maybe you're hiding it even from yourself.'

His eyes narrowed at that. 'I'm not following what—'

They both jumped at the sound of the intercom ringing.

She looked towards the front door. 'That will be my taxi.'

He pulled baguettes and cheese and ripe peaches from the basket. 'Stay. Have something to eat. I'll drive you to the airport.'

She walked away, grabbed hold of her suitcase.

He stopped her at the doorway. 'I don't want us to part like this.'

She stared into the brilliant blue eyes of the man she loved. And answered from her heart. 'I've told you my feelings…you've made it clear once again that there's no future for us.' She opened the door and, about to step into the bright light of the overhead sun, she turned and said, 'I hope you find happiness in the future. You deserve it. You just don't accept that right now.'

CHAPTER TEN

NOT FOR THE first time, Hannah looked blankly at another sales clerk in the airport duty-free who was waving a bottle of perfume and asking if she wanted to try a sample. The woman's smile faded when Hannah didn't respond. Realising how rude she must appear, Hannah took hold of the thin strip of sample paper, sniffed, made some appreciative noises before backing away. She felt numb, dumb and empty. And with hours to go before her flight, unable to read, unable to sit still, unable to bear being out in the packed waiting lounge near laughing families and excited couples, she felt as if the duty-free store and its bright colours and promises of contentment via cosmetics and alcohol and chocolate was the only place she could find refuge in.

She moved into a hidden corner that seemed forgotten by both staff and customers and vacantly inspected the stacked rows of lipsticks. She tried to read the improbable names—Moroccan Magic, Cupid's Bow, All-Nighter—but her brain soon zoned out and she stared at them vacantly.

What she wanted more than anything in the world was to be somehow magically transported back to her apartment. Back to her bedroom with the blinds pulled down. She picked up a silver eyeshadow. Her mum would love it. Recently her mum and dad had taken up ballroom dancing and her mum liked to wear dramatic make-up for their competitions. Hannah gave a faint smile, a fresh weight of heaviness clogging her throat when she remembered the time she was home visiting for the weekend and they'd arrived back from their first ever dancing competition, proudly announcing that they had come sixth. Hannah had clapped in delight. And then her parents had laughed and admitted that there had only been six couples in their category. They hadn't cared that they had come last. For them, taking part, dancing together, was all that mattered. They had been so animated in recalling the night and some of the extremes some of the couples had gone to to psych out their competition, finishing off each other's stories and sentences without even realising it. They loved each other so much. And never took that love for granted.

Hannah popped the eyeshadow in the small net shopping basket she'd picked up at the entrance, and realised it wasn't her apartment she'd choose to be transported to should a genie appear and grant her one wish. It was in fact her parents' house. There she might shake off the awful emptiness inside her through their calm and undemanding warmth and love. She wanted to be loved.

But she couldn't go home. Her parents, her mum especially, would notice her upset. And the last thing she wanted to do was worry her parents even more than they already were about her. They tried to hide it but even as a child she'd been aware of them studying her closer than they did Emily and Cora, more easily forgiving when she did something wrong. Now they worried over her lack of a relationship. They had never said anything but their delight and obvious relief when she'd told them that she was bringing Laurent home to meet them had said it all.

She wandered into the aftershave section. Was there something wrong with her? Was that why he couldn't love her? Was she too needy, too clingy, not pretty enough? Was it her background? Was the truth behind all his reasons for not wanting commitment the fact that he was waiting to meet someone from his own privileged background?

She eyed a familiar-shaped bottle of aftershave. Told herself to move away. But like an addict needing a hit, she lifted the lid and sprayed some onto her wrist. Closing her eyes, she inhaled the woody, musky scent. Laurent's aftershave. He never wore anything else. She blinked hard, a dense lump forming in her throat.

She didn't know what Laurent found lacking in her, but she could certainly identify one area of weakness—her judgement. How could she have allowed herself to get so tangled up with him again? She'd walked through this airport only three days ago determined that she was over him and was going to be nothing but professional and emotionally detached around him.

She'd made a complete mess of things. She moved into the alcohol section but even looking at the bottles made her queasy. Especially when she spotted the distinct blue-and-gold labels of Bonneval Cognac. She snatched her gaze away, a fresh wave of disbelief washing over her.

Had today really happened? First she'd asked him to sleep with her. Then to make love to her. Then later she'd more or less told him she loved him. Yip. Her judgement sucked.

She lingered by the confectionery section waiting for the embarrassment radiating from her cheeks to subside and trying not to give in to the temptation to buy a supersized bar of chocolate, before approaching the checkout.

Showing her boarding card to the cashier, she bought the silver eyeshadow.

She had a choice. Feel numb and dumb for the foreseeable future or try to pretend this weekend never happened. For her own sanity, she knew she needed to do the latter.

Finding a seat amongst a group of pensioners sitting at a gate displaying a Rome departure destination, she pulled out her phone and deleted Laurent's number and then, as quickly as her fingers allowed, every image of him in her picture gallery. Then, logging into the airport Wi-Fi, she began to research wedding celebrants in the Granada area of Spain.

Sitting in the boardroom of Bonneval Cognac, his father to one side, Nicolas Couilloud on the other, Laurent tried and failed to focus on the conversation of the two other men, who were arguing over the details of a five-year-old contract, which both were aggrieved about. He closed his eyes to the migraine lurking behind there.

'Laurent, is everything okay?'

He opened his eyes to Nicolas's terse question.

Nicolas sat back in his chair, a gleam entering his grey calculating eyes. 'You don't seem well. Perhaps you should leave these negotiations to your father and myself.'

He was about to answer but his father got there before him. 'Laurent is CEO now. It's he who has to finalise the contract. I'm only here to facilitate the negotiations.'

Laurent blinked, startled by his father's admission. He gave a brief nod of agreement and, for the first time in a very long time, they shared eye contact that wasn't more than a fleeting glance.

Nicolas cleared his throat. 'Has Mademoiselle Mc-

Ginley returned to England? You seemed particularly close at the wedding.'

'She left two weeks ago, immediately after the wedding.'

Nicolas shrugged, gave a knowing smile. 'There's plenty more attractive women out there keen to date you.'

Though he was tempted to stand, Laurent remained seated and, folding over his notepad and shutting down his laptop, he said to Nicolas, 'Considering that you are an old family *friend*, and our businesses have worked together for the past twenty years, you will get a two per cent contract increase.'

'We need at least eight per cent,' Nicolas spluttered.

Laurent stood. 'Two per cent.'

'Antoine, you can see that Laurent's offer is unreasonable,' Nicolas said, looking in appeal towards his father.

For a moment his father hesitated, his gaze shifting between Nicolas and him, but then with a shrug towards Nicolas he said, 'Laurent is CEO.'

His migraine worsening, and wanting these negotiations over and done with once and for all, Laurent stepped forward, thrown by his anger towards Nicolas for so casually dismissing Hannah, thrown by how suddenly he didn't give a damn about the business. All he could think about was Hannah. It felt as though he were living in a cloud of guilt and panic since she'd left.

He held out his hand, forcing himself to give Nicolas a conciliatory smile. 'I look forward to continuing our good working relationship that is so mutually beneficial.'

Nicolas's jaw tightened. After a long pause, he reluctantly reached out and shook his hand.

Leaving his father and Nicolas in the boardroom to discuss a vintage car that Nicolas was trying to persuade his father to sell to him, Laurent returned to his office.

He was irritably ploughing through his emails when his father appeared a while later.

'You look as tired as I feel.'

Laurent took in his father, his lopsided smile, the walking stick he was leaning on.

'I'm glad that you're finally listening to your physio's advice and using your walking stick.'

His father made a grumbling noise. 'I've decided I must look after myself now that you need my help with the business.'

Taken aback, Laurent studied his father and then had to bite back a smile at the teasing gleam in his father's eye.

He stood and pulled his visitor chair away from his desk so that his father could easily sit, before returning to his side of the desk.

'Well negotiated,' his father said.

'If you call giving an ultimatum negotiating.'

'Sometimes people need to have things spelt out loud and clear with no ambiguity.'

Laurent chuckled at that and his heart lifted when his father joined in. He cleared his throat. 'Thanks for the support in there.'

His father's attention shifted to something outside Laurent's office window. 'You're doing a good job.' Pausing, he tipped his walking stick against the floor a couple of times. 'You were born for the role.'

Laurent stared at his father, who cleared his throat noisily. 'Your mother said that you were asking about our...hmm...about our...about how we both left home.'

'Your affairs, you mean?'

His father nodded, and shifted his gaze to a point on the opposite wall, the colour in his cheeks rising. 'I was very unhappy back then.'

Laurent was about to interject and say that he didn't want to hear his excuses, but his father's guilt-ridden and anguished gaze met his and Laurent remembered Hannah's advice that he needed to listen to and try to understand his father.

'I couldn't cope in the role of CEO. I was out of my depth. I felt deeply ashamed and a failure. I met a woman who distracted me from all of that but it was a short-lived affair.'

With an impatient exhalation, Laurent interrupted, 'Hardly. It went on for years.'

His father's cheeks darkened even further and he swallowed hard. 'The times you thought that I was away continuing my affair, I was actually in hospital being treated for depression.'

For a long while Laurent stared at his father incredulously, wondering if he had heard right. 'Why didn't you tell me?'

His father bowed his head. When he eventually looked back up he grimaced. 'I'd like to say it was only because I didn't want to worry you, but I had seen your disgust when I returned after my affair—I couldn't bear to think of you having an even lower opinion of me, so I begged your mother not to tell you.'

Laurent gave an angry laugh. 'That makes no sense. You preferred for me to think that you were having an affair rather than tell me that you were unwell?'

'I didn't want you to think that I was weak.'

'Mental illness has nothing to do with weakness. I can't believe you kept it from me, robbed me of the chance of helping you. I could have helped. I would have wanted to support you.'

His father looked at him, perplexed. 'You would?'

'Of course I would. You're my father.'

'I thought I had lost my right to expect anything of you. I had let you and François down so badly.'

Laurent nodded. 'Yes, you did…but if I had understood how much you were struggling, I would have been there for you.'

Laurent swallowed when he spotted his father quickly wiping at his eyes and, looking down, studied the wood of his desk where generations of Bonneval had worked. He stared at a long paper-thin scratch in the wood. Hannah had been right. He did need to speak to his father. He lifted his gaze to see that his father, with bowed head, was looking towards the floor, his forehead creased, and wondered at his suffering and the extremes he must have gone to, to hide his illness from François and himself. All because he had feared their reaction.

His father lifted his head and, when their gazes met, in a flash Laurent realised just how deeply he had missed his father for the past twenty years.

He rolled his neck, trying to make sense of the fact that his parents' affairs were only part of the story. It was the feeling of being abandoned and shut out that had done the real damage. They'd never spoken to him before they'd left, explained what was going on, had been vague and distant in their sparse calls home. And when they had returned, they had always been preoccupied, never there for him.

His father slid a card across the desk to him, a pastel drawing of London Bridge on the front. 'I received this card in the post yesterday morning. It's from Hannah, thanking me for taking her on a tour of the House and apologising that she didn't get to say goodbye.'

Laurent picked up the card and studied her neat handwriting. She knew all about his parents but still showed them respect. At the wedding she'd slotted into the role of co-host, seeing that he needed support. Time and time again she'd shown her care for him. *'I really, really care for you.'* He'd panicked at her words, at the time thinking it was because he was averse to any form of commitment, but in truth it was because he was so scared of loving someone, and for them to leave him one day. He wanted to avoid at all costs having to ever face again the same grinding emptiness, the torrent of zero self-worth, the confusion, the self-blame, the panic of his teenage years.

His gaze shot back to his father when he shifted in his seat and attempted to stand while saying, 'I'd like to go home now if that's okay with you.'

Laurent went to his side but his father insisted on standing by himself. He escorted his father down to Reception, where the company car was waiting to bring him home.

At the car, his father once again refused his assistance, but as Laurent went to close the car door, his father leant forward and held out his hand.

Laurent took hold of it, his heart pulling when his father said, 'Thank you.'

On the way back to his office, bewildered, disappointed and exhausted by his conversation with his father, Laurent wondered what had it taken Hannah, given her background, their relationship history, to be so open and forthright with him? And he'd given her nothing in response. He inhaled a long breath, remembering her last words before she'd left, wishing him happiness in the future. He'd closed down on her but she'd still found it in herself to say those words to him.

Nothing about Hannah said she'd ever hurt him.

All along he'd thought he wasn't capable of giving love when in truth it really was about him not being able to accept love.

Back in his office he realised his father had forgotten Hannah's card to him. He looked at the handwriting again, loving its precision but also the quiet flourishes at the edges of the letters that spoke of Hannah's personality. He studied the words again too, that were thoughtful and kind and generous.

He loved her.

He'd loved her for such a long time but had hidden his fears behind denial. But twice he'd rejected her. What would that have done to her? Guilt and fury towards himself twisted in his gut. And then a fresh wave of panic had him pull at his tie, open his top button. Would she ever want to talk to him again?

Given the late hour and the fact that it was the school holidays, Hannah's Friday night train ride home from work to Richmond was for once almost pleasant. She'd found a seat and the man who had come to sit next to her was absorbed by his book, no loud headphones on, no shouting down the phone.

It was the perfect space for her to daydream about her future. To weigh up the pros and cons of staying in London or moving to Singapore or Granada.

For close to two weeks now she'd been trying to focus on making a decision, but her concentration was shot and her thoughts kept wandering off into a reel of flashing memories—how Laurent had silently contemplated her as he'd rowed them to the restaurant on her first night in Cognac, him fisting his hand in the air when he'd won the table tennis tournament before running over and high-fiving her, the wonder in his voice when he'd spoken of becoming an uncle, how closed he'd been when she'd tried to tell him what he meant to her.

The train rattled past row upon row of red-brick

houses, most with lights on in the downstairs rooms, given the gloom of the evening due to the low grey clouds hovering over the city.

Work were looking for an answer from her about the Singapore transfer. She had asked for a week's extension to consider it further and she needed to give them an answer on Monday. But she was finding it impossible to think straight. The hollowness, the aimlessness, the embarrassment inside her were too overwhelming.

She stared at the light drops of rain that were starting to splatter onto the window of the carriage, her cheeks reddening with not just humiliation, but the crushing memory of trying to reach out to Laurent and be honest about her feelings for him and then the humiliating realisation that he wasn't going to respond.

She pulled her gaze away from the window and studied the page of her notebook she'd divided into three columns—her two possible new lives along with her current position.

Her current life had so many pros. She liked her team. She liked her apartment. She was well paid and respected in her profession. London was a great place to meet new men. She grimaced at that. She wasn't going near another man for a very long time. She drew a definite X through London. It was time she moved on. Widened her horizons. Followed a life that felt true and meaningful.

She stood as the train pulled into Richmond station. And not for the first time scanned the platform for Laurent. Which she knew was crazy but she couldn't help herself. Or help how her heart went from being positioned in her throat with keen anticipation and sank faster than a pebble in water down to her stomach when she saw that he wasn't there.

It had been their thing. The first time she'd agreed to

go out for a drink with him, they had arranged to meet at seven the following Friday outside Richmond station when she would be arriving on her regular train home. But on the Thursday he'd been waiting for her, standing on the platform holding the most amazing bunch of pastel-pink-and-lemon tea roses he'd brought all of the way from his supposedly week-long trip to Paris.

He'd explained with an irresistible smile that he'd cut his trip short because he'd wanted to see her. And for the following ten months that they had dated, Hannah had never known when he would be there waiting for her, invariably with another gorgeous bunch of tea roses. And that unknown anticipation had given her days a sparkle that had had her practically bounce with good cheer through every meeting, every phone call, every mundane task of her job.

Outside the station she walked along the streets that took her home, a leaden weariness having her walk slowly despite the now persistent rain.

Stepping out onto the road to cross over to her street, she gasped at the blare of a horn and stepped back onto the footpath as a car whizzed by her, the young female driver and passenger laughing in her direction.

She stared after the car, her heart hammering, tears springing to her eyes. An elderly man stopped and asked her if she was okay and began to mutter about young troublemakers driving too fast.

She opened the communal front door to her apartment building with shaking hands. Closing it behind her, she rested against the wooden panels and resolved that, once and for all, she'd consign Laurent to the past.

Over the weekend she would make her decision on her future. And start mending her heart. She'd done it once before and could do it again.

CHAPTER ELEVEN

Slowing to a jog, Laurent came alongside Bleu, who had run ahead of him and was now lying flat on the ground outside the chicken coop, staring forlornly in the direction of the hen and her chicks.

Perhaps he was being foolish but he would almost swear Bleu only wanted to hang out with them. Reaching down, he stroked his coat. 'Maybe I need to get you a companion.'

Bleu twisted his head, his gaze as ever trusting and loyal, his tail now wagging over the grass.

'Time for bed, Bleu.'

Bleu stood and, after receiving his nightly rub that included having his ears scratched, ambled off in the direction of the stables.

Inside the château Laurent eyed his phone where he had left it on the hallway table. He'd texted Hannah before he'd left work for the weekend and again an hour ago before he'd gone for his run with Bleu.

He picked up the phone, willing her to have responded to his message saying he would like to talk with her. But there was only a single message from François.

In the oppressive silence of the château he tried to control his worry and frustration. He wanted to speak to her. Now. Tell her that he was sorry, that he loved her.

But he knew he needed to slow down. He had no idea of Hannah's feelings for him now. In all probability she would never want to see him again.

He should wait until the morning. Give her the night to think about his message. Some time and space would probably do him good too; he knew he loved Hannah but it felt as if part of him was still trying to play catch-up with that. For so long he'd refused to believe he'd ever allow himself to fall in love, and accepting he'd done just that wasn't proving easy to reconcile with.

He walked towards the stairs and lifted his gaze up to the domed stained-glass roof that had so entranced Hannah. Depending on the time of the day and the level of sunshine, different shades and patterns of light were reflected on the walls and the white marble treads of the stairs.

He turned back to the hall table. Picked up the phone. Found her number. Squared his shoulders and pressed the dial button.

It rang out to her voicemail. His heart pulled to hear her voice, clear with precise instructions on what details the caller should leave but also with a warmth that said you were welcome into her world.

He cleared his throat when the beep sounded, suddenly lost for words. 'Ah… *Oui...?* I left you some messages. I think we should talk. Call me back. Any time.' He was about to hang up but then blurted out, 'I'm coming to London tomorrow. I'd like to see you.'

He hung up. Travelling to London had never been his intention. He caught a glimpse of himself in the hallway mirror and was thrown by the aloneness of his reflection.

He climbed the stairs and wondered if she would respond.

Her answer was there when he got out of the shower, in a succinct text message.

I don't want to see you. There's nothing else to be said.

He rubbed a towel over his damp hair, his gaze on his bed. Hannah had been so right when she'd said that they had made love there. In truth, their intimacy had always been way more than just a physical act. It had always held a tenderness, an honesty. They had always exposed their true selves to one another during their lovemaking, but he'd been too blinkered by fear and a conviction that he was following the right path in life to recognise that.

He picked up his phone and called the executive travel agency employed by Bonneval Cognac and arranged his flights. Whether she wanted it or not, he was going to London.

Sunday morning, and Laurent's taxicab passed by the early morning joggers as he made his way towards Richmond. Once there, he rang Hannah's intercom, just as he had done endless times Saturday afternoon and evening. He held his breath, the knot of tension in his stomach tightening, willing her to answer.

But when she did answer with a hesitant, 'Hello,' he was so surprised after the frustration of yesterday that he jerked back and stared at the silver mouthpiece.

'Hello,' Hannah repeated.

'It's me.'

A long silence followed. He began to speak. 'Can I—' But the buzz of the front door opening interrupted him.

He walked past the bicycles belonging to the other tenants, stored in the hallway, and up the stairs to her first-floor apartment, remembering the time he'd carried her up to her apartment when she'd twisted her ankle one evening when stepping off a pavement wearing impossibly high heels.

She was standing at her door dressed in black yoga pants and a loose white top, a black and white sports bra visible underneath, her hair tied up in a bun, her expression and crossed arms screaming impatience and annoyance.

He paused a few feet from her, thrown at seeing her again, realising how much he'd missed her, not just during the past two weeks but for all the past year since they had split up. Yet another thing he'd deliberately blinded himself to in a bid to protect himself from ever exposing his heart to the world.

He clenched his hands, hating what an idiot he'd been.

Hannah shifted away from the doorframe she'd been leaning on, her expression growing ever more irritated.

Had he read too much into what she'd said about caring for him? What if that was all that she'd meant, that she cared for him, but she had not meant that she loved him as he'd assumed?

'Why so early?'

He tried not to recoil from her icy tone and answered, 'I called several times yesterday. I wanted to catch you before you left today.'

She didn't even try to argue that she hadn't planned on escaping from her apartment for the day in a bid to avoid him and said instead, 'I know I could spend the next ten minutes arguing with you about why I don't want you to come in, why there's no point in us talking, but I know how stubborn you can be.' Turning, she walked into the apartment, adding, 'You can have five minutes. After that I want to get back to my yoga.'

He nodded towards the yoga mat set on the floor beneath the opened sash window, the laptop on the kitchen table, the screen on pause showing a woman reaching her arms skywards, a foot pressed against the opposite thigh. 'Is that the yoga teacher you follow?'

'Yes, Kim Ackerman.' She went and sat on the piano stool in front of her upright piano, the farthest point from him in the combined kitchen and living space. 'What do you want to talk about?'

'I'm here to apologise.'

Her jaw tightened; her eyes took on a cold glint.

When he realised she wasn't going to say anything in response, he added, 'I've missed you…and I've come to realise how much you mean to me.'

She exhaled a disbelieving breath at that.

Uncomfortable, anxiety-induced heat flamed at the back of his neck. He wasn't sure of what to say, how to get across how he was feeling, trying to articulate it in his second language making it particularly difficult, and Hannah's cool scepticism wasn't helping either.

Thoughts rattled through his brain. In the end he decided to try to speak from his heart even though he felt like choking on the words that were so alien to him. 'You asked me at the beach house what I was so scared about. I had no idea what you were talking about. But since you left, my relationship with my father has changed, things aren't quite as tense.' He paused, gave her a wry smile. 'I listened to what you said about giving him a role in the company. He now works in an advisory position.'

Hannah's expression remained unmoved.

'We spoke about his affairs—he admitted to his first affair but I was wrong when I thought he was away having other affairs in the years that followed.'

'Where was he?'

'In hospital, receiving treatment for depression.'

Hannah gave a swift inhalation of surprise before saying, 'The poor man. That's terrible.'

'He said he didn't tell myself and François because he was ashamed. Which is bloody stupid.'

Hannah grimaced but then she regarded him with sad compassion. 'I'm guessing that he thought he was protecting you.'

A sizeable lump of emotion lodged in his throat when he saw tears in Hannah's eyes. He swallowed hard to dislodge it before adding, 'After he told me, I realised that it wasn't just his supposed affairs that devastated me but how abandoned I felt. When François and I were younger, our family was a happy one—a normal family. But then, when my father took over the business, it all unravelled. He became short-tempered, my mother preoccupied. We stopped being a family. And then the affair happened. And François and I were left in the dark from that point forward.'

He moved towards the window, suddenly feeling extremely restless. Outside a man was pushing a lawnmower along the footpath. He turned back to Hannah, rolling his shoulders against the ache in his shoulder blades. 'I wish they had told us that he was in hospital. Things could have been so different. I'd like to think I would have understood and been supportive—between my grandfather and me we could have helped him. As a teenager I felt responsible for François. I had no one I could speak to. I hated how alone I felt, how insecure, how out of control everything around me felt. I hated that lack of stability, feeling so vulnerable. And the constant roller coaster of my father coming and going only added to that. In truth I'm angry with both of my parents for robbing the rest of the family of the opportunity to support them, for not trusting us to care. But I can't change the past, I can only influence the present and hope for a better future for us as a family.'

Exhausted, he stopped. For long moments they stared at one another.

'Does any of this make any sense?' Then he exhaled. 'I must sound self-indulgent in everything I'm saying. I know I should have coped better in everything that happened, especially in comparison to everything that you went through.'

'Both of our backgrounds were pretty horrible. There's no point in comparing them. I'm so sorry that you were so alone back then.'

A jittery sensation ran through his legs at the compassion in her voice. 'And I'm sorry I reacted so poorly to what you said in Royan.'

Her gaze turned away from him towards her laptop screen. 'It hurt, but that's life, I guess.'

He moved across the room, coming to a stop by a low coffee table. Some pens and glue were piled neatly in a row on a dark wooden tray lying on top. 'Now, I can see how much it must have taken you to open up like that to me, given how I ended our relationship before, what you went through as a child.'

Hannah blinked. Her jaw working. 'Where's this conversation going?'

He pressed his leg against the coffee table, trying to gather his rambling thoughts and words. If any of his ex-banking colleagues who had always commended his negotiation skills saw him now they would scoff at his incompetence. He reeled back everything he'd said in his mind and then tried to answer her question as truthfully as he could, regardless of how uncomfortable it felt.

'I now realise why I was so set against relationships,

against ever falling in love. It isn't because I'm cynical, or have no interest in commitment. It's because I'm terrified of loving someone and for them to leave me. Up until now I haven't wanted to give another person that power over me.'

'I'm glad you've come to that understanding.'

He looked at her blankly for a moment. '*Dieu!* I'm really messing this up.' He cleared his throat. 'What I'm trying to say…' He moved around the coffee table and sat down on the nearest chair to her. 'The reason why I am here…' He stood back up. His heart felt as if it was going into arrhythmia. He circled back to the other side of the table. 'The reason we need to talk…' He closed his eyes and blurted out, 'We need to talk because I want you to know that I love you.'

Shooting off the stool, Hannah dodged around the sofa rather than having to pass Laurent, her heart hammering. At the kitchen table she flipped down the laptop screen where Kim Ackerman, the London-based online yoga superstar, had been instructing her audience in 'inhale love, exhale love.' It seemed to be a travesty to have Kim's image in the same room as her right now, because her blood was boiling with rage. And she was scared.

Scared of believing Laurent.

She swallowed down the temptation to laugh hysterically.

He was saying what she had longed for, that he loved her. But it felt wrong. It was too late. She was moving on from him. She glanced over to the mood board she'd spent yesterday creating in a café close to Richmond Park, where she'd hidden away from Laurent having guessed rightly that he would call at her apartment even though she'd said she didn't want to talk.

She'd also guessed he would turn up today. Just not this early.

'Hannah?'

She turned to him.

'Did you hear what I said? That I love you.'

She was almost taken in by the nervousness in his voice, how drawn and pale he suddenly looked.

Not that it made him in the slightest bit unattractive. That made her even crosser. Here she was standing in some tatty old gymwear, overheating from too many down dogs and warrior poses, and he looked as if he'd stepped out of a photo shoot for how Europe's top ten eligible CEOs dressed when off-duty.

Wearing dark jeans, a white open-neck heavy cotton shirt and a zipped navy bomber jacket, he was carrying himself with his usual understated sophistication. His hair had been recently cut and she hated how it emphasised the beautiful shape of his skull, the sharpness of his jawline, the brilliance of his blue eyes.

She went and yanked up the already open sash window to its maximum opening. Turning and trying to project a semblance of calmness, she said, 'I heard you, Laurent. But quite frankly I really don't understand what you mean when you say that you love me.'

He went to answer but the anger and fear inside her had her add, 'And can I point out that you seemed to find it hard to actually tell me that—to say those words? It seemed like you were having to force yourself, so please forgive me if I don't believe you.'

He stepped back, almost losing his balance when he banged against the coffee table.

Hannah turned away and went into the kitchen. She'd been sipping on green tea before he'd arrived but now she needed coffee. And not her usual instant, but strong percolated coffee.

She bent and searched the corner cupboard for her rarely used coffee maker, refusing to speak to Laurent. He clearly thought he could waltz in here and tell her he loved her and, hey presto, all would be rosy in the garden.

No way. Not by a long shot.

Eventually she found the machine at the furthest reaches of the cupboard and, dragging it out, cursed to herself when the cord and plug dropped to the floor, the plug whacking against her bare toes.

Her mood didn't improve when Laurent came and stood beside her. He said nothing but instead watched her wash out the jug and the water reservoir and then search her freezer compartment for some ground coffee.

When she couldn't take another minute of silence she turned to him and said, 'You're welcome to leave, you know.'

'Not until I tell you why I love you.'

She tried desperately to hold on to her anger, but the softness in his voice, the sincerity in his eyes was a much too strong opponent.

Backing against the counter, she eyed him sceptically, telling herself not to fall for his easy words, not to lose herself to her lousy judgement again. She needed to protect herself.

'When we first met, I was instantly attracted to you. You're the most beautiful and beguiling woman I have ever met. You project a cool calmness, a wariness, but behind that you're gentle, kind and forgiving. At times I wanted you to dislike my parents, I wanted to feel justified in my pain, but instead, while you understood my feelings towards them, you were also non-judgemental about them. Your openness to them, and especially now that I know about my father's depression, has made me stop and realise that I need to be more understanding, to realise that I haven't walked in their shoes.' He came closer. 'There's so much more I love about you—how in tune we seem to be with one another...' he smiled '...the synchronicity of our thoughts, our shared sense of humour. With you I feel complete, whole. Without you, I feel incredibly alone and lost. The past two weeks have been horrible.'

Hannah's heart felt as though it were a lead weight in her chest—the loneliness in his voice was so real. 'What has changed, Laurent? Why are you telling me now that you love me? Why not before?'

His gaze shifted to her fridge where there were numerous photos of her holding Diana, as a newborn, in her christening gown and at her dad's birthday party last month. Something altered in his expression and when he looked back at her it was with almost a pleading look.

'When we were together in London I was still carrying the emptiness and fear that had been in me for years.' As though anticipating how she was about to argue that he'd always seemed so confident, he added, 'My confidence, my self-esteem, despite outward appearances, was terrible. I hid that fact from myself as much as everyone around me. But being back home in Cognac, knowing that I'm making a difference to the business's future, understanding my parents a little better, have all helped restore how I feel about myself. All along I thought I wasn't capable of loving other people, when in reality the issue was that I couldn't accept love. I didn't think I was worthy of it and I worried about leaving myself open to pain. But your honesty at the beach house, knowing the courage it must have taken you to tell me that you cared for me, I now appreciate how much you must have meant those words.' His hand reached out as though to touch her but then, bowing his head, he pulled it back. 'I've messed you around, Hannah. I've hurt you. I'm truly sorry that I did. You said you wanted to be honest with me and I want to reciprocate that truthfulness. The honest truth is that I love you and want to spend my life with you.'

Hannah sank against the countertop, her legs shaking. It would be so easy to tell him that she loved him too. For a moment she felt dizzy with the wonder of what would happen if she did.

But just as quickly she dismissed that thought. 'Spend your life with me—what does that mean?'

'I've been thinking about how we could make this work. I know you want to change the direction of your career. Why not come to Cognac? You could run your wedding celebrant business from there. Or even join the House—your financial expertise would be of great benefit.' He stopped and gave her a hopeful grin. 'I'd get to take you out to lunch that way, commute to work together even.'

Hannah shook her head, trying to cling to the fragile excitement she'd felt yesterday when she'd finally come to a decision on her future.

She edged past Laurent and went and grabbed the poster-sized piece of cardboard that formed her mood board for her future.

She turned it to him, propping it on the kitchen table. 'I'm moving to Spain.'

'Why Spain?'

'I contacted an established marriage celebrant business in Granada and they're looking for a business partner. It's a husband-and-wife team at the moment, and they are struggling with demand. I've found an apartment in the city to rent.'

Running a hand over the image on the mood board of the one-bedroom apartment in an old Moorish building she'd found on the internet, she added in a low voice, 'I need a new start. Put the past behind me.'

'What about us?'

She held his gaze for the longest time, seeing bewilderment and hurt and pride all play out in his expression.

She looked away, trying to control a thousand different voices and emotions flooding her brain and body and soul, and spoke straight from her heart, being honest as he'd asked her to. 'I can't trust you. I don't want my heart broken again.'

Standing outside Hannah's door, Laurent felt as if he'd stepped into a vortex about half an hour ago and had just been spat back out again. Dazed, he wondered where he would go. What he would do.

A woman approached him, the straining Labrador on a leash making a beeline for him. The woman apologised as the Labrador's paws skidded on the pavement in his attempt to get close to Laurent. Crouching down, Laurent stroked the dog, who instantly calmed. Emotion caught him in the throat. He missed Bleu. He missed Cognac. He wanted to go back there. He'd never thought he would feel this way about his birthplace.

With one final hug for the Labrador, he waved him and his owner off.

He stepped out onto the road. Looked up to the first floor, the sound of Kim Ackerman's encouraging instructions just about audible.

He closed his eyes. He'd blown it. He'd waited too long in recognising what he felt for Hannah.

He breathed against the panic churning in his stomach. What if this was it? That there was no way back from this?

Part of him wanted to walk away, the part that always believed that relationships would be toxic and painful.

But the need to have Hannah in his life was too great. The need to prove to her what she meant to him pushed him towards the train station and then into a café in central London where he plotted for the next few hours how he would get her back. He was not going home without her.

CHAPTER TWELVE

MONDAY MORNING, AND with the dawn light creeping beneath her blinds Hannah knew she should get up, do something useful, but her body felt as if it belonged to a worn-out rag doll while her mind was spinning around and around, trying to make sense of yesterday, and unfortunately she was making very little progress.

He'd said he loved her. Had even thought through a future for them together. But it had all felt too easy for her to say she believed him, say that she loved him too and attempt to live happily ever after.

As much as Hannah wished it were, life simply wasn't like that.

She'd been honest yesterday when she'd said she didn't trust him. She didn't trust him not to change his mind, to realise that in fact he'd been right all along and love and commitment weren't for him.

Her birth parents, who instinctively should have loved and cared for her, had put their addictions and needs above hers. What if Laurent's love was equally fragile and no match for what life would throw at them?

She pushed herself up and off the bed and wobbled with light-headedness. She had a presentation to give to the board of a client company today and had no idea how she was going to pull it off.

She changed into her yoga pants and top, hoping that Kim Ackerman would once again help her focus on the day ahead.

Out in the living room she flicked through Kim's on-line videos and with a droll sigh picked one that was called, 'Yoga for a sore heart.'

She rolled out her mat and pressed play. Five minutes into the video, her mind still refusing to calm, she jumped when the intercom rang.

It had to be Laurent. Who else would be at her door this early? She refused to answer it but after three buzzes that had her startle each time, ruining Kim's guidance to 'free your mind of all that is troubling you,' she picked up the intercom hand piece and said curtly, 'There's no point in us talking.'

A soft, familiar-sounding female voice said, 'He said you'd say something like that.'

'Who's this?'

'Hannah, it's Kim, Kim Ackerman.'

Hannah swivelled around to stare at her laptop screen where Kim was frozen in a cat pose, wondering if her mind was playing tricks on her. Running to her window, she yanked it open and stared down towards the front door.

Standing there with her sleek black hair tied back into a ponytail, a yoga mat under her arm, was Kim Ackerman.

Stunned, Hannah went back to the intercom. 'Kim... hello!' She grimaced at her overexcited fan-girl reaction that hadn't dimmed despite having spent a whole week in Kim's company in India, before asking, 'What are you doing here?'

'Laurent contacted me yesterday via my website. I don't usually do private visits but he was very persuasive.' She stopped and after a light chuckle she added in a serious tone, 'He asked me to tell you that he wants to prove how much he understands you, how sorry he is that it has taken him so long to realise how much he loves you and the pain that has caused. He wants to prove to you that you can trust him.'

Hannah shook her head and dryly responded, 'Most men send flowers.'

Kim laughed. 'I'm guessing he has a lot of apologising to do.'

And his apologising didn't stop there. No sooner had Kim left after an hour of soul-reviving yoga, when her intercom rang again. This time it was a delivery from the French bakery in Putney Heath that had been her and Laurent's favourite in London. Even with her stomach in a knot, Hannah had been unable to resist the delivery of still-warm croissants and freshly brewed coffee.

After a quick shower she'd spent the entire journey to work looking over her shoulder, wondering if Laurent was about to appear at any moment.

But later in the day, when her dad phoned her at work, she realised she need not have worried because when she had been waiting at the station for her train, Laurent had been pulling into her parents' farm in a rental car.

Apparently he'd apologised for how he'd behaved on his previous visit. And confessed that he had hurt Hannah and wanted to make amends. Her dad chuckled down the phone at that point and told her he hadn't been prepared just to take Laurent's word on this and had presented him with a pair of wellington boots and tasked him with carrying out the hardest jobs on the farm for the morning—mucking out the yard outside the milking parlour, washing down the mud-encrusted tractor, carrying endless bales of hay from the trailer into the barn.

And all the while her dad had interrogated him, wanting to know how they could be sure he wouldn't hurt Hannah again, why he loved her and what his intentions were towards her with regards to marriage and children.

At this point Hannah closed her office door and pleaded down the phone, 'Oh, Dad, please tell me that you didn't ask him that.'

She could hear her dad's pride on the other side of the phone when he answered, 'I did. I saw how upset you were when you visited after he broke it off with you last year. I didn't say anything. I know your mother tried to ask you why you were so down but that you said that you didn't want to talk about it. And that's fair enough. Sometimes we all need space. But I tell you this, I wasn't going to let Laurent off lightly today.'

Hannah sat heavily onto her chair, glad she'd given her presentation before this bombshell had landed. 'I don't know...' She paused, feeling so lost and confused. 'I don't know what to do. I don't know if he really loves me. I love him, but I know I can't have my heart broken again.'

She heard a rustling on the line and imagined her father running his hand back and forth over the crown of his head, as was his habit when thinking things through. 'Your mother and I—' He broke away and spoke to her mother, who was obviously standing right next to him. 'Isn't that right, Jan?' Hannah could hear her mum murmur in assent. 'Your mother and I have spent the last hour since Laurent left discussing whether we should tell you that he visited us. He didn't ask us to. He said he just wanted to apologise to us and let us know how much he loves you.'

A sizeable lump formed in Hannah's throat to hear her dad say that Laurent loved her. She could hear the emotion in his voice, his concern. She squeezed her eyes shut and tried to concentrate on what her father was saying. 'I think we are good judges of character and believe he was being sincere.'

There was a shuffling on the other side of the phone and then her mum spoke. 'Follow your heart, Hannah. You'll know deep down if you can trust him. If you can love him with all your heart. Listen to your instinct. Be honest with yourself, both why you want to be with him, but also if you decide not to be with him. Is it Laurent or something inside you holding you back?'

Hannah ended the call wishing she could tap into that instinct her mother spoke about but it seemed to be encased in an ice pack of fear and doubt.

Leaving work that evening, Hannah was once again on high alert, looking out for Laurent. Which wasn't easy considering she had to peep over the biggest bunch of pastel-pink-and-lemon tea roses she'd ever seen. She had attempted leaving them in her office but as she'd walked to the lift, Amy, one of the juniors on her team, had run after her carrying them, exclaiming with an amused laugh that she couldn't believe that Hannah had forgotten them.

Hannah had been on the verge of telling Amy to keep the flowers but their arrival had caused enough consternation; Hannah didn't need the added speculation from her team as to why she didn't want to keep them.

Taking the escalator down to the underground platforms at Liverpool Street station, Hannah stumbled as she tried to get her footing and cursed Laurent.

He wasn't going away easily.

And in the crowded tunnels she cursed him again when she was thrown endless irritable looks from her fellow commuters, who clearly weren't impressed with being whacked by a bunch of flowers.

Then beyond a group of chattering and jostling visiting students she spotted a handmade sign posted onto the tunnel wall. Written on the plain white paper in thick black marker was one word.

HANNAH

Odd.
A few feet further on, she glimpsed another sign.

I

The writing was familiar and sent a shiver of apprehension down her spine. She wanted to stop and study it but the tide of commuters carried her on to another sign.

LOVE

And then another.

YOU

And at the entrance to the platform, where the crowd thinned out, there was yet another sign.

IT'S YOU WHO BRINGS ME HAPPINESS

Popping the flowers under her arm, not caring if they got squashed, Hannah pulled down the sign and then ran back and pulled down all the others, garnering strange looks as she did so, praying all the while that none of her colleagues had seen the signs.

She was shaking when she ran back to the platform in time to squeeze onto a carriage before the doors shut.

There were no seats available so she tucked herself into a corner and studied Laurent's handwriting.

At Waterloo station, she caught her train in a daze. And when she got to Richmond she braced herself to find him standing on the platform.

But she swallowed down a gulp of disappointment with each step she took towards the exit, realising that he wasn't there.

She wanted to see him.

His signs that she'd folded and placed inside her handbag, her disappointment that he was nowhere to be seen, were thawing her numbness.

Turning into her street, she braced herself again, her gaze shooting towards the front door of her house. But there was no sign of him.

Inside her apartment she crowded the tea roses into the three vases she owned and had no choice but to place the remaining flowers into a drinking glass.

She changed into her black jeans and a sleeveless white lace top and waited for him to ring her intercom.

An hour later she was angry and cross. What was he playing at?

By nine o'clock she was a bundle of nerves. Had something happened to him? She pictured him lying on a hospital trolley.

She picked up her phone. She needed to call him, make sure he was okay. She yelped when her intercom rang.

She picked up the hand piece. 'What the hell are you playing at, Laurent?'

A young hesitant male voice answered, 'Is that Hannah McGinley? I've a package for you.'

Hannah ran down the stairs and apologised to the startled-looking delivery driver, who handed her a poster-sized package and legged it back to his van.

Upstairs Hannah pulled off the plain brown paper wrapping to find a mood board beneath. She stared at the images on it, trying to understand what they all meant, a giddiness, a disbelief fizzing through her bloodstream. She gave a little cry when she spotted at the centre of the board a photograph of herself and Laurent high-fiving each other at Lara's wedding. Her breath caught at the shared affection and familiarity in which they were smiling at one another, at how unbearably handsome Laurent looked with his shirtsleeves rolled up, evening shadow adding to his dark looks.

She stared at the board, guessing what each photo and carefully written word might mean, desperate to hear Laurent's explanation.

She picked up her phone, realising he was going to wait for her to contact him.

He was waiting to see if she would trust and believe him when he said he loved her.

A hand resting on her stomach, she closed her eyes and listened to her instinct.

Then she rang his number. When he answered she struggled to speak, completely overwhelmed by how tenderly, how nervously he said her name.

Eventually she managed to ask, 'Where are you?'

'I can be with you within half an hour.'

Hannah sighed out her answer—'Good!'—and hung up.

Laurent willed the taxi driver to drive faster but knew that they were already at the upper speed limits.

Hannah had sounded upset on the phone.

What was he facing?

He lowered his window, needing some air.

When he arrived at her apartment she buzzed him up without him even having to press the intercom button.

He took the stairs slowly, dreading what might come.

She was at her door waiting for him and with an uncertain smile turned and led him inside.

It was only when she lifted the mood board he had delivered to her, and he saw how her hands were shaking, that he realised that she was as nervous as he was.

'Will you explain what all these images mean?'

He gave her a self-deprecatory smile. 'Given how poorly I managed to explain myself verbally yesterday, I decided to follow your lead and show you in images the future I dream of for us both.'

Taking hold of the board, he pointed to the various travel images on the top right-hand corner. 'These are the places I want to visit with you. Costa Rica, Whistler, St Petersburg…' Pausing to point to one image in particular, he added, 'The Soap Museum in Antwerp.'

He was gifted with an amused smile from Hannah and, taking courage from it, pointed to the image of four children on a beach, all looking cute but mutinous, their dark hair ruffled, clearly not impressed to have been forced to stop digging an enormous hole in the sand. 'These four represent the children I want us to have, strong, independent, spirited children.'

With trembling fingers she tucked a strand of her loose hair behind her ear and nodded for him to continue, her eyes bright, her cheeks flushed.

'And this couple, celebrating their fifth wedding anniversary with friends and family, I want that to be us. But of course we will be having champagne and brandy cocktails.'

Touching the photo of the children, Hannah said, 'Kim Ackerman, the croissants, the flowers, the signs, this board…are all incredible, but what means the most to me is that you went and visited my parents.'

He swallowed at the raw vulnerable emotion in her voice, felt his heart about give way with the tension of it all. 'Your parents deserved my apology. And I needed to show you how much I love you.'

She took the mood board from his grasp and placed it down on the table. Then, coming in front of him, she stared up into his eyes, as though she was trying to fully know him. 'You do love me, don't you?'

It wasn't a question but more a statement of wonder.

He wanted to reach out and touch her. But he stayed where he was, instinctively knowing he needed to give her space. 'I realised I loved you one evening when waiting for you at Richmond station. Your smile when you got off your train and saw me lit a fire of happiness in me that was extraordinary in its power but also terrifying.' He heard his voice crack and paused in a bid to gather himself before admitting, 'I was terrified of loving you and being hurt.'

She stepped towards him, her bare toes curling over the tops of his shoes. Her hand reached for his cheek; he closed his eyes at how tender her touch was. 'I will never hurt you.'

He opened his eyes and said the most honest words he'd ever spoken. 'I know you won't.'

He touched her cheek, their gazes holding, holding, holding, silently communicating the wonder, the beauty, the hope of this moment. Then he gently kissed her, his heart aching with the honesty between them, his bones dissolving at the sensation of being in the place where you belonged, where you could be the true version of yourself.

Reluctantly he pulled back, knowing they still had things to discuss.

Taking her by the hand, he led her over to the sofa. When they were both seated, angled into one another, he asked, 'Have you decided what you are going to do work-wise in the future?'

Hannah nodded. 'I told my senior partner that I'm leaving today.'

Laurent flinched. 'Are you still going to Granada?'

She dipped her head for a moment. He braced himself. She hadn't actually told him her feelings for him yet. She had never said that she loved him. When she looked back up, she tilted her head, gave him a shy smile. 'There's a château in Cognac that sounds more appealing.'

He grinned at that but then, shuffling on the sofa, he said quietly, 'I love you…but I still don't know how you feel about me.'

Hannah stared at him, perplexed, and then she started giggling. 'I love you, of course! How could you not know that?' Lifting a pillow, she hit him with it playfully. 'I love you, Laurent Bonneval. I love your loyalty to François, to your parents, to your family business. I love your kindness, your ability to read my mind, I love how sexy you look twenty-four-seven and I love the future you have mapped out for us. I love everything about you and will even tolerate the smelliest of cheeses in our fridge.'

Laurent grinned and grinned and then, placing a tender kiss on her forehead, he knelt before her.

Hannah paled.

He cleared his throat, suddenly really nervous again. 'I want to ask you something but I'm not sure if it's too early.'

Her eyes were glistening with tears. 'I'm not going to change my mind about anything. I love you and want to move to be with you in Cognac.'

'I spoke to your dad today, got his permission.'

At that a tear dropped onto Hannah's cheek. 'You did?'

'And when I got back to London this afternoon I went shopping.'

Hannah gasped when he took a pale blue box from his blazer jacket. Holding it out towards her, he said with the honesty that he wanted to be the trademark of their marriage, 'I'm still not sure I fully understand love, but I'm going to stop trying to understand it and just believe in it instead.' Opening up the ring box, he held his breath as Hannah stared at the five-stone diamond ring.

'It's so beautiful.'

He grinned at her softly spoken awe and, taking the ring out of the box, he took hold of her hand and asked, 'Hannah, will you be my wife?'

Hannah nodded, laughed, wiped away a tear from her cheek, laughed again, made a funny exclamation noise when he placed the ring on her finger and then grinned and grinned at him, her hands flapping in excitement.

And when she calmed, she edged forward on the sofa, her hands capturing his face, her nose touching his. 'I will love you for ever and ever, Laurent.'

EPILOGUE

It was a tricky manoeuvre, getting the full skirt of her wedding gown down the narrow steps of the farmhouse while carrying a heavy train. Hannah knew she could call for help but preferred to let her family and Lara chat and lark about in the kitchen instead.

At the bottom of the stairs, she paused to gather her breath and smiled at the consternation coming from the kitchen. Her mum and dad were arguing over how he should correctly knot his bow tie, Cora was pleading with her husband to stop Diana, who was now an adventurous fifteen-month-old, from crawling along the floor and Lara was cooing to her three-month-old daughter, Ruth.

Laurent had been right after all when he'd insisted that their wedding blessing take place on her parents' farm. At first Hannah had said no, that the château was a more suitable venue. Not only because of its size and facilities but also because it was the place where day by day they were becoming ever closer, where laughter rang out during their long weekend lunches with family and friends, where Hannah got to study Laurent and wonder at the security, the grounding, the absolute peace his love brought to her.

Now, though, she could see that the farm was the perfect place for them to marry. This house, so full of

warmth and love, had been integral in nursing the terrified child she once had been.

They had officially married earlier in the week at a
low-key but deeply intimate civil ceremony in Cognac
Town Hall before making the journey to England.

She listened to all the voices in the kitchen, all the people she loved so dearly, tears filling her eyes at the knowledge that their marriage was soon going to be blessed
in their presence.

She was excited, nervous and ever so slightly dazed.

But most of all she was grateful. Grateful that both
she and Laurent had been able to deal with their pasts
and focus on the future. Grateful that they had found
one another. Grateful that they were surrounded by so
much love and positivity and hope. She was grateful for
Laurent's love, his daily kindness and unwavering support as she established her celebrant business, his loyalty, his determination to create and maintain a strong
and honest marriage.

Hannah smiled when Lara opened the kitchen door.
Ruth, wearing a lilac dress in the same shade as her
mum's, was asleep in her arms. Lara along with Emily
and Cora were her bridesmaids today, Diana her flower
girl.

Lara gave a gasp. 'Oh, Hannah, I'm going to cry. You
look so beautiful.'

A rush from the kitchen ensued and Hannah giggled
at all the excited exclamations.

Coming towards her, tears in his eyes, her father
passed her bouquet of irises to her. The flowers of hope.

And then they were all on the way out through the
front walled garden, passing by the meadow with views
out to the green valley beyond, and around to the ter-
raced garden to the side of the house, her mum's pride

and joy, the borders surrounding the cricket-pitch-worthy lawn abundant with clematises, pastel tea roses, lilies and alliums.

Her heart kicked hard when she saw Laurent standing in front of the seated guests.

Gripping her dad's arm even tighter, she walked towards him, her heart brimming with love and hope.

When Cora and Diana reached him, Laurent scooped Diana up and pecked her affectionately on the cheek. Diana's giggles ran across the entire terrace and the guests laughed in response and suddenly the suspenseful tension of the day was gone.

And when Lara arrived at the top of the aisle, Laurent gently touched his hand against one of Ruth's tiny lilac socks and smiled in delight and pride at his niece.

And then it was her turn.

His brilliant blue gaze enveloped her.

She moved towards him, the momentous significance of declaring their love publicly causing a tear to float down her cheek.

Laurent hugged her father.

And then he was smiling down at her, his eyes reflecting her own nervousness and amazement, and then he pulled her into him.

'Don't cry,' he whispered against her ear.

She pulled back a fraction. Gave a little hiccup. 'It's my hormones.'

Laurent frowned and then his mouth dropped open. 'Are you…?'

Nodding, she whispered against his ear, her heart kicking at the security, the sense of peace that she found standing so close to him. 'Pregnant. Yes.'

His eyes dancing with wonder, he captured her face between his hands, was about to kiss her until Jamie, their wedding celebrant and a friend of Hannah's, cleared his throat loudly and said cheerfully, 'That's for later, folks.'

They grinned at one another and turned towards Jamie, Laurent lacing his fingers through hers.

Hannah turned for a moment to her family. She smiled at her dad and then looked at her mum, who gave her a knowing smile and nod that said that now Hannah was living life as it should be—trusting and hoping and loving and being honest with yourself.

She turned back to Laurent.

He dipped his head and said softly, 'I will treasure you, our baby, and every day of our marriage.'

* * * * *

ALWAYS THE BEST MAN

MICHELLE MAJOR

For Stephanie. You have the strongest, bravest spirit of any mother I know and you inspire me every day.

Chapter One

Some women were meant to be a bride. Emily Whitaker had been one of those women. For years she'd fantasized her walk down the aisle, imagining the lacy gown, the scent of her bouquet and the admiring eyes of family and friends as she entered the church.

When the day had finally arrived, there was no doubt she'd been beautiful, her shiny blond hair piled high on her head, perfect makeup and the dress—oh, her dress. She'd felt like a princess enveloped in so much tulle and lace, the sweetheart neckline both feminine and a little flirty.

Guests had whispered at her resemblance to Grace Kelly, and Emily had been foolish enough to believe that image was the same thing as reality. Her fairy tale had come true as her powerful white knight swooped her away from Crimson, the tiny Colorado mountain town where she'd grown up, to the sophisticated social circles of old-money Boston.

Too soon she discovered that a fantasy wedding was not the same thing as real marriage and a beautiful dress did not equate to a wonderful life. Emily lost her taste for both daydreams and weddings, so she wasn't sure how she'd found herself outside the swanky bridal boutique in downtown Aspen seven years after her own doomed vows.

"You can't want me as your maid of honor."

Katie Garrity, Emily's soon-to-be sister-in-law smiled. "Of course I do. I asked you, Em. I'd be honored to have you stand up with me." Katie's sweet smile faltered. "I mean, if you'll do it. I know it's short notice and there's a lot to coordinate in the next few weeks so..."

"It's not that I don't want to..."

Katie was as sweet as any of the cakes and cookies sold in the bakery she owned in downtown Crimson. She'd been a steadfast best friend to Emily's brother, Noah Crawford, for years before Noah realized that his perfect match had been right in front of him all along.

Emily was happy for the two of them, really she was. But if Katie was pure sugar, Emily was saccharine. She knew she was pretty to look at but after that first bite there was an artificial sweetness that left a cloying taste on the tongue. Emily didn't want her own bitterness to corrupt Katie's happy day.

"You have a lot of girlfriends. Surely there's a better candidate than me?"

"None of them are going to be my sister-in-law." Katie pressed her fingers to the glass of the shop's display window. "I remember the photos of your wedding that ran in *Town & Country* magazine. Noah and I don't want anything fancy, but I'd like our wedding to be beautiful."

"It will be more than beautiful." Emily swallowed back the anger that now accompanied thoughts of her marriage. "You two love each other, for better or worse." She took a breath as her throat clogged with emotion she'd thought had been stripped away during her divorce. She waved her hand in front of her face and made her voice light. "Plus all the other promises you'll make in the vows. But I'm not—"

"I'm a pregnant bride," Katie said suddenly, resting a hand on her still-flat stomach. She smiled but her eyes were shining. "I love your brother, Emily, and I know we'll have a good life together. But this isn't the order I planned things to happen, you know?"

"You and Noah were meant to be," Emily assured her. "Everyone knows that."

"Crimson is a small town with a long memory. People also know that I've had a crush on him for years and until I got pregnant, he had no interest in me."

Emily shook her head. "That's not how it happened." It had taken Katie walking away for Noah to realize how much she meant to him, but Emily knew his love for his fiancée was deep and true.

"It doesn't stop the talk. If I hear one more person whisper *shotgun wedding*—"

"Who?" Emily demanded. "Give me names and I'll take care of them for you." Since Emily had returned to Colorado at the beginning of the summer, she'd spent most of her time tucked away at her mother's farm outside town. She needed a do-over on her life, yet it was easier to hide out and lick her emotional wounds. But it wouldn't be difficult to ferret out the town's biggest gossips and grown-up mean girls. After all, Emily had been their ringleader once upon a time.

"What I need is for you to help me take care of the wedding," Katie answered softly. "To stand by my side and support me as I deal with the details. You may not care about the people in Crimson anymore, but I do. I want my big day to be perfect—as perfect as it can be under the circumstances. I don't want anyone to think I tried to force Noah or rush the wedding." She smoothed her fingers over her flowery shirt. "But I've only got a few weeks. Invitations have already gone out, and I haven't even started planning. Josh and Sara had one free weekend at Crimson Ranch this fall, and I couldn't wait any longer. I don't want to be waddling down the aisle."

"None of that matters to Noah. He'd marry you tomorrow or in the delivery room or whenever and wherever you say the word."

"It matters to me." Katie grimaced. "My parents are coming for the wedding. They haven't been to Crimson in years. I need it to be…" She broke off, bit down on her lip. "You're right. It doesn't matter. I love Noah, and I should just forget the rest of this. Why is a wedding such a big deal anyway?"

But Emily understood why, and she appreciated Katie's need for validation even if she didn't agree with it. So what if Emily no longer believed in marriage? She'd picked a husband for all the wrong reasons, but Katie and Noah were the real deal. If the perfect wedding would make Katie happy, then Emily would give her a day no one would forget.

"I could be the wedding planner, and you can ask one of your friends to—"

"I want *you*," Katie interrupted. "I'm an only child and now I'll have a sister. My family's messed up, but that makes me value the one I'm marrying into even more."

"I haven't valued them in the past few years." Emily felt her face redden, embarrassment over her behavior rushing through her, sharp and hot. "Until Davey was born I didn't realize how important family was to me."

"When your dad got sick, you helped every step of the way."

That much was true. Her father died when Emily was in high school. She'd taken over the care of the farm so her mom could devote time to Dad. Meg Crawford had driven him to appointments, cooked, cleaned and sat by his bedside in the last few weeks of home hospice care when the pancreatic cancer had ravaged his body.

It had been the last unselfish thing Emily had done in her life until she'd left her marriage, her so-called friends and the security of her life in Boston. As broken as she felt, she'd endure the pain and humiliation of those last six months again in a heartbeat for her son.

"You're a better person than you give yourself credit for," Katie said and opened the door of the store. The scent of roses drifted out, mingling with the crisp mountain air.

"I know exactly who I am." Emily removed her Prada sunglasses and tipped her face to the bright blue August sky. She'd missed the dry climate of Colorado during her time on the East Coast. It was refreshing to feel the warmth of the sun without miserable humidity making it feel like she'd stepped into an oven.

"Does that include being my maid of honor?" Katie asked over her shoulder, taking a step into the boutique.

"Shouldn't it be matron of honor?" Emily followed Katie, watching as she gingerly fingered the white gowns on the racks of the small shop. The saleswoman, an older lady with a pinched face, stepped forward. Emily waved her away for now. Shopping was one thing she could do with supreme confidence. Not much of a skill but today she'd put it to good use. "What's the protocol for having a divorcée as part of the bridal party?"

"I'm sticking with maid. There's nothing matronly about you." Katie pulled out a simple sheath dress, then frowned when Emily shook her head. "I think it's pretty."

"You have curves," Emily answered and pointed to Katie's full chest. "Especially with a baby on board. We want something that enhances them, not makes you look like a sausage."

Katie winced. "Don't sugarcoat it."

"We've got a couple of weeks to pull off the most amazing wedding Crimson has ever seen. You can be sweet. I don't have time to mess around."

"It doesn't have to be—"

Emily held up a hand, then stepped around Katie to pull a dress off the rack. "It's going to be. This is a good place to start."

Katie let out a soft gasp. "It's perfect. How did you do that?"

The dress was pale ivory, an empire waist chiffon gown with a lace overlay. It was classic but the tiny flowers stitched into the lace gave a hint of whimsy. The princess neckline would look beautiful against Katie's dark hair and creamy skin and the cut would be forgiving if she "popped" in the next few weeks. Emily smiled a little as she imagined Noah's reaction to seeing his bride for the first time.

"You're beautiful, Katie, and we're going to find the right dress." She motioned to the saleswoman. "We'll start with this one," she said, gently handing over the gown.

The woman nodded. "When is the big day?"

"Two weeks," Emily answered for Katie. "So we'll need something that doesn't have to be special ordered."

"Anything along this wall is in stock." The woman turned to Katie. "The fitting room is in the back. I'll hang the dress."

"Do I have to plan a cheesy bachelorette party, too?" Emily selected another dress and held it up for Katie's approval.

Katie ignored the dress, focusing her gaze on Emily. "Is that your way of saying you'll be my maid of honor?"

Emily swallowed and nodded. This was not a big deal, two weeks of support and planning. So why did she feel like Katie was doing her the favor by asking instead of the other way around? "If you're sure?"

"Thank you," Katie shouted and gave Emily a huge hug.

This was why, she realized, as tears pricked the backs of her eyes. Emily hadn't had a real friend in years. The women who were part of her social circle in Boston had quickly turned on her when her marriage imploded, making her an outcast in their community. She'd burned most of her bridges with her Colorado friends when she'd dropped out of college to follow her ex-husband as he started his law career. Other than her mom and Noah, she had no one in her life she could count on. Until now.

She shrugged out of Katie's grasp and drew in a calming breath. "Who else is in the bridal party?"

"We're not having any other attendants," Katie told her. "I'll try on this one, too." She scooped up the dress and took a step toward the back of the store. "Just you and Jase. He's Noah's best man."

Emily stifled a groan and muttered, "Great." Jase Crenshaw had been her brother's best friend for years so she should have expected he'd be part of the wedding. Still, Crimson's favorite son was the last person she wanted to spend time with. He was the exact opposite of Emily—warm, friendly, easy-to-like. Around him her skin itched, her stomach clenched and she was generally made more aware of her long list of shortcomings. A real prince among men.

Katie turned suddenly and hugged Emily again. "I feel so much better knowing you're with me on this. For the first time I believe my wedding is going to be perfect."

Emily took another breath and returned the hug. She could do this, even with Jase working alongside her. Katie and Noah deserved it. "Perfect is my specialty," she told her friend with confidence. Behind her back, she kept her fingers crossed.

"What the hell was that?" Noah Crawford held out a hand to Jason Crenshaw, who was sprawled across the Crimson High School football field, head pounding and ears ringing.

Jase hadn't seen the hit coming until he was flat on his back in the grass. He should have been paying more attention, but in the moment before the ball was snapped, Emily Whitaker appeared in the stands. Jase had done his best to ignore the tall, willowy blond with the sad eyes and acid tongue since she'd returned to town.

Easier said than done since she was his best friend's sister and…well, since he'd had a crush on her for as long as he could remember. Since the first time she'd come after Jase and Noah for ripping the head from her favorite Barbie.

Emily'd packed quite a wallop back in the day.

Just not as much as Aaron Thompson, the opposing team's player who'd sacked Jase before running the ball downfield. Jase brushed away Noah's outstretched hand and stood, rubbing his aching ribs as he did. "I thought this was flag football," he muttered as he turned to watch Aaron do an elaborate victory dance in the end zone.

"Looks like Thompson forgot," Noah said, pulling off his own flag belt, then Jase's as they walked toward the sidelines.

"We'll get 'em next time." Liam Donovan, another teammate and good friend, gave Jase's shoulder a friendly shove. "If our quarterback can stay on his feet."

"This is a preseason game anyway," Logan Travers added. "Doesn't count."

"It counts that we whipped your butts," Aaron yelled, sprinting back up the field. He launched the game ball at Jase's head before Logan stepped forward and caught it.

"Back off, Thompson," Logan said softly, but it was hard to miss the steel in his tone. Logan was as tall as Jase's own six feet three inches but had the muscled build befitting the construction work he did. Jase was in shape, he ran and rock climbed in his free time. He also spent hours in front of his computer and in the courtroom for his law practice, so he couldn't compete with Logan's bulk.

He also wasn't much for physical intimidation. Not that Aaron would be intimidated by Jase. The Thompson family held a long-standing grudge against the Crenshaws, and hotheaded Aaron hadn't missed a chance to poke at him since they'd been in high school. Aaron's father, Charles, had been the town's sheriff back when Jase's dad was doing most of his hell raising and had made it clear he was waiting for Jase to carry on his family's reputation in Crimson.

Jase took a good measure of both pride and comfort in living in his hometown, but there were times he wished for some anonymity. They weren't kids anymore, and Jase had long ago given up his identity as the studious band geek who'd let bullies push him around to keep the peace.

He stepped forward, crossing his arms over his chest as he looked down his nose at the brutish deputy. "Talk is cheap, Aaron," he said. "And so are your potshots at me. We'll see you back on the field next month."

"Can't wait," Aaron said with a smirk Jase wanted to smack right off his face.

The feeling only intensified when Aaron jogged over to talk to Emily, who was standing with Katie and the other team wives and girlfriends on the sidelines.

"Let it go." Noah hung back as their friends approached the group of women. "She wouldn't give him the time of day in high school, and now is no different."

"Nice," Jase mumbled under his breath. "Aaron and I actually have something in common."

Noah laughed. "Katie's asked Emily to be the maid of honor. You'll have plenty of excuses to moon over her in the next few weeks."

Jase stiffened. "I *don't* moon."

"You keep telling yourself that," Noah said as he gave him a shove. "It doesn't matter anyway. Emily has her hands too full with Davey and starting over even if she wanted a man." He gave Jase a pointed, big-brother look. "Which she doesn't."

"I'm no threat," Jase said, holding up his hands. "Nothing has changed from when we were twelve. Your sister can't stand me."

"I get that but you'll both have to make an effort for the wedding. Katie doesn't need any extra stress right now."

"Got it," Jase agreed and glanced at his watch. "I've got to check in at the office before I head home."

"How's the campaign going?"

"Not much to report. It seems anticlimactic to run for mayor unopposed. Not much work to do except getting out the vote."

"You're more qualified for the position than anyone else in Crimson," Noah told him, "although I'm still not sure why city council and all the other volunteer work you do isn't enough?"

"I love this town, and I think I can help it move forward."

Noah smiled. "Emily calls you Saint Jase."

Jase felt his jaw tighten. "How flattering."

"She might have a point. What are your plans for the weekend? Katie and I are going out to Mom's place for a barbecue tomorrow night. Want to join us?"

Jase rarely had plans for the weekend. Juggling both

his law practice and taking care of his dad left little free time. But Emily would be there and while the rational part of him knew he shouldn't go out of his way to see her, the rest of him didn't seem to care. If he could get his father settled early tomorrow...

"Sounds good. What can I bring?"

"Really?" Noah's brows lifted. "You're venturing out on a Saturday night? Big time. We've got it covered. Come out around six."

"See you tomorrow," he said and headed over to his gym bag at the far side of the stands. He stripped off his sweaty T-shirt and pulled a clean one from the bag. As he straightened, Emily walked around the side of the metal bleachers, eyes glued to her cell phone screen as her thumbs tapped away. He didn't have time to voice a warning before she bumped into him.

As the tip of her nose brushed his bare chest, she yelped and stumbled back. The inadvertent touch lasted seconds but it reverberated through every inch of his body.

His heart lurched as he breathed her in—a mix of expensive perfume and citrus-scented shampoo. Delicate and tangy, the perfect combination for Emily. Noah had accused him of mooning but what he felt was more. He wanted her with an intensity that shook him to his core after all these years.

He'd thought he had his feelings for Emily under control, but this was emotional chaos. He was smart enough to understand it was dangerous as hell to the plans he had for his future. At this moment he'd give up every last thing to pull her close.

Instead he ignored the instinct to reach for her. When she was steady on her feet, he stepped away, clenching his T-shirt in his fists so hard his fingers went numb. "Looks like texting and walking might be as ill-advised as texting and driving."

"Thanks for the tip," she snapped, tucking her phone into the purse slung over her shoulder. Was it his imagination or was she flushed? Her breathing seemed as irregular as his felt. Then her pale blue eyes met his, cool and impassive. Of course he'd imagined Emily having any reaction to him beyond distaste. "My mom sent a photo of Davey."

"Building something?" he guessed.

"How do you know?"

"I was at the hospital the day of your mom's surgery. I made Lego sets with him while everyone was in the waiting room."

She gave the barest nod. Emily's mother, Meg, had been diagnosed with a meningioma, a type of brain tumor, at the beginning of the summer, prompting both Emily and Noah to return to Crimson to care for her. Luckily, the tumor had been benign and Meg was back to her normal, energetic self.

The Crawford family had already endured enough with the death of Emily and Noah's father over a decade ago. Having been raised by a single dad who was drunk more often than he was sober, Jase had spent many afternoons, weekends and dinners with the Crawfords. Meg was the mother he wished he'd had. Hell, he would have settled for an aunt or family friend who had a quarter of her loving nature.

But she'd been it, and lucky for Jase, Noah had been happy to share his mom and her affection. With neither of her kids living in town until recently and Meg never remarrying, Jase had become the stand-in when she had a leaky faucet that needed fixing or simply wanted company out at the family farm. He'd taken the news of her illness almost as hard as her real son.

"I remember," she whispered, not meeting his gaze.

"Every time I've been out to the farm this summer, Davey was building something. Your boy loves his Lego sets. He's—"

"Don't say obsessed," she interrupted, eyes flashing.

"I was going to say he has a great future as an engineer."

"Oh, right." She crossed her arms over her chest, her gaze dropping to the ground.

"I know five is young to commit to a profession," he added with a smile, "but Davey is pretty amazing." Something in her posture, a vulnerability he wouldn't normally associate with Emily made him add, "You're doing a great job with him."

Her rosy lips pressed together as a shudder passed through her. He'd meant the compliment and couldn't understand her reaction to his words. But she'd been different since her return to Crimson—fragile in a way she never was when they were younger.

"Emily." He touched a finger to the delicate bone of her wrist, the lightest touch but her gaze slammed into his. The emotion swirling through her eyes made him suck in a breath. "I mean it," he said, shifting so his body blocked her from view of the group of people still standing a few feet away on the sidelines. "You're a good mom."

She stared at him a moment longer, as if searching for the truth in his words. "Thanks," she whispered finally and blinked, breaking the connection between them. He should step away again, give her space to collect herself, but he didn't. He couldn't.

She did instead, backing up a few steps and tucking a lock of her thick, pale blond hair behind one ear. Her gaze dropped from his, roamed his body in a way that made him warm all over again. Finally she looked past him to their friends. "Katie told me you're the best man."

He nodded.

"I've got some ideas for the wedding weekend. I want it to be special for both of them."

"Let me know what you need from me. Happy to help in any way."

"I will." She straightened her shoulders and when she looked at him again, it was pure Emily. A mix of condescension and ice. "A good place to start would be putting on some clothes," she said, pointing to the shirt still balled in his fist. "No one needs a prolonged view of your bony bod."

It was meant as an insult and a reminder of their history. She'd nicknamed him Bones when he'd grown almost a foot the year of seventh grade. No matter what he'd eaten, he couldn't keep up with his height and had been a beanpole, all awkward adolescent arms and legs. From what he remembered, Emily hadn't experienced one ungainly moment in all of her teenage years. She'd always been perfect.

And out of his league.

He pulled the shirt over his head and grabbed his gym bag. "I'll remember that," he told her and walked past her off the field.

Chapter Two

Emily lifted the lip gloss to her mouth just as the doorbell to her mother's house rang Saturday night. She dropped the tube onto the dresser, chiding herself for making an effort with her appearance before a casual family dinner. Particularly silly when the guest was Jase Crenshaw, who meant nothing to her. Who probably didn't want to be in the same room with her.

Not when she'd been so rude to him after the football game with her reference to his body. He had to know the insult was absurd. He might have been a tall skinny teen but now he'd grown into his body in a way that made her feel weak in the knees.

That weakness accounted for her criticism. Emily had spent the last year of her marriage feeling fragile and unsettled. Jase made her feel flustered in a different way, but she couldn't allow herself be affected by any man when she was working so hard to be strong.

Of course she'd known Jase liked her when they were younger, but she hadn't been interested in her brother's best friend or anyone from small-town Crimson. Emily'd had her sights set on bigger things, like getting out of Colorado. Henry Whitaker and his powerful family had provided the perfect escape at the time.

Sometimes she wished she could ignore the changes in herself. She glanced at the mirror again. The basics were the same—blond hair flowing past her shoulders, blue eyes and symmetrical features. People would still look at her and see a beautiful woman, but she wondered if anyone saw beyond the surface.

Did they notice the shadows under her eyes, the result of months of restless nights when she woke and tiptoed to Davey's doorway to watch him sleeping? Could they tell she couldn't stop the corners of her lips from perpetually pulling down, as if the worry over her son was an actual weight tugging at their edges?

No. People saw what they wanted, like she'd wanted to see her ex-husband as the white knight that would sweep her off to the charmed life she craved. Only now did she realize perfection was a dangerous illusion.

She heard Jase's laughter drift upstairs and felt herself swaying toward the open door of the bedroom that had been hers since childhood. Her mom had taken the canopy off the four-poster bed and stripped the posters from the walls, but a fresh coat of paint and new linens couldn't change reality.

Emily was a twenty-eight year old woman reduced to crawling back to the financial and emotional safety of her mother's home. She dipped her head, her gaze catching on a tiny patch of pink nail polish staining the corner of the dresser. It must have been there for at least ten years, back when a bright coat of polish could lift her spirits. She'd had so many dreams growing up, but now all she wanted was to make things right for her son.

"Em, dinner is almost ready," her mom called from the bottom of the stairs.

"Be right there," she answered. She scraped her thumbnail against the polish, watching as it flaked and fell to the floor. Something about peeling a bit of her girlhood from the dresser made her breathe easier and she turned for the door. She took a step, then whirled back and picked up the lip gloss, dabbing a little on the center of her mouth and pressing her lips together. Maybe she couldn't erase the shadows under her eyes, but Emily wasn't totally defeated yet.

Before heading through the back of the house to the patio where Noah was grilling burgers, she turned at the bottom of the stairs toward her father's old study. Since she and Davey had returned, her mom had converted the wood-paneled room to building block headquarters. It had been strange, even ten years after her father's death, to see his beloved history books removed from the shelves to make room for the intricate building sets her son spent hours creating. Her mother had taken the change easier than Emily, having had years alone in the house to come to terms with her husband's death. That sense of peace still eluded Emily, but she liked to think her warmhearted, gregarious father would be happy that his office was now a safe place for Davey.

Tonight Davey wasn't alone on the thick Oriental rug in front of the desk. Jase sat on the floor next to her son, long legs sprawled in front of him. He looked younger than normal, carefree without the burden of taking care of the town weighing down his shoulders. Both of their heads were bent to study something Jase held, and Emily's breath caught as she noticed her son's hand resting on Jase's leg, their arms brushing as Davey leaned forward to hand Jase another Lego piece.

She must have made a sound because Jase glanced up, an almost apologetic smile flashing across his face. "You found us," he said and handed Davey the pieces before standing. Davey didn't look at her but turned toward his current model, carefully adding the new section to it.

"Dinner's ready," she said, swallowing to hide the emotion that threatened to spill over into her voice.

Jase had known her too long to be fooled. "Hope it's okay I'm in here with him." He gestured to the bookshelves that held neat rows of building sets. "He's got an impressive collection."

"He touched you," she whispered, taking a step back into the hall. Not that it mattered. Her son wasn't listening. When Davey was focused on finishing one of his creations, the house could fall down around him and he wouldn't notice.

"Is that bad?" Jase's thick brows drew down, and he ran a hand through his hair, as if it would help him understand her words. His dark hair was in need of a cut and his fingers tousled it, making her want to brush it off his forehead the way she did for Davey as he slept.

"It's not…it's remarkable. He was diagnosed with Asperger's this summer. It was early for a formal diagnosis, but I'd known something was different with him for a while." Emily couldn't help herself from reaching out to comb her fingers through the soft strands around Jase's temples. It was something to distract herself from the fresh pain she felt when talking about

Davey. "Building Lego sets relaxes him. He doesn't like to be touched and will only tolerate a hug from me sometimes. To see him touching you so casually, as if it were normal…"

Jase lifted his hand and took hold of hers, pulling it away from his head but not letting go. He cradled it in his palm, tracing his thumb along the tips of her fingers. She felt the subtle pressure reverberate through her body. Davey wasn't the only one uncomfortable being touched.

Since her son's symptoms had first started and her ex-husband's extreme reaction to them had launched the destruction of their family, Emily felt like she was made of glass.

Now as she watched Jase's tanned fingers gently squeeze hers, she wanted more. She wanted to step into this tall, strong, good man who could break through her son's walls without even realizing it and find some comfort for herself.

"I'm glad for it," he said softly, bringing her back to the present moment. "What about his dad?"

She snatched away her hand, closed her fist tight enough that her nails dug small half-moons into her palm. "My ex-husband wanted a son who could bond with him tossing a ball or sailing. The Whitakers are a competitive family, and even the grandkids are expected to demonstrate their athletic prowess. It's a point of pride and bragging rights for Henry and his brothers—whose kid can hit a ball off the tee the farthest or catch a long pass, even if it's with a Nerf football."

Jase glanced back at her son. "Davey's five, right? It seems a little young to be concerned whether or not he's athletic."

"That didn't matter to my in-laws, and it drove Henry crazy. He couldn't understand it. As Davey's symptoms became more pronounced, his father pushed him harder to be the *right* kind of boy."

She pressed her mouth into a thin line to keep from screaming the next words. "He forbade me from taking him to the doctor to be tested. His solution was to punish him, take away the toys he liked and force him into activities that ended up making us all more stressed. Davey started having tantrums and fits, which only infuriated Henry. He was getting ready to run for congress." She rolled her eyes. "The first step in the illustrious political campaign his family has planned."

"Following in his father's footsteps," Jase murmured.

It was true. Emily had married into one of the most well-known political families in the country since the Kennedys. The Whitakers had produced at least one US senator in each of the past five generations of men, and one of Henry's great-uncles had been vice president. "I didn't just marry a man, I took on a legacy. The worst part was I went in with my eyes open. I practically interviewed for the job of political wife, and I was ready to be a good one." She snapped her fingers. "I could throw a party fit for the First Lady with an hour's notice."

Jase cleared his throat. "I'm sure your husband appreciated that."

She gave a harsh laugh. "He didn't appreciate it. He expected it. There's a big difference." She shrugged. "None of it mattered once Davey was born. I knew from the time he was a baby he was different and I tried to hide…tried to protect him from Henry as long as possible. But once I couldn't anymore, there was no doubt about my loyalty." She plastered a falsely bright smile on her face. "So here I am back in Crimson."

Davey looked up from his building set. "I'm finished, Mommy."

She stepped around Jase and sat on the carpet to admire the intricate structure Davey had created. "Tell me about it, sweetie."

"It's a landing pod with a rocket launcher. It's like the ones they have on *The Clone Wars*, only this one has an invisible force field around it so no one can destroy it."

If only she could put a force field around her son to protect him from the curiosity and potential ridicule that could come due to his differences from other kids. "I love it, Wavy-Davey."

One side of his mouth curved at the nickname before he glanced at Jase. "He helped. He's good at building. Better than Uncle Noah or Grammy."

"High praise," Jase said, moving toward the bookshelves. "If you make a bridge connecting it to this one, you'd have the start of an intergalactic space station."

Emily darted a glance at Davey as Jase moved one of the sets a few inches to make room for this new one. Her boy didn't like anyone else making decisions about the placement of his precious building sets. To her surprise, Davey only nodded. "I'll need to add a hospital and mechanic's workshop 'cause if there's a battle they'll need those."

"Maybe a cafeteria and bunk room?" Jase suggested.

"You can help me with those if you want." Leaving Emily speechless where she sat, Davey gently lifted the new addition and carried it to the bookshelf. With Jase's help, he slid it into place with a satisfied nod. "I'm hungry. Can we eat?" he asked, turning to Emily.

"Sure thing," she agreed. "Grammy, Uncle Noah and Aunt Katie are waiting." Her family was used to waiting as transitions were one of Davey's biggest challenges. Sometimes it took long minutes to disengage him from a project.

Her son stepped forward, his arms ramrod straight at his sides. "It's time, Mommy. I'm ready."

She almost laughed at the confusion clouding Jase's gaze. People went in front of a firing squad with more enthusiasm than Davey displayed right now. It would have been funny if this ritual didn't break her heart the tiniest bit. Embarrassment flooded through her at what Jase might think, but the reward was too high to worry about a little humiliation.

She rose to her knees and opened her arms. Davey stepped forward and she pulled him close, burying her nose in his neck to breathe him in as she gave him a gentle hug. A few moments were all he could handle before he squirmed in her embrace. "I love you," she whispered before letting him go.

He met her gaze. "I know," he answered simply, then turned and walked out of the room.

She stood, wiping her cheeks. Why bother to hide the tears? She'd left the lion's share of her pride, along with most of her other possessions, back in Boston.

"Sorry," she said to Jase, knowing her smile was watery at best. Emily might be considered beautiful, but she was an ugly crier. "It's a deal he and I have. Every time he finishes a set, I get a hug. A real one."

"Emily," he whispered.

"Don't say anything about it, please. I can't afford to lose it now. It's dinnertime, and I don't need to give my family one more reason to worry about me."

A muscle ticked in his jaw, but he nodded. "In case no one has said it lately," he said as she moved past, "your ex-husband may be political royalty, but he's also a royal ass. You deserve to be loved better." The deep timbre of his voice rumbled through her like a cool waterfall, both refreshing and fierce in its power.

She shivered but didn't stop walking out of the room. Reality kept her moving forward. Davey was her full reason for being now. There was no use considering what she did or didn't deserve.

Chapter Three

"Is that you, Jase?"

"Yeah, Dad." Jase slipped into the darkened trailer and flipped on the light. "I'm here. How's it going?"

"I could use a beer," Declan Crenshaw said with a raspy laugh. "Or a bottle of whiskey. Any chance you brought whiskey?"

His father was sprawled on the threadbare couch that had rested against the thin wall of the mobile home since Jase could remember. Nothing in the cramped space had changed from the time they'd first moved in. The trailer's main room was tiny, barely larger than the dorm room Jase had lived in his first year at the University of Denver. From the front door he could see back to the bedroom on one side and through the efficiency kitchen with its scratched Formica counters and grainy wood cabinets to the family room on the other.

"No alcohol." He was used to denying his dad's requests for liquor. Declan had been two years sober and Jase was hopeful this one was going to stick. He was doing everything in his power to make sure it did. Checking on his dad every night was just part of it. "How about water or a cup of tea?"

"Do I look like the queen of England?" Declan picked up the potato chip bag resting next to him on the couch and placed it on the scuffed coffee table, then brushed off his shirt, chip crumbs flying everywhere.

"No one's going to mistake you for royalty." Jase's dad looked like a man who'd lived a hard life, the vices that had consumed him for years made him appear decades older than his sixty years. If the alcohol and smoking weren't enough, Declan had spent most of his adult life working in the active mines around Crimson, first the Smuggler silver mine outside of Aspen and then later the basalt-gypsum mine high on Crimson Mountain.

Between the dust particles, the constant heavy lifting, operating jackhammers and other heavy equipment, the work took a physical toll on the men and women employed by the mines. Jase had tried to get his father to quit for years, but it was only after a heart attack three years ago that Declan had been forced to retire. Unfortunately, having so much time on his hands had led him to a six-month drunken binge that had almost killed him. Jase needed to believe he wasn't going to have to watch his father self-destruct ever again.

"Maybe they should since you're a royal pain in my butt," Declan growled.

"Good one, Dad." Jase didn't take offense. Insults were like terms of endearment to his father. "Why are you sitting here in the dark?" He picked up the chip bag and dropped it in the trash can in the kitchenette, then started washing the dishes piled in the sink.

"Damn cable is out again. I called but they can't get here until tomorrow. If I lose my DVRed shows, there's gonna be hell to pay. *The Real Housewives* finale was on tonight. I wanted to see some rich-lady hair pulling."

Jase smiled. Since his dad stopped drinking, he'd become addicted to reality TV. Dance moms, little people, bush people, swamp people, housewives. Declan watched them all. "Maybe you should get a hobby besides television. Take a walk or volunteer."

His dad let out a colorful string of curses. "My only other hobby involves walking into a bar, so I'm safer holed up out here. And I'm not spending my golden years working for free. Hell, I barely made enough to pay the bills with my regular job. There's only room for one do-gooder in this family, and that's you."

It was true. The Crenshaws had a long history of living on the wrong side of the law in Crimson. There was even a sepia-stained photo hanging in the courthouse that showed his great-great-grandfather sitting in the old town jail. Jase had consciously set out to change his family's reputation. Most of his life decisions had been influenced by wanting to be something different...something more than the Crenshaw legacy of troublemaking.

"I read in the paper that you're sponsoring a pancake breakfast next week."

Jase placed the last mug onto the dish drainer, then turned. "It's part of my campaign."

"Campaigning against yourself?" his dad asked with a chuckle.

"It's a chance for people to get to know me."

Declan stood, brushed off his shirt again. "Name one person who doesn't know you."

"They don't know me as a candidate. I want to hear what voters think about how the town is doing, ideas for the future—where Crimson is going to be in five or ten years."

His dad yawned. "Same place it's been for the last hundred years. Right here."

"You know what I mean."

"Yeah, I know." Declan patted Jase on the back. "You're a good boy, Jason Damien Crenshaw. Better than I deserve as a son. It's got to be killing Charles Thompson and his boys that a Crenshaw is going to be running this town." His dad let out a soft chuckle. "I may give ex–Sheriff Thompson a call and see what he thinks."

"Don't, Dad. Leave the history between us and the Thompsons in the past where it belongs." Jase didn't mention the hit Aaron had put on him during the football game, which would only make his father angry.

"You're too nice for your own good. Why don't you pick me up before the breakfast?" Declan had lost his license during his last fall from the wagon and hadn't bothered to get it reinstated. Jase took him to doctor's appointments, delivered groceries and ran errands— an inconvenience, but it also helped him keep track of Declan. Something that hadn't always been easy during the heaviest periods of drinking. "I'll campaign for you. Call it volunteer work and turn my image around in town."

Jase swallowed. He'd encouraged his father to volunteer almost as a joke, knowing Declan never would. But campaigning... Jase loved his dad but he'd done his best to distance himself from the reputation that followed his family like a plague. "We'll see, Dad. Thanks for the offer. Are you heading to bed?"

"Got nothing else to do with no channels working."

"I'll call the cable company in the morning and make sure you're on the schedule," Jase promised. "Lock up behind me, okay?"

"Who's going to rob me?" Declan swept an arm around the trailer's shabby interior. "I've got nothing worth stealing."

"Just lock up. Please."

When his father eventually nodded, Jase let himself out of the trailer and headed home. Although he'd driven the route between the trailer park and his historic bungalow on the edge of downtown countless times, he forced himself to stay focused.

Three miles down the county highway leading into town. Two blocks until a right turn onto his street. Four hundred yards before he saw his mailbox. Keeping his mind on the driving was less complicated than giving the thoughts and worries crowding his head room to breathe and grow.

He parked his silver Jeep in the driveway, since his dad's ancient truck was housed in the garage. It needed transmission work that Jase didn't have time for before it would run again, and Declan had no use for it without a license. But Jase couldn't bring himself to sell it. It represented something he couldn't name...a giving in to the permanence of caring for an aging parent that he wasn't ready to acknowledge.

He locked the Jeep and lifted his head to the clear night. The stars were out in full force, making familiar designs across the sky. He hadn't used his old telescope in years, but Jase never tired of stargazing.

Something caught his eye, and when he looked around the front of his truck everything in the world fell away except the woman standing in his front yard.

Emily.

He wasn't sure where she'd come from or how he hadn't noticed her when he pulled up. Out of the corner of his eye he saw her mom's 4Runner parked across the street.

She didn't say anything as he approached, only watched him, her hands clasped tight together in front of her waist. Her fingers were long and elegant like the rest of her. As much as he would never wish her pain, the fact that she wore no wedding ring made him perversely glad.

"Hi," he said when he was in front of her, then silently cursed himself. He was an attorney and a town council member, used to giving speeches and closing arguments to courtrooms and crowded meetings. The best he could come up with now was *Hi*? Lame.

"I owe you an apology," she whispered. "And I didn't want to wait. I hate waiting."

He remembered that about her and felt one side of his mouth curve. Her mother, Meg, had been an expert baker when they were kids and Emily had forever been burning her mouth on a too-hot cookie after school.

"You don't owe me anything."

She shook her head. "No, it's true. You were good with Davey tonight. Before bed he told me he wants to invite you for a playdate."

He chuckled. "I told you we bonded over plastic bricks."

"His father never bonded with him," she said with a

strangled sigh. "Despite my brother's best efforts, Noah has trouble engaging him." She shrugged, a helpless lift of her shoulders that made his heart ache. "Even I have trouble connecting with him sometimes. I understand it's the Asperger's, and I love him the way he is. But you're the first…friend he's ever had."

"He'll do fine at school."

"What if he doesn't? He's so special, but he's not like other boys his age."

"He's different in some ways, but kids manage through those things. I didn't have the greatest childhood or any real friends until I met your brother. I was too tall, too skinny and too poor. My dad was the town drunk and everyone knew it. But it made me stronger. I swear. Once I met Noah and your family took me in—"

"I didn't."

"No. You hated me being in your house."

"It wasn't about… I'm sorry, Jase. For how I treated you."

"Em, you don't have to—"

"I do." She stepped forward, so close that even in the pale streetlight he could see the brush of freckles across her nose. "I haven't been kind to you even since I've come back. It's like the nice part of my brain short-circuits when you're around."

"Good to know."

"What I said to you the other day on the football field about putting on your shirt."

He winced. "My bony bod…"

"Had nothing to do with it. You're not a skinny kid anymore. You must know…" She stopped, looked away, tugged her bottom lip between her teeth, then met his gaze again.

Something shifted between them; a current of awareness different than anything he'd experienced surged
to life in the quiet night air.

"The women of this town would probably pay you
to keep your shirt off." She jabbed one finger into his
chest. "All. The. Time."

He laughed, because this was Emily trying to be
nice and still she ended up poking him. "I'm popular
at the annual car wash, but I figure it's because most
of the other men on the council are so old no one wants
them to have a heart attack while bending to soap up
a front fender."

She didn't return his smile but eased the tiniest bit
closer. "I didn't want you standing bare chested in front
of me because I wanted to kiss you."

Jase sucked in a breath.

"I wanted to put my mouth on you, right there on the
sidelines of the high school field with half of our friends
watching." She said the words calmly, although he could
see her chest rising and falling. He wasn't the only one
having trouble breathing right now. "That's something
different than when we were young. You make me feel
things I haven't in a long time, and I don't know what to
do about it. But it doesn't give me the right to be rude.
I'm sorry, Jase. I can't—"

He didn't wait for her to finish. There was no way
he was going to listen to the word *can't* coming from
her, not when she'd basically told him she wanted him.
In one quick movement, he leaned down and brushed
his lips over hers.

So this was where she hid her softness, he thought.
The taste of her, the feel of her mouth against his. All
of it was so achingly sweet.

Then she opened her mouth to him and he deepened the kiss, threading his fingers through her hair as their tongues glided together. It was every perfect kiss he'd imagined and like nothing he'd experienced before. He wanted to stay linked with her forever, letting all of his responsibilities and the rest of the damn world melt away.

The moment was cut short when a dog barked—the sound coming from his house, and Emily pulled back. Her fingers lifted to her mouth and he wasn't sure whether it was to press his kiss closer or wipe it away. Right now it didn't matter.

"You have a dog?" she asked, glancing at his darkened front porch.

"A puppy," he said, scrubbing a hand over his jaw and trying to get a handle on the lust raging through him. "My former secretary Donna had a female Australian shepherd that got loose while in heat. They ended up with a litter of puppies, part shepherd and part who knows what?"

The barking turned into a keening howl, making him cringe. "Maybe elephant based on the size of their paws. But Ruby—my pup—was the runt. She was weaker than the rest and her brothers and sister tended to pick on her. They kept her, but it wasn't working with their other dogs. I went for dinner last week and…" The barking started again. "I need to let her out to do her business. Do you want to meet her?"

Emily shook her head and a foolish wave of disappointment surged through him.

"I need to get back to the farm. Mom thinks I was running to the store for…" She broke off, gave an embarrassed laugh, then looked at him again. "You rescue puppies, too? Unbelievable."

"It's not a big deal."

"Tell that to Ruby." She reached up on tiptoe, touched her lips to the corner of his mouth and then moved away. "You're damn near perfect, Jase Crenshaw."

"I'm not—"

"You are." She shook her head. "It's too bad for both of us that I gave up on perfect."

Before he could answer, she walked away. He waited, watching until she'd gotten in the SUV and pulled down his street. Until her taillights were swallowed in the darkness. Then the silence enveloped him once more, and he wondered if he'd dreamed the past few minutes.

An increasingly insistent bark snapped him back to the land of the wide-awake. He jogged to the front door and unlocked it, moving quickly to the crate in his family room. Her fluffy tail wagged and she greeted him with happy nips and yelps. He led her to the back door and she darted out, tumbling down the patio steps to find her perfect spot in-yard.

He sank down to the worn wood and waited for her to finish, lavishing praise when she wiggled her way back to him.

"I've got a story for you," he told the puppy as she covered him in dog slobber. "It's been quite a night, Ruby-girl."

Early Tuesday morning, Emily pasted a bright smile on her face before opening the door to Life Is Sweet, the bakery Katie owned in downtown Crimson. The soothing scent of sugar and warm dough washed over her as she automatically moved toward the large display case at the front of the shop.

The ambiance of the cozy bakery cheered her, even with the hellish morning of job interviews and application submissions she'd had. No surprise that businesses weren't lining up to hire an overqualified, single-mom college dropout who could only work part-time hours and needed to be able to take off when her son had a bad day. Yet it felt personal, as if the town she'd so easily left behind wasn't exactly opening its arms to welcome her back.

Life Is Sweet was different. With the warm yellow walls and wood beams stretching the length of the ceiling, the shop immediately welcomed customers both new and familiar. A grouping of café tables sat in one corner of the small space and the two women working the counter and coffee bar waved to her.

Katie pushed through the door to the back kitchen a moment later, carrying a large metal tray of croissants that she set on the counter.

"Should you be carrying pastries in your condition?" Emily asked with a laugh. Last weekend during dinner, Noah hadn't let Katie bring any of the serving bowls out to the table on the patio or clear the dishes. In fact, he'd all but insisted she sit the whole time they were at their mother's house. No matter what any of the women had told him about Katie and the baby remaining healthy despite normal activities, he couldn't seem to stop fawning over his wife-to-be.

Katie rolled her eyes. "I would have never guessed your brother had such an overprotective streak. He wants me to cut back even more on my hours at the bakery." She waved to one of the customers sitting at a café table, then looked at Emily. "I've hired a manager to run the front, but I'm still in charge of most of the baking. As long as my doctor says it's okay, I want to keep working."

"He'll get over it. I'll talk to him. Dad's death made him funny about keeping everyone he loves healthy." Her whole family had felt helpless when the pancreatic cancer claimed her father, and it had taken years for Noah to get over the guilt of not being around to help those last months.

When their mom had her health scare, Noah had returned to Crimson right away and remained at Meg's side for the duration of her recovery. But losing one parent and being scared for the other had taken a toll on him, and Emily understood his reasons for wanting Katie to be so careful.

"I know, and I love him for it." Katie sighed. "The morning sickness is done, so I feel great." She put all but two of the croissants in the case. "I'm just hungry all the time. Can I interest you in a coffee-and-croissant break? They're chocolate."

"How did you know I need chocolate?"

"Everyone needs chocolate." Katie set the remaining pastries on a plate, then poured Emily a cup of coffee and handed it to her. "You look like you've been through the job search gauntlet today." She got the attention of one of the women working the counter and mouthed "Five minutes." There was a line forming at the cash register so the worker gave her a harried nod. "Let's go to the kitchen. More privacy."

"You're swamped right now. I'm fine."

"Never too swamped for a snack," Katie answered and picked up the plate. She led Emily through a heavy swinging door into the commercial kitchen. "I'm going to sit on a stool while you take my picture and text it to Noah. You're the witness that I'm not working too hard."

Emily snapped the photo, sent it to her brother and then pulled off a piece of the flaky dough. "Fresh from the oven?" she asked as she popped the bite into her mouth. She climbed onto a stool next to Katie, trailing her fingers across the cool stainless steel counter.

"The best kind."

"If my brother becomes too much of a pain, I'll marry you," Emily said when she finished chewing. The croissant melted in her mouth, buttery and soft with the perfect amount of chocolate in the middle.

"Don't distract me with flattery," Katie answered but moaned as she took a bite. "What happened today?"

"No one feels a burning desire to hire the woman who publicly ridiculed the town on her way out."

Katie made a face. "It was a well-known fact that you had no plans to stay in Crimson any longer than necessary."

"Or maybe I got drunk one night and announced to a bar full of locals that I was too good to waste away in this…"

"*Hellhole mountain slum*, I think you called it."

"Right. Classy."

"And endearing," Katie agreed, clearly having trouble keeping a straight face.

"I'm stupid." Emily pressed her forehead to the smooth stainless steel, let it soothe the massive headache she could feel starting behind her eyes.

"You can make this better," Katie said, placing a hand on Emily's back. "Crimson has a long history of forgiving mistakes."

"And an even longer one of punishing people for them." She tipped her head to the side. "Look at how hard Jase has worked to make amends for trouble he didn't even cause."

"But people love him."

"Because he's perfect."

"Why are you so hard on him, Em?"

Emily shook her head, unable to put into words her odd and tumbling emotions around Jase.

"You could work for him," Katie said with a laugh.

"For Jase?" Emily asked, lifting her head. "What do you mean?"

"I'm joking," Katie said quickly. "From what I can tell it bothers you to be in the same room with him."

"That's not exactly true." Emily had really liked Jase kissing her. It had been easy to lose herself in the gentle pressure of his mouth. His hands cradling her face made her feel cherished. She'd wanted to plaster herself against him and forget she was alone, at least for a few minutes. She was definitely bothered by Jase, but not in the way Katie believed. "Is he hiring for his campaign?"

"No," Katie answered slowly, as if reluctant to share what she knew. "His secretary retired a few months ago."

"The one with the litter of puppies?"

"How did you know about that?"

Emily ignored the question. "Why hasn't he hired someone?"

"He won't say, but as far as I know he hasn't even interviewed anyone for the position." Katie took another bite of pastry. "There are plenty of people who would love to work with him."

"Plenty of single women," Emily clarified.

"He's pretty hot," Katie said, her smile returning. "Not as handsome as Noah, of course. He makes me—"

"I'm working on being a good friend." Emily held up a hand. "But I draw the line on listening to you ruminate on the hotness of my brother." She hopped off her stool and took a final drink of coffee. "Break's over, friend. I just got a tip on a job opening." She picked up the plate and walked it over to the sink.

"Are you sure that's a good idea?"

"Clearing my plate?"

"Asking Jase for a job."

Emily straightened her suit jacket and smiled, pretending the nervous butterflies zipping through her belly didn't exist. "I'm not sure, but when has that ever stopped me?"

She gave Katie a short hug. "Thanks for listening. You're a pro at this whole supportive girlfriend thing."

Katie returned her smile. "Good luck, Em."

"I've got this," Emily answered with more confidence than she felt. But bluffing was second nature to her, so she squared her shoulders and marched out of the bakery to get herself a job.

Chapter Four

Jase reached for the file folder on the far side of his desk just as he heard Emily call his name. His hand jerked, knocking over the cup of leftover coffee that sat on another stack of papers, dark liquid spilling across the messy top of his desk.

"Damn," he muttered, grabbing the old towel he'd stuffed under the credenza behind him. This wasn't the first time most of his work papers had been dyed coffee brown. The mug had been half-empty so this cleanup wasn't the worst he'd seen. He quickly wiped up the spill, then moved the wet files to the row of cabinets shoved along the far wall.

By the time he turned around, Emily stood inside the door to his office. Her blue gaze surveyed the disorder of his office before flicking back to him. "Is it always this bad?"

He kicked the dirty towel out of sight behind his

desk. "I've got things under control. It only looks like chaos."

She arched a brow. "Right."

Jase hadn't seen Emily since she'd walked away from him Saturday night. Letting her go had been one of the hardest things he'd ever done, but Emily wasn't the same proud, confident girl she'd been in high school. Whatever had happened when her marriage fell apart had left her bruised and tender. Jase had always been a patient man, and if she needed him to go slow he could force himself to honor that.

She didn't appear fragile now. This morning Emily wore a tailored skirt suit that looked like it cost more than the monthly rent on his office space. It was dark blue and the hem stopped just at her knee. Combined with low heels, a tight bun and a strand of pearls around her neck, Jase could imagine her on the stage next to her ex-husband, the perfect accessory for a successful politician.

He wanted to pull her hair loose, rip off the necklace that was more like a collar and kiss her until her skin glowed and her mouth turned pliant under his. Until he could make her believe she was more than the mask she wore like a coat of armor.

"Why haven't you hired a new secretary?"

He blinked, the question as much of a surprise as her appearance in his office. "I don't need one."

"Even you can't believe that." She nudged a precariously balanced pile of manila folders with one toe, then bent forward to right it when the stack threatened to topple.

"I haven't had time," he said, running a hand through his hair and finding it longer than he remembered. A haircut was also on his to-do list. "I did some interviewing when Donna first retired. She took a medical leave when her husband had a heart attack, and then they decided to simplify their lives and working here got cut. But she'd been with the practice when I took it over and ran this place and my life with no trouble at all. If I hire someone new, I'll have to train them and figure out if we can work together and..." He paused, not sure how to explain the rest.

"Let me guess." She arched a brow. "The women applying for the job think they're also interviewing for the role of your wife?"

"Maybe," he admitted, grabbing the empty coffee cup from his desk and walking toward her. There were plenty of single men in Crimson, so it was an irritating mystery how he'd ended up on the top of the eligible bachelor list. He didn't have time for dating, and even if he did...

"It would have been easier if Donna had helped screen the applicants."

One side of her mouth curved even as she rolled her crystal-blue eyes. "Because you have trouble hurting their feelings."

"You think you've got me all figured out."

She shrugged. "You're nice, Jase. Not complicated."

He touched the tip of one finger to her strand of pearls. "Unlike you?"

She sucked in a breath and stepped back so he could pass. There was a small utility sink in the kitchenette off the hallway, and he added the cup to the growing pile of dirty dishes. When he turned around, Emily was standing behind him, holding four more mugs by their handles.

"You forgot these."

He sighed and reached for them. Add washing dishes to the list.

"I appreciate the social call, but was there a reason you stopped by?" He turned and moved closer, into her space. "Unless you want to continue what we started Saturday night. That kind of work break I can use."

"No break and Saturday night was a mistake." She frowned. "You and I both know it."

He wanted to kiss the tension right off her face. "Then why can't I stop thinking about how you felt pressed against me?" He dropped his voice. "The way you taste…"

Color rose to her cheeks.

"I'm not the only one, am I? You walked away but you came back." His fingers itched to touch her. "You're here now."

"This isn't a social call." Emily straightened the hem of her jacket, looking almost nervous. "I think you should hire me."

Jase almost laughed, then realized she was serious. "No." He shook his head. "No way."

"Don't I at least get an interview?" Now her gaze turned mutinous. "That's not fair. I can do it." She spun on her heel and marched toward the front of his office. The space had a tiny lobby, two interior offices and a conference room. Jase loved the location just off Main Street in downtown Crimson.

The receptionist desk had become another place to stack papers since Donna'd left, and as he followed Emily toward the front door he realized how cluttered the area had become. Damn.

She picked up a thin messenger bag from one of the

lobby chairs and pulled out a single sheet of paper. "My résumé," she said, handing it to him. He stared at it, but didn't take it from her. Her mouth thinned. "During college I was an academic assistant for two law school faculty members. I managed calendars, helped with grant proposals and assisted in the preparation of teaching materials. I'm organized and will work hard. I can come in two days this week, and then make my hours closer to full-time once Davey starts school. I'd like to be able to pick him up, but my mom can help out if you need me later in the afternoons."

She kept pushing the résumé toward him, the corners of the paper crumpling against his stomach, so he finally plucked it out of her fingers.

"Emily," he said softly. "I need a legal secretary."

"Right now," she shot back, "you need a warm body that can do dishes."

She had a point, but he wasn't about to admit it.

"I can do this. I can help you." She kept her hands fisted at her sides, her chin notched up. It must have cost her to come to him like this, but Emily still made it seem like she was doing him a favor by demanding he hire her.

"This isn't a job you want." He folded the resume and placed it on the desk. "You're smart and talented—"

"Talented at what?" she asked, breathing out a sad laugh. "Shopping? Planning parties? Not exactly useful skills in Crimson. Or maybe I'm good enough to kiss but not to work for you."

He pointed at the sheet of paper. "You just told me why you're qualified. If you can work for me, you can find another job."

"Don't you think I've tried? I spent this entire morning knocking on doors. I'm a single mom with a son who has special needs, which is a hard sell even if someone did want to hire me." She bit down on her lip. "By the way, they don't. Because I wasn't nice when I was younger and that's what people remember. That's what they see when they look at me."

"I don't."

"You're too nice for your own good," she said, jabbing a finger at him. "That's why I'm here begging." A strangled sound escaped her when she said the word begging. He studied her for crying, but her eyes remained dry. *Thank God*. He couldn't take it if she started crying. "I'm begging, Jase, because I need to know I can support my son. When I left Henry, I wanted out fast so I took nothing. Hell, I'm borrowing my mom's car like I'm a teenager again. I have to start somewhere, but I'm scared I won't be able to take care of Davey on my own. He's about to start kindergarten, but what if something happens? What if he—"

"He's going to be fine, Em." He could see her knuckles turning white even as color rose to her cheeks.

"This was a horrible idea," she muttered, turning her head to stare out onto Main Street as if she couldn't stand to meet his gaze another second. "I'm sorry. I'm a mess."

Jase took a step toward her. It was stupid and self-destructive and a bad idea for both of them, but the truth was he didn't care if Emily was a mess. He wanted her to be his mess.

Emily felt the tips of Jase's fingers on the back of her hand. She couldn't look at him after everything she'd said. All of the shattered pieces of herself she'd just revealed.

But her fingers loosened at his touch, and she wanted to sway into him. Somehow he grounded her and just maybe...

The front door to the office opened, a rush of fresh mountain air breezing over her heated skin. "Jase, you're late."

Emily whirled around to see a short, curvy woman in an ill-fitting silk blouse and shapeless skirt staring at her.

"Sorry," the woman said quickly, glancing between Emily and Jase as she adjusted the bulky purse on her arm. "I didn't realize you had a meeting or..."

"It's fine," Jase told her, stepping away from Emily. "I'll grab my keys, and I'm ready. The Crimson Valley Hiker's Club today, right?"

The woman nodded. "If you're busy—"

He shook his head. "Mari, this is Emily Whitaker. She's Noah's sister and just got back to town. Em, Mari Simpson. Mari works at the library in town but has been kind enough to help keep me on track with my campaign." He gave Mari a warm smile, and Emily's throat tightened. Jase could smile at whomever he wanted. It didn't matter only...

"He'll be a great mayor," Mari chirped with a bright smile of her own. While the woman wasn't classically pretty, the smile softened her features in a way that made her beautiful. "I'm happy to do whatever I can." Her face was sweet and hopeful. The face of a woman who would make a perfect wife. Emily forced herself not to growl in response.

"Keys," Jase said again and disappeared into his office.

Mari continued to smile but it looked forced. "So you're Noah's sister?"

"I am."

"You moved back from Boston, right?"

A simple question but Emily knew it meant that although Mari Simpson wasn't a Crimson native, she'd been downloaded on Emily's past and reputation in town. "Yes," she answered, forcing herself to stay cordial. This was new Emily.

Emily 2.0. Nice Emily.

"It's good to be close to my family and friends again."

Mari tapped a finger to her cheek. "I think I saw your name on the application list for our reference desk opening."

Emily nodded. "I applied at the library."

"Too bad we filled the position already," Mari said a little too sweetly. "Lots of talented people want a chance to live in such a great little town. We only hire people with at least an undergraduate degree. I'm sure you'll find something."

Emily 2.0.

"Thanks for the vote of confidence," she said through clenched teeth. "I think—"

"Emily's going to work for me," Jase said, pocketing his phone and keys as he came back into the room. He kept his gaze trained on Mari.

Her jaw dropped and Emily was pretty sure her own reaction was the same.

"Here? But I've heard… I thought…she's—"

"Organized and hardworking," Jase said, repeating

Emily's words from earlier. "Just what I need to get the office back on track." He patted the tiny woman on the shoulder. "It'll be easier for you, too, Mari. You won't have to keep tabs on me all the time."

She gave a small nod but muttered, "I don't mind."

Finally Jase turned to Emily. "Does tomorrow work for an official start date? I can be here by eight. We'll keep your hours flexible until Davey starts school." For once his eyes didn't reveal any of his feelings. It was as if he hadn't said no and she hadn't broken down in an emotional rant. As if he wasn't offering her this job out of pity.

He held out his hand, palm up. On it sat a shiny gold key. "Just in case you're here before me." He flashed a self-deprecating smile. "Punctuality isn't one of my best qualities."

No, Emily thought, he didn't need to be on time. Jase had more important traits—like the ability to rescue distressed women with a single key.

She should walk away. He knew too much about her now. If there was one thing Emily hated, it was appearing weak. She'd learned to be strong watching her father lose his battle with cancer. She'd married a man who valued power over everything else in his life.

During her divorce she hadn't revealed how scared she'd felt. She'd been strong for Davey. Even when she'd been nothing more than a puddle of uncertainty balled up on the cool tile of the bathroom floor. Every time she got dressed, Emily put her mask into place the same way she pulled on a T-shirt.

But she'd kissed Jase like she wanted to crawl inside his body, then pleaded for a job as if he was her only hope in the world.

When she'd left behind her life in Boston, she'd promised herself she would never depend on a man again. She'd create a life standing on her own two feet, strong and sure.

But maybe strong and sure came after the first wobbly baby step. Maybe...

Forget the self-reflection. Right now she needed a job.

Her pause had been too long, and Jase pulled back his hand, his brown eyes shuttering. She snatched the key at the last moment and squeezed her fingers around it. The metal was warm from his skin and she clutched it to her stomach. "I'll be here in the morning," she told him and with a quick nod to Mari, ducked out of the office before he could change his mind.

A job. She had a job.

She took a deep breath of the sweet pine air. The smell of the forest surrounding Crimson always made her think of her childhood. But now as she walked down the sidewalk crowded with tourists, the town seemed a little brighter than it had been when she'd first returned.

A text came through from her mother, telling her Davey had fallen asleep on the couch so Emily should take her time returning home. What would she do without her mom? She hated asking for help when Meg had recently come through her own health scare, but her mother insisted she loved spending time with her grandson.

Baby steps. A job. Davey starting kindergarten. After things were settled, Emily could think about finding a place of her own. Jase hadn't mentioned a salary, and she didn't care. The job was enough.

The weather was perfect, brilliant blue skies, bright sun and a warm breeze blowing wisps of hair across her cheek. She shrugged out of the suit jacket and folded it over her arm. Just as she walked by a small café, her stomach grumbled.

When was the last time she'd eaten at a restaurant? Not since leaving Boston and then it was always for some law firm party or campaign event. She and Henry hadn't gone on a proper date since their honeymoon. Here in Crimson, Davey liked the quiet and routine of her mother's house.

She sent a quick text to her mom and walked into the restaurant. It was new in town, which she hoped meant unfamiliar people. This space had been a small clothing store the last time she'd been in Crimson. The inside was packed, and she wondered if she'd even get a table in the crowded dining room. It was a disappointment, but not a surprise, when the hostess told her there was nothing available. Just as she turned to leave, someone called her name.

A woman with flaming red hair was waving at her from a booth near the front window.

"You're Emily, right?" the woman asked as she stepped closer. "You must think I'm a crazy stalker, but I recognize you from the Fourth of July Festival. I'm April Sanders, a friend of Katie's."

"The yoga teacher out at Crimson Ranch?"

April nodded. "I got the last empty booth. No pressure, but you're welcome to join me."

Emily thought about declining. She knew Katie had a big group of friends. Hell, everyone in town loved her future sister-in-law. But even though she'd grown up in Crimson, Emily had no one. That's the way she'd wanted it since she got back to town. It was simpler, less mess.

But now the thought of a full meal with adult conversation actually appealed to her. So did spending time with April. The woman was a few years older than Emily but with her gorgeous copper hair and bright green eyes, she looked like she just stepped off the pages of a mountain resort catalog. "Are you sure you don't mind?"

"I'd love it," April said, gesturing to the empty banquette across from her. "It feels strange to be eating alone when there's a crowd waiting for tables."

Emily slid into the booth. "Thank you."

A waitress came by the table almost immediately with a glass of water and another menu. Thankfully, the young woman was a stranger to Emily.

"Are you interested in staying incognito?" April asked when they were alone again. "You looked terrified the waitress might recognize you."

Emily blew out a breath. "I don't have the best reputation in town."

"A sordid past?" April leaned forward and lifted her delicate brows. "Do tell."

"Nothing exciting," Emily answered with a laugh. "Simple story of me thinking I was better than I should have as a girl. Life has a way of slapping you down if you get too big for your britches." She shrugged. "People in small towns like to bear witness to it."

"Life throws out curveballs whether you're big or small," April agreed.

The waitress returned to the table and, as she took

April's order, Emily studied the other woman. April wore no makeup but her fair skin was smooth, and her body fit under a soft pink T-shirt. She looked natural and fresh—perfect for Crimson. After Emily ordered, April smiled. "I met your mom a couple of times at Katie's bakery. She's lovely."

Emily nodded. "One of the most amazing women I know."

"How is she feeling?"

"She gets tired more quickly, but otherwise is back to her normal self. We were lucky the tumor was benign and they could remove it without damaging any other part of her brain."

"She was lucky to have you and Noah come back to help her."

"I wouldn't have been any other place but by her side. That's what family is for, you know?"

"I've heard," April answered softly. "My friend Sara is the closest thing I have to family."

Sara Travers, who ran the guest ranch outside town with her husband, Josh, had moved to Crimson a couple years ago from Los Angeles. Sara had been a famous child star and still acted when the right project came along. Otherwise, she and Josh—a Crimson native and one of Noah's good friends—spent their time managing Crimson Ranch. "Did you come to Crimson with Sara?"

April nodded. "We didn't plan on staying, but then she met Josh and…"

"The rest is history?"

"She had a tough couple of years and deserves this happiness."

"If my brother is any indication, Crimson is *the* place

for happy endings." She smiled. "Have you found your happy-ever-after here?"

"It's a good place to build a life," April said and Emily realized the words weren't an answer to the question.

"Or rebuild a life." The waitress brought their orders, a club sandwich for Emily and a salad for April. Emily leaned across the table. "I like you and I appreciate the invitation to lunch, but after seeing what you eat I'm not sure we can be friends." She pointed to the bowl of dark greens. "Your salad is so healthy I feel guilty picking up a fry from my plate. You don't even have dressing."

The willowy redhead stared at her a long moment and Emily did a mental eye roll. She had the uncanny ability to offend without meaning to by tossing off comments before she thought about them. Her family was used to it and she'd managed to tame the impulse during her marriage but now...

April burst out laughing. "You remind me of Sara. She gives me grief about how I eat, too. I've always been healthy but became more diligent about what I put in my body when I was diagnosed with breast cancer a few years ago."

Emily thumped her palm against her forehead. "Now I feel like an even bigger jerk."

"Don't," April said, still smiling. "I've been cancer-free for over five years."

"My dad died when I was in high school. Pancreatic cancer." She took a bite of sandwich, swallowing around the emotions that always bubbled to the surface when she thought about her father. "I still miss him."

"It's difficult for you being back in Crimson."

"I thought I'd made a life beyond this little town. Returning to Colorado has been an adjustment."

April snagged a fry and popped it in her mouth. "So is divorce."

"Are you…"

"My ex-husband left me during my cancer treatments," April answered. She shrugged. "He couldn't handle me being sick."

"Jerk," Emily muttered.

"And yours?"

"Another jerk." Emily pushed her plate closer to the center of the table, a silent invitation for April to take another fry. When she did, Emily figured this friendship might stand a chance. "I was the one who did the leaving, but it was because my ex couldn't handle that our son wasn't the child he expected or wanted. Henry needed everything to appear perfect, and I bought into the lie."

"And lost yourself in the process?" April's voice was gentle, as if she'd had experience in that area.

Emily bit down on her lip, then nodded.

"I don't have the same history with this town as you, but I can tell you it's a good place to rediscover who you are." April nabbed another fry. "Also to reinvent yourself."

"Is that what you've done?"

"I'm working on it. In addition to Crimson Ranch, I also teach yoga at a studio on the south side of town. You should come in for a class." April leaned closer. "I like you, but I'm not sure I can be friends with someone whose shoulders are so stiff they look like they could crack in half."

Emily laughed, feeling lighter than she had in months. "I may," she told April. "If only to support a friend."

April held up her water glass. "Here's to new friends and new beginnings."

Chapter Five

Jase walked toward the front door of his office at 8:05 the following morning. His tie was slung over his shoulder, his hair still damp from the quick shower he'd taken, but he'd made it almost on time.

Downtown was quiet this early in the morning, one shopkeeper sweeping the sidewalk in front of his store as another arranged a rack of sale clothes. Life Is Sweet bakery would be crowded, so Jase hadn't bothered to stop for his daily dose of caffeine.

He'd been second-, third- and fourth-guessing his decision to offer Emily a job since the words had left his mouth yesterday. He wasn't sure how he was going to handle being so close to her every day, especially when she'd told him their kiss had been a mistake. But he'd also woken up with a sense of anticipation he hadn't felt in years. Not much else could ensure that he was *almost* on time.

He opened the door, then stopped short, checking his watch to make sure he hadn't lost a full day somewhere. The entire space had been transformed. The reception desk was clear other than the papers stacked neatly to one side. The wood furniture in the waiting area had been polished, and the top of the coffee table held a selection of magazines. There was even a plant—one that was green and healthy—on the end table next to the row of chairs where clients waited.

He caught the faint scent of lemon mixed with the richer smell of fresh coffee. His office hadn't looked this good in all the years he'd been here. There was a freshness to the space, as if it had been aired out like a favorite quilt.

He was still taking it all in when Emily appeared from the hallway.

"I hope you don't mind," she said, almost shyly. "I started cleaning up before we talked about how you wanted it done."

He rubbed a hand over his jaw, realizing in his haste to be on time he'd forgotten to shave this morning. "I didn't even know it needed to be done. Are you some kind of a witch who can wiggle her nose and make things happen?" He shook his head. "Because I'm five minutes late and what you've done here looks like it took hours." He glanced at the closed door to his office.

"I didn't touch anything in there. Yet." She reached behind her and shook out her loose bun, blond hair falling over her shoulders. Jase was momentarily mesmerized, but then she gathered the strands and refastened the bun. "I came in early," she told him, moving to stand behind the receptionist's desk.

"How early?"

She moved the stack of papers from one side of the desk to the other before meeting his gaze. "Around five thirty."

"In the morning?" he choked out. "Why were you awake at that time?"

"I don't sleep much," she said with a shrug. "I've gone through the filing system Donna set up and think I understand how it works. We need to talk about how you record billable hours."

He stepped close enough to the desk that his thighs brushed the dark wood. "We need to talk about you not sleeping. How often does that happen?"

"A few times a week," she said quietly. "It's no big deal."

"How many times is a few?"

Her mouth pressed into a thin line. "Why do you care, Jase?"

"How many?"

"Most nights," she answered through clenched teeth. "My doctor in Boston gave me a prescription for pills to help, but I haven't refilled it since I've been back. Davey had trouble adjusting when we first got here, and I wanted to hear him if he needed me."

"And now?"

She shrugged. "I watch him sleep. He's so peaceful, and it makes me happy. This morning my mom's schedule allowed her to watch him for me when he woke up, so I came into the office to get a few things done." She looked up at him, her gaze wary. He noticed something more now, the shadows under her eyes and the tension bracketing her mouth. It didn't lessen her beauty or her effect on him, but he kicked himself that he hadn't seen it before. This woman was exhausted.

"You didn't have to do this," he said, gesturing to the shiny clean space. "But I'm glad you did."

She rewarded him with a small smile. "It was a pit in here, Jase. It's like you don't even care."

"I do care," he argued. "I care about my clients and this town. So what if the office isn't spotless?"

"You're a business owner and you're running for mayor. People have expectations."

He choked out a laugh. "Tell me about it." He didn't mind taking grief from her because the brightness had returned to her gaze. The Emily he remembered from high school had been so sure of herself and her place in this world. She'd held on to that pretense since returning to Crimson, but the more time he spent with her the more he could see the fragile space between the cracks in her armor. A part of him wanted to rip away all of her defenses because they were guarding things that held her heart captive. But he hated seeing her troubled and knew she hated revealing any weakness.

"Thank you for this job. I know you didn't want to hire me."

No. He wanted to kiss her and hold her and take care of her. The kissing and holding weren't going to be helped by working with her, but he could take care of her and that was a start.

"You were right," he admitted. "I needed help. There are too many things on my plate right now, so I've been ignoring the office. It's starting to show in my work, and that's not going to help anyone."

"The town loves you. They'll cut you some slack."

"They love what I do for them."

"You do too much."

He shook his head. "There's no such thing. Not for someone with my history."

"The Crenshaw family history isn't yours, Jase. The weight of a generations-old reputation shouldn't rest on one man's shoulders."

If only that were true. "My dad isn't going to help carry the load." He didn't want to talk about this. Emily was here so he could help her, not the other way around. "I have to be at the courthouse at nine, so we should talk about what else needs to be done. I'm going to get a cup of coffee first, and you're an angel for making it. For all of this. Thank you, Em."

She tapped one finger on the screen of the desktop computer. "Eight thirty."

"Already?" He glanced at his watch.

"No, you have to be at the courthouse at eight thirty." She moved around the desk, her hips swaying under the fitted cropped pants she wore. She'd paired them with a thin cotton sweater in a pale yellow along with black heels. It was more casual than yesterday but still professional. "I'll get your coffee."

"You don't have to—"

"I want to." She tipped up her chin, as if daring him to contradict her. "So you can get ready to go."

Before he could argue, she disappeared around the corner.

This place wasn't good enough for someone like Emily. His office, even though it was clean, was too shabby for her crisp elegance. He imagined that she'd fit perfectly into the upper echelons of Boston society. Emily looked like a lady who lunched, a fancy wife who could chair events and fund-raisers and never have a hair out of place. Yet as he followed her, he watched wisps of blond hair try to escape from the knot at the back of her head.

She poured coffee into a travel mug, and Jase was momentarily distracted by the fact that the clean dishes and coffee mugs were put away on the shelf above the utility sink.

Emily turned, thrusting the stainless steel mug toward him. Her fingers were pink from the water and had several paper cuts on the tips. Not as delicate as she looked, his Emily.

No. Not his. Not even for a minute.

But she was here. Although he'd done her a favor, he needed her. He wanted her. Any way he could have her.

"You're welcome in my office while I'm gone." He brushed a lock of hair behind her ear and felt a small amount of satisfaction when she sucked a breath. "I should be back by noon."

"You have a meeting with Toby Jenkins here at one thirty."

He nodded, thankful he'd set up the calendars on his cell phone and office computers to sync automatically. He was in the habit of entering meetings in his calendar, but that didn't mean he remembered to check it every day.

"I told my mom I'd be home by two today. Davey still naps in the afternoons, and I like to be there when he wakes up."

"I can pick up lunch on my way back. Any requests?"

"You don't need to—"

"It's the least I can do, Emily. The way you transformed the office went beyond anything Donna could have done. It feels good not to be surrounded by my usual mess."

One side of her mouth curved. "I'm glad to be use-ful."

What had her ex-husband done to beat down the spir-ited girl he'd known into this brittle, unsure woman? Jase wasn't a fighter, but he would have liked to punch Henry Whitaker.

Instead, he gave Emily a reassuring smile. "You're the best."

Her smile dimmed, but before he could figure out why, she tapped her watch. "You need to go or you're going to be late."

"They're used to me being late."

"Not with me running the show." She pointed to the door. "Now go. I've got your inner sanctum to tackle."

He laughed, then wished her luck and headed back out into the bright sunshine. It was the best start to a morning he'd had in ages.

By the time he parked in front of his father's trailer a few minutes before noon, Jase's mood had disintegrated into a black hole of frustration. Even though he expected it from Emily's text, seeing the Crawfords' 4Runner at the side of the mobile home only made it worse.

He didn't want Emily here. This part of his life was private, protected. Most people in town knew his father, or knew of him if they'd lived in Crimson long enough. But even as a kid, Jase had never let anyone visit the run-down home where he'd lived. Not even Noah.

He stood on the crumbling front step for a moment trying to rein in his clamoring emotions. Then he heard Emily's laughter spill out from the open window and pushed through the door.

Her back was to him as she faced the tiny counter

in the kitchen. "Canned spaghetti is not real food," she said with another laugh.

"It's real food if I eat it and like it," his dad growled in response, but there was humor in his tone. His father sat in one of the rickety wooden chairs at the table. He watched Emily like she was some sort of mystical being come to life inside his tumbledown home.

"I'm not a great cook," she shot back, "but even I can make homemade meatballs. I'll teach you." He could see she was dumping the can of bright red sauce and pasta into a ceramic bowl.

"If we're having Italian night," his dad said, pronouncing Italian with a long *I*, "you'd best bring a bottle of wine with you."

Jase let the door slam shut at that moment. Emily whirled to face him, her smile fading as she took in his expression. Declan shifted in the chair, his own smile growing wider.

"Just in time for lunch," his dad said, even though he knew how much Jase hated any food that came from a can.

"How was the courthouse?" Emily covered the bowl with a paper towel and put it in the microwave shoved in the corner of the counter.

Taking a breath, he caught Emily's scent overlaid with the stale smell of the trailer. The combination was an assault on his senses. The hold he had on his emotions unleashed as he stalked forward, shouldering Emily out of the way to punch in a minute on the microwave timer. "What the hell are you doing here?" he asked, crowding her against the kitchen sink.

"My fault," his father said from behind him. "I forgot I had a doctor's appointment this morning. When you didn't answer your cell phone, I called the office. Emily explained you were unavailable but was nice enough to drive me."

Jase looked over his shoulder. "You should have rescheduled the appointment."

"It wasn't a problem," Emily said. "Your office was organized and I—"

"I offered you a job as a legal secretary," he bit out. "That's work with professional boundaries. Inserting yourself into my personal life isn't part of the job description."

Those blue eyes that had been so warm and full of life iced over in a second. He expected her to argue but instead her lips pressed together and a moment later she whispered, "My bad. Won't happen again."

"Jase, what's crawled up your butt?" his dad asked, his voice booming in the tense silence that had descended between him and Emily.

She lifted one eyebrow. "I'm not going to stick around to find out." Skirting around him, she gave Declan a quick hug. "Enjoy your spaghetti. I'm going to hold you to that cooking lesson. But grape juice, no wine."

"Thank you, darlin'." His dad's voice softened. "You're a good girl. I'm sorry about this."

"It's not on you," she whispered.

Jase didn't turn around, his hands pressed hard to the scarred Formica. He heard the creak of the door as it opened and shut, not the angry bang he expected but a soft click that tore a hole in his gut. Still he didn't move.

The chair scraped as his father stood. He moved behind Jase to take the bowl out of the microwave. For several minutes the only sound was the spoon clinking and the rustle of a newspaper.

"She doesn't belong here," Jase said finally, rubbing his hand over his face as he turned. "Emily works for me now. That's all, Dad. She isn't part of this."

"That girl has been a part of you for years," Declan answered, setting down the spoon in the empty bowl.

Jase felt his eyes widen before he could stop the reaction. He'd never talked to anyone, especially his father, about his feelings for Emily. He understood Noah knew but had never spoken it aloud.

"I'm a bad drunk," Declan said with a shrug. "But I was never blind, and you're my son. I know you better than you think."

"Emily's in a rough place now. I'm helping her get back on her feet. That's all."

"You're embarrassed about me and how you grew up."

Another bit of unspoken knowledge better left in the shadows. "You're in a better place, Dad. I'm proud of you for staying sober."

Declan choked out a laugh. "I'm the one who's proud, Jase. But you take on too much that isn't yours. My reputation and our family history. The way you were raised. You've overcome a lot, and you don't need to be ashamed of it. You don't have to make it all better."

Jase thought about his ancestor's picture in the town jail and how he wanted his family legacy to be something more than it was. "If you won't let me move you to a better house, I respect that decision. But I don't want her here. You need to respect that."

"From what I can tell, Emily Crawford is plenty capable of making her own decisions."

But she was *working* for him now. It was what she'd wanted, and it changed things. Not his need or desire, but his inclination to act on it. "Her name is Emily *Whitaker*, Dad. She was married. She has a son. Neither one of us is who we were before."

His father smiled. "I think that's the point."

Chapter Six

Emily looked up from the old rocker on her mother's front porch at the sound of a car coming down the gravel driveway. It was almost nine at night, and Davey had been asleep close to an hour.

She hadn't expected her mother to return from her date with Max Moore so soon. But when Emily recognized Jase's Jeep, her first inclination was to run to the house and shut the door.

He'd hurt her today, and she hated that anyone—any man—had the power to do that. While she understood that Jase's reaction had been about his own issues, a part of her still took the blame he'd placed on her. Her faults sometimes felt so obvious it was easy to hold herself accountable for any perceived slight. Flawed as she might be, Emily had never been a coward.

So she remained on the rocker, her legs curled under

the thin blanket she'd brought out to ward off the evening chill of the high mountains. Although she couldn't concentrate on the actual words, she kept her eyes trained on the e-reader in her lap as a door slammed shut and the heavy footfall of boots sounded on the steps.

"What are you reading?"

She ran one finger over the screen of the e-reader but didn't answer.

"You can ignore me," he said as he sank into the chair next to her, "but I won't go away."

"There's always hope," she quipped, her fingers gripping the leather cover of the e-reader tighter at his soft chuckle.

They sat in silence for a minute, and Emily's grasp began to relax. As if sensing it he said, "I'm sorry, Em."

"It's fine," she lied. "Point taken. I overstepped the bounds." There she went, instinctively making his mistake her fault.

"My reaction wasn't about you. What you did for my dad today was kind. It made him happier than I've seen him in a long time to have a beautiful woman caring for him."

"No big deal."

"Don't do that." His hand was around her wrist, warmth seeping through the fleece sweatshirt she'd pulled on when the sun disappeared behind the mountain. "It was special to him, and it should have been to me, as well." He stood, releasing her, and paced to the edge of the porch. "I love my father, but I hate the man he was when I was younger. He was mean and embarrassing. Everyone knew the problems he had, but that didn't stop me from being humiliated when I'd have to get him home after a night at the bars."

She could see the tension in his shoulders as he gazed out into the darkening night. "He showed up one year for a parent-teacher conference so drunk he ended up puking all over the first-floor bathroom. I never let him come to another school function."

She flipped closed the cover of her e-reader, her heart already melting for this man's pain. "Jase—"

He turned to her, folded his arms across his chest. "It killed me to live in that trailer growing up. The only saving grace was that no one but me had to see him at his worst. Even Noah, all the times he picked me up, has never been inside. That place represents my greatest shame, and my dad refuses to move. To see you there with all of the memories that seem to seep out of the walls to choke me... I couldn't stand it. It felt like you'd be contaminated by it."

Emily stood, placed the blanket and e-reader on the chair and walked toward him.

Jase shook his head. "You're too good for that, Em. Too good for him. I'm sorry I lashed out, but I still hate that you—that anyone—has seen that piece of who I am."

"No." She stepped into his space until she could feel his breath whispering over the top of her head. "You're too good to give in to that shame. Where you came from doesn't change who you are now."

"Are you kidding?" He didn't move away from her but leaned back against the porch rail as if he needed space. "That trailer and what it represents *made* me who I am. The night in my front yard, you said I was perfect, and I know what my reputation is around town. Nice Jase. Sweet Jase. Perfect Jase. No one sees anything else because I don't let them. Everyone thinks I work so damn hard despite my family's reputation in Crimson. I work hard *because* of where I came from. Because I'm scared to death if I don't, the poison that has crushed the self-respect of so many people in my family will take me down, too."

Something dark and dangerous flashed in his eyes and she saw who he was under the Mr. Perfect veneer he'd spent years polishing to a bright shine. He was a man at the edge of his control and a part of her wanted him to shuck off his restraint. With her. Yes. She could handle it. She would welcome whatever he had to offer.

He blinked, and the moment was gone. His chest rose and fell like he'd sprinted up Crimson Mountain. She placed her hand on it, fingers splayed, and felt his heartbeat thrumming under her touch. "You aren't your father." She said the words softly and felt his breath hitch. "I know what it's like to want to prove something so badly it makes you into someone you're not. Someone fake and false. You're real, Jase. Not perfect. Real."

"I'm sorry," he said again, lifting his palm to press it over her hand. "For what I said and how I treated you."

She let a small smile curve her lips. "I think this makes us even."

"You did good today. In my office and with my dad. Thank you."

This was the part where she should step away. If they were even, it was a fresh start. But she couldn't force herself to move. Emily might not believe in perfect, but she had learned to appreciate real. The knowledge that Jase was different than she'd assumed both humbled and excited her. Of all people, she should have known not to judge a person by who they were on the outside.

She'd built an entire life on outward impressions only to watch it crumble around her.

The connection she felt with Jase, her awareness of him, suddenly flared to life stronger than it had before. She moved her hand up his chest and around to the back of his neck. At the same time she lifted onto her tiptoes so she could press her mouth to his. He tasted like night air and mint gum, and she loved how much he could communicate simply through the pressure of his mouth on hers.

He angled his head and ran his tongue across her bottom lip. His hands came to rest on her hips, pulling her closer until the front of her was plastered against him. Unlike other men she'd known, he didn't rush the kiss. It was as if learning her bit by bit was enough for him. He savored every taste, trailing kisses along her jaw before nipping at her earlobe.

"Your ears are sensitive," he whispered when she moaned softly. His breath feathered against her skin. "You touch them when you're nervous."

"I don't," she started to argue, then he bit down on the lobe again and she squirmed. "You're observant," she amended.

"I want more. I want to know everything about you," he said and claimed her mouth again.

Her brain was fuzzy but the meaning of his words penetrated the fog of desire after a few moments. "No." She lifted her head and tried to step away but he held her steady.

"Why?" A kiss against her jaw.

"I can't think when you do that."

"Then I'll do it more."

She opened her mouth to argue, and he took the opportunity to deepen the kiss. One thing she'd say for Jase Crenshaw—the man was persistent. Even though she knew she should stop it, she gave in to the need building inside her. Her body sang with desire, tremors skittering over her skin. Jase ran his fingers up under the hem of her sweatshirt and across her spine. Everywhere he touched her Emily burned. Her breasts were heavy and sensitive where they rubbed against his T-shirt and she wanted more.

So much more.

So much it scared her into action. As Jase's hands moved to the front of her waist and brushed the swell of her breasts, she wrenched away from him. With unsteady hands, she grabbed on to the front porch rail to prevent herself from moving back to the warmth she already missed.

"We've determined I'm not perfect," Jase said, his tone a mix of amusement and frustration. "So what's the problem now?"

"I work for you."

"Are you asking to be fired?"

She glanced at him and saw he was teasing. Her shoulders relaxed. "I don't want to complicate things, Jase. I know you gave me the job because you felt sorry for me and this..." She pointed between the two of them. "Would only muddy the waters more."

"I don't feel sorry for you." He came closer and she didn't resist when he cupped her face in his hands. "I respect you, and I want you. But neither of those emotions involves pity."

"Why are you running for mayor?"

His hands dropped to his sides. "I think I can help

the town move forward. I've been on city council long enough to understand what needs to be done and—"

"You have a responsibility," she finished for him.

"You say that like it's a bad thing."

"It's not, but your life is filled with obligations. I don't want to be another one."

"You're—"

"I'd like to be your friend."

He stared at her for several seconds, then blew out a breath. "I'd like that, too, but it doesn't have to mean—"

"Yes, it does," she interrupted, not bothering to hide her smile at the crushed puppy-dog look of disappointment he gave her.

With a small nod, he moved around her. "Good night, Emily."

"Good night, Jase." She watched his taillights disappear into the darkness, then turned for the house. For the first time in forever, she fell asleep within minutes of her head hitting the pillow.

Friday morning, Jase walked the three blocks from his office to the Crimson Community Center and thought about how nice it was not to be rushing through town. He was speaking to the downtown business coalition and probably would have been late for the meeting if Emily hadn't shoved him out the door.

She was a stickler for punctuality, something that had never been a strength of his. He cared about being on time, but he often got so lost in whatever he was doing that he stopped paying attention to anything else. She hadn't been in the office yesterday, and despite how organized she'd left things on Wednesday, he'd found he missed knowing she was sharing his space.

She was a distraction but the best kind possible, and now he spent the minutes going over what he planned to say to the group of business owners. Ever since Emily had asked the question, Jase had been pondering the answer to why he was running for mayor. It wasn't as if he didn't have enough to keep him busy with his law practice.

He came around the corner and noticed Mari pacing in front of the entrance to the community center. Automatically he checked his watch, since his one campaign worker tended to pace when she was anxious.

"We have a problem," she said, adjusting her heavy-rimmed glasses as she strode toward him.

He held up his hands. "I'm not scheduled to speak for another ten minutes. It's good."

"Your opponent got here first," she answered, shaking her head. "It's *really* bad, Jase."

"What opponent?"

"Charles Thompson."

Jase's stomach dropped to the pavement like a cement brick. "Charles Thompson isn't running for mayor. I'm unopposed in the election."

"Not anymore. He has the signatures he needs to put his name on the ballot and filed as a candidate with the courthouse before yesterday's deadline. I don't understand why he's doing this."

"Because it's me." Jase rubbed a hand over his eyes. "Charles has been at loose ends since he retired as sheriff. I bet my dad called and rubbed the election in his face. If there's anything the Thompsons can't stand, it's a Crenshaw getting ahead."

"That's plain spiteful."

Spiteful and stupid and why was he doing this again?

Because he owed it to the town? Because he had something to prove?

"You have to get in there and prove you're a better candidate." Mari tugged on his arm, but Jase stood his ground. He didn't want to face Charles and everything the older man knew about his childhood. If there was one person who knew where all the Crenshaw skeletons were hidden, it was Charles Thompson. "Jase, let's go."

He could walk away right now, withdraw his candidacy. Charles would be a fine mayor, maybe even better than Jase. The older man had nothing but time to devote to the job. But if Jase won, maybe he could stop trying so hard to make amends for a past he didn't own. Perhaps it would finally be enough—he would be enough—to excise the ghosts of his past.

Jase wasn't his father or any of the infamous men in his family. He'd paid more than his dues; he'd tried to atone for every sin committed by someone with the last name Crenshaw. Now was his time to bury the past for good. He couldn't walk away.

Taking a deep breath, he straightened his tie and smoothed his fingers over the hair curling at the nape of his neck. A haircut was still on the to-do list, right after fighting for his right to lead this town.

He followed Mari into the crowded meeting room where Charles Thompson stood at the podium. A ruthless light snapped in his eyes as he met Jase's gaze over the heads of the members of the coalition. Jase knew he had friends in this room, but facing Sheriff Thompson turned him into the scared, cowering boy he'd been years ago. He'd dreaded seeing the patrol car parked in front of his dad's trailer and knowing what it meant.

Those days were a distant memory for most people,

Declan Crenshaw having faded into the background of
the Crimson community. But for Jase they were like a
razor across an open wound—raw and painful.

"My esteemed opponent has arrived," Charles announced into the microphone, his deep voice booming
through the room.

People in the audience turned to where Jase stood
at the back and he forced a neutral look on his face. He
made eye contact with a couple of friends, Katie Garrity, who was representing her bakery, and Josh Travers from Crimson Ranch. Katie gave him a sympathetic
smile and Josh looked almost as angry as Jase felt.

Their support bolstered his confidence but his courage took a nosedive at Thompson's next words. "Come
on up here, boy," Charles said, his gaze boring in Jase's
taught nerves. "I want to talk to you about the future of
this town and family values."

Jase banged through the front door of his office an
hour after he'd left, holding on to his temper by the
thinnest thread. Emily jumped in her chair, glancing
up from the computer screen.

"How did it go?"

"Fine," he bit out, not stopping. He could feel the
mask he wore beginning to crumble and needed the
safety of being behind a closed door when it did. "I
have a meeting with Morris Anderson at eleven. Let
me know when he gets here."

He dropped his briefcase on the floor, slammed his
office door shut behind him and stalked to the window behind his desk, trying to get his breathing under
control as he stared out to the parking lot in back of
the building.

"All those slamming doors don't sound like *fine* to me."

He didn't bother turning at Emily's cool voice behind him. "Do you understand what a closed door means?" he asked.

"Better than you'd imagine," she answered with a small laugh. "But in this case, I don't care. Either you tell me what happened at the meeting, or I can call Katie. Which do you prefer?"

Jase closed his eyes and concentrated on making his lungs move air in and out. He knew there were no secrets in Crimson, at least not for long. His phone had started ringing and beeping with incoming calls and texts as soon as he walked out of the community center.

"Charles Thompson is running against me for mayor. He announced his candidacy to the downtown coalition this morning."

She didn't say anything, and Jase finally turned. Emily stood just inside the doorway to his office. After his secretary retired, Jase convinced himself that he preferred running the entire office on his own. So much of his life was filled with people and responsibility. This space had become a sanctuary of sorts, a place where he was in total control. He answered to no one.

In only a few days, Emily's presence had become the answer to a secret need he didn't know how to voice. Not only was she organized and efficient, but she breathed new life into an existence that had become so predictable Jase couldn't seem to force its path out of the familiar ruts.

This morning she wore a simple cotton dress with a light sweater thrown over her shoulders and strappy sandals. Her hair was held back with a clip but the length of it tumbled over her shoulders. The scent of her shampoo mixed with perfume tangled in the air, and Jase had noticed on Wednesday the hint of it lingered even after she left for the day.

"So what?" she asked when he finally met her gaze. "You've done more for this town than Charles Thompson. People love you."

He shook his head. "He was sheriff," he told her, as if that explained everything. The word *sheriff* captured the past Jase had worked so hard to bury under the duty and responsibility he shouldered in town.

"You've been the de facto leader on town council for several years. Noah told me you were instrumental in convincing Liam Donovan to move his company's headquarters to Crimson."

She stepped farther into the room and, like he was magnetized, Jase moved around the desk toward her. Toward the certainty of her unmistakable beauty and the sound of her voice. Maybe if he listened to her long enough, he could believe in himself the way she seemed to.

"From what I remember, Thompson was a decent sheriff, but this town has never had a big problem with crime. Business and keeping things moving forward have been a struggle for some of the older generation. Things are different now than when I left, and people say you're the reason."

If only it were that simple. "He knows everything about me."

Her delicate brows came down, as if she couldn't understand the significance of what he was saying.

"Charles ran the department when we were kids," he explained. "During the time when my grandpa died and Mom left with Sierra. My dad was still working at the mine, and he was at his lowest. It was worse than anyone knows." He paused, cleared his throat to expel the emotions threatening his airways. "Except Charles. He knows every sordid detail."

"That past has nothing to do with you."

"That past *is* me," he argued.

She shook her head. "Charles can't use anything he knows because of his position as sheriff in this election."

"He already has. Most of what he talked about at today's meeting was family values. He had his wife of thirty-four years and his two sons sitting in the front row. Hell, Miriam brought muffins to hand out."

"You want muffins? Katie will make you dozens of them. We can hand out baked goods to every voter in this town."

"That's not the point. You know how perception plays into politics. He's sowed the seeds of doubt about me. Now people will start talking…about me and my family and our history in Crimson."

"They'll understand he's running a smear campaign."

"No, they won't." He ran his hands through his hair, squeezed shut his eyes. "He was so smooth. Charles actually talked about how much he admired me, how much I'd overcome. He claimed he'd always felt protective of me because my mother abandoned me and my dad was so messed up. Would you believe he even compared me to his own sons?"

"Aaron and Todd?" Emily snorted. "Those two caused more trouble as teens than anyone else in the school. I haven't seen Todd, but from what I can tell, Aaron hasn't changed a bit. He's still a big bully. I don't know how many times I have to say no to a date before he quits calling me."

"He's calling you?" As angry as Jase was about Charles, temper of a different sort flared to the surface of his skin, hot and prickly. It was almost a relief to channel his frustration toward something outside himself. Something he could control. Above all else, Jase understood the value of control. "I'll take care of it."

"Hold on there, Hero-man. I don't need you to handle Aaron for me. I can take care of annoying jerks all on my own."

"You can handle everything, right?"

He regretted the rude question as soon as it was out of his mouth. Emily should snap back at him because he was lashing out at her with no cause. Instead, she flashed him a saucy grin. "Takes one to know one."

The smile, so unexpected and undeserved, diffused most of his anger, leaving him with a heaping pile of steaming self-doubt. He sat on the edge of his desk and leaned forward, hands on his knees.

"I'm sorry. I know you can take care of yourself." His chin dropped to his chest and he stared at the small stain peeking out from under one of the chairs in front of the desk. "But it's a lot easier to worry about other people than think of how quickly my own life is derailing."

A moment later he felt cool fingers brush away the hair from his forehead. He wanted to lean into her touch but forced himself to remain still. "Did you ever meet Andrew Meyer who used to run this office? I took over his practice four years ago, and I haven't changed a thing." He pushed the toe of his leather loafer against the chair leg until the stain was covered. "Not one piece of furniture or painting on the wall. You can still see the frame marks from where he took down his law school diploma and I never bothered to replace it with mine. I inherited his secretary and his clients, and I haven't lifted a finger to make this place my own. Hell, I think the magazines in the lobby are probably four years old. Maybe even older."

"I switched them for current issues," she said softly.

Her fingers continued to caress him and it felt so damn good to take a small amount of comfort from her. Too good. He lifted his head, and she dropped her hand.

"Why haven't you changed anything?" She didn't move away, and it was the hardest thing Jase had ever done not to pull her closer.

"Because this place isn't mine."

"It is," she said, her tone confused. "It's your office. Your clients. Your reputation." She laughed. "Your mortgage."

"This is the oldest law practice in the town. It was founded in the early 1900s and passed down through the Meyer family for generations. Andrew didn't have kids, so he offered a partnership position to me when I was still in law school. He wanted a Crimson native to take over the firm. This is his legacy. Not mine."

"Jase, you are the poster child for the town's favorite son. Charles Thompson can't hold a candle to the man you've become. Whether it was despite where you came from or because of it, the truth doesn't change."

"What if who people see isn't the truth? What if I've become too good at playing the part people expect of me?"

"You don't have to reflect the town's image of you back at them. You're more than a two-dimensional projection of yourself. Show everyone who you really are."

Staring into Emily's crystal-blue eyes, it was tempting. The urge to throw it all away, create the life he wanted, curled around his senses until the freedom of it was all he could see, hear and taste. Right behind the whisper of release came a pounding, driving fear that cut him off at the knees.

Who he was, who he'd been before he'd started down the path to redeeming his family name was a lost, lonely, scared boy. The memories he'd secreted away in the parts of his soul where he didn't dare look threatened to overtake him.

He stood abruptly, sending Emily stumbling back a few steps. "I'm going to win this election. I need people to see the best version of me, not the grubby kid Charles remembers."

Her eyes were soft. "Jase."

"I've worked toward this for years. It's what people expect…" He paused, took a breath. "It's what I want."

"Are you sure?"

"Charles isn't right for this. I'm going to be mayor."

She placed a light hand on his arm. "I'm going to help you."

He looked at her elegant fingers wrapped around his shirtsleeve. "Because you work for me."

"Because we're friends."

His eyes drifted shut for a moment. "Right. I forgot."

He felt a poke at his ribs. "Liar."

She had no idea. "I saw Katie at the meeting," he told her, needing to lighten the mood. He was too raw to go down that road with Emily. As much as he craved her kiss, he couldn't touch her again and not reveal the depth of his feelings. He thought he could control how much he needed her, but not when he was carrying his heart in his hands, ready to offer it to her if she asked. "She asked about plans for the bachelor and bachelorette parties."

Emily pulled a face. "No strippers."

He laughed in earnest. "I wasn't even thinking that."

"All men think that."

"You've got the whole male population figured out?"

"Like I said before, you're not complicated."

When it came to Emily, he wished it were true. His feelings for the woman standing in front of him had been simple for years. He wanted her. An unattainable crush. Unrequited love. End of story.

But a new chapter had started since she'd returned to town, and it was tangled in ways Jase couldn't take the time to unravel. Not if he was going to stay the course to his duty to Crimson.

"Then we're talking beer and poker night?"

Emily opened her mouth, then glanced over her shoulder as the door to the outer office opened. "Your appointment's here."

"Admit it, you like beer and poker."

She shook her head. "Come over for dinner tonight and we'll brainstorm better options." Her hand flew to cover her mouth as if she was shocked she'd extended the invitation.

"Yes," he said before she could retract the offer. "What time?"

Emily blinked. "Six."

"I'll be there."

"Jason, are you here?" a frail voice yelled from the front office.

"In my office, Mr. Anderson," Jase called. "Come on back."

"I should go…um…"

"Finish editing the brief I gave you?" Jase suggested, keeping his expression solemn.

"Exactly," she agreed.

As Morris Anderson tottered into the room, Emily said hello to the older man and disappeared.

"That Meg Crawford's girl?" Morris asked after she'd gone. Morris was here to revise the terms of his will, which he did on a monthly basis just to keep his four children on their toes.

Jase nodded, taking a seat behind his desk.

"I went to school with her grandmother back in the day. Spunky little thing."

"Good to know where Emily gets it." Jase pulled out Morris's bulging file. "Who made you angry this month?"

"Who didn't make me angry?" Morris asked through a coughing fit. "My kids are ungrateful wretches, but I love them." He pointed to the door, then to Jase. "The spunky ones are trouble," he said after a moment.

"Do you think so?" Jase felt his hackles rise. His protective inclination toward Emily was a palpable force surrounding him.

"I know so," Morris answered with a nod. "Trouble of the best kind. A man needs a little spunk to keep things interesting."

"I'd have to agree, Mr. Anderson," he said with a smile. "I'd definitely have to agree."

Chapter Seven

Emily wasn't sure how long she'd been sitting on the hallway floor when a pair of jeans and cowboy boots filled her line of sight.

"Emily?" Jase crouched down in front of her, placed a gentle hand on her knee. "What's wrong, sweetheart?"

"Nothing," she whispered. "Except dinner might be a little delayed. Sorry. I didn't realize you were here."

"I could see you through the screen door. I knocked but…"

"Hi, Jase." Davey's voice was sweet. Her boy didn't seem the least concerned to see his mother having a meltdown on the hardwood floor. "I built the space station hospital. Want to see it?"

"In a minute, buddy," Jase told him. "I'm going to hang out here with your mom first."

She tried to offer her son a smile but her face felt brittle. "Are you getting hungry, Davey?"

"Not yet." Small arms wrapped around her shoulders. "It's alright, Mama." The hug lasted only a few seconds but it was enough to send her already tattered emotions into overdrive. If her son was voluntarily giving her a hug, she must be in really bad shape.

She expelled a breath as Davey went back into the office. The tremors started along her spine but quickly spread until it felt like her whole body shook.

"Let's get you off the floor." Jase didn't wait for an answer. He scooped her into his arms and carried her toward the family room. Jase was strong and steady, the ends of his hair damp like he'd showered before coming over. She breathed in the scent of his shampoo mixed with the clean, woodsy smell she now associated with him alone. How appropriate that the man who was the poster child for Crimson would smell like the forest. As much as she wanted to sink into his embrace, Emily remained stiff against him. If she let go now, she might really lose it. "Where's your mom?"

"Book club," she managed between clenched teeth. "We should probably reschedule dinner for another night."

"I'm not leaving you like this." He deposited her onto the couch. "Not until you tell me what's going on."

Emily fought to pull herself together. She was so close to the edge it was as if she could feel the tiny spikes of hysteria pricking at the backs of her eyes. The cushions of the couch were soft and worn from years of movie nights and Sundays watching football. She wanted to curl up in a ball and ignore the constant pounding life seemed determined to serve up to her.

She couldn't look at Jase and risk him seeing the humiliation she knew was reflected in her eyes. She

stood, moving around the couch in the opposite direction. The kitchen opened to the family room, separated
by a half wall and the dining room table. "I'd planned to
make steaks," she said quickly, ignoring the trembling
in her fingers. "But I didn't get them out of the freezer,
so we may be stuck with hot dogs. Do you mind turning on the grill?"

He let himself out onto the flagstone patio as she
opened the pantry door and scanned the contents of the
cupboard. She heard him return a few minutes later but
kept her attention on the cupboard. "How do you feel
about boxed mac and cheese? I don't know how Mom
managed to make a home-cooked meal every night
when we were younger. She worked part-time, drove
us around to after-school activities, and still we had
family dinners most evenings. You remember, right?
She loved cooking for you and Noah."

He was standing directly behind her when she
turned, close enough she was afraid he might reach
for her. And if he did, she might shatter into a million
tiny fragments of disappointment and regret. "I know
I'm babbling. It's a coping mechanism. Give me a pass
on this one, Jase."

His dark eyes never wavered. "What happened?"

Her fingers tightened on the small cardboard box so
hard the corners bent. "An overreaction to some news.
My meltdown is over. I'm fine."

"What news?"

"Does it matter?" She shook her head. "I lost the
privilege of a major freak-out when I became a mother.
Moms don't have a lot of time for wallowing when dinner is late."

"Tell me anyway."

She slammed the box of mac and cheese on the counter, then bent to grab a pot out of a lower cabinet. "I liked you better when you were nice and easygoing and not all up in my business."

Elbowing him out of the way she turned on the faucet and filled the pot with water. "Apparently, my ex-husband got remarried last weekend. One of my former friends in Boston was nice enough to text me a photo from the wedding."

She set the pot of water on the stove and turned on the burner. The poof of sound as it ignited felt like the dreams she'd had for her life. There one minute and then up in flames. "It was small—nothing like the extravaganza I planned—only family and close friends."

She laughed. "My friends are now her friends. She was a campaign worker. What a cliché." She glanced over her shoulder, unable to stop speaking once she'd started. "You know the best part? She's pregnant. A shotgun wedding for Henry Whitaker III. It's like Davey and I never existed. We're gone and he's remaking our life with someone else. Our exact damn life."

"I'm sorry."

"Don't be sorry." She ripped off the top of the box with so much force that an explosion of dried macaroni noodles spilled across the counter. "I'm not."

"You don't have to pretend with me."

"I'm not sorry, Jase. I'm mad. It's mostly self-directed. I let myself be sucked into that life. I was so busy pretending I couldn't even see Henry for who he was." She scooped up the stray noodles, dropped them in the water and then dumped the rest of the box's contents in with them. "My son has to pay the price."

"Your ex-husband is an idiot."

"To put it mildly."

"There are other words going through my mind," Jase said, his tone steely. "But I'm not going to waste my energy on a man so stupid he would let you go and give up his son because of a political image."

Emily took a deep breath and released it along with much of her tension. "I don't miss him." It had been a shock to get the text about Henry but she hadn't been lying to Jase when she told him she was most angry at herself. "How did I marry a man who I can feel nothing but revulsion for five months after leaving him?"

"He hurt you," Jase answered simply.

"I should have seen him for who he was. My parents had a good marriage. There was so much love in this house."

He reached out, traced a fingertip along her jaw. "There was also a lot of pain when your dad died."

"Yes, and it left scars on all of us. But Noah managed to fall in love with an amazing woman. Mom is now dating someone who makes her happy. I seem to be the one with horrible taste."

Jase smiled. "Did you meet any of the women your brother dated before Katie?"

"From what I've heard, *date* is a fairly formal term for Noah's pre-Katie relationships."

"Exactly."

"He's one of the lucky ones." She sighed and stepped away from Jase. Staring into his dark eyes made her forget he wasn't for her. Jase Crenshaw was all about duty and responsibility. Whether he was willing to admit it or not, his image was a big part of his identity. He wasn't motivated by the hunger for power and prestige that had influenced her ex-husband. But it didn't change the fact he would eventually want more than Emily was willing to give.

She opened the refrigerator and grabbed a pack of hot dogs from the shelf. "Man the grill, Mr. Perfect. We're eating like kids tonight."

Jase watched her for a long, heavy moment before his lips curved into a grin. "The only thing perfect about me is my grilling skills."

She smiled in return, knowing he'd given her a pass. Maybe he'd sensed her frazzled emotions couldn't take any more deep conversation. "Let's see if your hot dogs can beat my mac and cheese."

"I'm up for the challenge," he said and let himself out onto the patio.

Alone in the kitchen, Emily went to check on her son. He was still busy with his Lego structures and she watched him for a few minutes before giving him a fifteen-minute warning for dinner. Davey's difficulty with rapid transitions had driven Henry crazy. Her ex-husband had loved spontaneity when he wasn't working or campaigning. A game of pick up football with the neighbors, a bike ride into town for dinner or an impromptu weekend at the shore. Henry had to be moving at all times, his energy overpowering and bordering on manic.

She'd kept up with him when Davey was a baby but as the boy grew into a toddler, he liked notice if things were going to change. Henry had never been willing to accept the difficulty of swooping in and changing Davey's schedule without warning. Davey's difficulty with change only got worse over time, and it had become a huge source of tension with Henry.

Since returning to Crimson, Emily had done her best

to keep her son on a regular schedule. Her mother and Noah had quickly adapted, making her understand the issues her ex-husband had were his own and not her or Davey's fault.

She filled a plastic cup with milk for Davey, then pulled out two beers for her and Jase. As she was setting the table, Jase let himself back into the house. "Perfect dogs," he said, holding up a plate.

"Do you know Tater?"

Emily turned to find Davey standing behind her, looking at Jase.

"She's my uncle Noah's dog," the boy explained. "Her fur is really soft, but she has stinky breath and she likes to lick me."

"Tater is a great dog," Jase answered, setting the hot dogs on the kitchen table.

"Let's wash hands," she said to her son. "Mac and cheese and hot dogs for dinner."

He climbed on the stool in front of the sink, washed his hands, then went to sit next to Jase at the table. "Tater used to live here with Uncle Noah. Now they both live with Aunt Katie. Do you have a dog?"

Jase nodded. "I have a puppy. Her name is Ruby."

"Does she have soft fur?"

"She sure does and I bet she'd like you. She's six months old and has lots of energy. She loves to play."

"I could play with her," Davey offered, taking a big bite of mac and cheese.

"Would you like to meet her sometime?"

Davey nodded. "We can drive to where you live after dinner."

"If that's okay with your mom," Jase told him.

"A short visit," Emily said, trying not to make Davey's

suggestion into something bigger than it was. Which was difficult, because her son never volunteered to go anywhere. She planned outings to local parks and different shops downtown, and Davey tolerated the excursions. But there was no place he'd ever asked to go. Until now. She wondered if Jase understood the significance of the request.

He tipped back his beer bottle for a drink and then smiled at her. "I love mac and cheese."

She rolled her eyes but Davey nodded. "Me, too. And hot dogs. Mommy makes good cheese quesadillas."

"I'll have to try for an invitation to quesadilla night."

"You can come to dinner again." Davey kept his gaze on his plate, the words tumbling out of his mouth with little inflection. "Right, Mommy?"

"Of course," she whispered.

Jase asked Davey a question about his latest Lego creation. Once again, her son was talking more with Jase than he normally would to his family. Henry had a habit of demanding Davey make eye contact and enunciate when he spoke, both of which were difficult for her quiet boy. The last six months of her marriage had been fraught with tension as she and her ex-husband had waged a devastating battle over how to raise their son. The arguments and tirades had made Davey shrink into himself even more, and she'd worried the damage Henry was unwittingly doing might leave permanent scars on Davey's sensitive personality.

The way he acted toward Jase was a revelation. When Jase smiled at her again, his eyes warm and tender, Emily's heart began to race. How could she resist this man who saw her at her worst—angry or in the middle of an emotional meltdown—and still remained at her side, constant and true?

The answer was she didn't want to fight the spark between them. For the first time since returning to Crimson, Emily wondered if she hadn't squandered her chance at happiness after all.

"She needs to go out and do her business, and then you can play with her." Jase unlocked the front door of his house as he spoke to Davey.

The young boy stayed behind Emily's legs but nodded.

Emily gave him an apologetic smile. "He always takes a few minutes to acclimate to new places."

"Take all the time you need, buddy." As soon as the door began to open, Ruby started yelping. "She's usually pretty excited when I first get home."

"Davey, let's go," Emily said, her voice tense.

Jase looked over his shoulder to see the boy still standing in front of the door, eyes on the floor of the porch.

She crouched down next to her son. "It's okay, sweetie. You wanted to meet the puppy. Remember?"

"Take your time," Jase called. "I'm going to bring her to the backyard because it's fenced. Come on out whenever you're ready." The yelping got more insistent, a sure sign Ruby needed to get to the grass quickly. He lifted the blanket off the crate in the corner and flipped open the door, grabbing the puppy in his arms as she tried to dart out. She wriggled in his arms and licked his chin, but as soon as he opened the back door she darted for her favorite potty spot near a tree in the corner. He followed her into the grass with a glance back to the house. Emily and Davey hadn't emerged yet.

Ruby ran back to him and head-butted his shin before circling his legs. He didn't bother to hide his smile. Even after the worst day, it was hard not to feel better as the recipient of so much unconditional love. It didn't matter how long he'd been gone. She greeted him with off-the-charts enthusiasm every time.

After a few minutes, Ruby stopped, her whole body going rigid as her focus shifted to the back of the house. Jase went to grab her but she dodged his grasp and took off for the porch. He called for her but she ignored him as a six-month-old puppy was apt to do.

To his surprise, she slowed down at the top of the patio steps and didn't bark once at Emily or Davey. His puppy normally gave a vocal greeting at every new person or animal she encountered. She trotted toward Emily, stopping long enough to be petted before moving closer to Davey.

The boy was standing ramrod stiff against the house's brick exterior, his gaze staring straight ahead. Jase could almost feel Emily holding her breath. Ruby sniffed at Davey's legs, then nudged his fingers with her nose. When he didn't pet her, she bumped him again, then sat a few feet in front of him as if content to wait. After a moment, Davey's chin dipped and he glanced at the puppy. She rewarded him by prancing in a circle, then sitting again. He slowly eased himself away from the house and took a hesitant step toward her.

Ruby whined softly and ran to the edge of the porch and returned to Davey with a tennis ball in her mouth, dropping it at his feet. The ball rolled a few inches.

"She's learning to play fetch," Jase called. "Do you want to throw the ball for her?"

Davey didn't give any indication he'd heard the question other than picking up the ball gingerly between his fingers and tossing it down the steps. Ruby tumbled after it, and in her excitement to retrieve the ball, she lost her balance and did a somersault across the grass. With a small laugh, Davey made his way down the steps toward the grass.

Ruby returned the ball to him and the boy threw it again.

"She'll go after the ball all night long," he told the boy. "Let me know when you get tired of throwing it."

Davey walked farther into the yard.

Jase turned for the patio to find Emily standing on the top step, tears shining in her blue eyes. "What's wrong?" he asked, jogging up the stairs to her side.

She shook her head. "Davey laughed. Did you hear him laugh?"

"Puppies have that effect on people."

"I can't remember the last time he laughed out loud," she whispered, swiping under her eyes. "It's the most beautiful sound."

"I'm glad I got to hear it."

Ruby flipped over again as she dived for the ball and this time when Davey giggled, Emily let out her own quiet laugh. She clapped a hand over her mouth.

Jase wrapped an arm around her shoulder. "It's been a while since I've heard his mother laugh, too."

"I don't know whether to laugh or cry." She sank down to the top step and Jase followed, his heart expanding as she leaned against him. "He used to laugh when he was a baby. Then things went sideways... He became so disconnected."

"You're a good mom, Em. You'll get him through this."

She turned to look at him. "Do you really believe that? You don't think I messed him up by leaving Henry and moving him across the country?"

"You protected him. That's what a mom is supposed to do." He tried not to let decades-old bitterness creep into his voice but must have failed because Emily laced her fingers with his.

"How old were you when your mother left town?"

"Nine. My sister was seven. I haven't seen either of them since the day Mom packed up the car and drove away."

"Have you ever looked?"

"My mother made it clear any man with the last name Crenshaw was bound for trouble."

"She was wrong. You've changed what people in this town think of your family. She needs to know who you've become."

"It's too late."

"What about your sister?"

"I don't blame her. Who knows how my mother poisoned her against my dad and me. I'm sure Sierra has a good life. She doesn't need me."

Emily squeezed his hand. "I didn't think I needed my family when I left Crimson. I was stupid."

He glanced down at their entwined fingers and ran his thumb along the half-moons of her nails. "You used to wear polish."

"You're changing the subject." She waved to Davey

with her free hand when he turned. The boy gave her a slight nod and went back to throwing the ball.

"I don't want to talk about my family tonight." He threw her a sideways glance. "My turn for a pass?"

"Fine. Let's go back to my former beauty routine, which is a fascinating topic. I had my signature nail color and perfume. I was determined to be someone people remembered."

"You were."

"For the wrong reasons," she said with a laugh. "It's pretty sad if the thing I'm recognized for is a top-notch manicure and a cloud of expensive perfume."

"Now they'll recognize you as a strong woman and an amazing mother." He leaned closer to her until his nose touched the soft skin of her neck. "Although you still smell good."

Her breath hitched. "I wish I hadn't been so mean to you when we were younger."

"I suppose you'll have to make it up to me."

She turned, and he was unnerved by her serious expression. "I'm not the right woman for you, Jase."

The certainty of her tone made his gut clench. "Shouldn't I be the one making that decision?"

"I'm doing you a favor by making it for you."

"I don't want favors from you." He narrowed his eyes. "Unless they involve your mouth on me. Isn't that what you told me you wanted?"

Color rose to her cheeks and she dropped her gaze. "Wanting and needing are two different things."

He *wanted* to haul her into his lap and kiss that lie off her mouth. It was becoming more difficult to be patient when she was sitting so close that the warmth of her thigh seeped into his skin.

"We should talk about plans for the prewedding parties." She tugged her fingers out his and inched away from him until the cool evening breeze whispered in the space between their bodies. Jase hated that space. "Since so many of Noah's and Katie's friends overlap, I think the bachelorette and bachelor parties should be combined."

"Makes sense. Party planning is not exactly my strong suit."

"You're lucky I'm here."

There were many more reasons, but she was already spooked, so he didn't mention any of them. "I can tell you have an idea."

She flashed him a superior grin. "A scavenger hunt."

"Like we did as kids?"

"Sort of. We'll put together groups and give everyone clues to search for items important to Noah and Katie. They both grew up here so there's plenty of things to choose from."

"I like it," Jase admitted.

"Because it's brilliant."

"That's the Emily I know and…" He paused, watched her eyes widen, then added, "like as a friend."

She bumped him with her shoulder. "Mr. Perfect and a comedian—quite a combination."

"We've already established I'm not perfect."

"I like you better as a real person." She nudged him again. "And a friend."

As the sun began to fade, they watched Davey throw the ball over and over to the puppy.

"I wonder who will give up first," Jase muttered. The answer came a few minutes later when Ruby dropped the ball on the grass in front of Davey, then flopped down next to it.

"Wavy-Davey, it's time to head home," Emily called to him. "Bedtime for puppies and little boys."

The boy ignored her and sat next to Ruby, buried his face in the puppy's fur and began to gently rock back and forth.

Emily sighed. "Too much stimulation," she said, a sudden weariness in her eyes. "You might want to go inside. Chances are likely he'll have a tantrum."

"How do you know?"

"The rocking is one of his tells." She pressed her hand to her forehead. "I should have monitored him more closely but..." She gave Jase a watery smile. "I was having fun."

"Me, too," he told her and lifted his fingers to the back of her neck, massaging gently. "I'm not going to leave you. He's a kid and if he has a tantrum, so be it."

"I don't want the night to end like this." She walked down the steps slowly, approaching her son the way she might a wounded animal. Jase followed a few paces behind.

"Davey, we're going back to Grandma's now."

The rocking became more vigorous.

"Do you want to walk to the car or should I carry you?"

"No."

"You can decide or I'll decide for you, sweetheart." Emily's tone was gentle but firm. "Either way we're going home. You can visit Ruby again."

Davey's movement slowed. "When?"

"Maybe this weekend."

He shook his head and Jase stepped forward. "Hey,

buddy, you did an awesome job tiring out Ruby. I bet she's going to sleep the whole night through."

"She likes the ball," the boy mumbled.

"She likes you throwing the ball," Jase told him. "But even as tired as she is, I bet she'll wake up tomorrow morning with a ton of energy."

Davey gave him a short nod.

"Do you think it would be okay if I brought her out to your grandma's farm in the morning? You can puppy-sit while I go to a meeting."

The boy glanced up at him, then back at Ruby. He nodded again.

Jase crouched down next to Davey. "I'll ask your mom if it's okay with her, but you have to get a good night's sleep, too. That means heading home now and going to bed without a fuss. Do you think you can do that?"

Davey got to his feet and lifted his face to look at Emily before lowering his gaze again. "Can Ruby come over in the morning, Mommy?"

Emily reached out as if to ruffle her son's hair, then pulled her hand tight to her chest. "You'll have to eat breakfast early."

"Okay."

"Then it's fine with me. Your grammy will love to meet Ruby."

"She can walk with us." Without another word, he turned for the house. "Let's go home, Mommy."

Jase bent and scooped the sleeping puppy into his arms. Ruby snuggled against him.

Emily ran her hand through the dog's fur, then cupped Jase's cheek. "Thank you," she whispered and pressed a soft kiss to his mouth.

"A better way to end the night?" he asked against her lips.

"Much better. Good luck at the breakfast tomorrow." She kissed him again, then ran up the back steps.

Jase followed with the dog in his arms, watching as Emily buckled her son into his booster seat. He waved to Davey as they drove away.

"You did good," he whispered to the puppy sleeping in his arms and walked back to his house.

Chapter Eight

"You're looking at those pancakes like they're topped with motor oil instead of syrup."

Emily smiled as Jase spun toward her, almost spilling his cup of coffee in the process.

"You came," he said.

She glanced around at the basement reception room of one of Crimson's oldest churches. The last time she'd been here was after her father's funeral, but she tried to ignore the memories that seemed to bounce from the walls. Instead she waved a hand at the display of Sunday school artwork. "Where else would I be on a beautiful Saturday morning?"

"I don't really need to answer that, do I?"

"No, but I would like to know why the candidate who sponsored this breakfast is hiding out in the corner? Are you familiar with the term *glad-handing*?"

"I'm eating breakfast," he mumbled, pointing to the paper plate stacked with pancakes that sat on the small folding table shoved against the wall. "They're actually quite good." He set down his coffee cup and picked up the plate, lifting a forkful of pancake toward her mouth.

"I had oatmeal earlier."

"Edna Sharpe is watching. You don't want her to think you're too good for her pancakes."

Emily rolled her eyes at the glint of challenge in his gaze. But she allowed him to feed her a bite. "Yum," she murmured as she chewed. Her breath caught as Jase used his thumb to wipe a drop of syrup from the corner of her mouth.

"Jase," she whispered, "why aren't you talking to everyone?"

He dropped the plate back to the table and folded his arms across his chest. "I hate how they look at me."

"Like you're Crimson's favorite son?"

"Like I'm the poor, pathetic kid with the mother who abandoned him to his drunken dad." He held up a hand when she started to speak. "I understand most people in town know my family's history. But I've worked hard to make sure they see me and not the Crenshaw legacy. Now Charles Thompson is leaking small details about my childhood—dirty laundry I don't want aired—to anyone who will listen. You know how fast those bits of information travel through the town grapevine."

"So you're going to let him have the last word? Give up on everything you've done for Crimson?"

"Of course not."

She pointed toward the crowded tables. "Then go visit with these people. Shake hands. Kiss babies."

"Kiss babies," he repeated, one side of his mouth curving. "Really?"

"You know what I mean. I understand what happens when you let someone else's perceived image guide your actions. That's not who you are."

"They expect—"

"You're not perfect. Neither is your history. People can deal with that. But you have to put yourself out there."

"Is that what you're doing?"

"I'm supporting a friend," she said and straightened his tie.

His warm hands covered hers. "I'm glad you're here, Em. I could use a friend right now."

"What you could use is a kick in the pants."

His smile widened. "Are you offering to be the kicker?"

She nodded. "Katie and Noah are stopping by in a bit and I left a message for Natalie."

"You didn't need to. It's a Saturday morning and they have lives."

"Support goes both ways, and you've given plenty to your friends. They're happy to return the favor."

He took a deep, shuddering breath. "There wasn't supposed to be this much scrutiny."

"Welcome to the joys of a political campaign."

"And part of a life you left behind." He bent his knees until they were at eye level. "This isn't the plan for rebuilding your life." His fingers brushed a strand of hair away from her face. A flicker of longing skittered across her skin, one that was becoming all too familiar with this man.

"I can help," she said with a shrug. "It's what I know how to do."

He glanced over her shoulder and cursed. "My father is here," he said on a harsh breath.

Emily could feel the change in Jase, the walls shooting up around him. "You mingle with the voters," she said quickly. "I'll talk to your dad."

"You don't have to—"

"Too late," she called over her shoulder. She hurried to the entrance of the reception hall, where Jase's father stood by himself. A few of the groups at tables nearby threw him questioning looks. Emily knew Declan Crenshaw's history as well as anyone. The man had been on and off the wagon more times than anyone could count.

Once Jase and Noah had become friends, Emily's whole family had been pulled into the strange orbit circling Declan and his demons. Jase had slept over at her parents' farm most weekends, and she remembered several times being woken in the dead of night to Declan standing in their front yard, screaming for Jase to come home and make him something to eat.

As a stupid, spoiled teenage girl, Emily had hated being associated with the town drunk. She'd unfairly taken her resentment out on Jase, treating him like he was beneath her. Shame at the memory rose like bile in her throat. She'd been such a fool.

Now Declan's gaze flicked to her, wary and unsure behind the fake smile he'd plastered across his face. Without hesitating, Emily wrapped him in a tight hug.

"Jase is so glad you could make it," she said, loud enough so the people sitting nearby were sure to hear.

"You're a beautiful liar," Declan murmured in her ear, "and I know you hate these events as much as I do."

She pulled back, adjusted the collar on his worn dress shirt much as she'd straightened his son's tie. Declan would have been a distinguished man if the years hadn't been so hard on him. "Maybe not quite as much. I wasn't very nice, but at least I never embarrassed the people who loved me."

"Good point," he admitted with a frown, his shaggy eyebrows pulling low. "But things are different now. I'm sober for good. Am I ever going to live down the past?"

"I'm more concerned Jase feels the need to live it down for you." She led him toward the line at the pancake table.

"I know what Charles Thompson is trying to do." Declan picked up a paper plate and stabbed a stack of pancakes with a plastic fork. "It's my fault and it's not fair."

"Life rarely is." Emily took one pancake for herself. "We both know that."

"You're good for him."

She shook her head. "I'm not. As small of a community as Crimson is, the life Jase has here is still more public than I'm willing to handle."

Declan greeted the older man standing behind the table wiping a bottle of syrup. "Morning, Phil."

The other man's eyes narrowed. "Surprised to see you out of bed so early, Crenshaw."

Emily braced herself for Declan's retort, but he only smiled. "I'm full of surprises. How are Margie and the kids?"

Phil blinked several times before clearing his throat. "They're fine."

"I heard you have a grandbaby on the way." Declan poured syrup over his pancakes.

"My daughter-in-law is due around Thanksgiving," the other man answered, his face relaxing.

"I can't wait for Jase to find the right girl," Declan said. He nudged Emily's plate with his, which she ignored. "But until then, he's giving everything he has to this town. Do you know how many times he's taken payment for his services as a lawyer with casseroles or muffins?"

"I don't," Phil admitted. Several other volunteers had gathered around him.

Declan leaned over the table and lowered his voice, as if he was imparting a great secret. "More than I can count. He shares the food with me, and while I appreciate it, blueberry muffins don't pay the bills. But Jase wants to help people. There's his work on city council and getting Liam Donovan to move his company headquarters here." Declan glanced toward the doors leading into the hall. "There's Liam now, along with Noah Crawford. My son is good for this town, you know?"

The group on the other side of the table nodded in unison. "We know," Phil said.

With a satisfied nod, Declan turned to Emily, his dark eyes sparkling. "Shall we sit down and have breakfast, darlin'?"

She nodded, stunned, and followed him to a table, waving Noah and Liam over toward them. "You were amazing."

He threw back his head and laughed. "That's the first time I've ever heard that adjective used to describe me."

"I thought you'd get angry when Phil made the comment about you getting out of bed early."

"I don't get mad about hearing the truth. Phil and I go way back. It may have taken me a whole morning to climb out of bed in my hangover days, but at least I wasn't wearing my wife's undies when I did."

Emily felt her mouth drop. "What are you talking about?" she asked in a hushed whisper.

He winked at her. "I know plenty about the people in this town. For years, there was only one bar the locals liked. My butt was glued to one of the vinyl stools more nights than I care to admit. Most folks like to talk and they figure a drunk isn't going to remember their secrets." He tapped the side of his head with one finger. "But I got a mind like a steel trap. Even three sheets to the wind, I don't forget what I hear."

"There's more to you than anyone knows," Emily murmured with a small smile. She wouldn't forget what this man had put Jase through because of his drunken antics, but she could tell Declan was sincere in his desire to support his son.

"I think we have that in common," Declan told her.

A moment later Noah put an arm around her shoulder. "Hey there, sis. Trading one politician for another?"

She shoved him away, panic slicing up her spine.

"I'm joking, Em," Noah said quickly. "Didn't mean to strike a nerve."

"You should let Katie do the talking while you stick to looking the part of a handsome forest ranger." Emily tried to play off her reaction, but the way Noah watched her said he wasn't fooled.

He smiled anyway, smoothing a hand over his uniform. "I *am* a handsome forest ranger." His expression sobered as he looked over her shoulder. "Hello, Mr. Crenshaw."

"Noah." Declan nodded. "Congratulations on your upcoming wedding."

"Thanks. I owe a debt of thanks to Jase for helping me realize the love of my life had been by my side for years." He moved back a step to include Liam in the conversation. "Have you met Liam Donovan?"

Declan stuck out his hand. "I haven't but I've heard you're rich enough to buy the whole damn mountain if you wanted it."

Noah looked mortified but Liam only smiled and shook Declan's hand. "Maybe half the mountain," he answered.

As she greeted Liam, Emily could feel her brother studying her. She and Noah hadn't been close after their father's death, especially since they'd each been wrestling with their own private grief, and neither very successfully. They'd begun to forge a new bond since returning to Crimson, but Emily wasn't ready to hear his thoughts on her being a part of Jase's life.

Pushing back from the table, she grabbed her plate and stood. "You two keep Declan company. I see an old high school friend." She leaned down to give Jase's father a quick hug. "Thanks for breakfast," she said with a wink.

"Best date I've had in years."

Noah looked like he wanted to stop her, but she ducked around him and headed for the trash can in the corner. She waved to a couple of her mother's friends, then searched for Jase amid the people mingling at the sides of the reception hall.

Of course he was in the middle of the largest group, gesturing as he spoke and making eye contact with each person. They all stood riveted by whatever he was saying, nodding and offering up encouraging smiles.

A momentary flash of jealousy stabbed at her heart.

She understood what it was like to be on the receiving end of Jase's attention, sincere and unguarded. He was the only man she knew who could make his gaze feel like a caress against her skin, and this morning was proof of why that was so dangerous to her.

Even when he was living up to other peoples' expectations, Jase was comfortable in the role. He belonged in the spotlight and in the hearts of this town. Emily had left behind her willingness to trade her private life for public favor. Davey had changed her. She'd never put anyone else's needs before his. Even her own.

She slipped out the door leading to the back of the church, needing a moment away from the curious eyes of the town. The midmorning sun was warm on her skin. She closed her eyes and tipped up her face, leaning back against the building's brick wall.

A moment later the door opened and shut again.

"What happened to catching up with old friends?" Noah asked, coming to stand in front of her.

"You're blocking my sun," she told him.

"Because from what I remember of how you left this town, you don't have many friends here."

She opened her eyes to glare at him. "Don't be mean."

He sighed. "I don't understand what you're doing. For years you couldn't stand Jase—"

"That's not true." The protest sounded weak even to her own ears.

"You certainly gave him a hard time. I stopped out at the farm this morning and saw Mom and Davey with his puppy."

"Davey bonded with Ruby right away, so Jase was nice enough to bring her by so they could play."

"Of course. Jase is a nice guy."

"Too nice for someone like me?"

Noah stepped out of her line of sight, turning so he stood next to her against the wall. "You know he's had a crush on you for years."

"It's different now. I'm working for him."

"Which means you two are spending a lot of time together. He'd moved on until you came back. Jase has a lot of responsibility in this town. Between his practice, his father and now dealing with a real campaign—"

"I understand, Noah." She hated being put on the spot and the fact her brother was doing it. "Are you telling me to stay away from him?"

Noah shook his head. "You're coming off a bad divorce. I'm saying don't use Jase as a rebound fling. Both of you could end up hurt."

Pushing off the wall, she spun toward him. "It's Jase you're worried about, not me."

"Emily—"

"No. You don't know anything about my marriage."

"Why is that?" He ran a hand through his hair. "How the hell am I supposed to understand anything about your life? You cut me out after Dad died."

"That was mutual and you know it."

"I thought we were doing better since Mom's illness?"

"We are, Noah. But it might be too soon for brotherly lectures on my private life."

"Nothing is private in Crimson. You know that. Besides, I thought you came back to here to heal?"

"Maybe Jase is a part of me healing." Until she said the words out loud, she hadn't realized how true they were. Tears sprang to the backs of her eyes and she swiped at her cheek, refusing to allow herself to break down. She'd promised herself she was finished with crying after she'd left Henry.

Noah cursed under his breath. "I'm sorry. Don't cry."

"I'm not crying," she whispered and her voice cracked.

"You really care about him."

"We're friends. It's not a fling. Not a rebound. I don't know what is going on between us, but I'm not going to hurt him. I think…" She paused, forced herself to meet Noah's worried gaze. "I think I'm good for him. It goes both ways, Noah. I know it does."

"Okay, honey." Noah pulled her in for a tight hug. She resisted at first, holding on to her anger like an old friend. But her brother didn't let go, and after a few moments she sagged against him, understanding that even if he made her crazy, Noah was far better comfort than her temper could ever be.

"I'm sorry," he whispered into her hair.

"You're a good friend to Jase."

"But I need to be a better brother to you. You're important to me. You and Davey both."

"You have to say that because I helped your bride pick out a wedding dress that will bring tears to your eyes."

"I can't wait," he said with a lopsided grin and a dopey look in his eyes that made her smile. "But I'm *choosing* to tell you the truth about supporting you more. I mean every word."

"Then will you help me find my own place to live?"

"Mom loves having you at the farm." He frowned. "She loves helping with Davey and having you close."

"I'll still be close, but I want a home of my own, even

if it's a tiny apartment somewhere. After the wedding will you help me look?"

"Of course."

"Do you have any prewedding nerves?" she asked, stepping out of his embrace. "You spent a long time avoiding commitment."

"I was a master," he agreed.

"Marriage is a big deal, especially when there's a baby on the way."

"I felt the baby kick the other night."

"Oh, Noah."

"It made this whole thing feel real. I mean, I know it's real but…yes, I'm nervous." He looked over her shoulder toward the mountains in the distance. "Not about marrying Katie. I can't believe I was blind for so long, but now I've got her and I'm never letting go." He took a breath, then said, "Even if I don't deserve her."

"You do." She nudged him with her hip. "You're a pain in my butt, but you deserve happiness."

"What if I mess up? What if I can't be as good as Dad?"

"Don't compare yourself." She gave a small laugh. "Do you think I could ever hold a candle to Mom?"

"You're an amazing mother."

"You'll be an amazing dad." She held up her hand, fist closed. "We've got this, bro."

"Are you trying to be cool?"

She shrugged and lifted her hand higher. "Don't leave me hanging."

With a laugh, Noah fist-bumped her, then pulled her in for another hug. "We'd better head back inside. I have a feeling Declan and Liam together are a danger-ous combination."

* * *

Jase's lungs burned as he ran the final stretch to the lookout point halfway up the main Crimson Mountain trail. At the top, he bent forward, sucking in the thin mountain air.

The late-afternoon trail run was supposed to clear his head, but his mind refused to slow down. Images of Emily and his dad swirled inside him, mixing with thoughts of the questions he'd answered at this morning's campaign breakfast.

How do you feel about Charles Thompson running against you?

Do you have too much going on to add mayor to your list of responsibilities?

When are you going to settle down and start a family?

Are you worried about not having time to take care of your dad?

What if Declan starts to drink again?

He'd answered each of the inquiries with a nod and an understanding smile, but he'd wanted to turn and run from the crowded church hall. Those questions brought up too many emotions inside him. Too much turmoil he couldn't control. Jase's greatest fear was losing control and it seemed he had less of a grasp on it with each passing day.

He sank down to one of the rock formations and watched as Liam Donovan came over the final ridge, a few minutes behind Jase. Liam's dark hair was stuck to his forehead and his athletic T-shirt plastered to his chest. The run up to the lookout point was almost three miles of vertical switchbacks. Jase had been running this trail since high school but today even the beauty of the forest hadn't settled him.

"Are you crazy?" Liam asked, panting even harder than Jase. "You were running like a mountain lion was chasing you."

Jase wiped the back of one arm across his forehead. "A mountain lion would have caught you instead of me. I thought you wanted a challenge."

"A challenge is different than a heart attack. You'd have a tough time explaining to Natalie that you left me on the side of the mountain."

"I wouldn't have left you." Jase grinned. "I'm too afraid of your wife."

"The strange thing is she'd take that as a compliment." He sat on a rock across from Jase. "You had a good turnout at the breakfast this morning."

"I appreciate you stopping by."

"Always happy to do my part with a plate of pancakes. Your dad is a character."

Jase laughed. "That's one word for him."

"He's really proud of you." Liam used the hem of his shirt to wipe the sweat off his face. "My dad never gave a damn about anything I did. Not as long as I stayed out of his way."

Liam's father owned one of the most successful tech companies in the world. It had been big news in the technology world when Liam broke off to start his own GPS software company and chose Crimson as the headquarters for it.

"I couldn't exactly stay out of Declan's way. I was too busy cleaning up behind him."

"A fact your new opponent in the mayor's race is exploiting?"

Jase blew out a breath. "Sheriff Thompson has seen me at my lowest. He and my dad grew up together in town and the Thompsons and Crenshaws have always been rivals—sports, women, you name it." He stood and paced to the edge of the ridge, taking in the view of the town below. "Anytime a situation involved my dad, Thompson made sure he was on the scene. Didn't matter if it was the weekend or who was on duty. The sheriff always showed up to personally cuff Dad."

"Declan seems sincere about changing."

"He's always sincere." From up here, Jase could see downtown Crimson and the neighborhoods fanning out around it. The creek ran along the edge of downtown, then meandered through the valley and into the thick forest on the other side.

As a kid, he'd battled the expectations that he'd follow in his father's footsteps. People always seemed to be waiting for him to make a misstep, to become another casualty of the Crenshaw legend. He'd worked so hard to prove them wrong. When would he be released from the responsibility of making up for mistakes he hadn't made?

Liam came to stand next to him. "I know what it's like to have to claw your way out from a father's shadow. Our backgrounds are different, but disappointment and anger don't discriminate based on how much you have in the bank."

"But you've escaped it."

"Maybe," Liam said with a shrug. "Maybe not. My dad is known all over the world. I've created a different future for myself but his legacy follows me. I choose to ignore it and live life on my terms."

Jase wasn't sure if he'd even know how to go about

setting up his own life away from the restrictions of his past. "When I graduated from law school, a firm in Denver offered me a position. I turned it down to come back to Crimson and take over Andrew Meyer's family practice."

"Do you regret the choice you made?"

Jase picked up a flat stone from the trail and hurled it over the edge of the ridge. It arced out, then disappeared into the canopy of trees below. "I don't know. Back then, I was so determined to return to Crimson as a success. Part of it was feeling like I owed something to the people in this town. As much as they judged my family, they also came forward to take care of us when things were rough. After my mom left, we had food in the freezer for months."

"Nothing says love in a small town like a casserole."

"Exactly," Jase agreed with a laugh. "There were a couple of teachers who looked after me at school. Once it became clear I was determined to stay on the straight and narrow, the town was generous with its support. I was given a partial scholarship during undergrad and always had a job waiting for me in the summer. I wanted to pay back that kindness, and dedicating myself to the town seemed like the best way to do it."

"But…" Liam prompted.

"I've started to wonder what it would have been like to go to work, come home and take care of only myself. Maybe that's selfish—"

"It's not selfish." Liam lobbed a rock over the side and it followed the same trajectory as Jase's. "It's also not too late. I was going to ask if you need support with the campaign. Financial support," he clarified.

"But now I'm wondering if becoming mayor is what you really want?"

"Does it matter? I've committed to it."

"You can back out. Charles Thompson isn't a bad man. He would do a decent job."

Jase cocked a brow.

"Not as good as you, of course. But the future of Crimson doesn't rest on your shoulders, Jase."

"I'll think about that." As if he could think about anything else. "We should head back down. I'll take it easy on you."

Liam barked out a laugh. "A true gentleman."

Jase started for the trail, then turned back. "Thanks for the offer, Liam. I appreciate it, but I don't want to owe you. Having you at my back is plenty of support."

"I'd think of it as an investment," Liam answered. "And the offer stands if you change your mind."

"Thank you." Jase started running, the descent more technical than climbing the switchbacks due to the loose rocks and late-afternoon shadows falling over the trail. It was just what he needed, something to concentrate on besides the emotional twists and turns of his current life.

Chapter Nine

Monday morning, Emily jumped at the tap on her shoulder, spinning around in her desk chair to find Jase grinning at her.

She ripped the headphones off her ears. "You scared me half to death," she said, wheezing in a breath.

"You were singing out loud."

"You were supposed to be in court all day." She narrowed her eyes.

"What exactly are you listening to?" He reached for the headphones, but she grabbed them, then spun around to hit the mute button on her keyboard.

"Music," she mumbled. "Why are you back so early? I didn't hear the bells on the door when it opened."

"I came in through the door to the alley out back."

"You snuck up on me," she grumbled.

"What kind of music? I didn't recognize it."

"Broadway show tunes, okay?" She crossed her arms over her chest and glared. "*Evita* to be specific. I like musicals." The words came out like a challenge. "You're a lawyer—sue me."

His grin widened. "Don't cry for me, Emily Whitaker."

"Asking for trouble, Jase Crenshaw."

He held up a brown paper bag. "Here's a peace offering. I brought lunch from the deli around the corner. That's why I came through the back. Have you eaten?"

She held up an empty granola-bar wrapper. "I'm working through lunch since I'm leaving early today." Tomorrow was Davey's first day of kindergarten so tonight they were going to the ice cream social at the elementary school. Her son didn't seem worried about the change, but Emily had been a bundle of nerves since the moment she'd woken up this morning.

She'd had a meeting at the beginning of the week with the kindergarten teacher and the school's interventionist to discuss the Asperger's and how to help Davey have a successful school year. For a small school district, Crimson Elementary School offered many special education services. This would mark the first time he'd been away from her during the day.

She'd enrolled him in preschool in their Boston neighborhood, having added Davey's name to the exclusive program's wait list when he was only a few months old. Despite the expense of the private program, the teachers had been unwilling to work with his personality quirks.

Much like her husband, they'd expected him to manage like the rest of the children, which led to several frustrated tantrums. Davey had lashed out, throwing a toy car across the room. It had hit one of the other students on the side of the head and the girl had stumbled, then fallen, knocking her head on the corner of a bookshelf. There'd been angry calls from both the teacher and the girl's mother and even a parent meeting at the school to allay other families' concerns about Davey continuing in the program.

Henry had been furious, mostly because two of his partners had kids enrolled at the school so he couldn't brush the incident under the rug. In the end, Emily had pulled Davey, opting to work with him herself on the skills he'd needed to be ready for kindergarten.

She couldn't control the way Asperger's affected his personality and his ability to socialize with both adults and other kids. Or how he was treated by people who didn't understand how special he was.

"Come to the conference room and eat a real lunch," Jase said gently, as if he could sense the anxiety tumbling through her like rocks skidding down the side of Crimson Mountain.

"I have work to do."

"Em, you are the most efficient person I've ever met. You've already organized this whole office, updated the billing system, caught up on all my outstanding correspondence and done such a great job of editing the briefs that Judge McIlwain at the courthouse actually commented on it."

Pride, unfamiliar and precious, bloomed in her chest. "He did?"

"Yes, and he's not the only one." Jase rested his hip against the corner of her desk. "Do you remember the contract you drafted for the firm I'm working with over in Aspen?"

She nodded.

"The office manager called to see if I'd used a service to hire my new assistant. She wanted to find someone just like you for their senior partner. He's a stickler for detail and notoriously hard on office staff."

"She called me, too." Emily swallowed.

"Why?" Jase's tone was suspiciously even.

"To offer me a job."

"What was the starting salary?"

She told him the number, almost double what he was paying her.

Jase cursed under his breath. "Why didn't you take it? It's one of the most prestigious firms in the state."

"I know. I researched them."

"They can offer you benefits and an actual career path. You have to consider it, even if it makes me mad as hell hearing someone tried to poach you."

She shook her head. "I don't want to work in Aspen. I like it here with you." She flashed what she hoped was a teasing smile. "You'd be lost without me."

His brown eyes were serious when he replied, "You have no idea."

"Jase…"

"At least let me feed you. I've been thinking of ideas for the prewedding scavenger hunt."

She stood at the same time he did, too shocked to protest any longer. "You have?"

He looked confused. "Wasn't that the plan?"

"Well, yes," she admitted as she followed him to the conference room at the far end of the hall. "But I wasn't sure you'd take it seriously. You have so much going on, and it's a silly party theme."

There was an ancient table in the middle of the conference room, with eight chairs surrounding it. On her second day in the office, Emily had taken wood soap and furniture wax to the dull surface, polishing it until it gleamed a rich mahogany. She liked that she could make a difference here in Jase's small law practice.

He held out a chair for her and she sat, watching as he emptied the contents of the bag. He set a wax-paper-wrapped sandwich in front of her, along with a bag of barbecue potato chips. "Noah is my best friend. Making his wedding weekend special isn't silly, and neither was your idea. You need to give yourself more credit."

She nodded but didn't meet his gaze, running one finger over the seam of the wax paper. "What kind of sandwich?"

"Turkey and avocado on wheat," he answered absently. "Do you want a soda?"

"Diet, please," she said, unable to take her hand off the sandwich.

He left the room and Emily sucked in a breath. He remembered her favorite sandwich.

The small gesture leveled her, and the barriers she'd placed around her heart collapsed. This man who was wrong for her in every way except the one that mattered. He seemed to want her just the way she was. Her ex-husband would have brought her a salad, forever concerned she might not remain a perfect size six.

Perfect.

Her life since returning to her hometown had been anything but perfect, yet she wouldn't trade the journey that had brought her here. She was a better person for her independence and the effort she'd put into protecting Davey from any more suffering and rejection.

* * *

She did her best to gather her strength as she pulled up to the elementary school parking lot later that evening. The playground and grassy field in front of the building were crowded with people, and she wished she'd gotten to the event earlier.

Instead she'd changed clothes several times before she and Davey left her mother's house. Difficult to find an outfit that conveyed all the things she needed.

I'm a good mother. Like me. Like my son. Accept us here so I can make it a true home.

Straightening her simple A-line skirt, she got out of the SUV and helped Davey hop down from his booster seat. The desire to gather him close almost overwhelmed her. She wanted to ground herself to him with touch but knew that would only make him anxious. She dropped the car keys into her purse and gave him a bright smile. "Are you ready to meet your new teacher?"

His eyes shifted to hers, then back to the front of the school. "Okay," he mumbled and emotion knitted her throat closed.

"Okay," she repeated and moved slowly toward the playground. Several women looked over as they approached, and she recognized a couple who'd been in her grade. They waved and she forced herself to breathe. If she panicked, Davey was likely to pick up on her energy. Already she could feel him dragging his feet behind her.

"We've got this," she said, glancing back at him.

He crossed his arms over his chest and stared at the ground.

Emily's heart sank but she kept the smile on her

face. All she wanted was to protect her sweet boy, but so often she didn't know how to help him.

Suddenly she heard a female voice calling her name. She looked up to see a tiny woman with a wavy blond bob coming toward her.

"I hoped you'd be here," Millie Travers said as she wrapped Emily in a tight hug. Millie was a recent addition to the community, having moved to town last year to be close to her sister Olivia. Both sisters were married to Crimson natives. Millie's husband, Jake Travers, was a doctor at the local hospital and Emily knew he had a daughter from a previous relationship who was around Davey's age.

Emily had met Millie, along with Katie's other girlfriends, at a breakfast Katie had coordinated shortly after her engagement. Her future sister-in-law was doing her best to make sure Emily felt included in her circle of friends, which she appreciated even if it was difficult for her to trust the bonds of new friendships after her experience in Boston. But she couldn't deny Millie was an easy person to like. "Katie told me to look out for you," the other woman said with a smile. "Your son is starting kindergarten this year, right?"

Emily swallowed. "Yes." She turned to where Davey stood stiff as a statue behind her. "Davey, this is Mrs. Travers, a friend of mine."

Her son stared at the crack in the sidewalk. Around the dull roar in her head, Emily heard the sound of laughter and happy shouts from the other kids on the playground. She wondered if Davey would ever be able to take part in such carefree fun.

If Millie was bothered by Davey's demeanor, she didn't show it. Instead, she sank down to her knees but kept her gaze on the edge of the sidewalk. "It's nice to meet you. My stepdaughter, Brooke, is starting first grade this year. She can answer any questions you have about kindergarten. Mrs. MacDonald, the kindergarten teacher, is really great."

"Whatcha doin', Mama-llama?" A young girl threw her arms around Millie's neck and leaned over her shoulder. Emily saw Davey's eyes widen. The girl wore a yellow polka-dot T-shirt and a ruffled turquoise skirt with bright pink cowboy boots. Her blond curls were wild around her head.

"I'm talking to my new friend, Davey," Millie said, squeezing the small hands wrapped around her neck. "He's starting kindergarten this year."

Brooke stood up and jabbed a thumb at her own chest. "I'm an expert on kindergarten." She stepped around Millie and held out a hand. "Ms. MacDonald has a gecko in her room."

"I have a question," Davey said quietly.

Brooke waited, reminding Emily a bit of Noah's puppy. Finally she asked, "What's your question?"

"Is it a crested gecko or a leopard gecko?"

"It's a leopard gecko and his name is Speedy," Brooke told him. "Come on. I'll take you to see the classroom."

Millie straightened, placing a gentle hand on Brooke's curls. "We need to make sure it's okay with Davey's mommy."

Emily was about to make an excuse for why Davey should stay with her when he slipped his hand into Brooke's. The girl didn't seem bothered by his rigid shoulders or the fact he continued to stare at the ground.

"I'll go, Mommy," Davey said softly.

Emily opened her mouth, but only a choked sob came

out. Biting down hard on the inside of her cheek, she gave a jerky nod.

"We'll be right behind you," Millie said, moving to Emily's side and placing an arm around her waist. "Go slow, Brookie-cookie. Show Davey the room and we'll meet you there so both Davey and his mommy can meet Ms. MacDonald."

"Okeydokey," Brooke sang out and led Davey through the crowd.

"Do you need a minute?" Millie asked gently.

Emily shook her head but placed a palm to her chest, her heart beating at a furious pace. "He doesn't usually…" She broke off, not sure how to explain what an extraordinary moment that had been for her son.

"Brooke will take care of him." Millie smiled. "He's going to be fine here. I know you don't have any reason to believe me, but something in this town rises up to meet the people who need the most help."

"I've never been great at taking help," Emily said with a shaky laugh. "I'm more a 'spit in your eye' type person."

"That's not what I hear from Katie. She's a very good judge of people. We'll follow them." Millie led her along the edge of the crowd, smiling and waving to a number of people as they went. But she didn't stop so Emily was able to keep Brooke and Davey within her sight. Millie's smile widened as she looked over Emily's shoulder. "And she's not the only one."

Emily turned to see a tall, blond, built man she recognized as Dr. Jake Travers, Millie's husband, walking through the parking lot with Jase at his side. Jase was a couple inches taller than Jake and his crisp button-down shirt and tailored slacks highlighted his broad shoulders and lean waist. Her heart gave a little leap and she smiled before she could stop herself.

"My husband is the hottest guy in town," Millie said, nudging Emily in the ribs. "But soon-to-be Mayor Crenshaw holds his own in the looks department. Wouldn't you agree?"

Emily shifted her gaze to Millie's wide grin and made her expression neutral. "He's my boss," she murmured.

The other woman only laughed. "I was Brooke's nanny when I first came to Crimson. That didn't stop me from noticing my *boss*." She gently knocked into Emily again. "Don't bother to deny it. Your game face isn't that good."

"My game face is flawless," Emily countered but the corners of her mouth lifted. Maybe not flawless when it came to Jase. The two men were almost at the playground. She leaned down to Millie's ear and whispered, "I'll only admit Dr. Travers is the second-hottest guy in town."

Millie hooted with laughter, then grabbed her husband and pulled him in for a quick kiss. "Jake, do you know Noah's sister, Emily?"

Jake Travers held out his hand. "Nice to see you, Emily."

"Your daughter was really nice to my son tonight," Emily told him. "She's a special girl."

He laughed. "A one-child social committee, that's our Brooke."

"She's giving Davey a tour of the kindergarten classroom," Millie told him. "How's the campaign, Jase?"

"Pretty good." Jase inclined his head toward the mass of kids on the playground. "But it's never too early to recruit potential voters." He smiled but Emily could see it was forced. Millie and Jake didn't seem to notice.

"Speaking of recruitment," Millie said, glancing up at Jake, who'd looped an arm around her slender shoulders. "I told the classroom mom you'd help coordinate a field trip to the hospital to see the Flight For Life helicopter." She turned to Emily. "She's working the volunteer table now so I'd like to stop by for a second. We'll see you in the kindergarten room. Brooke's classroom is right next door."

Emily nodded and kept moving toward the building. She saw Davey follow Brooke Travers inside.

"Campaign stop?" she asked Jase. He'd taken up Millie's post at her side and more people waved to him as they approached the school.

"I thought you and Davey might like some moral support." He shrugged, ducked his head, looking suddenly embarrassed. "Clearly, you've got it under control. He's made a friend and you—"

"I'm glad you're here," she said, letting out an unsteady breath. "Davey left my side, which was the whole point of this, and I almost broke down in tears on the spot." She stopped and pressed her open palm to his chest. His heart beat a rapid pace under the crisp cotton of his shirt. "Thank you for coming," she whispered.

He covered her hand with his, and then interlaced their fingers. "Anytime you need me," he said, lifting her hand and placing a tender kiss on the inside of her wrist.

Emily felt color rise to her cheeks, and she glanced around to find a few people staring at them. "Jase, we're…"

"At the elementary school," he said with a husky laugh. "Right." He lowered her hand but didn't release it.

Butterflies swooped and dived around Emily's stomach, and she felt like a girl holding hands with her first boyfriend. It took her mind off the worry of fitting in with the other mothers. Between Millie's exuberant welcome and Jase's gentle support, Emily felt hopeful she could carve out a happy life in the hometown that had once seemed too small to hold all of her dreams.

But the biggest dreams couldn't hold a candle to walking into the bright classroom to see her son solemnly shaking hands with his new kindergarten teacher.

"I'm glad Davey will be joining our class this year," the teacher said to Emily as she and Jase approached. "It's great he has a friend like Brooke to introduce him to the school."

Davey darted a glance at Emily and she saw his lips press together in a small smile when he spotted Jase next to her. "They have a Lego-building club," he mumbled, his eyes trained on Jase's shoes.

Jase crouched low in front of Davey. "That's excellent, buddy. Are you excited about school?"

Davey took several moments to answer. Emily held her breath.

Her son looked from Jase to her and whispered, "I'm excited."

Emily felt a little noise escape her lips. It was the sound of pure happiness.

Chapter Ten

Jase pulled up to his house close to nine that night. He parked his SUV in the driveway, then opened its back door for Ruby to scramble out. After the ice cream social, he'd gone directly to his dad's house with dinner.

Declan had gotten his cable fixed so they watched the season finale of some show about dance competitions, the point of which Jase couldn't begin to fathom. But his dad seemed happy and more relaxed than he'd been in ages. Ruby had curled up between them on the sofa and the quiet evening was the closest thing Jase could remember to a normal visit.

As soon as her legs hit the ground, Ruby took off for the house. Jase quickly locked the car, then came around the front, calling the puppy back to him.

But Ruby ignored him, too busy wriggling at the feet of the woman sitting on the bottom step of his front porch.

Emily.

She'd changed from the outfit she wore to the ice cream social to a bulky sweatshirt and a pair of…were those pajama pants?

"Hey," he called out, moving toward her. "These after-dark visits are becoming a habit with us."

She didn't answer or smile, just stood and stared at him.

Worry edged into his brain, beating down the desire that had roared to life as soon as he'd laid eyes on her.

"What's going on?"

She walked forward, her gaze intent but unreadable. When she was a few paces away, she launched herself at him. Her arms wound around his neck and he caught her, stumbling back a step before righting them both. She kissed him, her mouth demanding and so damn sweet. All of the built-up longing he'd tried to suppress came crashing through, smothering his self-control.

He lifted her off the ground, holding her body against his as he moved them toward the house. Ruby circled around them, nipping at his ankles as if she resented being left out of the fun. Emily's legs clamped around his hips as he fumbled with the house key. She continued to trail hot, openmouthed kisses along his jaw and neck.

"Are you sure?" he managed to ask as he let them in, then slammed shut the front door. "Is this—"

"No talking," she whispered. "Bedroom." She bit down on his lip, then eased the sting by sucking it gently into her mouth. Jase's knees threatened to give way.

He moved through the house with her still wrapped around him, and then grabbed a handful of dog treats from the bag on the dining room table as he passed.

He tossed them into the kitchen and Ruby darted away with a happy yip.

He felt Emily smile against his mouth. "Always taking care of business."

"You're my only business," he told her, moving his hands under the soft cotton of her sweatshirt as he made his way down the hall. He claimed her mouth again. "I want to taste every part of you." He pushed back the covers and lowered her to the bed, loving the feel of her underneath him.

"Later," she told him. "I need you, Jase. Now."

He lifted his head to meet her crystal-blue gaze but found her eyes clouded with passion and need. The same need was clawing at his insides, making him want to rip off her clothes like a madman. To think she was as overcome as he was changed something inside him. His intention of savoring this moment disappeared in an instant.

Straightening, he toed off his shoes, then pulled his fleece and T-shirt over his head in one swift move. Emily sat up, tugging at the hem of her sweatshirt and he was on the bed in an instant.

"Let me." As she lifted her arms, he pulled off the sweatshirt, leaving her in nothing but a pale pink lace bra. Lust wound around his chest, choking off his breath as he gazed at her. He felt like a fumbling teenager again, unable to form a coherent thought as he stared.

Her eyes on his, Emily reached behind her back and unclasped the bra, then let it fall off her shoulders and into her lap.

"Beautiful," Jase murmured as her breasts were exposed. He reached out to touch her and she scooted forward, running her hands over his chest.

"Right back at you," she said.

"Emily—"

"I want this," she told him. "I want you. Please don't make me wait any longer."

He wanted to laugh at her impatience. He'd been waiting for this moment for as long as he could remember. He stood again, shucked off his jeans while she shimmied out of her pajama bottoms and panties.

"Condom?" she asked on a husky breath when he bent over her again.

He started to argue, to insist they take their time but the truth was he didn't know how long he'd last if she continued to touch him. He opened the nightstand drawer and grabbed a condom.

She reached for it but he shook his head. "I better handle this part or the night will really be over before it starts."

Emily smiled and bit down on her lip, as if pleased to know she affected him so strongly. Was there really any question?

A moment later he kissed her again, fitting himself between her legs, capturing her gasp in his mouth as he entered her.

Nothing he'd imagined prepared him for the reality of being with Emily. She drew him closer, trailing her nails lightly down his back as they found a rhythm that was unique to them.

Everything except the moment and the feel of their bodies moving together fell away. All of life's complications and stress disappeared as passion built in the quiet of the room. In between kissing her, he whispered against her ear. Not the truth of his heart. Even in the heat of passion he understood it was too soon for that.

Instead he murmured small truths about her beauty, her strength and the complete perfection of being with her. She moaned against him, as if his words were driving the desire as much as the physical act. Her grasp on him tightened and he felt her tremble at the same time she cried out. She dug her nails into his shoulders and the idea that she might mark him as hers made his control shatter.

He followed her over the edge with a groan and a shudder, and she held him to her, gentling her touch as their movements slowed.

Balancing himself on his elbows, he brushed away loose strands of hair from her face. She looked up at him, the blue of her eyes so deep and her gaze painfully vulnerable. She blinked several times, her mouth thinning but her eyes remained unguarded. It was like the normal screens she used to defend herself wouldn't engage. He understood the feeling, so when she closed her eyes and turned her head to one side, he simply placed a gentle kiss on the soft underside of her jaw.

"No regrets," he murmured, then rose and walked to the bathroom. He glanced back to her from the doorway. Emily Whitaker was in his bed, the sheet tucked around her, her long blond hair fanned across his pillow like a golden sea. Tonight reality was indeed much better than his dreams.

Run, run, run.

The voice in Emily's head wouldn't shut up, and she pressed her fists against her forehead trying to press away the doubts blasting into her mind. She felt the wetness on her cheeks and couldn't stop the sobs that coursed through her body.

She wasn't sure how long she lay there before Jase returned. His fingers were cool around her wrists as he tugged them away from her face.

"No, Em." His voice was hollow. "No tears."

"I don't want to hurt you," she whispered, knowing she already had.

"If you mean hurt me with the best sex of my life, bring on more pain."

His kindness at this moment when he should hate her only made her cry harder. All the pain and sorrow and guilt and anger she'd bottled up during her marriage and before came pouring out. It was like being with Jase had torn away all of her emotional barricades.

"So not your best experience I take it," he said with a strained laugh.

She shook her head. "The best ever."

"Look at me and say that."

After several moments, she did. "It was amazing. You were amazing, Jase. I don't regret tonight, but I'm sorry."

"Remember I'm a simple man," he told her. "You're going to need to be a little clearer."

"I'm a mess." She used the edge of the sheet to wipe the tears from her face.

He nodded. "But a beautiful mess."

She poked at him. "You're not supposed to agree with me," she said but laughed at the fact that he had.

"Then I'm sorry. And we're even."

"We're not even." She didn't know how they ever could be. "You've been nice to me when I didn't deserve it, given me a job and connected to my son in ways not even his father could. I'm so grateful to you."

Jase raised an eyebrow. "So that was thank-you sex?"

She gasped and shifted away from him.

"I'm not complaining," Jase added, pulling her back again. "Just trying to figure out where we are here."

"You make me feel things," she whispered, scooting up so her back was against the headboard. She tucked the sheet more tightly under her arms, wishing she'd put on clothes while Jase was in the bathroom. He was wearing a pair of athletic shorts low on his hips but she still had the surprisingly awesome view of his ripped chest and broad shoulders. "Things I thought I put away to concentrate on the serious business of raising a son with special needs."

"Things like?"

She swallowed, worried her fingers together, traced the empty space on her left hand where she'd worn her wedding ring. She'd been so sure of herself when she'd met Henry. Positive that force of will could make her life perfect. Keep her heart safe. Impenetrable.

"Things like...joy...hope." There were other feelings that terrified her, but she wasn't ready to admit to anything more. She drew in a breath. "I came here tonight because I needed..."

"A release?"

"You."

The silence stretched between them, heavy with all they'd both left unspoken. He turned so he was sitting next to her and stretched his long legs out over the bed. "That's the nicest word I've ever heard."

He gathered her into his arms, sheet and all, his strong arms reminding her there was another kind of safety. The type that came from allowing another person to see her true self.

"I wanted you," she told him, circling one finger

through the sprinkling of dark hair across his chest. "I've wanted you since that day at the football game. Maybe since the morning of my mom's surgery when you came to the hospital."

She could feel his smile against the top of her head. "I've wanted you for as long as I can remember."

"But I'm empty, Jase. On the inside. There are a million broken pieces scattered there. I don't know how to fix them." She slid her hand up to his jaw, running her thumb over the rough stubble. "You deserve someone who is whole. I can't be that person yet, and I may never be the woman who can support you in all you do for this town. All people expect of you."

"You already have." He ran a finger along her back at the edge of the sheet. The simple touch was both soothing and strangely erotic. "You've organized my life, focused my campaign when I needed it and smoothed over the rough edges of having my dad involved. I've learned to rely on only myself, which is a difficult habit to end. But I trust you."

She shook her head. "I'll help with your message, not be part of it. I'm comfortable with a behind-the-scenes role. A friend. It's different."

"It doesn't have to be."

"I came here because you mean something to me, but I can't be the person you need." She reached up, pressed her mouth to his and repeated, "I *don't* want to hurt you." She meant the words but she couldn't admit the bigger truth—that she was terrified of her heart being the one to break. The more she cared, the harder the loss was to bear.

"There's more," Jase said softly. "Tell me why you're afraid."

"*I* don't want to be hurt," she admitted on a harsh breath. "I can't give you my heart because having it break again would kill me, Jase."

"I won't—"

"You can't know that." She tucked her head into the crook of his arm, unable to meet his gaze and say the words she needed him to hear. "My dad certainly didn't plan to die from cancer and leave my mom alone. I never thought I'd marry a man who couldn't accept his own son."

"I'm not your ex-husband." Jase's voice was pitched low.

"Henry isn't a villain. He's someone who needs his life to look perfect." She gave a strangled laugh. "I have no room to judge when it's what attracted me to him in the first place. Having a baby opened my heart in ways I didn't expect. I never wanted to feel that way, to be vulnerable. Davey is everything to me. But there isn't room for anyone else. I want you, and I don't regret coming here. But we can't let it go any further." She tried to pull away, but his arms tightened around her.

"What if this is enough?"

She stilled, risked a glance up to find him smiling at her. "Is that possible?" A piece of hair fell across his forehead, and she pushed it back, loving the feel of his skin under her fingers.

"I know it's not possible that once with you is enough for me." He lowered his mouth to hers, his lips tender. Desire pooled low in Emily's belly and she moved in his arms. The evidence she wasn't the only one affected pressed against her hip. She shifted again.

"Emily," he groaned against her mouth. "You're killing me."

"In a good way, I hope. I like being in your arms, Jase. I want to feel something. I'm tired of the nothingness. I want more. With you."

He moved suddenly and she was on her back again with Jase's body pressed to hers. "Then no worries, regrets or expectations."

"Expectations?"

"Expectations most of all." He pulled the sheet down, then skimmed his teeth over the swell of her breast. "I'm drowning under them, Em. But not with you. With you I can just *be*. And I promise you the same. We can be friends and more. But only as much as feels right. No other promises. No blame. No stress."

Another layer of joy burst to the surface inside her. It felt as if her chest was filled with bubbles, fizzy and light. She felt drunk with the exhilaration of it.

Right now, every part of her life was filled with stress. It was part of being a single mother. Even with her family's support, she could never truly let go. What Jase was offering felt like a lifeline. And the best part was she could give the same thing back to him. Pleasure for the sake of pleasure. No expectations.

It felt like freedom.

She wrapped her arms around his neck. "You've got yourself a deal, counselor."

"Sealed with a kiss," he said and nipped at the edge of her mouth.

"Sealed with a thousand kisses," she whispered and set about adding them up.

Chapter Eleven

The following Friday morning, Emily was busy untangling a strand of tiny twinkle lights being used to decorate the wide patio at Crimson Ranch, where tomorrow's wedding would be held. Sara worked on a separate length of lights while April Sanders arranged mason jars that would be filled with wildflowers on the tables set up around the patio.

Jase had closed the office today so they could both concentrate on wedding plans. Her mother was picking up Davey after school while April led a private yoga class for Katie and her girlfriends. The group would then go for facials and massages at a spa near Aspen before joining the men for the scavenger hunt Emily and Jase had organized. Emily had worked to make sure the activities leading up to the wedding were fun, personal and helped celebrate who Katie and Noah were as a couple.

She understood why they'd selected the ranch as their wedding venue. Located on the outskirts of town, the property had been beautifully restored in the past few years to become one of the area's most popular destinations.

In addition to the rough-hewn-log main house, there was a large red barn and several smaller cabins spread around the property. Clumps of pine and aspen trees dotted the landscape, giving the buildings a sense of privacy. Each time the breeze blew Emily enjoyed the sound of aspen leaves fluttering in the wind. She could see where the property dipped as it got closer to the forest's edge and knew the creek ran along the divide.

"You had sex." Sara grinned at Emily.

Emily spit the bite of muffin she'd picked up from the basket sitting on the table. "Excuse me?" She choked on muffin crumbs.

April patted her on the back. "Don't take offense. The more outlandish Sara's comments, the more she likes you."

Sara laughed and continued to string lights. "For the record, I like you a lot, Emily Whitaker. Not as much as I like your brother. When I first came to town, Noah flirted with me every chance he got."

"Noah flirted with everything with a pulse before Katie," Emily muttered.

"But with me he was trying to make Josh jealous." Sara's smile was devious. "You have points in your favor for being related to Noah, but there are other reasons I like you."

"You barely know me." Emily wiped the back of her hand across her mouth. "You definitely don't know me well enough to comment on my sex life." She heard the pretentiousness in her voice that she'd perfected during her short marriage.

Sara only laughed again. It was a rich, musical sound that projected across the vast pasture spreading out behind the house. Sara was petite with pale blond hair and luminous blue eyes. Her bigger-than-life presence made her hard to ignore. Emily supposed the "it girl" vibe contributed to Sara's fame from the time she'd been a child actor.

"We met at the dinner to celebrate your mom's recovery," Sara told her. "You were there with your son, and it's clear you're devoted to him. Another plus in your favor."

"I remember but—"

"You looked tense and defensive, like you might snap in two at any moment." Sara waved a hand toward Emily. "Now you're relaxed and you can't control the good-sex grin on your face—"

"I can control my smile," Emily argued, then thought of Jase and felt the corners of her mouth tug upward. She pressed her fingers to her mouth and glanced at April.

"Don't look at me. I'm certainly not smiling like that."

"Which is what we're working on next," Sara said, moving to April's side. "You've been alone for too long, my friend."

April shook her head, a tangle of red curls bouncing around her face. "One marriage was quite enough, thank you. I'm perfectly content without a man in my life."

"Don't forget I was married, too." Emily wasn't sure

why she felt compelled to argue this point. The idea that these women she was only beginning to know could read her was scary as hell. "I have a son and he's my priority. I don't have time for anything else."

"But you've been making time," Sara said.

April's voice was gentle. "You do seem happier, which is a good thing."

"Maybe it's the yoga." Emily pointed at April. "I've been coming to your classes. Maybe you should take credit for my newfound calm, if that's what I have."

"It's more than calm," April told her with a smile. "It's a glow. I'd love to believe it was the yoga but—"

"It's sex." Sara winked. "You don't have to admit it for it to be true."

"Don't tell Katie," Emily mumbled after a moment. "She and Noah will want there to be more to it than there is." She bit down on her lip, then grinned. "And it's great the way it is."

It had been more than great and her stomach did a slow, sweet roll at the thought of the time she'd spent with Jase. It was easy to have him come to the farm with Ruby after work under the guise of discussing wedding plans or the mayor's race, and he'd become a fixture at their dinner table. Emily's mother had even insisted he bring Declan to join them for several evening meals.

At first it amazed her how seriously he seemed to value her opinion. Whether on reception details or the more important campaign strategies, he listened to her ideas and often used them as the foundation from which to build his own.

Emily liked being someone's foundation. And she loved the private, stolen moments when Jase would wrap her in his arms and shower her with kisses. She felt the telltale goofy smile tug at her mouth again.

Sara threw an arm around April's shoulder. "Yoga classes are lovely but nothing is better than the restorative powers of great sex." She pointed at Emily. "Are you going to tell us who it is?"

"Do I have to?"

Sara thought about that for a moment. "No, but if you don't I'll be forced to ask your soon-to-be sister-in-law."

April lifted her hand to clamp it over Sara's mouth. "Forgive her. She means well. You don't have to tell us anything." April's voice was gentle, her tone so motherly it made Emily warm inside. "For the record," April added, "I think Jase is great."

"He is..." Emily narrowed her eyes. "Wait. That was sneaky." A gorgeous earth mother with a little edge.

"April's the worst," Sara said when April dropped her hand. "She's gentle and sweet, so people don't realize she's also whip smart and far too observant. The thing that makes it less annoying is she'll protect your secrets to her grave."

"Is Jase a secret?" April asked, her eyes all too perceptive.

"Yes." Emily shook her head. "I mean, no. We're friends."

"April needs a friend like that," Sara said with a laugh.

"Why don't you worry about your own love life and leave mine alone?" April crossed her arms over her chest and did her best to glare at Sara. She still looked sweet.

"No worries in my life." Sara wiggled her brows. "Josh is absolutely perfect. In fact, just last night..."

"Save it," April said quickly. "We're talking about Emily."

"Feel free to move on," Emily told them, then held up a hand to Sara. "I'm not asking for details about your private life."

Sara grabbed a muffin off the table and dropped into a chair. "You don't seem like a sell-it-to-the-tabloids type of person."

"No."

"Of course she's not," April agreed. "So you and Jase are friends." April pointed at Emily. "The kind of friends that have seen each other naked."

"That's one way to put it," Emily answered, making a face.

"You like him?"

Emily nodded.

"A lot?" Sara asked.

"Yes."

"Everyone in town loves him," April offered. "Why just friends and why the secret?"

"Because," Sara added, popping a bite of muffin in her mouth. "You understand this town can't keep a secret? People will find out."

"If they don't already know," April said.

"We want something that belongs to us."

Now Sara's face softened. "Oh, yes. I understand." She glanced at April. "We both do."

Sara stood and came to give Emily a hug. She glanced over her shoulder at April. "Come on. Group embrace."

The willowy redhead, who smelled of vanilla and cloves, wrapped them both in a tight hug. "What is between you and Jase is yours," she whispered. "But don't hold on to it too tight. Love is like a garden, Emily. It needs light and air to breathe, or it will shrivel before it has a chance to grow strong."

Emily gasped. "It's not love," she murmured. "It can't be."

Neither Sara nor April answered. They only tightened their hold on her.

By the time the last team came through the doors of the brewpub in downtown Crimson, Jase's mood was as dark as the mahogany paneling lining the walls.

Luckily his friends didn't seem to notice. Everyone had loved Emily's scavenger hunt. The teams had raced through Crimson collecting mementoes that were special to Noah and Katie.

Now they were sharing stories about the couple, laughing and toasting the impending nuptials as the bride and groom held court at one of the large tables in the center of the bar. The entire evening had been a success if he ignored the fact that Emily was doing her best to avoid him.

With so many of their friends around, it was easy to accomplish. No matter how many times Jase tried to meet her gaze or talk to her alone, she managed to slip away. He knew she'd spent the day working out at Crimson Ranch with Sara and April, but he couldn't imagine how things could have changed between them so quickly.

He watched her step away from the main group to take a call on her cell phone, her brows puckering at whatever was being said on the other line. The conversation only lasted a few minutes, and he moved behind her as she ended the call.

"Everything okay?"

She jumped, pressing a hand to her chest. "Sneak up much?"

"Avoid people much?" he countered.

Color rose to her cheeks and she looked everywhere but into his eyes. The sudden distance between them made him angry. This had been the best week of his whole damn life. Even with the campaign, work and all the other pressures of regular life, Jase had felt happier than he could remember. He wanted more from Emily. He wanted the right to give more *to* her.

Maybe it was excitement around the wedding or so many of his friends in relationships, but he was convinced Emily was meant for him. He'd always made decisions in his life based on what was smart and responsible. Duty had governed his actions for as long as he could remember. Being with Emily was about making himself happy. Making her happy. For the first time, he wanted to commit to something more than this town and restoring his family name.

He wanted something of his own.

He wanted Emily.

"It's been a hectic day," she said, her tone stiff. "I want everything to be perfect for Noah and Katie."

"I thought we agreed perfection is overrated."

She looked at him now, her eyes sad. "Not for the two of them. They deserve it."

"You deserve—"

She held up a hand. "I can't have this conversation now. My mom called. One of Davey's completed sets fell off the shelf and broke. He's having a meltdown." The sound of laughter and music carried to them and she glanced over his shoulder at their friends. She looked so alone it made his gut twist. "I've got to go, but I don't want to worry Noah. Will you cover for me?"

"Let me come with you."

"It's better if you don't," she whispered. "People will talk."

"I don't give a damn what anyone says."

She wrapped her arms tight around her middle. "I do."

Those two words killed him. He'd told her he wouldn't push her, and he had to honor that. When she turned to walk away, it took everything in him not to stop her.

Even more when Aaron Thompson slid off his bar stool as she moved past. The man put a meaty hand on Emily's arm and she flinched. Jase saw red as Aaron leaned closer and Emily's face drew into a stiff mask.

Jase was striding forward by the time she shook free and ran out the pub's front door.

"What the hell did you say to her?" He pushed Aaron's broad chest, and the man stumbled into the empty bar stool, knocking it on its side with a clatter.

Jase felt the gazes of the crowded bar on him, but for once he didn't care. He stepped into Aaron's space as the other man straightened.

Aaron leaned closer and lowered his voice so only Jase could hear. "I told her she'd have a hard enough time raising that weirdo kid of hers in this town without hitching herself to the Crenshaw wagon." His beady eyes narrowed farther. "When she's ready for a real man, she should give me a call. Your dad couldn't keep a woman satisfied, and I doubt you're any different."

It didn't matter that Emily was gone. Jase knew Aaron's words would have prodded at her fears, the same way they slithered into his. "Don't ever," he said on a growl, "speak to her again."

"Oh, yeah?" Aaron smirked. "Whatcha going to do about it?"

Jase hauled back his fist and punched Aaron, his knuckles landing against skin with an audible thud. The burly man staggered a few steps before righting himself. Noah and Liam had already grabbed hold of Jase.

"Dude," Aaron shouted into the sudden quiet of the bar. "I'm sorry. My dad wants what's best for this town. You don't have to threaten our family."

"Settle down, man," Noah said when Jase strained against him.

"He's lying." Jase felt blood pounding against his temples. He glanced around the bar to find himself the center of attention from every corner. He was so used to being universally liked, it took him a minute to recognize the emotions playing in the gazes of the friends and strangers who stared at him.

Anger. Disappointment. Pity.

"He's a liar," Jase yelled and felt a heavy hand clasp on to his shoulder.

"What's the problem?" Cole Bennett, Crimson's sheriff, stepped between Jase and Aaron.

Aaron winced. "I made an offhand comment about the election to Jase," he said, holding a hand to one eye. "You know, *may the best man win* and whatever. He went crazy on me." He looked at the sheriff all righteous indignation. "Must have hit a nerve. My dad can tell you plenty of stories about the Crenshaws going ballistic for no reason."

Anger radiated through every cell in Jase's body. He

shifted, then realized Noah and Liam were still holding him. "I'm fine," he said, shrugging away.

"You sure?" Noah's voice was concerned.

"Yeah." He pointed at Aaron. "That's not what went down and you know it."

Sheriff Bennett stepped closer to him, placing one hand on his chest. "You want to tell me a different side of the story?"

Jase opened his mouth, then snapped it shut again. He caught Aaron's smug gaze over Cole's shoulder and realized tonight was no accident. He'd been set up in this scene and had fallen right into the trap. He couldn't contradict Aaron's story without revealing specifics of the truth, which would humiliate Emily.

"No." He closed his eyes and tamped down his temper. "I've got nothing to say."

Cole heaved out a sigh. "Are you sure?"

Jase met the other man's gaze. "I am."

"What if I want to press charges?" Aaron asked.

Cole gave Jase an apologetic look, then turned to the other man. "Do you?"

"I should. It was a cheap shot." The bartender handed Aaron a bag of ice and he groaned a little as he pressed it to his eye. "But I guess we can't expect anything else from a Crenshaw."

Noah took a step forward, anger blazing in his eyes. "Don't be a—"

"It's okay," Jase interrupted, grabbing hold of his friend. "If he wants to press charges—"

"I don't. My father taught me to be the better man."

"Okay, then. Let's move on. Everybody back to their regularly scheduled evening." Cole turned to Jase. "I assume you're heading out?"

Jase nodded.

"I don't know what he did to deserve that punch," Cole said, "but I can guarantee it wasn't the story he told about the election. You sure you don't want to tell me anything else?"

"Positive."

With a nod, Cole moved away. Liam and Noah took his place.

"What the hell, Jase?" Noah asked. "I don't think I've ever seen you take a swing at somebody."

"I've got to get out of here," Jase muttered. "Sorry about causing a scene during your party."

Liam placed a hand on his shoulder. "You want company?" When Jase shook his head, Liam nodded and walked back toward their group of friends.

"Come back to our table," Noah told him. "Don't let this ruin the night."

"I'm not going to," Jase answered, "but I need to go now. Give Katie a hug for me. I'll pick you up in the morning to head out to Crimson Ranch."

Noah looked like he wanted to argue but only said, "No one expects you to be perfect, Jase."

"I know." But both of them knew it was a lie. People in this town expected perfection, duty and self-sacrifice from Jase, all of it offered with a smile. He understood that in the way of small towns, the news of the punch would spread like dandelion fuzz on the wind. The news, while inconsequential in its retelling, only needed to be nurtured a bit before it took root and grew into the start of a weed that could derail everything he'd worked to create.

At this moment he couldn't bring himself to care.

He left the bar and kept his head down as he walked to his parking space in the alley behind his office building. Driving out of town, he was tempted to take the turnoff toward the Crawfords' farm. Thoughts of Emily and her reaction to Aaron's taunts consumed him, but he'd promised not to ask her for more than she was willing to give. In his current mood he might drive a wedge between them if he pushed her.

Instead he steered his SUV toward the trailer park and pulled into his father's small lot. The blue-tinted glow from the television was the only thing lighting the inside of the trailer.

Declan hit the mute button on the remote when Jase walked in. "I thought the big party for Noah was tonight?"

"It is," Jase said, lowering himself to the sofa. "What happened to our family, Dad? Why are we so messed up? Mom leaving with Sierra, you and Uncle Steve drinking, Grandpa in jail. Why does every generation of our family have a sad story to tell?"

His father leaned back against the recliner's worn cushion. "Not every generation. Not you."

"Not yet," Jase shot back. "It's like there's a curse on us, and I don't know if I'm strong enough to break it."

"You already have."

"I decked Aaron Thompson tonight."

"Hot damn," Declan muttered. "That little jerk has been giving you grief since grade school."

"You noticed?"

"I'm a drunk, not an idiot. Hitting Aaron does not make you cursed. Hell, I've taken a swing or two at Charles over the years."

"And gotten yourself cuffed for the trouble."

"Worth it every time."

"I'm not you."

Declan laughed. "Praise the Lord." He leaned forward, placed his elbows on his knees. "In a town like Crimson, people see what they want. Once a reputation is set, it's hard to change it. I don't know how the trouble with our family started, but I do know it's easier to live down to expectations than to try to change them. At least it was for me. Your grandpa went to jail for the first time when I was ten. My brother and I had our first beers when we were eleven. Working in the mine didn't help. Nothing much good comes from sticking a bunch of ornery men inside a mountain."

Jase asked the question he'd been afraid to discuss with his dad for almost twenty years. "What about Mom?"

"Your mom was right to go. I was a mess back then."

"Yeah, Dad," Jase answered, "I know. I was the one taking care of you."

"You don't remember, do you?"

"Mom leaving?" Jase shrugged. He remembered crying. He remembered being alone at night staring at the empty bed where his sister had slept next to him.

"She wanted you to go with her."

"No. She took Sierra and left me behind."

"Because you told her I needed you more." When Declan met Jase's gaze, his eyes were shining with unshed tears. "She had your little suitcase in the trunk but you refused to get in the car. It killed her but eventually she agreed to let you stay. That's how I know you're not like the rest of us. You've never done a selfish thing in your life. You take care of this town like you've taken care of me all these years. With every ounce of who you are. You're not part of the curse. You're our family's shot at breaking it."

Jase closed his eyes and tried to remember the details of the night his mom had driven away. All he could see was Sierra's face in the car window and the taillights glowing in the darkness. The days after were a blur of tears and anger and his father going on a major bender.

"One punch doesn't make you a troublemaker, Jase."

"Tell that to the people who witnessed it."

"What I should do is talk to the man who's the cause of all your recent stress. This is Charles Thompson's fault. If he—"

"It's fine." Jase stood, ran a hand over his face. "Don't go after Thompson again. You're right. The Crenshaw curse ends with me."

He started to walk past his dad, but Declan reached out with a hand on Jase's arm. "It's what you want, Jase. Right?"

"Sure, Dad." Jase didn't know how else to answer and he was too tired to sort out his muddled emotions, either to his father or himself. "I'm picking up Noah early tomorrow to drive out to the ranch. Call if you need anything, okay?"

"Save me a piece of cake," his dad said, sitting back in the recliner. Declan had been invited to the wedding but since alcohol was being served, he'd decided to forgo the celebration. Jase appreciated his dad's effort to stay sober but hated that it isolated Declan even more than he already was.

"Are you sure you don't want me to get you for the ceremony?"

"Enjoy yourself tomorrow, son. Don't worry about me."

Jase gave the smile he knew his dad wanted to see. "Call if you change your mind."

Chapter Twelve

"Are you nervous?" Emily paced the guest cabin where she and Katie were waiting for the wedding to start. "You don't look nervous." She turned to Katie, who was glowing in the ivory gown they'd chosen at the bridal salon in Aspen. "You look beautiful." The satin gown had a sweetheart neckline and a lace overlay that was both delicate and modern. Katie's dark hair was pulled away from her face in a half-knot, with gentle curls tumbling over her shoulders. "Noah is going to lose his mind when he sees you. But, seriously, shouldn't you be nervous?"

Katie smiled and patted the bed next to her. "I don't need to because you've taken care of everything. It's perfect, Em. My dream day." As Emily sat down on the patchwork quilt, Katie took her hand. "Thank you for everything."

"It was easy." She gave a strangled laugh. "My mother-in-law and I were at the reception hall until two in the morning the night before my wedding redoing seating arrangements. There were so many stupid details to focus on but none of them involved preparing Henry and me to make a life together." She squeezed Katie's fingers. "You and Noah are doing this right."

"Unrequited love, fear of commitment, friendship and a baby after a breakup," Katie said with a laugh. "We might have had the order a little off."

"The love is what counts," Emily answered. She stood when Katie sniffed and Emily grabbed the box of tissues from the dresser, handing Katie a wad of them. "No crying. Your makeup is perfect."

"Then don't say sweet things to me." Katie dabbed at the edge of her eyes with a tissue. "I asked you for my dream wedding, and you've given it to me."

"Not quite yet."

A knock sounded on the door. "Ladies, are you ready?" Sara called.

"Perfect timing," Emily said with a smile.

Katie stood, her eyes widening as she pressed a hand to her stomach. "Wow. Just got nervous. Major butterflies."

"You've got this." Emily opened the door and followed Katie out, smiling as Sara oohed and aahed over the dress. Katie's father was waiting at the edge of the barn, out of sight of the chairs set up in front of the copse of aspens where the ceremony would take place. It was a perfect fall day, cool and sunny with just the slightest breeze.

She knew Katie and her parents weren't close, but her father became visibly emotional at the sight of his daughter. It made Emily's heart ache missing her own dad and all the moments she'd never get to share with him.

But this wasn't a day for sorrow, and she was honored to be Katie's maid of honor. She adjusted Katie's train and then stepped away. When the processional music began, she turned the corner from the barn toward the wedding guests. All Katie's and Noah's closest family and friends were in attendance. Emily's gaze sought Davey first, her son looking so handsome in his suit, standing next to his grandma in the front row. His eyes flicked to hers and she saw the stiffness in his small shoulders ease the tiniest bit.

The knowledge that seeing her gave him some comfort made her heart squeeze. She looked up to her brother standing in front of the grapevine arbor and smiled before her eyes met those of the man standing next to him.

She had to work to control her expression as Jase looked at her, his gaze intense. Her knees went weak and she clutched the bouquet of wildflowers tighter. One foot in front of the other, she reminded herself. Breathing in the warm mountain air, she felt her heart skip as Jase's mouth curved up at one end. As much as she'd tried to avoid him the previous night, now she couldn't break eye contact, even as she took her place in front of the assembled guests.

The music changed and Katie came into view. Emily glanced at the beautiful bride but then watched her brother's face as Katie moved closer. There was so much love in Noah's eyes. It was as if the whole world went still for a moment and there was only her brother and his bride. Emily was suddenly grateful for the tissue she'd stuffed under the ribbon of her bouquet.

She continued to need the tissue as the short ceremony progressed. By the time Noah leaned down to kiss his bride, Emily swore she could hear the whole valley choking back tears. Then there were only smiles and cheers as Noah and Katie walked back down the aisle hand in hand.

Jase offered her his elbow and she tucked her hand in it, blushing as he leaned close to her ear and whispered, "You look beautiful." She sucked in another breath and smoothed one hand over the pale pink cocktail gown she wore. She felt beautiful and happy and lighter than she had in ages. As they started down the aisle together, Emily was proud to meet the approving gazes of the people she'd come to think of as her community.

But Jase paused before the first row. "You two belong with us," he said to her mother and Davey.

Emily's heart, already so full, expanded even more at her mother's watery, grateful smile. Jase tucked Meg's arm into his other elbow and nodded at Davey. "Why don't you lead us down, buddy?"

The boy looked at the ground and Emily wanted to curse her own stupidity. She knew her son didn't like people looking at him and was afraid Jase's sweet gesture would backfire.

Davey chewed on his lower lip for a few seconds and finally muttered, "I'll follow you."

Emily breathed a sigh of relief and saw her mother do the same. Jase nodded and the four of them made their way past the other guests.

Emily didn't have a chance to speak to Jase alone until the dancing started. Meg and her new beau had taken Davey home after the cake was cut. To Emily's surprise, Davey had seemed to actually enjoy himself at the wedding, running around through the field behind the tables with the other kids.

He stuck close to Brooke Travers and didn't yell or play fight the way the other boys at the reception did, but he was definitely a part of the group and she couldn't have been prouder.

As the sky darkened over the mountain, silhouetting the craggy peaks against the deep blue of evening, a three-piece bluegrass band began to play. Noah pulled Katie onto the makeshift dance floor near the edge of the patio and other couples followed. Emily was just about to head inside to see if the caterers needed help packing up when strong arms slipped around her waist.

"Dance with me?" Jase asked but was already turning her to face him.

"I should check on things," she said but didn't protest when he lifted her hands to his shoulders.

"It's fine," he said, beginning to sway with her to the lilting sound of the fiddle drifting toward them. "Better than fine. All of your hard work made this a perfect day."

"We both worked hard," she corrected and rested her head against his chest. "You and I make a pretty good team." She was starting to trust the happiness she felt, to rely on it.

One of Noah's high school friends walked by, then stopped and clapped Jase on the shoulder. "Good to see you've grown a spine, Crenshaw."

Emily felt Jase tense and lifted her head.

He said a few words to the man, then tried to turn her away.

"Makes me want to vote for you all the more," the

man said with a chuckle. "I like a mayor with a strong right hook." With another laugh, he walked away.

Emily pulled back enough to look up at Jase. "What was that about?"

He shook his head. "Nothing."

"A strong right hook isn't nothing," she argued. "Did you hit someone?" She couldn't imagine a circumstance where Jase would throw a punch.

"Let's just dance."

"Tell me."

He blew out a breath. "Aaron Thompson," he muttered.

"What about him?"

"I saw him talking to you at the bar last night. You were upset when you left, so I asked him about it."

The happiness filling her moments earlier evaporated like a drop of water in the desert. Shame took its place, hot and heavy, a familiar weight on her chest. She hated that anyone, especially Jase, knew the awful things Aaron had said to her. But even more...

"You hit him?" she asked and several people nearby turned to look at them. She stepped out of Jase's arms and lowered her voice. "I didn't need you to defend me."

"He was out of line. No one has the right to speak to you that way." He reached for her, but she jerked back, giving herself a mental headshake. What was between her and Jase was supposed to be casual. Emily had let it turn into something more because he made her happy. But the way Aaron had taken advantage of that was the unwelcome reminder she needed. She couldn't let this go any further.

She caught Noah's gaze and flashed her brother a

small smile as she waved. "I'm going to check if the caterers need help."

"Emily," Jase whispered, "don't walk away."

But she hurried into the cabin before Jase could stop her. She told herself it was because she was angry at Jase, although it felt more like fear clawing at her stomach. Panic at the thought of depending on someone and allowing herself to be vulnerable again. Of needing Jase and then having him leave her. It was one thing when they were on equal ground, but if she began to rely on him and truly opened her heart…what was to stop him from breaking it?

April was supervising the last of the cleanup so Emily pitched in where she could. Her hands trembled as she moved vases of flowers to the kitchen's large island but she didn't stop working.

"I think we're almost finished in here," April said eventually. "I don't have a hot guy waiting to dance with me, so I can handle the rest."

"It's fine," Emily muttered. "I'm not in the mood to dance."

"Uh-oh." April stepped in front of her as she turned for the sink. "What's wrong?"

"Nothing."

"What kind of nothing?"

Emily sighed and met the redhead's gentle gaze. "Is it really possible to start over?"

April opened her mouth, then shut it again as if she didn't actually know how to answer the question.

"It seems easy in theory," Emily continued. "Cut out the bad parts from your life and move on. Let go. Tomorrow's a new day. I can spout out greeting-card sentiments until I run out of breath. But is it possible?

How can I leave the past behind? Life isn't simple, you know?"

"I do know," April said with a sad smile. "Maybe it's not about a fresh start as much as it is continuing to try to do better."

"Learn from your mistakes?" Emily laughed. "Another cliché, but I have plenty to choose from."

April picked up a flower and twirled the stem between her fingers. "Play it cool as much as you want, but it's obvious you really care for Jase, and he's crazy about you."

Emily swallowed. "I wasn't looking for…"

"For love?"

"It isn't—"

April tapped Emily on the nose with the wildflower's soft petals. "I have no history in this town, Emily. No expectations of who either of you are supposed to be. You can be honest with me."

"Which may be easier than being honest with myself."

"Start with saying the words out loud."

Emily swallowed then whispered, "I love him."

"I have a feeling he feels the same."

"He can't," Emily said, shaking her head. "We want different things from life. I can't be the woman he needs."

"Maybe what he needs is the woman you are."

Emily felt tears clog the back of her throat. A tiny sliver of hope pushed its way through the dark layers of doubt she'd heaped on top of it. "Are you always this good at giving pep talks?"

"To other people," April told her, "yes."

The catering manager walked back into the kitchen with the final bill.

"I'll take care of this," April said. "You find Jase."

"I can't tell him yet." Emily fisted her hands until her nails left marks on the center of each palm. "It's too soon. I don't know—"

"You might start with showing him how you feel," April said and nudged her toward the patio door.

"Right. Show don't tell. I think I can do that." At the thought of being in Jase's arms again, her stomach buzzed and fluttered like a thousand winged creatures were taking flight inside it. "I think I'd like that very much."

As she stepped back outside, she saw that Jase and the other guests had gathered in the center of the patio to say goodbye to Noah and Katie. The newlyweds were staying in one of the guest cabins at Crimson Ranch overnight before driving to the Denver airport tomorrow to fly out for their honeymoon to a Caribbean island.

"I'm so happy to have a sister," Katie said as Emily hugged her.

"Me, too," Emily whispered, then turned to her brother. "I'd tell you to get busy making me a little niece or nephew," she said, punching him lightly on the arm, "but for once in your life, you're an overachiever."

"Always the clever one." Noah chuckled and pulled her in for a hug. "Call if you need anything."

"I absolutely won't," Emily shot back. "You've earned these two weeks in paradise. Enjoy them."

"I intend to and thanks again, Em." Noah tipped up her chin. "You made my bride very happy."

"Go." Emily made a shooing motion. "I've laid all the groundwork for you to get lucky tonight."

Noah leaned in close and kissed Emily on the cheek. "Maybe I'm not the only one," he whispered with a wink, then turned and scooped Katie off her feet.

Everyone cheered as the couple disappeared down the pathway toward the far cabins. As the music started again, guests drifted back toward the patio. Emily continued to stare into the darkness for several minutes, nerves making her skin tingle as she thought about finding Jase in the crowd.

With a fortifying breath she turned and bumped right into him. She yelped and stumbled back. Jase grabbed hold of her arms to steady her.

"Were you some kind of a cat burglar in another life?" she asked, trying to wrestle her pounding heart under control. "You're far too good at being quiet."

He let go of her, dropping his hands to his sides. "My dad wasn't much fun with a hangover. I learned to be quiet so I wouldn't wake him."

"Oh." Her comment had been meant as a joke. The way he answered made her remember they'd each been shaped by their past. "I'm sorry."

"No need," he said quickly. "It's a fact."

"I meant for earlier. Even if it wasn't necessary, thank you for defending my honor with Aaron."

"Again, no need. You don't deserve to be dragged into the long shadow cast by my family's reputation." The music picked up tempo and Jase turned for the house. "Should we head back?"

Emily didn't move. "What do you mean your *family's reputation*? Aaron told me I might as well be campaigning for his father since I was distracting you from the usual attention you pay to Crimson and its residents. He insinuated that a relationship with a divorced mom of a kid with special needs would work against your bid for mayor."

"I'm going to kill him," Jase muttered. "I wish I would have knocked him out cold." He ran his hands through his hair, leaving it so tousled Emily couldn't resist reaching up to straighten it.

"No," she told him. "You shouldn't have hit him at all."

He pulled her hands away from his hair, clamping his fingers gently around her wrists. "Emily, what is the real problem here?"

Where to start?

Your dreams. My fears.

Falling in love with you.

Definitely don't lead with that one.

She raised up on tiptoe and slid her lips along his, the knot of tension inside her unfurling at the warmth of his mouth and the roughness of his stubble when their cheeks brushed. He smelled like the mountains and tasted of mint and sugary wedding cake. Right now, he was everything she wanted in the world.

Show don't tell.

"The only problem is we're not undressed."

Jase gave a harsh laugh. "You're trying to distract me."

"Is it working?"

"Hell, yes." He glanced over his shoulder toward the lights of the party, which was still going strong even in the absence of the bride and groom. "Think anyone will notice if we sneak away?"

"Let them notice." She would deal with the consequences of her feelings for Jase another time. When he laced his fingers with hers, Emily almost forgot her doubts. She simply let them go.

Giving in to the happiness fizzing through her made her giggle.

Jase glanced down at her but didn't stop moving toward his SUV. "What's so funny?"

She shook her head. "Nothing. I'm glad to be with you."

He opened the passenger door and she slipped in. "You just made me the second-happiest guy on this ranch." He pulled the seat belt around her, using it as an excuse to kiss her senseless.

She took out her phone and punched in a quick text to her mother as Jase came around the front of the SUV. "Everything okay?" he asked, turning the key in the ignition.

Emily waited to speak until her mother's answering text came through. Then she smiled at him. "I've got permission for a sleepover."

"The whole night?" His voice was husky.

"Yep. I mean, I'd like to be home in the morning for breakfast. Davey usually sleeps until about eight on the weekend so that gives us…"

"All night long," Jase finished, taking her hand and lifting it to his mouth. Then he cringed a little. "Unfortunately, the puppy doesn't like to sleep in so late."

"I guess you're going to have to make waking up early worth my while."

Of course, Ruby needed some attention when they got back to the house. "One of my neighbors came over a couple of times today to let her out and play with her." Emily laughed as Ruby exploded out of her crate, yipping and running circles around Jase as he struggled to clip on her leash. "Clearly, she's ready for more. I'm sorry. This isn't exactly a great start to a romantic evening. I need to take her for a short walk so she won't be so wound up."

"I'll come with you." They followed the puppy into the front yard toward the sidewalk.

As Ruby sniffed a tree, Jase shrugged out of his coat and wrapped it around Emily's shoulders. She loved being surrounded by his scent and the warmth of him. They started down the sidewalk with Ruby happily trotting next to them. She seemed in no hurry to do her business tonight, making Jase groan and Emily laugh.

"I'm sor—"

"Don't say it." She took his hand as they walked. "This is nice. I love the quiet of your neighborhood and this time of night, especially after the past week of planning the wedding. It feels normal."

"Normal is underrated," he said with a laugh. "Every birthday wish when I was a kid was for a normal family like yours."

"As I remember, a lot of those birthdays were spent at our house."

"Your mom would bake a red velvet cake and you'd refuse to come out of your room to sing."

Emily pressed her free hand to her face. "I was horrible to you."

"You were pretty mean to Noah, too, so I took it as a compliment."

"Only you, Jase."

Ruby finally found the perfect patch of grass and they turned back toward the house. They walked in silence for a few feet until Emily felt Jase's body tense.

"What is it?"

"I wanted to ask you something, a favor really," he told her. "You know city council is holding a town hall meeting in two weeks. Charles and I are both supposed to be there. People will have a chance to ask us questions about our plans as mayor."

She nodded.

"They'll want us to introduce our families as part of the meeting. I think it was Charles's idea as a way to discredit me. He can stand up there with his wife and sons as proof he's an established family man and I'll just be…alone."

"I'm sure your dad will come if you ask him."

Jase shook his head. "He doesn't like crowds. They make him anxious and that makes him want to drink." He let out a small laugh. "Well, everything makes him want to drink but so far he seems committed to his sobriety this time around. I don't want to mess that up."

"You've supported him in so many ways over the years," Emily argued. "He can do this for you."

"Honestly, I'm not sure if having my dad there would be a help." Jase stopped at the bottom of his porch steps as Ruby nosed around in the bushes in front of the house. "I was hoping you and your mom and Davey would stand up for me."

Emily felt her mouth drop open and quickly snapped it shut at the look of disappointment that flashed in Jase's eyes.

"Never mind. Stupid idea." He let go of her hand to scoop up the puppy. "When you mentioned me celebrating my birthdays at your parents' farm, it made me think the Crawfords were almost more of a family to me than my own." Ruby wriggled in his arms and licked his chin. "But you aren't my family, and I know how you feel about being in the spotlight. I'll bring Ruby." He laughed, but it sounded forced. "Puppies are always crowd pleasers."

He turned for the house, then stopped when she placed a hand on his arm.

Show don't tell.

Emily had assumed April meant those words from a physical standpoint, which was easy enough. She wanted Jase more than she could have imagined— longed to be in his arms. She thought about all the little things he'd done for her, from allowing her full control of his office to letting her take the lead on the wedding plans to showing up at the school ice cream social to check on her and Davey.

Despite her fears and doubts, she wanted to give something back to him. The town hall meeting was big, but she was coming to realize starting over was a mix of baby steps and giant leaps. Not pretending the past didn't happen but moving through the old hurts to create new happiness.

"We'll be there," she said and had the pleasure of watching gratitude and joy wash over his features. It felt so good to give this to him. It felt right.

"You don't have to," he told her. "I mean it. I'll be fine."

"You're not alone," she whispered. She leaned forward to kiss him but stopped when Ruby licked her right on the mouth.

Jase groaned as Emily laughed.

"You should still bring the dog," Emily said as she wiped her mouth. "She's your ace in the hole."

"Right now I want her out of my arms." He nudged

open the front door and deposited the puppy on the hardwood floor. "And you in them." He pulled Emily against his chest.

"I take priority over Ruby?" she asked with a laugh. "I feel so important."

"You take priority over everything," he whispered against the top of her head. His words made sparks dance across her skin. "Thank you, Em. I know what I'm asking is a lot." He tipped up her head, cupping her face between his hands. "If you decide it won't work, I'll understand."

His touch was tender. "I'll make it work," she told him and somehow she would.

Ruby scampered toward her basket of toys, picked up a stuffed bunny with her, teeth then walked into her crate to curl up with it.

"She's tired," Emily said.

"Finally."

Jase went over and locked the crate, then returned to Emily. "So how about a sleepover?"

Emily giggled. "Maybe you shouldn't call it that. It reminds me of being a kid…you know, pillow fights and nail-painting parties."

"Pillow fights, yes." Jase kissed the corner of her mouth. "Nail painting, no." He moved closer and deepened the kiss. She held on to him and he lifted her as if she weighed nothing, moving down the hall toward his bedroom. "Do you want to have a pillow fight?" he asked as he set her down on the bed, then covered her body with his.

"Maybe later."

"I'll hold you to that," he told her. "After I hold you to me."

She laughed again, loving how Jase made everything fun. She'd never thought of the bedroom as a place for laughter until the tall, sweet man watching her from chocolate-brown eyes had come into her life.

She slipped off her shoes and reached behind her back for the zipper of the cocktail gown she wore. Her fingers paused as Jase pulled his tie over his head, then undid the buttons of his tailored shirt. His broad chest made her mouth water.

He moved to the edge of the bed and slid his palms up her bare legs. He grasped the hem of her dress and she lifted up onto her elbows as he tugged it off her. His eyes darkened as they raced over her.

"The lingerie," he said in a half growl, "I like it."

Emily whispered a silent prayer of thanks to her new sister-in-law. Katie had insisted she buy the matching bra and panties during one of their prewedding shopping trips to Aspen. At the time it had seemed like a foolish expense, but now the lavender lace made her feel beautiful. Or maybe it was the way Jase was looking at her. Her whole body grew heavy with need.

She crooked a finger at him. "Come closer, Mr. Almost Mayor, and take it off me," she whispered.

He toed out of his shoes and took off his suit pants, then climbed onto the bed, lowering his weight over her as he claimed her mouth. No more joking or laughter. His kiss was intense and demanding, and she moaned as his fingers skimmed across her breast. Emily arched off the bed as his mouth followed, grazing the sensitive peak with his teeth.

Then they were a tangle of arms and legs, sighs and whispered demands. The demands came mostly from her. She was impatient for him but he insisted on moving slowly, savoring each moment and lavishing attention on every inch of her body.

This man wrote the book on show don't tell. She'd never felt so cherished or been so fully possessed. As much as she longed to say the words *I love you*, Emily still held back. But when they moved together as the pleasure built and built and finally shattered them both, all of her defenses crumbled in a shimmer of light and passion. She knew things could never go back to the way they'd been, at least not for her. Jase Crenshaw well and truly owned her heart.

Chapter Thirteen

Jase could feel Emily's heart beating steady against his chest early the next morning. She was wrapped around him, snuggled in tight and sleeping soundly.

She'd told him sleep was often elusive for her, so he reveled in the fact that she was snoring softly as morning light peeked in between the slats of the wood shutters that covered his bedroom windows.

He'd never allowed a woman to spend the night at his house before Emily. This place was a sanctuary to him, and he hadn't been willing to share it with anyone else. The satisfaction he felt at waking up with her beside him should be terrifying. It proved he was already in far too deep when he still expected her to break his heart.

Yet his smile wouldn't fade. It felt so damn *right* to have her here. He'd put the down payment on the modest bungalow shortly after taking over the law practice.

It had been a rite of passage to buy a home he could call his own. But he wasn't sure how to be a host and the women he dated invariably wanted to take over the role. Minutes in the door and they began rearranging sofa pillows and suggesting wall colors.

So he'd stopped inviting anyone over but his guy friends. They didn't care his walls were bare and he had nothing but leftover carryout and beer in the fridge. To his surprise, Emily hadn't either. He'd even solicited her opinion on what he should do to make it homier. She'd told him to keep it as it was, which had been both refreshing and disconcerting. Especially given the ruthlessness with which she'd taken over his office.

At first he'd thought she was respecting his space but over the past few weeks, when she'd stop by but never stay, he'd wondered if it was more about her keeping what was between them casual. Now she was here, and it seemed like a damn good first step.

"I can hear you thinking," she mumbled sleepily, rolling off him.

"Good morning," he said and kissed her cheek.

She yawned, her eyes still closed. "What's got the wheels turning so hard this early?"

"Paint colors."

"Is that code for kinky morning sex?"

He laughed and pulled her close again. "Would you like it to be?"

"Talk to me about paint colors."

He combed his fingers through her hair, loving its softness and the way the scent of her shampoo drifted up to him. "I need to update the house, make it more mine. I was thinking about what color to use for the family room and kitchen."

She rose onto her elbows. "While we're in bed together? What does that say about me?" She frowned but amusement flickered in her blue eyes.

"It says you inspire me to be a better person. Painting has been on the list for years, but I've ignored it. Even though I bought the house, I couldn't quite believe I deserved it. You make me believe."

Her gaze softened. "You make the most unromantic topics into love poems."

He tapped one finger against her nose. "Again, I give credit to you for inspiring me. Can we get back to kinky morning sex?"

"Dorian Gray."

He thought about that for a moment and then shook his head. "As in *The Picture of...*? The creepy book and movie?"

"Yes and no." She flipped onto her back again. "It's also a paint color, the perfect gray. You should use it for your family room and a shade lighter in the kitchen. It faces north so needs more light."

Jase felt a smile curve his lips. "You've been thinking about colors for my house."

Clearly misunderstanding, she crossed her arms over her chest. "You asked," she said on a huff of breath.

He levered himself over her and kissed the edge of her jaw. "Paint talk as foreplay. Works for me. What do you know about the color wheel?"

"I know you're crazy," she said, rolling her eyes.

"Only for you, Em."

She suddenly turned serious. "This isn't casual anymore."

He thought about lying so he wouldn't chase her away, but he couldn't manage it. "It's not casual for me," he agreed. "It never has been. We can still take it slow and I—"

She pressed her fingers to his mouth. "I like it slow." Her hand curled around to the back of his neck and she drew him down for a hot, demanding kiss. "I like it most ways with you."

"Emily," he said on a groan. "Tell me you're good with where this is going." He lifted his head and stared into her eyes. "I need to know."

She closed her eyes for a moment and took a deep breath. Then she looked at him again. "I'm scared of feeling too much. But I…" She paused, bit down on her lip, then whispered, "I want it to be more than casual. I want to try with you, Jase. For you."

"For us," he said. There was more he wanted to tell her, but she wasn't the only one afraid of being hurt. Jase was used to keeping the things he wanted most locked up tight. It was when he said the words out loud that his life usually went to hell.

Mommy, don't leave. Don't take Sierra.

Dad, stop drinking before it ruins you.

His requests met with disappointment so he didn't make them, and he wasn't going to now. He needed time to believe this precious thing between them wasn't going to be taken away.

He smiled and kissed her again. "We've got approximately not many minutes until the puppy starts whining," he said, glancing at the clock on the nightstand. "We've established slow is good. Now let's see how we do with fast."

The next two weeks flew by for Jase. One of his biggest cases went to trial early at the courthouse in Aspen, so he was out of the office most of the time. He'd never been as grateful for Emily, who managed his practice with so much efficiency he didn't worry about anything falling behind while he was in court.

He was even more grateful for her when he got home at the end of each long day. She'd taken over Ruby's care, picking up his energetic puppy in the morning on her way to the office and keeping her all day. She claimed both Davey and Tater, Noah's dog that was staying at the farm during Noah and Katie's honeymoon, loved having the puppy around.

When he could manage it, Jase drove directly to the farm after work. It was like he was a teenager again, showing up for dinner at Meg's big table, only now Emily greeted him with a kiss each time he arrived.

Everything in his life was exactly where he wanted it. Everything but the mayor's race. Charles was taking full advantage of Jase's busy schedule by planning campaign events all over town. Almost overnight, yard signs with the slogan Charles Thompson, A Family Man You Can Trust had popped up on every corner. Jase got calls from friends and business owners, suggesting he ramp up his efforts with the election date quickly looming.

The problem was he didn't want to take time away from the rest of his life to focus on the campaign. He couldn't stop questioning the reasons he'd decided to run for the position in the first place. Yes, he was dedicated to Crimson, but he didn't need to be mayor to prove that. Or did he?

He was getting pressure to be seen around town when all he wanted was to spend his free time with Emily and Davey. Although the boy was adjusting to school, he still preferred the quiet of home. Jase had set up a Lego construction area in the corner of his family room so Davey was becoming more comfortable at his house. That didn't solve the issue of Emily needing a quiet life with her son, while Jase's obligations to the town pulled him to be more visible with every passing day.

He checked his watch for the fifth time as he waited for the city council meeting to end late on Tuesday, one day before the big town hall event. Monthly council meetings were held in the evenings because so many of the members also had day jobs. Jase had never minded before because his life was the town. But Emily had texted that Davey wanted to show him his latest Lego structure, and he'd hoped to get out early enough to make it to the farm.

The council members continued to debate the date for the lighting of the town Christmas tree in December while Jase's mind raced from thoughts of Emily to the trial to the doctor's appointment he needed to reschedule for his father to the campaign he was pretending didn't exist.

"Jase, do you have anything to add?" One of the longtime council members lifted a thick brow.

Jase blinked and glanced around at his fellow council members, reluctant to admit he had no idea where the thread of the conversation had gone. Liam Donovan met his gaze and gave a subtle shake of his head.

"No," Jase said firmly, as if he knew what the hell they were talking about now. "I agree on this one."

Thankfully, the general comment was enough to satisfy everyone and the meeting adjourned. He checked his phone, disappointment washing through him. He'd missed a text from Emily, telling him Davey was going to bed and they'd keep Ruby overnight at the farm. She'd added an emoji face blowing a kiss at the end, which only made him want to hurl the phone across the room.

Jase didn't want emoji. He wanted Emily in his arms.

He punched in a quick text promising to stop by in the morning before heading to Aspen.

"You realize you can't speed up or slow down time by watching the clock," Liam said from behind his shoulder.

Gathering his things, Jase turned and shook his head. "It's a damn shame, too. Thanks for saving my butt just now."

Liam nodded. "You weren't exactly dialed in for this meeting. I'll walk out with you."

Jase watched a group of council members standing on the far side of the conference table, heads together as they talked. Charles Thompson was in the middle, as if holding court, and the sight made a sick pit open in Jase's gut. One of the men glanced back at Jase, guilt flashing in his gaze before he waved.

"Looks like you weren't the only one to notice." He followed Liam out into the cool autumn night. He should be sitting on his back porch with Emily right now. Instead he was heading over to his office to work a few more hours on the cross-examination he was preparing for tomorrow.

"Also looks like your campaign is in the toilet," Liam said without preamble. "Before you got to the meeting, Charles made a pretty convincing speech about you being pulled in too many directions to give your full attention to the duties of mayor."

"Which is not true—"

"He also hinted that your dad is having problems and you've got too many distractions right now."

Jase cursed under his breath and turned on his heel. The town meetings were open to the public so Charles had every right to be there. But not to spread lies about Jase's father. "My dad is fine," he ground out, moving back toward the courthouse. "I'm going to—"

"Whoa, there." Liam placed a hand on Jase's shoulder. "It's not a coincidence Charles showed up tonight, made the comment and now is hanging out after the meeting. He's playing dirty, Jase."

"Why the hell did you tell me, then?"

"Because *you* have a choice to make."

Jase shrugged away from Liam's grasp and paced several steps before turning and slamming his palm against the side of the brick building. He cursed again and shook out his hand. "I've made my choice."

"I'm new to the council," Liam said, "but from what I've heard, the choice was made for you. When the former mayor took off, Marshall Daley stepped in as mayor pro tem. He was never going to seek another term, so the town council members suggested you run."

"That's the basic gist," Jase admitted. "It wasn't supposed to be this complicated."

"Did you ever really want to be mayor?"

"Of course I did. I can do the job."

"I'm not debating that."

"I love this town."

"Again, you'll get no argument from me there. Hell, you had a major impact on my decision to make Crimson the headquarters for LifeMap. But it felt different. You were on a mission to make a name for yourself. I didn't understand it then…"

"And now you do?" Jase sagged against the building, tired at the thought of rehashing his family history one more time. "Everyone around here thinks they know me."

Liam shrugged. "It's clear you don't want it the way you once did."

"Is it so wrong to also want a life for myself, as well?"

"No."

"I won't let Charles win."

"Even if it means you lose in the long run?"

Jase straightened. "I'm going to make sure that doesn't happen."

"How?"

"Can I make a suggestion?"

Both men turned as Cole Bennett stepped out around the street corner.

"Evening, Sheriff," Jase said. "Out for a stroll downtown or is this official business?"

Cole moved closer. He wore jeans and a T-shirt and held up his hands, palms out. "Off duty tonight. I was hoping to talk to you before the town hall meeting this week." He glanced at Liam. "It's private."

Jase started to argue but Liam held up a hand. "I need to get home anyway. Let me know if I can help. No matter what you decide."

"Thanks, man." Jase shook Liam's hand, then watched him walk across the street to where his truck was parked.

"You have some advice for me?" he asked the sheriff.

"Information," Cole clarified. "Your office is on this block, right?"

Jase nodded.

The sheriff glanced over his shoulder. "Let's go there."

"Why do I have a bad feeling about this?" Jase asked as he led Cole a few storefronts down until they reached his office.

"Because you're not stupid," Cole answered bluntly.

With a sigh, Jase unlocked the door and flipped on the light in the reception area. The scent of vanilla from the candle Emily burned at her desk filled the air, and his heart shifted. The subtle changes she'd made to his life mattered and he hated that his sense of duty to the town was keeping them apart.

It wasn't only his schedule. They'd agreed their relationship wasn't casual, but he could feel Emily holding back. He assumed it was because of his increasing commitments to work and the campaign. While he wanted to tell her it would pass, how could he make that promise if he won the election?

"Since you're not on the clock, how about a drink?" Jase asked, moving toward his office. "I've got scotch or…scotch."

Cole chuckled low. "I'll have a scotch. Thanks."

Jase motioned him into the office, then went to the kitchenette area and poured two squat glasses with the amber-colored liquid. Back in the office, he handed one to Cole, then sat behind his desk.

Cole took a slow sip before placing the glass on Jase's desk. "How bad do you want to win the election?"

The question of the hour. "Not bad enough to do something illegal for it." It was the most honest answer Jase could give without exposing the doubts plaguing him.

"What about exposing something your opponent had

done?" the sheriff asked. "Not exactly illegal but it's definitely borderline. Turns out Thompson had been going easy on his friends and neighbors for years. Anytime there was a problem with someone he knew personally, the issue disappeared."

Jase actually laughed. "Everyone except my father."

Cole shrugged. "There's a lot of politics involved in small-town law enforcement. I'm overhauling the department, but I do have records that certain procedures weren't exactly…aboveboard when he was in charge."

"What are you going to do with the information?"

"That's why I'm here. Charles Thompson was supposed to retire and go fishing or whatever the hell else he wanted. I didn't take his bid for mayor too seriously at first." He picked up his glass of scotch and tipped it toward Jake. "You had the blessing of the council, so there was no question you'd be elected."

Jase didn't shy away from Cole's scrutiny. "Now there is?"

The sheriff finished off his scotch before answering. "Thompson is pushing you hard and you're letting him. I don't know if it's because the garbage he's throwing is getting to you or because you've decided you don't care about winning."

"Maybe I'm tired of my whole life revolving around Crimson."

"Fair enough, but I'm asking you to get your head back in the game. We need you, Jase. We need somebody decent in charge of this town." Cole placed his glass back on the desk and stood. "I can leak what I know about Thompson, make him go away, but it won't change how he's trash-talking you or what it means if you don't answer the accusations. You have a chance to tomorrow night. I hope you take it, but if you need something more let me know."

"Thank you," Jase said and watched the sheriff walk out the door. He threw back the rest of his scotch, welcoming the burn in his gut. Maybe he had been ignoring the campaign in the hope the decision would be taken from him. But that wasn't who he was, and Cole's visit proved it.

Why couldn't he have Emily and the mayor's position? Yes, she had doubts but he'd worked too hard to give up now. He needed to prove that she and Davey fit into his life, every part of it. The town hall meeting would be the perfect place to do just that.

Emily stopped in front of the entrance to the Crimson Community Center where the town hall meeting was about to start. She smoothed a hand over the fitted dress she hadn't worn since she'd stood next to her ex-husband when he'd made partner at his law firm.

"I should have picked something else. This is way too formal."

Her mother squeezed her hand. "You look lovely and the sweater softens the look." Meg glanced down at Davey, who stood a few steps behind Emily, his hands tightly fisted at his sides. "You are very heroic tonight."

Emily shared a look with her mom, then smiled at Davey. He'd insisted on changing into his superhero costume after school today and refused to put on a different outfit for the meeting. She understood that sitting still in a crowd of strangers was going to be a challenge, so hoped Jase understood Davey's wardrobe choice. Her purse was stocked with Davey's favorite snacks, a small bag of Lego pieces and the fail-safe iPad loaded with a few new apps. She prayed it would be enough to keep him content during the meeting.

As her mother held open the door, Emily put a hand on Davey's shoulder to guide him, then drew back as he flinched away from her touch.

Breathe, she told herself. Smile.

She'd come back to Crimson for a quiet life, and now she was putting herself on display for the entire town. Her mother led them up the side aisle to the front row of chairs marked Reserved. Emily glanced over her shoulder as she took her seat and saw several of her new friends sitting together a few rows back. April waved and Natalie Donovan gave her a thumbs-up sign. A little bit of the tension knotted in her chest eased.

A tap on her shoulder had her swinging back around.

"It's not Halloween," Miriam Thompson, Charles's wife, said in a disapproving hiss as she made her way into the seat next to Emily, with Aaron's brother, Todd, on her other side. Aaron wasn't with them, a fact for which Emily was grateful. "You should show some respect to the seriousness of this election."

Red-hot anger rushed through Emily. Anger at Miriam for making the comment, at Jase for asking her to do this but mostly at herself for still caring what people thought of her and her son. Before she could respond, her mother whipped around in her seat.

"You should shut your mouth, Miriam," Meg said. "Before I come over there and do it for you. My grandson can be a superhero every day if it makes him happy." She wagged a finger at each of the Thompsons. "We could use more heroes in this town, not people who feel like it's their right to taunt and bully others."

Miriam gasped but turned away, her cheeks coloring bright pink as she made her son shift seats so she wasn't sitting right beside Emily.

Emily tried to hide her shocked smile as she leaned over Davey toward her mother and spoke low. "'Come over there and do it for you'?"

Meg sniffed. "I never liked that woman."

A hush fell over the room as Liam Donovan walked onto the stage, along with Jase and Charles. Liam was moderating the meeting. A few general announcements were made first and then Liam formally introduced Jase and Charles, although Emily couldn't imagine there was anyone in the room who didn't know either man. Crimson had grown in the years since she'd been gone, but it seemed as though everyone in attendance tonight had some history with the town.

The thought made her encouraged for Jase, as so much of Crimson's recent boom could be attributed to work he'd done as part of the city council. No wonder he was torn between making decisions for his own happiness and his duty to the town.

Charles took the mic first, detailing his background as former sheriff. Emily gritted her teeth as he made special mention of his long marriage, and his family's history of service and philanthropy in Crimson.

Jase didn't seem bothered, though, and stepped to the podium after shaking Charles's hand. He smiled as he looked out over the audience.

"It's great to see so many friendly and familiar faces in this crowd," he began. "This town means a lot to me and no matter what our differences, we can all agree that we want the best and brightest future for Crimson." After a ripple of applause, he spoke again. "I'd like to personally thank Charles for his contributions to our town over the years. Families like the Thompsons gave us a strong foundation. As many of you know, my family's history runs in a different direction." He chuckled softly. "Which is why I'm especially grateful for this town and the people in it."

Emily didn't turn around but she could feel the energy building in the crowd as Jase spoke. He was sincere and articulate, not shying away from where he came from but taking the power of his family's troubled history away from Charles by owning it himself. She'd never been prouder. Then she felt Davey shift next to her. It was hard to tell whether he was reacting to the excitement of the crowd or Jase's voice booming through the room or one of any number of things that might disturb his equilibrium.

The reason didn't matter. Something was also building inside Davey. He fidgeted, tugging on the tights of his superhero costume and humming softly under his breath. She reached in her purse and grabbed the bag of Lego pieces.

"Here, sweetie," she said, placing them gently in his lap. Keeping her voice calm and trying to regulate her own energy was key for keeping him from moving any closer to a meltdown.

Her mom shot her a look but Emily shook her head. It didn't matter what anyone thought at the moment. She had to keep Davey calm or everything she'd worked so hard to create would blow up in her face.

Davey opened the bag and methodically pulled out building pieces.

Emily breathed a tentative sigh of relief and focused on Jase. He was looking directly at her.

"With me tonight," he said, "is a family who have

made me a part of their own over the years." His gaze left hers, but she could still feel the warmth of it across her skin. "What makes this town special is that we take care of each other. Meg and Jacob Crawford took care of me when I needed it most. As mayor, I want to make sure we continue to move Crimson forward and, more importantly, that we continue to look out for one another."

"I guess your own father isn't part of your grand plan?" The loud, slurring voice rang out in the quiet of the meeting room. Emily heard the crowd's collective gasp but kept her eyes on Jase. His expression registered shock, confusion and finally a resigned disappointment as he looked out past the audience toward the back of the room. His gaze flicked to hers for a moment. The silent plea in his chocolate-brown eyes registered deep in her heart even as he schooled his features into a carefully controlled mask once again.

"You count, Dad," he said calmly into the microphone. "But we should talk later."

Emily turned to the back of the room to see Declan making his way up the center aisle. The door to the hallway was swinging closed and she caught a glimpse of a figure moving to the side as it shut. Aaron Thompson.

She got up immediately and moved toward Jase's dad.

"Why the hell aren't I up there with your fake family?" Declan yelled. "I'm part of this town, too. Or have you forgotten why you wanted to become such a do-gooder in the first place, Jase?"

"Declan, don't do this," she said as she got closer. The smell of liquor coming off him hit her so hard she took a step back. She had to get him out of this meeting. "This isn't you talking." She tried to make her voice gentle. "It's the alcohol. Jase needs you to get it under control. Now."

His bloodshot eyes tracked to her. "Oh, yeah, sweetheart. My son loves control. He can't tolerate anything less than total perfection." He motioned a shaky finger between himself and Emily. "The two of us are bound to disappoint him."

The words struck a nerve but she smiled and reached for his hand. "Then let's get out of here."

She could see Sheriff Bennett moving around the edge of the room toward them. A glance over her shoulder showed Jase stepping out from behind the podium toward the edge of the stage. She shook her head, hoping to diffuse Declan's alcohol-filled rant before it had a chance to gather steam.

She took his arm just as she heard Davey cry out, "Mommy, my spaceship. It broke." Her son's voice was a keening cry. "It broke!"

"I won't be handled," Declan yelled and tore his hand away from her grasp.

But Emily's attention was on Davey so instead of letting go she stumbled forward, plowing into Declan's chest and sending them both into the edge of the chair at the end of the row.

Edna Sharpe occupied the chair, and as it tipped, the three of them tumbled to the floor. Emily saw stars as her head slammed into the chair.

All hell broke loose.

People from the nearby rows surrounded them. Edna screamed and flailed at the bottom of the pile. "My ankle. You broke my ankle."

Declan moaned. "I think I'm going to be sick."

Emily scrambled to get out from under him but his thigh was pinning her down.

"Mommy!" Davey screeched, his voice carrying over the din of noise to her. "I lost a piece to my spaceship."

She pushed at Declan, recognizing the mounting hysteria in Davey's tone. Cole Bennett was there a second later, but it was too late. Jase's father coughed, then threw up, the vile liquid hitting Emily's shoulder as she tried to turn away.

He was hauled off her then and she stood, the crowd surrounding them parting as she pushed her way through. One bonus to being puked on—it cleared a path quicker than anything else.

Jase was trying to shoulder his way down the aisle, yelling at people as he moved.

Davey had started shrieking now, and she knew a full-blown meltdown could last for several minutes to close to an hour. Meg met her gaze and whispered, "I'm sorry." Meg picked a screaming Davey up and carried him out the side door of the meeting room.

Emily shook her head as she followed. There was nothing her sweet mother could have done to prevent this moment. The responsibility was Emily's. And she failed. Miserably.

Jase was in front of her a second later. She expected understanding. Instead, he glared at her. "What the hell, Em? You tackled my dad. Is Edna really hurt? This is a mess."

She blinked, unable to process the accusation in his tone, let alone to respond. "I've got to get to Davey," she whispered.

His muffled screams echoed from the hall.

Jase ran a hand through his hair. "Can you get control of him? The screaming is only making this disaster worse."

She reeled back as if he'd slapped her. A disaster. That's how Jase saw her attempt at helping him. Her head was ringing from where she'd hit the corner of the chair. Her son was having a public meltdown. And she was covered in vomit.

"We've got to pull out of this," Jase said, searching her gaze as if he expected her to have a magic solution.

"I'm going to my son," she said, pushing at him. "He's not part of a disaster. He's a scared little boy who shouldn't have been put in this situation in the first place."

"The sheriff has your dad out the door," Liam called from where he stood on the stage. "I'm going to get everyone back to their seats."

Jase closed his eyes for a moment and his gaze was gentler when he opened them again. "I didn't mean it like that. Em…"

"No." She pushed away. It was too late. She knew better. Davey was all that mattered, her only priority. "I've got to get him out of here. Take care of your image or your dad. I don't care. I'm not your problem, Jase. We're not yours."

She hurried down the row, bending to pick up a stray Lego piece as she walked. She found Davey and her mother at the end of the hallway, Davey standing stiffly in front of the wooden bench where her mother sat. She crouched in front of him. "I have the missing piece," she said. He continued to scream, his eyes shut tight and his cheeks blotchy pink as he heaved breaths in and out between shrieks. "Davey, sweetie. Look at Mommy. I have the Lego piece. You can finish the spaceship."

His screaming subsided to an anxious whine as he looked at the small yellow brick she held in front of him. Emily held her breath. He hiccuped and reached for it, holding it gently between his first two fingers. "Thank you, Mommy." He wiped at his cheeks with the back of his sleeve. "Can we go home now? You're stinky."

She let out a ragged laugh. Or maybe it was a sob. Hard to tell with the emotions swirling inside her. "Yes, Wavy-Davey, we can go home now."

She straightened, meeting her mother's worried gaze. "I'm so sorry," Meg whispered.

Emily shook her head. "No kind words, Mom. I need to keep it together until we get back to the farm."

Meg's mouth thinned but she nodded. "You might want to take off the sweater."

Emily carefully pulled the nasty sweater over her head, gagging a little as the scent of vomit hit her again. It had been easy enough to ignore when adrenaline was fueling her. But now the reality of everything that had happened—in front of most of the town and everyone who mattered to her—made her want to curl up in a tiny ball. But she still had her son to take care of, which was the only thing keeping her going.

She stuffed the sweater into a nearby trash can. The memories of this horrible evening would prevent her from ever wearing it again.

"Let's go home," she said and her mother took her hand and led them toward the car.

Chapter Fourteen

Jase had returned to the stage after Emily left and Declan had been hauled away. He'd remained calm even though he'd wanted to walk to the front of that room and rip Charles Thompson to shreds. Everything he'd worked for had been destroyed, but he'd seen Aaron Thompson slip into the hallway as the door closed to the back of the meeting room. At that moment he realized how personal the Thompsons felt about his failure and what lengths they were willing to go to make sure he wasn't elected mayor.

None of that really mattered. All he cared about was the hurt in Emily's eyes as he'd demanded she quiet Davey. It had been his shame talking. She didn't deserve the pain he'd caused her. He'd wanted to follow her to the Crawfords' farm right away, but there had been so much fallout to deal with after the scene his dad had caused.

Jase publicly apologized for his dad's behavior. He wanted to call out Charles Thompson, but he wouldn't stoop to Thompson's level or make excuses for Declan. It had been even more difficult to keep his temper in check when Charles complained as Liam officially ended the meeting and sent the crowd home.

Several of Jase's friends had offered words of encouragement and support, but he could barely hear them over the roar in his head. Jake Travers deemed Edna's ankle only a sprain but she insisted on going to the hospital for an X-ray, so Jase stayed with her until her daughter arrived to take her home. Cole offered to let Declan ride out his bender in one of the town's holding cells.

Jase didn't bother to comment on the irony of his father in jail as he was trying to make a bid to lead the town. It was his worst nightmare come to life.

At least he'd thought it was until arriving at the ranch. Meg had come to the door before he'd knocked.

"I need to see her," he said and opened the screen.

Meg crossed her arms over her chest. "No, Jase."

"I only need a minute," he pleaded, letting the emotions he'd tried to tamp down spill into his tone. "I'll wait if she's putting Davey to bed. Maybe I could—"

"No." Meg's normally warm gaze was frigid as she met his. "She was trying to support you tonight even though it wasn't what she wanted. You hurt her when things went bad." She shook her head. "My daughter has been down that road before, and she's only begun to recover from the pain of it. I won't let her be treated that way again. She deserves better."

"I know." He felt desperate in a way he hadn't in years. He could feel the person he loved slipping away from him, only this time it was his own fault. "I let the moment get the best of me. I love her, Meg."

"You want her, Jase. You have for years. I get that, but it isn't the same as love. What happened tonight wasn't love."

"I made a mistake."

"You might not be the right man for her."

"You're wrong."

"I hope I am, and if Emily decides to allow you back into her life, I won't stop her. But for now she doesn't want to see you. You have enough to deal with in your own life. Focus on that."

"I don't care about anything else." The words came out louder than he'd intended and he forced himself to take a calming breath. "At least tell her I was here. Tell her I'm sorry. Please, Meg."

After a moment she nodded. "You're a good man, Jase. You don't have anything to prove to this town but it's time you start believing it." She backed up and shut the door, leaving him alone on the porch.

This house was the one place he'd always felt safe and welcome, and now he'd messed that up along with his relationship with Emily.

It was close to midnight by the time Jase walked into the sheriff's office. He would have been there earlier, but Cole had texted that his dad was sleeping and he'd alert Jase when Declan woke up. Jase had gone home after leaving the Crawfords' and let Ruby into the yard. As the puppy chased shadows around in the porch light, Jase had sat on the top step and left messages for each of the town council members to apologize for the spectacle his father had created at the meeting.

Declan was sitting on the bench in the holding cell when Jase walked into the office.

"It isn't locked," Cole told him, getting up from his chair, "but he said he wouldn't come out until you got here." He patted Jase on the arm. "I'm going to give the two of you some time. I'll be out front. Let me know if you need anything."

Jase walked forward, wrapped his fingers around the cool iron of the holding cell's bars. "You ready, Dad?"

Declan snorted. "That's all you've got to say to me?"

"If you're looking for me to apologize," Jase ground out, his temper sparking even through the numbness of his exhaustion, "forget it. Drying out in this cell was the safest place for you tonight. After the stunt you pulled—"

"You shouldn't be here." His dad stood, paced from one end of the small cell to the other. "You don't owe me anything, least of all an apology. Why the hell aren't you with Emily?"

"Let's go home."

"I puked on her."

"Yep."

Declan rubbed a hand over his face. "I'm sorry."

"Emily is the one who's owed an apology. Maybe she'll talk to you."

"She won't speak to you?"

Jase shook his head. "Come on, Dad. I'm tired and done with this day."

His father lowered himself back down to the metal bench. "You see me here."

"I see you," Jase said quietly, hating the memories the image conjured.

"This is *me* in here, Jase. Not you. I did this to myself, like my dad and his dad before him. Our trouble is not your responsibility."

"It sure as hell felt like it when you barged into the town hall meeting drunk out of your mind."

"I slipped," Declan said. "I let people get to me and I took one drink."

"One drink ended in the bottom of the bottle. I've seen it too many times, Dad. You can't stop at one drink."

"I know, and I didn't want to. I wanted to lose myself. To forget about everything for a little while."

"Aaron Thompson brought you to the meeting."

"It wasn't his fault, even as much as I'd like it to be. I was at the bar when he found me. Yeah," Declan admitted, "he said some things that set me off more."

"They wanted me to be humiliated."

"I brought tonight's shame on you, Jase. Not the Thompsons. I'm the reason you can't have a life of your own."

"I have a life," Jase argued, but his voice sounded flat to his own ears. Because without Emily he had nothing. "I thought we agreed the town hall meeting was too much for you. If I knew—"

"It wasn't the meeting." Declan stood, reached into the back pocket of his jeans and pulled out a small envelope. "Nearly twenty years later and she can still set me off." He handed the envelope to Jase. "It's a letter from your mom, son."

Jase stared at the loopy cursive on the front of the envelope, disbelief ripping through him. "Why didn't she track down my email or cell number? No one sends letters anymore."

"Your mother was always an original." Declan

moved toward the door to the cell. "I don't know what she wrote, but I hope whatever it is gives you some closure."

"Why after all this time?"

"I don't know." He stopped, cupped his rough hand around Jase's cheek. The smell of stale liquor seeped from his skin, both familiar and stomach churning. "What I hope she says is that leaving had nothing to do with you. That she regrets not taking you with her and giving you the life you deserve." His smile was sad as he ruffled Jase's hair. "That's what I hope she says, but I don't want to know. Bennett let me use the phone when I woke up. My AA sponsor is coming by the house in the morning. Whether you believe me or not, this was a one-time mistake."

Jase stood there staring at the envelope for a few more seconds, then turned. "Dad."

Declan turned back, his handle on the door to the outer office. "Yeah?"

"I don't regret staying with you."

"Are you sure you won't stay with Mom?" Noah pulled out from the farm's driveway and started toward town. He and Katie had been home from their honeymoon for a few days so Emily had asked him to go apartment hunting with her.

"I can't keep hiding out there." Emily read the address to the first building, which was in a new development on the far side of town. She watched the midday sun bounce off the snow-dusted peak at the top of Crimson Mountain. The weather was cooler now, and while there hadn't been any snow yet in town, winter would be closing in soon.

"That's not how she thinks of it."

"Doesn't make it less true." She shifted to look at her brother, still tan from his honeymoon on the beach. "I'm staying in Crimson, Noah. I need to start making a life for Davey and me."

"He still likes school?"

She smiled. "He loves it. Since I'm now working in the elementary school front office, I can check in on him during the day." The kindergarten teacher, Erin MacDonald, had made a visit to the farm when Emily kept Davey home from school the day after his public meltdown. While Davey had spent the day building Lego sets and baking cupcakes with his grandma, Emily'd barely been able to get out of bed.

The teacher's sensitivity to Davey's outburst had made its way through Emily's fragile defenses and she'd broken down with all the details of her messed-up life. Erin had immediately called the school principal. The new secretary he'd hired had quit after only two weeks. Emily had an interview the following afternoon and started work the next day. "Millie Travers told me Ms. MacDonald was a great teacher, but she's more. She's a great person." She nudged her brother. "Turns out Crimson is full of great people. Davey is getting access to the resources he needs. He's made a friend—"

"In addition to Brooke?"

"Brooke is his *best* friend," Emily clarified. "But, yes, another boy who loves Lego building. They mainly play side by side, but it's a start."

"Does Henry know how he's doing?"

"I sent him an email," Emily admitted with a shrug. "I don't know what I was hoping for, but he's Davey's father so I thought…" She sighed. "His assistant responded to it."

"The guy is a total idiot."

"Agreed. But we're doing okay without him."

Noah turned onto the road that led into town. The aspen leaves were turning brilliant yellow, shimmering in the sunlight. It gave Emily a bright and shiny glow inside her.

"What about the other idiot in your life?" Noah glanced over at her.

"Jase isn't in my life." She paused, then whispered, "and he's not an idiot."

"You haven't talked to him?"

"You know I haven't, Noah." She'd asked April to go to his office the morning after the meeting to give him Emily's resignation letter. Maybe she should have been brave enough to face him, but the humiliation she'd felt after that night had been too raw.

"Why?"

"There's nothing to say. We want different things." She kept waiting for the pain to ease, the vise around her heart to release. Every time she thought of Jase, her whole body reverberated with the deep ache of missing him. "I hear the election is going well." She'd tried not to hear, not to listen but it was difficult in a small town where people were happy to pass around gossip like it was breaking news.

Noah nodded. "Hard to believe the stunt his dad pulled at the town hall meeting actually helped him in the campaign."

"Not hard with Jase."

"Everyone is talking about how much he's overcome and how he's a self-made success."

"He deserves every bit of his success," Emily said quietly. The Thompsons' plan to discredit Jase in the eyes of voters had backfired. She wasn't the only one who'd seen Aaron as he sent Declan into the town hall meeting. Apparently, Charles had a reputation of bending the rules while he'd been sheriff and no one wanted a man with a twisted moral compass in charge of the town.

"You missed the turn." She straightened in her seat as Noah took a right toward Crimson High School.

"I have a quick stop to make."

"What stop?"

He pulled over to the curb at the edge of the football field. "I'll show you. Hop out."

There were a few teenagers throwing a ball on the field but the stands were empty.

"Do you see it?"

She climbed out of the truck, scanning the bleachers for something familiar. "See what, Noah?"

The truck's engine roared to life and she whirled around. Noah had rolled down the passenger window. "See me making you really angry."

"Have you lost your mind?"

He grimaced. "According to my new wife. I hope you'll forgive me, and I'll be back in ten minutes."

"What are you talking about?"

Noah blew her a kiss and drove off, leaving Emily standing on the sidewalk. She didn't even have her phone. "I'm going to kill him," she muttered.

"It's not his fault," a voice said behind her. She went stock-still even as her knees threatened to sag. "He owed me for something and I called in the favor. He didn't have a choice."

She turned to face Jase, letting anger rise to the top of the mountain of emotions vying for space in her heart. "Of course he had a choice," she said on a hiss of breath. "The same way I have a choice as to which one of you I'm going to murder first."

He took a step toward her and she backed up. "Don't come any closer."

"We need to talk."

She shook her head. What she needed was to get the hell out of there before she gave in to the temptation to plaster herself against him. "No. We don't."

"I need to talk," he clarified.

"Talk to someone who wants to listen to what you have to say."

He ran his hands through his hair, looking as miserable as she felt. "Don't you understand? I only ever cared about you. From the start, Emily."

She closed her eyes and stuck her fingers in her ears, repeating the words *I can't hear you* in a singsong voice.

His hands were on her arms a moment later. She flinched away but secretly wanted to melt into him. She'd missed his warmth. Missed the scent of him, pine and soap and man. Missed everything about him.

"Open your eyes," he said, his tone an irresistible mix of amusement and desperation.

She did, keeping her gaze trained on the football field. Davey would like the symmetry of the lines dissecting the green grass.

"This was where I fell in love with you the first time," Jase whispered, following her gaze. "Every weekend you were at the football games, surrounded by a group of friends. You took great pleasure in ignoring me."

"You were my older brother's best friend. I had no use for you." She glanced back at him and her heart skipped a beat. He was watching her as if it was the first time he'd seen her. As if she really was the only thing he cared about in life.

"And still I was ruined for any other girl." His fingers brushed her hair away from her face. "I remember you on those cool fall nights, bundled up in sweaters and boots, your blond hair like a calling card as you held court in the bleachers. You were the most perfect girl I'd ever seen."

She took a step back, out of his grasp and tried to get a handle on her emotions. "I was a brat."

"I didn't care." His chocolate-brown gaze never wavered as he spoke.

"Why are you telling me this now?"

"Because you need to understand it was always you, Em. You were the first and only thing I ever wanted." He flashed a wry smile and toed his boot against the gravel. "Back then it was because you embodied the perfection that was never a part of my life."

"I wasn't perfect and—"

He pressed his finger to her lips. "Then you returned and *I* got a chance to make you happy. No, you're not perfect. Neither am I. But *real* is better than perfect." He scrubbed a hand over his face and the scratch of his stubble made her melt. Just a little. "I messed up, and I'm sorry. Sorrier than you'll ever know. I let the shame I felt about my own family change me."

"I understand."

"How can you understand when I don't?" He shook his head. "There's no excuse, Emily. I love that boy. Hell, I found myself putting together a Lego town the other night with the bin of blocks you left at the house. I miss him. I miss you."

"I understand life is messy. I wanted it to be put in easy compartments. Even Davey, especially Davey."

"You came here to protect him. I get it."

She shook her head. "I came here to hide. Henry wasn't the only one who failed him. Mothers have dreams for their kids. To-the-moon whoppers like, *Will he grow up to be President?* And the dreams that really mattered. *Will he have friends? Will he be happy?* I felt like I lost control of those the first time I noticed Davey's differences."

He stared at her, patiently waiting as always.

"I want to live life celebrating who he is."

Just when she thought it couldn't get any more painful, Jase ripped open another layer of her heart. "I want that, too, Em. I love you both so much."

And another layer. "I'm pulling out of the mayor's race."

"No," she whispered. "You wouldn't."

"I have a meeting with the council later this afternoon to officially withdraw my name."

"But you're going to win. Charles Thompson—"

"The reasons Charles is running for mayor are as convoluted as mine." The half smile he gave her was weary and strained. A different type of heartache roared through her knowing his distress was her fault. Jase had helped her regain her confidence and spirit, and she'd repaid him by allowing her fears to bring both of them low.

"Your reasons aren't convoluted." She moved to him then, put a hand on his arm. "You are straightforward and selfless. You've done so much already—"

"Trust me, I know what it's like to have fear rule your life. No matter how much I do, I'm scared it isn't enough to make amends for all the mistakes. I worry I'll never be enough."

"Those mistakes weren't yours, but the choice to make a different future for yourself has been." He was standing before her, willing to give up everything he'd built in this town. His whole life. The searing thought that this was exactly what her ex-husband had expected of her almost brought her to her knees.

"My mother contacted me," he said softly. "Her letter is what made Dad drink again."

"Oh, Jase."

He ran a hand through his hair, his jaw tight. "She's sick, and she wants to see me. After so many years, she apologized for leaving."

"You deserve that."

He trailed his fingers over hers, his touch sending shivers of awareness across her skin. "I want to deserve you, Em. We deserve happiness. Together. Give me another chance to prove how much you mean to me. How much I love you."

She pressed a hand to her chest as if she could quell the pounding of her heart. He was willing to give her exactly what she'd wanted from Henry, but it was so wrong. She loved him for his dedication and sense of duty, for the very *rightness* of who he was. She couldn't allow loving her to destroy his dream. "You can't give up the campaign, Jase."

"I will if it means a chance with you."

"It isn't… You don't…" She took a breath, trying to give her words time to catch up with her racing thoughts. "I wanted to make my life manageable again, but love isn't manageable and neither is everything that comes with it. Life is messy. If I hide from the pain, I risk never having the love. So I'm going to stop hiding. I love Davey the way he is—"

"Me, too," he whispered, his voice raw.

"I know." She reached up, cupped his face with her hands. "You must know you're already enough for the people in this town. For me. You're the one who has to believe it now. I want to support you, even when it's a struggle. We'll find a way. I may not be the perfect politician's wife but—"

"I don't want you to be perfect. I want you, all of you. Your bossiness and your skyscraper-tall defensive walls—"

"Hey." She poked him in the chest.

"I want the way you love Davey so fiercely, the way you bullied me into stepping into my own life." He lifted a hand to trail it across her jaw. "I want you when you're fragile and vulnerable, when you're strong and stubborn. I want Davey and a house full of Lego creations." He dipped his head so they were at eye level. "I want you every day for the rest of our lives."

"You're going to win this election, Jase." She felt tears slip down her cheeks. "You are the best thing I never expected to happen in my life." She wrapped her arms around his neck and brushed her lips across his. "How did I miss seeing you for so long?"

"The only thing that matters is we're here now." He lifted her into his embrace. "Tell me you'll give us another chance."

She laughed. "A thousand chances, Jase. Because if you take me on, it's going to be for good."

"For good and forever," he agreed. "Be mine forever."

"Yes," she whispered. "Forever."

He took over the kiss, making it at once tender and fully possessive. Emily lost herself in the moment, in the feel of him and the happiness bubbling up inside her like a newly unearthed spring.

A honking horn had her jerking away a moment later.

"Get a room," Noah called as he slowed the truck. He grinned at her. "I hope this means you're not mad at me."

"I'm not mad," she called. "But you're still in trouble."

His gaze flicked to Jase. "Are you going to help me with her?"

Emily growled as Jase laughed. "I wouldn't be dumb enough to try."

Emily patted him on the shoulder. "Which is why you get a thousand chances." She pointed at her brother. "You get none."

He blew her a kiss and she couldn't stop her smile.

"Are we still going apartment hunting?" Noah asked.

"She's got a home," Jase answered. "With me."

"And I get to pick the paint colors?" Emily asked, raising a brow.

"You get to do whatever you want."

She kissed him again. "What I want is to spend the rest of my life with you." She felt color rise to her cheeks, realizing she'd said too much too soon.

Jase only smiled. "I've only been waiting most of my life," he said, dropping to one knee and pulling a small velvet box out of his jacket pocket. "Emily, will you marry me?"

She swallowed, struggled to take a breath and nodded. He slipped the ring on her finger and stood to take her in his arms once more.

"Katie is going to be so mad she missed this moment," she heard her brother yell. "Good thing I got the whole event on video. Congratulations, you two crazy kids." Noah honked once more, then drove out of the parking lot.

"I love you, Em," Jase whispered. "Forever."

"Forever," she repeated and felt her heart fill with all the happiness it could carry.

* * * * *

WEDDING DATE WITH THE ARMY DOC

LYNNE MARSHALL

Many thanks to Flo Nicoll, with her uncanny gift of pinpointing the missing link in my manuscripts and for giving me the freedom to explore diverse and difficult stories.

Also, I'd like to dedicate this book to the 'Dr Gordon' I remember so well from my first job, working in a pathology department. I learned so much and was given many opportunities all those years ago! Knowing 'Dr Gordon' changed the direction of my life. May he rest in peace.

CHAPTER ONE

CHARLOTTE JOHNSON MADE the necessary faces to chew the amazing chocolate, nut and caramel candy she'd just shoved into her mouth between looking at pathology slides. Mid-nut-and-caramel-chew, she glanced up to see a hulking shadow cover her office door. Her secret surgeon crush, Jackson Ryland Hilstead the Third, blocked the fluorescent light from the hallway, causing her to narrow her eyes in order to make out his features. *Be still, my heart, and, oh, heavens, stop chewing. Now!*

Except she couldn't talk unless she finished chewing and swallowed, and she figured he'd come for a reason, as he always did Friday afternoons. Probably because of his heavy schedule of surgeries on Thursday and Friday mornings. He'd ask her questions about his patients' diagnoses and prognoses, and she'd dutifully answer. It had become their routine, and she looked forward to it. After all, as the staff surgical pathologist at St. Francis of the Valley Hospital, it was her job to be helpful to her fellow medical colleagues, even while, in his case, thinking how she'd love to brush that one brown, wavy lock of hair off his forehead. Yeah, she was hopelessly crushing on the man.

She lifted her finger, hoping her sign for "One moment" might compute with the astute doc, then covered her mouth with the other hand as she chewed furiously. Finally, she swallowed with a gulp, feeling heat rise from her neck upward. *Great impression.*

"Don't let me interfere," he said, an amused look on his face. "The last thing I want to do is come between a woman and her chocolate." Obviously he'd noticed the candy-bar wrapper on her desk.

She grabbed a bottle of water and took a quick swig. "You're sounding sexist. How unlike you," she teased, hoping she didn't have candy residue on her teeth. Of all the male doctors she dealt with on a daily basis, this surgeon was the one who made her feel self-conscious. It most certainly had a lot to do with his piercing blue eyes that the hospital scrubs seemed to highlight brighter than an OR lamp. She pulled her lab coat closed when his eyes surreptitiously and briefly scanned her from head to toe. Or as much as he could see of her with her sitting behind her double-headed microscope.

"Ah, Charlotte..." He sat down across from her. "How well you *don't* know me. If you weren't my favorite pathologist, I'd be offended." Finally responding to her halfhearted "sexist" slur.

The guy was a Southern gentleman from Georgia, and she wasn't above stereotyping him, because he was a walking billboard for good manners, charm and—perhaps not quite as appealing considering the odds in a competitive and overstocked female world, in California anyway—knowing how to relate to women. The word *smooth* came to mind. But it was balanced with sincerity, a rare combination. Plus there was no escaping that slow, rolling-syllable accent, like warm honey down her spine, setting off all sorts of nerve endings she'd otherwise forgotten. He spoke as though they had all the time in the world to talk. She could listen to him all day, and if she'd owned a fan she'd be flapping it now.

"Well, if you weren't *one* of my favorite surgeons," she lied, as he was her absolute favorite, "I would've eaten the rest of it."

One corner of his mouth hitched the tiniest bit. "I think you already have, but don't worry, your gooey-chocolate choice would be number ten on my list of top three favorite candy bars."

Busted, she batted her lashes, noticing his spearmint-and-sandalwood scent as he moved closer. She inhaled a little deeper, thinking he liked to change up his aftershave, and that intrigued her.

"And since you brought up the subject of sexism, I've got to say you look great today. Turquoise suits you."

He regularly paid her compliments, which she loved, but figured he was like that with all the women he encountered, so she never took them too seriously. Though she had to admit she longed for him to mean them. What did that say about her dating life? Something in the way his eyes watched her and waited for a response whenever he flattered her made her wonder if maybe she was a tiny bit more special than all the other ladies in the hospital. She liked the idea of that.

"Thank you," she said, sounding as self-effacing as ever.

"Thank *you*," he countered.

Their gazes held perhaps a second longer than she could take, so she pretended the slide on the microscope tray required her immediate and complete attention. "So what do you need?"

Intensely aware of his *do-you-really-want-to-know?* gaze—this was new and it was a challenge that shook her to the bone—she fought the urge to squirm. Yeah, sexist or sexy or whatever it was he just did with those eyes was way out of her comfort zone. So why did that look excite her, make her wish things could be the way they had been before her operation? Where was that invisible fan again? Shame. Shame. Shame. And she called herself a professional woman.

"Do you have the slides yet for Gary Underwood? A lung biopsy from yesterday afternoon. I've got an impatient wife demanding her husband's results."

"The weekend is coming, so I can understand her concern." Charlotte hadn't yet finished the slides from yesterday morning's cases, but she was always willing to fish out a few newer ones for interested doctors. Jackson was as concerned about his patients as they came. Another thing she really liked about the guy.

She turned on the desk lamp, sorted through the pile of cardboard slide cases, each carefully labeled by the histology technicians, and found the slides in question. They settled in to study them, their knees nearly touching as they sat on opposite sides of the small table that held her dual-headed teaching microscope. She put her hair behind her ears and moved in, but not before seeing him notice her dangly turquoise earrings that matched her top. She could tell from the spark in his eyes that he liked them, too, but this time kept the fact to himself.

Yes, he was a real gentleman, with broad shoulders and wavy brown hair that he chose to comb straight back from his forehead. And it was just long enough to curl under his ears. Call him a sexy gentleman. *Gulp.* Very, very sexy.

Being smack in the heart of the San Fernando Valley was nothing new for an original Valley girl like her, but she figured it had to be total culture shock for a man from Savannah. *Talk to me, baby. I love that Southern drawl.* Why did she have such confidence inside her head but could never dare to act on it? She didn't waste a single second answering that question. Because things were different now. She wasn't the woman she'd used to be. Enough said.

In his early forties with a sprinkling of gray at his temples, Jackson had only been in Southern California for a year. Word was, if she could believe everything she heard from Dr. Dupree, Jackson had needed a change after his divorce. Which made him a gentleman misfit in a casual-with-a-capital-C kind of town. She liked that about him, too—the khaki slacks and button-down collared shirts with ties that he'd obviously given some time to selecting. Today the shirt was pale yellow and the tie an expensive-looking subtly sage-green herringbone pattern. Nice.

She turned off the desk light so they could view the slide better. They sat in companionable silence as they studied it. Hearing him breathe ever so gently made the hair on the back of her neck stand on end. Good thing she'd worn it down today. Hmm, maybe that was what he liked? *Stop it, Charlotte. This will never go anywhere.* Maybe that was why she enjoyed the fantasy so much. It was her secret. And it was safe.

She fine-focused on the biopsied lung tissue, increasing the magnification over one particular spot of red-dyed swirls with minuscule black dots until the cells came into full view. They studied the areas in question together. "Notice the angulated nuclear margins and hyperchromasia in this area?" She spoke close to a whisper, a habit she'd got into out of respect for the solemn importance of each patient's diagnosis.

"Hmm," he emitted thoughtfully.

She moved the slide on the tray a tiny bit, then refocused. "And here, and here." She used the white teaching arrow in the high-grade microscope to point out the areas in question.

He inhaled, his eyes never leaving the eyepiece.

"Here are mitotic figures, and here intercellular bridges. Not a good sign." She pulled back from her microscope. "As you can see, there are variations in size of cells and nuclei, which adds up to squamous cell malignancy. I'll have to study the rest of the slides to check the margins and figure out the cancer staging, but, unfortunately, the anxiously awaiting wife will have more to be anxious about."

"Bad news for sure." Jackson pushed back from the microscope, but not before one of his knees knocked hers, and it hurt her kneecap, feeling almost like metal. Maybe he was Superman in disguise? "I'll get in touch with Oncology to get a jump on things."

The situation caused an old and familiar pang in her stomach. Charlotte knew how it felt to be a family member waiting for news from the doctor. She'd gone through the process at fifteen, the year her mother had been diagnosed with breast cancer. That was the day she'd first heard the term *metastatic* and had vowed to figure out what it meant. And after that she'd vowed to learn everything she could about her mother's condition.

"Is he young and otherwise healthy?"

"Yes," Jackson said. "Which will help the prognosis."

She nodded, though not enthusiastically. Her mother had been young and supposedly healthy, too. The loss of her mother soon after bilateral mastectomies had broken her family's heart. Her father had never recovered, and within a span of three years of his downhill slide, he'd also died. From alcoholism, his self-medication of choice to deal with the emotional pain. She'd already stepped in as the responsible one when her mother had first been diagnosed, and after she'd died Charlotte had kept the family functioning. Barely. At eighteen, along with applying to colleges, she'd signed on to be the guardian of her kid sister and brother, otherwise they'd have ended up in foster homes.

Her mother's cancer had changed the course of her life, steering her toward medicine, and later, with her never-ending quest to understand why things happened as they did, sending her into the darker side of the profession, pathology.

"Well, I've got to run," Jackson said, bringing her out of her thoughts. "I've got a dinner I can't miss tonight, and Mrs. Underwood to talk to first." He stood and took a couple of steps then turned at her office door and looked at her again thoughtfully. "Do you happen to know offhand the extension for social services? I think the Underwoods could use some added support this weekend."

Having put the desk light back on, she scanned her hospital phone list cheat sheet and read out the numbers, admittedly disappointed to know he had a dinner engagement.

"Thanks," he said, but not before giving her a thorough once-over again. "Really like those earrings, too." Then he left, leaving her grinning with warming cheeks.

Wanting desperately to read more into his light flattery than she should, she groaned quietly. The guy had a dinner date! Plus the man probably said things like that to all the women he encountered in his busy days. It had probably been drilled into him back in Georgia since grade school, maybe even before that. Treat all women like princesses.

Who was she kidding, hoping she might be more special than other women he knew? She was five feet nine, a full-figured gal, or had used to be anyway, a size ten, and not many men appreciated that in this thin-as-a-rail era. Besides, even if he did find her attractive, nothing could ever come of it. She'd pretty much taken care of that two years ago with her surgery.

Odds were most men wouldn't want to get involved with her. She pulled her lab coat tighter across her chest. Her ex-boyfriend had sure changed his mind, calling off their short engagement. They'd been all set to go the conventional route, and she'd loved the idea of having a career, marriage and kids. Her mouth had watered for it. Then...

She'd cut Derek some slack, though, since her decision had been extreme and radical even. They'd talked about it over and over, argued, and he'd never really signed on. He hadn't wanted to go there. He'd wanted her exactly as she had been.

The memory of her mother suffering had been the major influence on her final decision.

Her hand came to rest on her chest. The realistic-feeling silicone breast forms—otherwise known as falsies—she wore in her bra sometimes nearly made her forget she'd had a double mastectomy. Elective surgery.

She fiddled with Mr. Underwood's slides, lining them up to study them more thoroughly.

She'd accidentally found her own damn cancer marker right here in her office. Along with the excitement and anticipation of getting engaged and the plans for having a family, some deeper, sadder dialogue threaded through the recesses of her brain. One morning she'd woken in a near panic. What if? She'd shivered over the potential answer. Then, unable to move forward with a gigantic question mark in her future, she'd had the lab draw her blood and do the genetic marker panel. The results had literally made her gasp and grab her chest. Her worst nightmare was alive and living in her DNA.

Knowing her mother's history, the near torture she'd gone through, well, having preemptive surgery had been a decision she'd known she'd have to make. Why not take care of it before it ever had a chance to begin? She'd begged Derek to understand. He'd fought her decision, but he'd never seen what her mother had gone through.

Jackson appeared at her door again, making her lose her train of thought. He inclined his head. "You okay?"

"Oh, yes." She recovered quickly, and he obviously accepted her answer since the concern dissolved from his face.

"Hey, I forgot to ask just now. Are you going to that garden party Sunday afternoon?"

Her old concerns suddenly forgotten, the hair on her arms joined the hair on the back of her neck in prickling. Was it possible that the handsome Southern doctor was actually interested in her?

"Yes. I kind of thought it was mandatory." It was July, the newest residents would all be there and it was a chance to put names to faces.

"Good. I'll see you there, then." And off he went again, his long legs and unusual gait taking that Southern stroll to a new level.

For an instant she let her hopes take flight. What would it be like to date again, especially with a man's man like Jackson Hilstead the Third? But he'd made no offer to go to the garden party together, and after all the thoughts she'd had just now, she wasn't a bit closer to making her secret crush real. No way.

Feeling the fallout from rehashing her past, she exchanged the instantaneous hope for reality. There was no way anyone would want her. Not with the anything-but-sexy scars across her nearly flat chest.

She sat staring into her lap, letting the truth filter through her.

Dr. Antwan Dupree appeared at her door, a man so full of himself she wished she could post a "closed for business" sign and pretend no one was home.

"I brought you some Caribbean food from a little place nearby. Thought you might like to try a taste of your heritage."

"I'm not from the Caribbean."

"Yes, you are. You just don't know it. Look at your honey-colored skin and the loads of wavy, almost black hair. Darlin', you've got Caribbean brown eyes. There's no question."

"It's brown. My hair is dark brown. Both my parents were from the States. My grandparents were from the States. My great-grandparents were from the States. I'm typical Heinz Fifty-Seven American. The name John-son is as American as it gets."

"I see the islands in you."

"And that makes it so? Must be nice to live in your world." She suppressed a sigh. She always had to try her best not to be rude to the young, overconfident sur-geon, because she did have to work with him.

"I'm just trying to help you get in touch with your roots. Try this. It's rice and peas and jerk chicken. You'll love it."

"I don't do spicy." She opened the brown bag, pulled out the take-out container and peered inside. Black-eyed peas were something she'd never tried before, but the rice was brown, the chicken looked juicy and, since the doctor had gone to the trouble to bring the food, she figured she should at least taste it. "But I'll give this a try."

"When you eat that you'll be singing, 'I'm home, at last!'" He had an okay voice, but she wasn't ready for a serenade right then.

"I doubt it, but thanks for the thought." Her number one thought, while staring at her unrequested lunch, was how to get rid of Antwan Dupree.

Just as Antwan opened his mouth to speak again Jackson appeared once more at the door, which pleased her to no end.

Would you look at me, the popular pathologist? The thought nearly made her spew a laugh, but that could get messy and spread germs and it definitely wouldn't be attractive and Jackson was standing right there. She kept her near guffaw to herself and secretly reveled in the moment, though inwardly she rolled her eyes at the absurdity of the notion. Popular pathologist. Right.

Antwan was a pest. Jackson Hilstead, well, was not!

"Give it a try, let me know what you think." Antwan turned for the door. "You have my number, right?" He made a point to look directly at Jackson when he said that.

"Thank you and good-bye." She'd never found swagger appealing. She'd also learned that with Antwan it was best to be blunt, otherwise the guy imagined all kinds of improbable things. The thing that really didn't make sense was that he was better than decent looking and had loads of women interested around the hospital. Why pester her?

He nodded. "We'll talk later," he promised confidently, and did his unique Antwan Dupree walk right past Jackson, who hadn't budged from his half of the entrance.

"Doctor." Jackson tipped his head.

"Doctor." Dupree paid the same respect on his way out. No sooner had he left than Charlotte could hear Antwan chatting up Latoya, the receptionist down the hall. What a guy.

"Sorry to interrupt," Jackson said.

"Not at all. In fact, thank you!"

Jackson smiled and her previously claustrophobic office, with Dr. Dupree inside plus him now being gone, seemed to expand toward the universe.

"Spicy beans and rice give me indigestion, but I guess I have to try this now. I was actually kind of looking forward to my peanut butter and jelly sandwich."

That got another smile from him, and she longed to think of a thousand ways to keep them coming. She also felt compelled to clarify a few things. "For the record," she said as she closed the food container and put it back in the bag, "there is nothing at all going on between me and Dupree. He, well…he's a player and I really don't care for men who are full of themselves, you know?"

"He does like the ladies." Jackson hadn't budged from his spot at the door, and she began to wonder why he'd made another visit. "But in this case he does exhibit excellent taste."

Really? He thought she was attractive? Before she let herself get all puffed up about his comment, it occurred to her that Jackson must have come back to her office for a reason. Maybe he wanted to ask her to go with him to the garden party? "Did you need something?"

"Yes."

She mentally crossed her fingers.

"I was just talking to Dr. Gordon. He said he'd like to speak to you when you have a chance."

The head of pathology, Dr. Gordon, was her personal mentor, and admittedly a kind of father figure, and when he called, she never hesitated. "Oh. Sure, thanks." She stood and walked around her desk, then noticed the subtle gaze again from Jackson covering her from head to toe. If only she hadn't chosen sensible shoes today! But she thanked the manufacturer of realistic-looking falsies for filling out her special mastectomy bra underneath her turquoise top.

Charlotte strolled side by side with the tall doctor down the hall. She pegged him to be around six-two, based on her five-nine and wearing low wedge shoes, plus the fact her eyes were in line with his classic long and straight nose, except for that small bump on the bridge that gave him such character. She forced her attention away from his face, again noticing his subtly unusual gait, like maybe one shoe didn't fit quite right. When they reached Dr. Gordon's office door, she faked casual and said good-bye.

When he smiled his good-bye, she secretly sighed—what was it about that guy?—and lingered, watching him leave the department.

"You coming in or are you going to stand out there gawking all afternoon?" As head of pathology, Dr. Gordon had taken her under his wing from her very first day as a resident at St. Francis, and she owed him more than she could ever repay. She also happened to adore the nearly seventy-year-old curmudgeon, with his shocking white hair and clear hazel eyes that had always seemed to see right through her. His double chin helped balance a hawk-like nose.

"Sorry. Hi." She stepped inside his office. "You wanted to talk to me?"

He grew serious. "Close the door."

His instruction sent a chill through her core. Something important was about to happen and the thought made her uncomfortable. He'd better not be retiring because she wasn't ready for him to leave! She did what she was told, closed the door, then sat across from him at the desk, hoping she wasn't about to get reprimanded for something.

He gave his fatherly smile, and immediately she knew she had nothing to worry about. "I'm not going to mince words. My prostate cancer is back and Dr. Hilstead is going to do exploratory surgery on me Monday. I want you to read the frozen sections."

Stunned, she could hardly make herself speak. "Yes. Of course." She wanted to run to him and throw her arms around him, but they didn't have that kind of relationship. "Whatever you want." His wife, Elly, had passed away last year, and he'd seemed so forlorn ever since. The last thing the man needed was a cancer threat. Her heart ached for him, but she fought to hide her fears. "I'll go over those specimens with a fine-tooth comb."

"And I'll expect no less." Stoic as always. Pathology had a way of doing that to doctors.

"Is there anything I can do for you this weekend?"

"Thank you but no. My son is flying in from Arizona for a few days."

"I'm glad to hear that."

"Oh, wait, there is something you could do. I guess you could fill in for me on Sunday afternoon at that new resident garden party deal."

"Of course." Not her favorite idea, since she'd hoped she could find a way to comfort him, like make a big pot of healthy soup or something, but she'd planned to go to the Sunday event anyway.

The good doctor winked at her. "Whatever we find, we'll nip it in the bud, right?"

"You bet." With her heart aching, she wished she could guarantee that would be the case, but they passed a look between them that said it all. As pathologists, they knew when cancer reared its head the hunt was on. It was their job to be relentless in tracking it down, the surgeons' job to cut it out, and the oncologists' to find the magic healing potion to obliterate anything that was left.

Medical science was a tough business, and Charlotte Johnson had signed on in one of the most demanding fields. Pathology. She'd never get used to being the bearer of bad news. Usually the doctors had to take it from there once she handed over the medical verdict. She considered Jim Gordon to be a dear friend as well as colleague and any findings she came up with he'd know had come directly from her. The responsibility unsettled her stomach.

Now that she'd dealt with her own deepest fear— and Jim Gordon had condoned her radical decision two years ago at the age of thirty-two—she was damned if she'd give up being an optimist for him.

Come Monday morning she'd be ready for the toughest call of her career, and it would be for Dr. Gordon. Her mentor. The man she'd come to respect like a father. But first she'd have to make it through the garden party on Sunday afternoon, and the one bright spot in that obligation was the chance to see her secret surgeon crush again. Dr. Jackson Hilstead.

CHAPTER TWO

CHARLOTTE DIDN'T WANT to admit she'd picked the Capri blue patterned sundress only because Dr. Hilstead had liked her turquoise top on Friday, though the thought had entered her mind while searching her closet for something to wear on Sunday morning.

It had been a long time since she'd even considered wearing a dress cut like this, which made her feel uncomfortable, so she'd compromised with a white, lightweight, very loosely knit, three-quarter-sleeved summer sweater. To help cover the dipping neckline, she chose several strings of large and colorful beads. On a whim, she left her hair down, letting the thick waves touch the tops of her shoulders and making no excuses for the occasional ringlet around her face. And this shade of blue sure made her caramel-colored eyes stand out.

With confidence, later that afternoon, she stepped into the St. Francis of the Valley atrium, which connected to an outdoor patio where dozens of doctors had already begun to gather. At the moment she didn't recognize a single face, all of the residents looking so young and eager. But there was Antwan with a young and very attractive woman on his arm. Relieved he wasn't alone, she glanced around the cavernous room.

She recognized several large painted canvases and

they drew her attention to the bright white walls as she realized the ocularist down the hall from her office, Andrea Rimmer, had painted them. In fact, she'd bought several of her early paintings at an art auction because she'd loved her style so much, but these paintings were signed with a different name because Andrea had married a pediatrician, Sam Marcus, so her name had changed now. Anyway, the paintings of huge eyes peeking through various openings were amazing, each iris completely different from the next, and Charlotte was soon swept up in imagining their meaning.

Totally engrossed with admiring the newest paintings of her current favorite artist, she jumped when someone tapped her shoulder. That flutter of excitement flitted right on by when she realized it was Dr. Dupree.

"You're looking extra fine today," he said, making a show of looking her up and down.

"Thank you. Where's your date?"

"Getting some refreshments." His line of vision stayed on her chest. "All those necklaces remind me of the Caribbean."

"They're just some beads I threw on, that's all. Oh, look." She really wanted to divert his interest from her chest. "Your lady friend is searching for you."

"If I didn't assume you'd have a date today, I would have asked you myself."

"I'm here as the representative of the pathology department. This garden party is all business for me."

"Such a shame. If you ever want to actually have a good time, let me know. You don't know what you're missing until you've gone out with me."

Seriously? "If this is any example of how you treat your dates, count me out. Now go spend some time with the very attractive woman you've brought. Shoo." She used her hands to shoo him away, like the pest he was. Man, it ticked her off how he treated women as interchangeable objects.

Frustration and anger interfered with her enjoying the artwork, and though she already really wanted to leave, she had promised Dr. Gordon to be the face of Pathology today. So she forced herself to head toward the refreshment table, where several of the new doctors stood talking among themselves. She glanced up in time to see something to make her get excited. Jackson Hilstead was easy to spot, being a head taller than others in his group, as he moved into the atrium. Charlotte found her smile come to a halt when she noticed that to Jackson's right was the assistant head of the hospital laboratory, Yuri Ito. His hand rested on her shoulder, like he was guiding her. Obviously they'd come together.

Why had Jackson asked if she was coming to the party if he was bringing a date? Her previous excitement turned to disappointment, making the thought of eating sour on her tongue. What else was new? Why had she even let herself follow her fancy in the first place? Antwan may have been right about the surgeon. Maybe he was as much of a lady's man as Dupree. What was up with surgeons?

Halfheartedly, she moved on to the buffet and picked a few items to pretend she was busy, rather than try to make eye contact with Jackson. What was the point? She greeted a few of the new residents, introducing herself and inviting them to stop by anytime for a quick tour of the department. The two young women and one guy all seemed very receptive, maybe even a little too enthusiastic. The dip may have looked great but it tasted bland, matching her mood, since eyeing the tall surgeon with Yuri, but she forced herself to partake.

Another tap on the shoulder sent her heart skittering once more, until she turned to face Antwan again. How did he keep ditching his date?

"Here," he said, handing her a glass of punch. "You'll like this—it's for grown-ups. And it reminds me—"

"Let me guess—of the Caribbean? Evidently everything does today." She took the drink and sipped, pleasantly surprised by the sweet taste with a kick, as it was definitely a grown-up beverage. "Thanks." She forced a smile and received a much-too-eager grin in return. The sight made her eyes immediately dance away in time to connect with Jackson's where he stood a few feet away.

"Hi," he said, over the crowd.

"Hello," she mouthed back.

Jackson couldn't miss Antwan standing right beside her, which was probably why he quickly looked away. But she'd been clear with him about having nothing going on with Dr. Dupree, and hoped he'd believed her. Which further proved that looks could be deceiving.

So much for getting all dolled up for a man. Except Antwan seemed to appreciate her efforts. Backfire! "Oh, look, there's your date. Isn't she one of the new surgical residents? I'm going to introduce myself."

Antwan's smile faded quickly, and that brought hers back to life as she made her way over to the pretty African-American doctor across the room. She particularly enjoyed watching the too-sure-of-himself doctor squirm.

As the afternoon wore on and she got to know a few of the new batch of residents, who'd just begun working at the hospital July first, she secretly kept tabs on Jackson, who never left Yuri's side, though it sure didn't seem like they had much to say to each other. As in her case with Antwan, could looks be deceiving there, too?

Don't get your hopes up. She felt the urge to adjust her specially made bra but fought it. *This further proves the uselessness of secret crushes. Oh, they're fine when you keep them secret, but start letting them out on a rope and disasters like this happened.* Reality was like looking into a magnifying mirror. *What I see up close is never pleasant.*

She glanced up to find Jackson watching her, and, as crazy as her thoughts had been seconds before, that mere eye contact from the man she'd let her guard down over got her hopes right back up again. She had it bad for the guy, which meant one thing—she needed to get over it!

When she'd felt she'd spent the obligatory amount of time mingling with the new doctors, inviting them to visit Pathology, and also with several of her staff colleagues, she decided to skip out, admittedly feeling disappointed. With no chance for witty conversation with her doctor of choice, that Southern charmer who appeared to be taken anyway, there was no point in sticking around another minute. Unfortunately, her path of exit brought her by Jackson and Yuri, who looked like they were edging their way out, too.

Yuri gazed at her, tension in her eyes. "Hi, Charlotte."

"Hi, Yuri." No hard feelings. Yuri was a nice woman. "See you Monday." She scurried on by but not before someone tapped her on the shoulder. A third time! That Antwan didn't know when to give up. She swung around, less-than-kind thoughts in her mind and probably flashing in her eyes, to see Jackson's laid-back smile.

"You going already?"

Switching gears fast, she skidded into sociable. "Oh,

uh, yes. Got a big day tomorrow, with Dr. Gordon's surgery and all. Well, you obviously know that."

"Yeah, I'll be leaving shortly, too."

Hmm, he'd said "I'll," not "we'll." Stop it. Don't continue to be a fool. "Well, good-bye, then. I'll be ready with the cryostat bright and early. I promise to get those frozen sections cut, stained and read in record time."

"I'm sure you will. Well, listen, I just wanted to make sure you knew how stunning you look today. I could hardly take my eyes off you."

Was he saying this right in front of Yuri? What was with men these days? But Yuri smiled up at him approvingly.

"Well, thank you." Her head was officially spinning with confusion. "I guess." She glanced at Yuri again, who continued to smile. "Good-bye now."

Jackson grinned and nodded and let her leave with a wad of conflicting thoughts clumping up her brain. What was going on?

Once she hit the street and got some fresh air, she inhaled deeply to clear her head, then gave herself a stern talking-to. *That's what I get for letting a man get under my skin. I should know better!*

On Monday morning Charlotte came into work early, hoping to see Dr. Gordon in the hospital before he'd been given his pre-op meds. Unfortunately, he already had, but he wasn't yet so out of it that he couldn't squeeze her hand and give her a smile and a thumbs-up as they rolled him from his hospital room toward surgery. His slightly intoxicated grin nearly broke her heart.

The vision of him stripped down to a bland hospital gown, with a little blue "shower cap" covering over his abundant white hair, lying on the narrow gurney as the transportation clerk pushed him toward the elevator, made her eyes blur and her chest squeeze. It also brought back sad memories of seeing her mother in the same position years ago, and reinforced why she'd chosen the safety of the isolated pathology department to the hospital wards after medical school.

To distract herself, she stopped at the cafeteria and bought a large coffee, then headed to the basement to her department, where she'd double-check the cryostat before Dr. Gordon's first specimen arrived.

Jackson planned to send down from surgery a sentinel node for her initial study, and depending on her findings, they would proceed from there.

By eight-fifteen the OR runner appeared in her lab with the first node from Dr. Gordon. The specimen came with exact directions as to where it had been resected and she made a note of that with a grease pencil on the textured side of the first of several waiting glass slides. She carefully put the specimen in a gel-like medium and placed it in a mold for quick freezing in the cryostat. She helped the process along with special fast-freeze spray, then within less than half a minute mounted the fully frozen specimen on the chuck and set up the microtome to her exact specifications.

After dusting the initial cut away from the blade with a painter's brush, she made the next cut and got the full surface of the node on the microtome then pressed her labeled glass slide to pick it up. She used H&E stain for immediate results since the hematoxylin and eosin stains worked best for her purposes, then placed a coverslip.

Whisking the now stained slide to the lab microscope, she began her study, and soon her hope for a benign node was dashed. Within five minutes of receiving the first specimen, she had to report the bad news over the intercom that connected surgery to her little corner of the world. The protocol was not to get into histologic details with frozen sections, instead sticking to a "just the facts, ma'am" approach.

"Dr. Hilstead, this is Dr. Johnson reporting that the first lymph node is positive for metastatic cancer." The words tangled in her throat, and she had to force them out, refusing to let her voice waver in the process.

"I see," Jackson replied. "I'll proceed to the next lymph node. Stand by."

"I'll be here."

Jackson continued with abdominal lymph node dissection, and she dutifully and quickly made her cryosurgical cuts and examined each and every specimen under the microscope, tension mounting with each specimen. The head of histology poked her head in the door, wearing a sad expression. Word soon spread in the small laboratory section about Dr. Gordon. Charlotte worked on in silence. After three positive-for-cancer lymph nodes, her voice broke as she reported, "This one is also positive."

A lab tech standing silently behind her in the tiny cryostat room moaned and left, grabbing a tissue on the way out. Dr. Gordon was well liked by his staff because he treated everyone decently, and in Charlotte's case, taking her under his wing and mentoring her when she'd been a green-behind-the-ears pathologist. She owed so much to him, yet all she could do today was be the bearer of bad news on his behalf.

There was no hiding the fact her findings were

tearing her up, and her favorite surgeon must have felt compelled to console her. "We're almost done here, Charlotte. Just a few more, I promise."

"Of course." She recovered her composure, knowing the entire surgical team could hear her over the intercom. "I'll be here, Doctor."

And so it went until they found a benign node after six specimens.

Early afternoon, stowed away in the comfort of her dark office, studying yesterday afternoon's surgical slides, Charlotte sipped chamomile tea. With her heart loaded down with emotions, feeling like a brick around her neck, it would be a long day that she'd just have to force herself through. She'd had plenty of experience willing herself through days at a time, beginning as a teenager and more recently two years ago after her surgery had been done and she'd had to deal with the reality of her decision. She'd stripped herself of part of her female identity and hadn't yet figured out how to move forward. Derek's reaction the first time they'd made love after surgery, his expression when he'd seen her, would forever be tattooed in her mind.

A light double tap on her closed door drew her out of the doldrums she'd been intent on wallowing in. "If it isn't important, I'd rather be left alone." She went the honest route, hoping the staff would understand, especially since they all seemed to already know about Dr. Gordon's diagnosis.

The door opened, and Jackson, ignoring her request to be left alone, stepped inside. He was still in OR scrubs, his wavy hair mostly covered with the OR cap as he closed the door behind him. "I thought you could use a friend right about now."

Not giving Charlotte a chance to respond, he walked to her desk, took one of her hands and, finding little resistance from her, pulled her to standing like a reluctant dance partner, then into his arms. He hugged her tightly and sincerely and the warmth washed over her like a comforting cloud, all soft and squishy, with every surface of her skin reacting to his embrace in goose bumps. Yes, she did need this, and Jackson had no idea how much it meant to her.

They stood together like that for several moments, her breathing in his scent and finding it surprisingly not sterile-smelling at all, even though he'd just come from surgery. She leaned into his solid body, enjoying it, knowing this was a man she could literally lean on. One of his hands wandered to her hair, as if unable to resist the opportunity to feel it. She liked that he was so obvious about it, and smiled against his shoulder.

Before standing in the dim light and holding each other became awkward, Jackson spoke. "Chemotherapy can work wonders these days. I've already got Marv Cohen working on Jim's case, and I feel that already shifts the prognosis into a more positive direction."

Who was he kidding, trying to cheer her up? He was talking to a pathologist. She was a doctor from the end-of-the-road department where patients wound up after all the great medical plans hadn't panned out. The thing that hurt was that she knew Dr. Gordon himself had taught her to think that way. "We have to be realistic, Charlotte," he'd say. How would he feel when he woke up and got the news?

With all her dreary thoughts, she appreciated Jackson's desire to make her feel better. But this fight wasn't about her, it was Jim Gordon's to fight, and she promised she'd do everything in her power to help him. "I'll read the slides first thing in the morning, and report directly to Marv, after you, of course, so he can come up with a magic potion and stop this mess." *No matter what,* her mother had insisted to the very end, *don't lose hope.* Becoming a pathologist had made her cynical.

"I'm sure you will." His hands slid to either side of her face, fingers gently cupping her ears. Then he studied her eyes. She'd never been this close to him before, and loved looking up into his angled features and, in her opinion, handsome face, into those often world-weary eyes. Distracted by the thickness of his eyelashes, she didn't see what was about to happen until his mouth lightly kissed hers. Surprising herself, she let him, relaxed and enjoyed the feel of his lips pressing on hers. This kind of comfort she could get used to really fast.

But wait. This couldn't happen! It meant things, like getting close to another human being again. A man. Which could lead to, well, sex. Which wouldn't happen because once Jackson found out about her surgery and the fact she'd stripped herself of many a man's favorite playground, the breasts, he'd be like Derek. Not able to accept her as she was—still a woman, but scarred and different.

The pain from Derek's walking away had sliced too deep.

She ended the kiss, not abruptly, just not allowing it to go any further. She prepared a quick cover, with a single thought planted in her head since yesterday. "Didn't I see you with Yuri yesterday?" By his confused expression, it seemed like she had the perfect antidote to stop this kiss cold.

"You did. I was doing her a favor."

Charlotte was very aware that even though they were

no longer kissing, he hadn't let her out of his arms. "A favor?" Did he really expect her to believe that line?

"She's got a thing for Stan Arnold."

"The head of the medical lab?" Trying to picture petite Yuri with tall, gangly Stan made Charlotte smile.

"He would be the one. Apparently she's had a thing for him for years, and recently found out his wife had dumped him. So she cooked up this plan to make him jealous."

"I don't remember seeing Stan at the party yesterday."

"That's the joke. Yuri sets up this elaborate plan, me pretending to be her date, and the guy doesn't show up." He smiled and shook his head. "She's got it bad."

"I guess I shouldn't listen to everything Antwan tells me."

His eyes widened, as if amazed she'd listen to *anything* Antwan said, let alone everything. "Like what?"

"That you're a ladies' man, and you've dated a lot of women from St. Francis."

An odd look crossed his face. "Not at all true. I've had only a couple of dates since I've moved here, no one from the hospital, and once they got to know me, neither lady bothered to stick around." What was he telling her? Was there a Mr. Hyde to his charming Dr. Jekyll? Before she could delve into that loaded statement, Jackson spoke again. "And by the way, I noticed Dr. Dupree hanging around you a lot yesterday. If you hadn't already told me you don't have anything going on with him, I might have thought you were there together." He'd expertly changed the subject.

"Oh, no! I hope no one else thought that." She was well aware of still being in Jackson's arms, and was also dying to know if she'd made him feel jealous yesterday, even though she knew it was pointless, just a little ego bump.

"I don't really care what anyone else thinks, but *I'm* relieved." He kissed her again, this one far from a comfort kiss and sending shivers dripping down her spine. If she'd had any doubt about his interest before, he'd sure proved her wrong now. This kiss felt intimate, like they kissed like this every day, and she liked it. Kissing Jackson shut down her never-ending thoughts and questions, allowing her to stay in the moment and enjoy the soft yet persistent feel of his lips on hers. At first he kissed like a gentleman, but something she did—she'd got carried away and opened her mouth and pushed her tongue between his lips, to be exact—had fired him up. She reeled with the feel of him getting a little wild with the kisses because of something she'd set off. How long had it been since she'd done this to a man?

As his mouth worked down the side of her neck, finding many of her trigger points and setting loose chills, his hands began to wander over her shoulders and down her arms, soon skimming the sides of her chest down to her waist and back up. As much as she was enjoying everything, he'd moved into "the zone" and it shocked her back to reality.

This can't happen. Not here. Not now. Not ever?

She pulled herself together and stepped back, letting him know they'd crossed a line for which she wasn't ready. She searched for and found her voice, barely able to whisper the words. "Though this is really nice, it probably isn't the best way to work out my concerns for Dr. Gordon."

"Seems like a pretty damn good replacement, though." Jackson, like the perfect gentleman that he usually had been until about five minutes ago, took a second to pull it together. "I'm pretty sure Jim will be out of Recovery by now. Want to go visit him with me?" It had been spoken as if nothing monumental had just happened between them, like he kissed women in their offices all the time.

"I'd love to." She'd also love to continue kissing him, but only in her dreams could she have what she really wanted from Jackson. Just like the reality of Dr. Gordon with metastatic cancer, some things weren't easily worked out.

With more questions about Jackson than she'd ever had before, and a boatload of mixed-up feelings, both mental and physical, for him, she still managed a daring last kiss. She'd call it a gratitude kiss. Granted, it followed a quick hug of thanks and was only a buss of the cheek, but at least it was something.

After graciously accepting her parting gift, and searching her stare for an instant, he headed for the door and she followed him toward the elevators for the post-op ward. Something significant had happened between them. Figuring out what it meant would be left for another time.

Before just now, never in her wildest imagination could she have seen that kiss coming.

Dr. Gordon's eyes were closed. The head of the hospital bed was elevated slightly, and the white over-starched sheets seemed to bleach what little color he had from his face. Oxygen through a nasal cannula helped his shallow breathing. The sight of her mentor looking so vulnerable made her stomach burn. She took his hand, the one with the IV, and his eyelids cracked open. He needed a few seconds to focus before he smiled.

"Hello, Jim. Glad to see you survived surgery," Jackson said, as if he'd had nothing to do with it.

"Yeah, some lunatic tried to kill me today." His gaze shifted to Charlotte rather than look at Dr. Hilstead any longer, and his tough facade softened as he did.

"How're you doing?" She could hardly hear herself.

"Besides feeling like I've been shot with BBs in my gut, okay, I guess."

"When was the last time you had pain medicine?"

"I lost track of time a while ago. I'm supposed to push this." He nodded toward the medicine dispenser attached to his IV pole, which allowed the patient to regulate pain control on the first day post-op. He pressed it. If enough time had passed since the last dose, he'd get more now, which of course would put him back to sleep.

"Can I give you some ice chips?"

"Sure." He let her feed the ice to him from a plastic spoon, and it struck her how over the past few years he'd spoon-fed her knowledge as her mentor. Helping now was the least she could do. She found a pillow on the bedside chair, fluffed it and exchanged it for the flattened one behind his head, just like she'd learned to do with her mother. He groaned with the movement but let her do it.

Their eyes met briefly. Appreciation, with flecks of hard-won wisdom, conveyed his thoughts. Jackson had probably already talked to him about the findings, and Dr. Gordon had assigned her to the frozen sections for the surgery. They all knew the outcome. There was no point in bringing it up.

She tried to keep sadness from coloring her gaze as they shared a sweetly poignant moment, almost like father and daughter. Emotion reached inside her and gripped until her throat tightened and she feared she'd start to cry. She inhaled as reinforcement. "You probably feel like sleeping."

He let her use the excuse, squeezed her hand one last time and let her go. "Thanks for coming by."

"I'll be back later, okay?"

He nodded, snuggled back on the pillow and shut his eyes again.

Jackson guided Charlotte at the small of her back from the bedside out the door to the nurses' station. "He knew before going in what the likelihood was of his having mets."

She hated this part of her job, verifying the worst outcome. Seeing her mentor's tired face just now, looking nothing like the strong head of the department she'd always looked up to, had knocked some of the air from her. She gulped and the swelling emotions she'd tried to ward off with little bedside tasks took hold. Her eyes burned, and her chest clutched at her lungs. Memories from nearly twenty years ago threw her to the curb, and she broke down.

Jackson swept her under his arm and walked her to a quiet side of the ward, back near the linen cart. "Let's go get a cup of coffee, okay?"

Trying her best to get hold of her runaway feelings, she nodded and swiped at her eyes. He handed her some nearby tissues, and she used them. Then, with his arm around her waist, he led her back to the elevator, which they had all to themselves.

"I didn't realize how close you are to Jim."

"He's been like a father figure to me. I lost my mother to breast cancer when I was fifteen, and my dad a few years after that. Dad just couldn't go on without her, I guess. I still miss them." Jackson's grasp tightened around her arm. "Dr. Gordon pretends he's an old grump, but I knew the first time I met him that he was a teddy bear. I guess I let him step into that vacant parental role. I don't know what I'll do—"

"Don't go down that path. We've got a lot of options at this point."

She nodded, further composing herself in preparation for their exit from the elevator. "My mother's missed diagnosis and subsequent illness was the reason I went into medicine and pathology."

"I wondered why a beautiful woman like you had chosen that department."

His honest remark helped lighten her burdens for the moment, and she smiled. He thought she was beautiful? "Do you think I'm ghoulish?"

It was his turn to grin, which definitely reached his eyes, and he laughed a little, too. "I can safely say you and that word have never come to mind at the same time."

"Whew." She mock-wiped her brow. "Wouldn't want to make the wrong impression." *Because I really like you.*

They entered the cafeteria and, taking the lead, he grabbed a couple of mugs and filled them with coffee, after verifying with caffeine or not for her. Then he picked up a couple of cookies on a plate, and after he'd signed off on the charge, they went to the doctors' seating in a smaller and quieter room than the regular cafeteria. Leading the way, he chose a table and removed the items from the tray then waited for her to sit before he did. Yeah, a take-charge gentleman all the way.

"You feel like talking more about what tore you up back there?" He got right to the point.

She inhaled, poured some cream into her coffee and thought about whether or not she wanted to revisit those old sad feelings about her parents any more, and decided not to. "I'm good. Just worried about Dr. Gordon."

He reached across the table and squeezed her hand. "I understand."

She hoped her gratitude showed when their gazes met. From his reassuring nod she figured it did. She accepted a peanut-butter cookie and took a bite. "Mmm, this is really good."

He picked his up and dipped it in his black coffee before taking a man-sized bite. His brows lifted in agreement. "So," he said after he'd swallowed, "since we're going to change the subject, I have an observation. I'm thinking you might be dating someone?"

Her chin pulled in. "Why would you think that?" Hadn't they been making out in her office earlier?

"You put a quick stop to our..." He let her finish the sentence in her mind, rather than spell it out.

She lifted her gaze and nailed his, which was, not surprisingly, looking expectant. He was definitely interested in her, which caused thoughts to flood her mind. She'd gone through a long, tough day already, and it wasn't even two o'clock. She'd once again seen firsthand how things people took for granted, like their health, could change at any given moment. It made her think how much more out of life she longed for. Shouldn't she grab some of what it had to offer, especially when it, or rather, he, was sitting right across from her, dunking his cookie like it was the best thing on earth? Instead of day in and day out spending most of her time with the biggest relationship in her life, her microscope?

But would Jackson want her as she was? Admittedly, she'd always been proud of her figure, never flaunting herself too much but not afraid to show some cleavage if the occasion and the dress called for it. Now every day when she showered she saw her flat chest, the scars. There wasn't anything sexy about that. Yet she was a woman, lived, breathed and felt like a woman, but one who strapped on her chest the symbols of the fairer sex every day before she came to work. Pretending she was still who she'd used to be.

The decision had seemed so clear when she'd made it. Get rid of the tissue, the ticking time bomb on her chest. Never put herself in a position to hear the words that had devastated her mother's life. *You have breast cancer.*

Because of lab tests and markers, she'd thought like a scientist, but now she had to deal with the feelings of a woman who was no longer comfortable in her body.

Then there was tall, masculine and sexy-as-hell Jackson sitting directly across from her, smiling like he had a secret.

She bet his secret was nowhere as big as hers. "You took me by surprise earlier."

"I took myself by surprise."

She liked knowing that the kiss had been totally spontaneous. "So, since you asked, I'm not seeing anyone. Today's just been hard. That's why I—"

"I understand." His beeper went off. He checked it. "Let me know when you're leaving later and after we pop in on Jim again I'll walk you to your car."

It wasn't a question. She liked that about him, too. "Okay."

Except later, when Jackson walked her to her car, after visiting the hospital and finding Dr. Gordon deeply asleep and looking like he floated on air, Jackson reverted to perfect-gentleman mode. No arm around her shoulder or hand-holding as they walked. Whatever magic they'd conjured earlier had worn off. He simply smiled and wished her good night, told her to get some rest, more fatherly than future boyfriend material, and disappointingly kept a buffer zone between them as she got into her car.

As she drove off, checking her rearview mirror and seeing him watch her leave, his suit jacket on a fingertip and hanging over his shoulder, looking really sexy, she wondered if he'd had time to come to his senses, too. Something—was it her?—held him back. Then, since she knew her secret backward and forward, and how it kept her from grabbing at the good stuff in life, she further wondered what his secret was.

CHAPTER THREE

JACKSON TOSSED HIS keys onto the entry table in his West-lake condo, thinking a beer would taste great about now, but knowing he'd given up using booze as an escape. It had cost what had been left of his marriage to get the point across.

A long and destructive battle with PTSD had led to him falling apart and quitting his position as lead surgeon at Savannah General Hospital just before they'd planned to fire him three years ago. The ongoing post-traumatic stress disorder had turned him into a stranger and strained his relationship with his teenage sons, frightening them away. It had also ensured his wife of twenty years had finally filed for divorce.

He'd lost his right lower leg in an IED accident in Afghanistan. It had been his second tour as an army reservist. He'd volunteered for it, and for that his wife had been unable to forgive him. She'd deemed it his fault that the improvised explosive device had caused him to lose his leg. He'd returned home physically and emotionally wounded, and, piled onto their already strained marriage from years of him choosing his high-maintenance education and career over nurturing their life together, she couldn't take it.

His fault.

Their marriage had been unraveling little by little for years anyway. High-school sweethearts, she'd then followed him on to college. His grandfather used to tease him that she was majoring in marriage. Then they'd accidentally got pregnant the summer before he'd entered medical school. With their respective families being good friends, there was no way he could have let her go through the pregnancy alone. So he'd done the honorable thing and they'd got married right before he'd entered medical school.

It hadn't been long before they'd realized they may have made a mistake, but his studies had kept him too busy to address it, and the new baby, Andrew, had taken all of her time, and, well, they'd learned how to coexist as a small family of three. In his third year of medical school she'd got pregnant again. This time he'd got angry with her for letting it happen when he'd found out she'd stopped taking birth control pills. Evaline had said she wanted kids because he was never around. And so it had gone on.

Then at the age of twenty-seven and in the second year of his surgical residency, he'd signed up for the army reserves. One weekend a month he'd trained in an army field medical unit, setting up mobile triage, learning to care for mass casualties. When he'd finished his surgical residency and had been asked to stay on at Savannah General, his wife had thought maybe things would get better. But he'd started signing on with his reserve unit for two-week humanitarian missions for victims of natural disasters at home in the States. Soon he'd branched out to other countries, and when he'd been deployed to Iraq, Evaline had threatened to leave him.

He'd made it home six weeks later in one piece, his eyes opened to the need of fellow US soldiers deployed in the Middle East, and also finally accepting the trouble his marriage was in. They sought out marriage counseling and he'd focused on working his way up the career ladder at Savannah General, and things had seemed to get better between them. He'd stayed on in the army reserves doing his one weekend a month, catching hell from Evaline if it fell on either of his sons' sports team events, but he hadn't been able to pick and choose his times of service. They'd limped on, keeping a united front for their boys and their families, while the fabric of their love had worn thinner and thinner.

Then, after a brutal series of attacks on US military personnel, they'd needed army reserve doctors and he'd volunteered to be deployed to Afghanistan. He had been one week short of going home when the IED had changed everything.

His fault?

He'd come home, had hit rock bottom after that, then eventually had got help from the veterans hospital, and had spent the next year accepting he'd never be the man he'd once been and cleaning up his act. He'd been honorably discharged from the army, too. But the damage to Evaline and his sons and his reputation as a surgeon had already been done. She'd filed for divorce.

As time had passed his PTSD had settled down and he'd felt confident enough to go back to work. That was when he'd figured there wasn't anything for him back home in Georgia anymore. His wife had divorced him. His oldest son had wanted nothing to do with him. So since his youngest son would be attending Pepperdine University in Malibu, California, he'd sought employment in the area, hoping to at least mend that relationship. St. Francis of the Valley Hospital had been willing to give him a chance as a staff surgeon. With less responsibility, not being the head of a department but just a staff guy for a change, not having to deal with his ex-wife and her ongoing complaints anymore and enjoying the eternal spring weather of Southern California, his stress level had reached a new low.

Until today, when he'd had to tell his friend Jim Gordon some pretty rotten news—that he had metastatic cancer—and they both knew there'd be one hell of a battle ahead. Then, in a moment of weakness, seeing the distress Charlotte Johnson had been in, he'd let his gut take over and he'd moved in to comfort her. But it hadn't worked out that way, because he'd played with fire. He knew he'd thought about her far, far differently than any other colleague. That he'd been drawn into her dark and alluring beauty while sitting across from her, looking at patient slides, for the last year. Come to think of it, could he have been any slower? How long had he had a thing for her anyway? At least three-quarters of the last year, that was how long.

Could he blame himself for kissing her when she'd fit into his arms so perfectly, and she'd shown no signs of resisting him? Still, it had been completely improper and couldn't happen again because he wasn't ready to have one more woman reject him because his lower leg had been replaced with a high-tech prosthetic. Maybe it wasn't sexy, but it sure worked great, and he'd been running five miles a day to prove it for the last two years. In fact, he'd never been in better condition.

Ah, but Charlotte, she stirred forgotten feelings, that special lure of a woman that made him want to feel alive again. Something about her mix of confidence on the job and total insecurity in a social setting made him hope what they had in common might be enough to base a new relationship on. When he'd kissed her, because of her response, he'd got his hopes up that maybe she felt the same way. But she'd stopped the kiss and an invisible barrier had seemed to surround her after that. He'd pretended everything had been fine when he'd walked her to her car—he hadn't noticed her need to be left alone—but the message had got through to him. Loud and clear.

He wandered into his galley kitchen and searched the refrigerator, hoping there might be something halfway interesting in the way of leftovers. He grabbed a bottle of sparkling water and guzzled some of it, enjoying the fizzy burn in his throat. Today he'd kissed the woman who held his interest more than any other since his high-school sweetheart. That was the good news. The bad news was he knew he couldn't do anything further about it. Her invisible force field wouldn't let him through, and if that wasn't enough, his boatload of baggage held him back.

Out of curiosity, though, he did have one little— okay, monumental—test for Charlotte, one that would really determine her mettle before he totally gave up.

Saturday was the annual charity fund-raiser five- and ten-kilometer run for St. Francis of the Valley trauma unit. Charlotte had signed up a while back and had forgotten to train for it, but she showed up anyway in support of the event. What they'd neglected to tell her was that this year they'd added zombies. Someone had got the bright idea to raise more money by getting employees to pay professional makeup artists, who'd donated their time for the event, to be made up as the undead. The sole purpose, besides getting their pictures taken, was to chase down the runners and tag them with washable paint, and hopefully improve some personal best times for some participants in the process.

Being a good sport, Charlotte ran with the five-kilometer crowd, squealing and screaming whenever zombies crawled out of bushes or from behind nearby trees, heading straight for her. She checked her sports watch. Out of fright she had cut her running time—well, the last time she'd run, which had been a month ago—by a couple of minutes at the halfway point. Impressive. Go zombies!

Running always made her think, and today was no different. Since Monday, with Dr. Gordon's surgery and the amazing kiss from Jackson, the man had been missing in action. He hadn't even shown up for their usual Friday afternoon slide show. Had the fact that she'd stopped him from kissing her the way he'd wanted been the reason? Or was her hunch right about him having his own reasons for keeping distance between them? She didn't have a clue, but one thing was certain—she missed him even though she felt safer when he wasn't around. Talk about being mixed up.

Oh, man, here came another small cluster of zombies, heading right for her and the group of three runners in front of her. The rules said that if a zombie left a red mark on you, you had to subtract thirty seconds from your final time. Even though she knew they weren't real, they still freaked her out. She shot into sprint mode and caught those runners up ahead, nestling herself in the middle of them as protection. She had no pride when it came to fear. They all screamed and swerved together as the slow-moving zombies up ahead got closer. They fanned out to avoid their zombie touch, especially if they carried red spray paint. She darted around another zombie, leaving the group of nurses behind and winding up running solo again, checking every bush and tree ahead for any surprises.

Soon things calmed down, so she slowed her pace and relaxed, enjoying the early morning sunshine and mild temperature. If she kept up like this she'd actually have a shot at finishing the run.

Already having finished his ten-kilometer race and finishing in the top twenty, Jackson had doubled back, deciding to run the five-kilometer route, too. He wasn't kidding himself. He knew that doing the shorter run as well had everything to do with searching for Charlotte, because he'd heard through Dr. Gordon she'd signed up to run.

Up in the distance he saw a woman with long legs and rounded hips, wearing tight running gear, with a high ponytail swishing back and forth with each stride. Her lovely light olive-colored legs and arms helped make the call that, yes, it was undeniably Charlotte. She wasn't what he'd call a sporty type, but was fit for sure, though with full-figure curves, and in his mind she looked fantastic. Man, he'd missed her this week and really liked spying on her now.

He picked up his pace, realizing there was no hiding his big secret since he was wearing jogging shorts. He'd noticed the looks all morning from hospital employees as he'd sprinted by with his carbon graphite transtibial prosthetic, including a flex foot that looked suspiciously like the tip of a snow ski. Their interest in his running blade didn't bother him, he'd had to get used to it over the past couple of years, but that little yet monumental test he was about to give Charlotte—finally finding out what she'd think of his prosthetic and below-the-knee amputation—made his stomach tighten.

He hoped she wouldn't be like the only two women he'd dated since moving out West, neither of whom had been able to get past his missing leg. He'd once played the pity-me game and had lost his marriage and family, and since then had promised himself to never let it affect him again. So why was he so nervous now, jogging up behind Charlotte?

Well, here goes nothing. He lunged forward and reached out then grabbed her shoulder.

A hand grabbed Charlotte's shoulder. She screamed and nearly jumped out of her highly padded sports bra. Being so close to the finish line, would she be disqualified by a fake zombie bite?

With her heart nearly exploding in her chest, she turned to see how ugly the zombie who'd taken her out was. Instead she found a face that managed to take what was left of her breath away. It was Jackson's, and she wanted to throttle him!

"You nearly gave me a heart attack," she squeaked, soon forgiving him when she noticed those broad shoulders and the fit physique beneath the tight T-shirt, and how handsome he looked in the early morning sunshine, his hair damp and curling around his face from his workout. She smiled.

"Sorry, couldn't resist it." He slowed down his pace to stay with her.

"Well, I'm amazed I've made it this far without being attacked."

"I'll protect you."

Oh, how those amazingly masculine words put new spring in her step. She couldn't resist and took a quick glance at his shorts and those strong athletic legs. And, holy cow, the man had a prosthetic limb! And he ran like an Olympic athlete, with smooth, even strides and barely any effort at all, not out of breath in the least. He looked like a wounded warrior running on that shiny high-tech blade.

Her mind worked at laser speed. He usually came to her office wearing scrubs or street clothes. Once or twice she'd noticed his masculine arms, muscles that'd come from weights at the gym, but she'd never had the opportunity to see his amazing abdomen and those runner's muscled legs. Had she mentioned, holy cow, that he had a below-the-knee amputation on the right?

That explained his slightly unusual gait.

So her crush for the better part of a year had been on a man who had more in common with her than she could have ever dreamed! They were both missing something. The next question was, why had he grabbed her just now, obviously slowing down his pace to run with her?

It had to be because he liked her, too. Hadn't he proved it Monday afternoon when they'd hugged and kissed? The fact that he'd stayed far away from her and her department ever since, so very unlike him, had made her think differently and had proved he had reservations about starting a relationship. Welcome to the club, buddy. At least now she understood why and it didn't hurt so much that he'd been avoiding her. But it scared her, and not in a zombie-chasing way but much deeper. Because it was as plain as the sun right there in the sky making her squint. This. Was. A. Test.

She took another glance at his leg, more blatant this time, keeping her expression blasé, and making sure he noticed. Then she acted like there was absolutely nothing unusual about him.

He gave her a relaxed smile. She noted relief in his gaze, letting on how much he appreciated her casual acceptance of his amputation. Yeah, her mind was spinning out of control in record time with thoughts and deductions, but she couldn't help it. This was such a surprise. And it leveled the playing field, which sent a shiver across her skin, warm and damp from running almost five kilometers.

"So now you know," he said matter-of-factly, sounding like it was a challenge.

Think fast for the perfect answer, because if there was ever a time for the right words, it was now. She tried not to remember how cutting Derek's words had been to her the first time he'd seen her chest. *That's pretty extreme, Charl, and to think it wasn't even necessary.* Who was she kidding? It wasn't just what he'd said but the shocked, nearly horrified and unaccepting expression that had accompanied it. Pain radiated through her chest as all these thoughts and memories flashed past in less than a second. Think fast! *He's waiting for a response to his comment.* "That you're not perfect? I think I already knew that, Doctor, the day you said you didn't like my all-time-favorite chocolate bars."

He laughed, and she felt good about dismantling the bomb he'd expected to leave her with.

Then, like the fact he was missing part of a leg meant nothing, they forgot about it and ran on, Jackson prodding her along and scooping her away from another zombie attack as they closed in on the last half-kilometer mark. For someone who hadn't trained, she'd make sure to finish this race if it killed her, rather than let her new running partner down.

"I take it you run a lot," she said, having to gasp the words since she was so out of breath.

"It's the best stress reliever I know."

"Hey, Dr. Hilstead, isn't this your second time

around?" one of the OR techs called from the crowd on the sidelines as they approached the finish line.

"I'm helping my friend be safe from the zombies," he shouted back.

"Wait, so you've already finished this race?"

"I ran the ten kilometers." He looked straight ahead, rather than rub it in with a self-satisfied look.

Yeah, I run five in my sleep. She mocked how she figured what his smug thoughts were about now, though using the last of her quickly disappearing breath. Now she'd have to finish this race even if she had to crawl over the line, just to save face.

He laughed again, and she was happy a guy who'd taken a big chance and shown the entire hospital his secret was in such a good mood. She hoped she'd had something to do with it, too, because she wanted to think the biggest risk he'd taken had been with her re-action. That would make her special, and she'd passed with flying colors. She hoped so anyway. Was she special?

"Got any steam left?" he asked. "Let's finish strong."

She understood the "let's" meant "her" and he wanted her to kick it up for the next several meters. Typical guy. Show him a finish line and he'd have to make a run for it.

She nodded, lying, and pushed into a sprint, well, her version of a sprint anyway—no hint of form, arms nearly flailing and her feet kicking up in a girlie run way behind her. But in her world she finished strong, simply because she finished!

He grinned and grabbed her shoulder again, this time not scaring the life out of her but guiding her to the SAG station for water and a banana. Her knees were wobbly, she gulped for air, and her pulse tore through her chest, but other than that she felt great.

"Good job, Dr. Johnson!" several of the hospital volunteers said in unison.

She wasn't able to speak just yet, so she smiled and sipped some water to prove she was still alive. Jackson stood there grinning at her, his chest hardly moving, only a sheen of exertion on his skin. She, on the other hand, was sweating big fat drops, her sports bra with the "natural-looking" silicone padding nearly sliding out of place. He nabbed a towel from the volunteers' table and put it around her neck.

"Thanks." She could finally talk.

"You did great."

"You made me."

"Then I'm glad I found you."

Oh, the things she could imagine with that statement. *I'm glad I found you.* Wait, he'd been looking for her? Further proof he might be interested, and now that she'd passed the test, why not go for it? She'd finished the run, was now high on endorphins, or was it light-headedness from low blood oxygen? Who cared? She felt good right now, and she could talk again, so she decided to go for it. "Hey, you want to have dinner with me later?"

After all they'd been through together for the last few minutes—his surprise test, her passing it, his forcing her to excel at a sport she could honestly live without, her probably setting a new "slowest five-kilometer" world record, him acting proud of her anyway, and probably for many reasons—he hesitated.

Every part of his facial expression put on the brakes, and it took her aback. So she thought fast and covered. "I've got an autopsy to do later this afternoon, and I thought if you weren't doing anything around five, you might join me in the cafeteria for a quick and easy dinner? Nothing special or anything. No big deal." Had that sounded professional enough? It was nothing like a *dat*e date, just dinner with a running buddy who'd shown her his BKA for the first time today.

Jackson's mind wandered in a half-dozen different directions. Why was a great and attractive girl like Charlotte spending Saturday afternoons doing autopsies and offering last-minute dinner invitations? Hell, yeah, he wanted to spend time with her, but tonight was a rescheduling of his usual Friday night dinner and a movie with his son. He couldn't back out from that, they still had too much to work through, and things continued to be strained. But they were making progress. His son attending Pepperdine had been his main motive for moving to California in the first place. What was left of his family had to come first.

Reality clicked in. Tonight wasn't the night. His fascination with the lovely pathologist, who now knew about his leg, would have to wait.

"Can I take a rain check on that invitation?"

James, the near-to-retirement morgue attendant, was ready and waiting after Charlotte had showered and changed into scrubs. By the time she'd donned the gown, shoe covers, face mask and clear plastic face shield, plus two pairs of gloves, he'd already weighed the body and placed it on the stainless-steel gurney-style table, complete with irrigation sink and drainage trough. A large surgical table was nearby with the tools of her trade—bone saw, rib cutter, hammer with hook, scalpel, toothed forceps, scissors, Stryker saw and more.

A family had requested an autopsy on their loved

one, a twenty-five-year-old man, who'd arrived in the hospital three days earlier with signs of a bacterial infection. The hospital had agreed to the postmortem examination to identify any previously undiagnosed condition that may have contributed to his death, and to pin down what bacterium had suddenly run rampant throughout his system.

As a clinical pathologist, not to be confused with forensics like people saw on TV dramas just about every night of the week, her job was to see for herself what may or may not have caused his death. Knowing that up to a quarter of performed autopsies revealed a major surprise other than the notated cause of death, over the next two to four hours she'd systematically examine the outside and inside of this young man's body to get to the best and most logical diagnosis.

James, her diener, stood by ready to assist with each aspect of the autopsy. Turning on her Dictaphone, Charlotte described what she saw externally. Then she used a scalpel to make a Y-shaped incision. Before her afternoon was done she'd weigh and measure every major organ, take systematic biopsies and place them in preservation solution. She'd also collect blood and fluid for laboratory specimens, snap pictures and preserve the brain in fixative for future dissection. She wondered what the zombies would think of her now.

James labeled as they went along and would, after the autopsy, submit all specimens to the histology lab for Monday, when they resumed their work week. Once the autopsy was complete, James would wash the body and make it ready for the funeral home.

Though the family might want and expect immediate results, like they'd come to expect on those infamous TV dramas, it might be an entire month before she'd have the final report completed. Autopsies needed and deserved the extra time to make the right diagnoses.

Her beeper went off. Ah, damn, it was Dr. Dupree. Since he'd called on her official hospital beeper, she answered.

"I need a favor," he said, before she could even say hello.

She'd grown to expect the worst whenever Antwan said he needed anything. "Yes?"

"They told me you're on call, and I just got an okay from a family for an autopsy. Can you do it for me tonight?"

"Tonight? Why the rush?"

"The family gave me twenty-four hours until they send their daughter to the mortuary. I need this favor, please."

She wasn't used to hearing sincerity in his voice. "When did the patient die?"

"Just now. I operated on her two weeks ago. Removed her appendix. Everything went great. Two days ago she was readmitted for loss of consciousness at home. Medicine was doing a work-up on her. She seemed to be fine. Then a nurse found her unresponsive in the hospital bed. She was already dead."

"Okay. Send her to the morgue. I'll tell James about the add-on."

"Thank you. I owe you a special dinner out."

"No, you don't. This is my job." Why was it that every time she spoke to Dr. Dupree her hackles rose? Because he was such a player, hitting on every woman in a skirt or hospital scrubs. But just now he'd shown a new side, genuine caring for a young patient who'd died of mysterious causes that may or may not have had something to do with the recent surgery. He was either being extra thorough or covering his backside… CYA, as the saying went.

For the sake of the family and the concerned doctor, Charlotte would do her usual thorough examination, and if she got lucky tonight, she might solve an unfortunate mystery.

Four hours later, having completed the long and complicated second autopsy, with strong suspicions that the young female patient had most likely died from an undetected brain aneurysm, she opted to shower in the doctors' lounge. It was nearly ten by the time she was dressed and ready to go home, but she decided to make a quick stop at her office first to call Security.

The elevator dinged as she unlocked the door to the pathology department, which was a few doors down from the morgue. She glanced over her shoulder in case it was Security, in which case it would save her a call, but out came Jackson. Though tired from a long day, her mood immediately lifted.

"Hi," he said, looking as surprised as she was. "I took a chance and got lucky."

"Hi, yourself. What are you doing here?" She unlocked the door and opened it. He followed her inside.

"I realized I didn't have your personal cell-phone number, and thought I'd see if you were still around so I could get it."

He'd come back to the hospital at…she glanced at her watch…ten-fifteen p.m., hoping to run into her? Sure, she was happy the man was pursuing her, but it also made her wonder about his dinner date. She gave him her number and watched as he entered it into his cell phone. Then he insisted she take his. A good sign.

"How'd the autopsy go?"

"I wound up doing two."

"No kidding. You must be beat."

"Yeah, it's been a long day, starting with getting chased by zombies and ending with, well, you know." Out of respect for the dead she always recalled the Latin phrase—*Hic locus est ubi mors gaudet succurrere vitae. This is the place where death rejoices to help those who live.* It was her way of reframing the tough job she did as a pathologist, especially when both of the autopsies she'd performed tonight had been on young people, which always seemed wrong.

His hand came to her shoulder and lightly massaged. "Yeah, I know. It must be hard."

"No harder than what you do in surgery." She turned and looked up at him. Though he stood behind her, she got the distinct impression he might like to kiss her again, and admittedly, with that warm hand caressing her tight shoulder muscle, the thought appealed.

But he didn't. "You've got a point. Why don't I stick around while you do whatever you've got to do? Then I'll walk you to your car."

The rule at St. Francis Hospital was for every female employee—or any employee who preferred to be escorted, for that matter—to call Security after dark for the walk to the parking lot. Charlotte had used the service many times. In fact, it was the sole reason she'd come back to her office, to make the call and wait until a security guard arrived. Now she wouldn't have to.

"Thanks for saving me a call to Security. It usually takes twenty minutes for anyone to show up, so I was going to look at a few slides while I waited."

"I'll stick around if you still want to check those slides."

"To be honest, I'd really like to get home."

"Let's go, then."

As they walked, Charlotte couldn't let her question remain silent. "So how'd your evening go?"

"It was good. I had dinner with my youngest son, Evan—or Ev, as he prefers to be called these days."

Relieved that his mysterious dinner date had been with his son, she smiled. "You get together often?"

"Yeah, usually on Friday nights, but he had other plans last night."

So that was who he rushed off to every Friday afternoon. Her spirits kept lifting with each tidbit of information Jackson dropped. "That's great." And she really meant it.

He grimaced. "Well, we've got a lot to work out. The divorce was hard on both my sons but particularly on Evan. I've got to rebuild his trust, and we're getting there little by little."

She admired how much Jackson's family meant to him. It put him in a good light—a man who loved his family. The more she learned about him the more she liked, and the fact he had a BKA had zero impact on his appeal. If only she could trust that her situation would be as easily dealt with by him as his was for her. Unfortunately, her experience with Derek had set her up to expect the worst.

Sooner than she expected, because they always found conversation easy, he delivered her to the car.

"So thanks, and good night, then," she said, and as she unlocked the door and prepared to slide behind the wheel, he pecked her on the cheek. It surprised her, but in a good way, though she'd kind of wished for more and sooner than now.

"So I'll call you later, okay?"

"Sure." She grinned, enjoying being pursued by a man she was definitely attracted to. Maybe that was why the second part of her thought slipped out. "I'd really like that."

From the look on his face, he really liked that, too. Good!

Once inside her car, as she placed the seat belt over her shoulder and across her chest, her elation ebbed a bit. What was she thinking, acting like she was just a regular woman living a regular life, hoping to have a regular relationship with a new guy? That was ancient history for her—love, marriage, a career and family— a dream she could never achieve now.

Mindlessly, her hand brushed over her silicone pads. She was anything but regular.

But forty-five minutes later, when Charlotte was home and in her pajamas, Jackson didn't waste any time before using his newly acquired phone number. He said he'd called just to make sure she'd got home okay and to bid her good night again. She went to bed wearing a smile and thinking of his handsome face. Maybe taking a risk on a man like Jackson made perfect sense. Who could possibly be better than a guy with a BKA to understand her sense of feeling incomplete?

CHAPTER FOUR

MONDAY MORNING, CHARLOTTE visited Dr. Gordon, who was still in the hospital. He was undergoing aggressive chemotherapy and the oncological team decided it would be best for him to be monitored round the clock for the first couple of doses.

She put on her optimistic face, hoping her mentor didn't see right through her, since she secretly worried the therapy might be too little too late. Surprisingly, Dr. Gordon seemed in good spirits, and though the chemo had to be tough on him, he didn't complain.

Already Charlotte could see his hair and white caterpillar fuzzy brows thinning, the shine in his always inquisitive hazel eyes dulled. Memories of her mother losing her beautiful light brown hair nearly broke her heart, and how toward the end a raging fever had changed her mother's eyes to a glassy stare. At moments like these, the harsh reminders, she was glad she'd had the radical surgery to ensure she'd never have to go through what her mother had. Deep down she also knew there was no guarantee against cancer.

Charlotte fluffed Dr. Gordon's pillow, assuring him his department hadn't yet gone to hell in a handbasket, to use one of his favorite phrases, thanks to a few other pathologists pitching in along with her to cover for him. She gently replaced the pillow behind his head.

"I would expect no less, Charlotte," he said gratefully. "I only mentor the best and brightest."

His confidence in her skills had always amazed her, and right now a warm sense of fondness expanded to the limits of her chest as she made sure his call light was within reach and the pitcher of ice water was nearby. "Thank you," she said, fighting back the tears that always threatened whenever she was around him these days.

"No." He inhaled, as if continuing to talk would soon be a burden. "Thank you." He gave a frail squeeze of her hand and she leaned forward and kissed his forehead.

"Don't tell anyone I did that."

He winked. "It'll be our secret."

She smiled and quickly left because her vision was blurring and she didn't want Dr. Gordon to see her cry. No sooner had she stepped outside his room than her cell phone vibrated. It was Jackson. She headed for the elevator and answered.

"Have dinner with me," he said the instant after she answered. "We'll call it our rain check. I've found a great place in Westlake and it's no fun to eat out by myself."

Well, it wasn't exactly the most romantic offer for a date, but she liked it that he'd thought of her. "Tonight?"

"Got plans?"

"I've got extra work to clear out, what with Dr. Gordon being off, and—"

"Tomorrow night, then. We'll take a rain check on our rain check."

It only took a second to make her decision. "That should work. Sure, I'd love to."

"Great! I'll need your address."

The guy clearly wasn't big on chitchat. Did she want him coming to her town house in Thousand Oaks to pick her up? If he was any other first date, or someone like Antwan, she'd insist on meeting somewhere. On second thought, she'd never consent to meeting Dr. Dupree anywhere! But this was Jackson Hilstead the Third, her secret crush, the one guy in the hospital who might possibly understand her fragile body image, because he'd fought the same demons. "What time?" she asked, after giving him her street address.

"Seven."

"That'll work."

She hung up, grinning, her mind whirring. She had a little over twenty-four hours to clear her desk, clean up her house and find something sexy but not too revealing to wear. She hadn't been this excited about going out with a man in a long time.

Now, if she could just ignore that insecure whisper, *He won't accept you as you are*, starting up in her mind and concentrate on enjoying herself on their first date. Her first date in...she couldn't remember when.

Jackson finished his Tuesday afternoon surgery early and made hospital rounds on his patients, updating the doctor's orders on some and discharging a few others. Feeling a long-forgotten ball of excitement winding up inside over the thought of dinner with Charlotte, he grinned all the way to his car. He'd take a long run as soon as he got home to work off the edge. He hadn't looked forward to getting to know a woman like this in a long time.

He'd dated a couple of different women over the last year in California when he'd been feeling lonely and had needed a woman's company. His self-image had taken a serious hit when he'd lost part of his leg. But then, he hadn't expected to get a divorce at the time either. And when it had become obvious that his two dates hadn't been ready for an imperfect guy, he'd stopped looking around, because the rejections only a few months apart and the subsequent effect on his ego had turned out to be major. He'd been in the prime of his life and the thought of being alone from here on out had sometimes been too depressing to consider. So he'd pushed his feelings down and had gone about his days working hard and trying to put things right with his sons.

And he'd hated to admit it wasn't enough. Enter Charlotte.

He'd always taken solace in the safe haven of Dr. Charlotte Johnson's office. Reading slides with her had turned into his one indulgence with the opposite sex in the last year. He liked sitting close enough to notice whatever new perfume she chose to wear, and to catch the fire in her rich caramel-brown eyes whenever she found something interesting on one of his patients' slides to share with him. He liked it that she didn't lead with her sex, like so many other women around the hospital. They had it and they flaunted it, and it often made his basic urges get all fired up, which sometimes made it hard to concentrate.

Did a man ever grow out of that? He was forty-two, so apparently not.

But Charlotte was different. She had a fuller figure than many of the women at St. Francis Hospital, which he preferred to a woman being too thin, and though she dressed in a very feminine way, she was careful not to show too much skin. That made her interesting, and alluring in a far less blatant way than the others.

Call it intriguing. But what appealed to him most of all was her no-nonsense personality. She clearly had her head on straight, and after the long, slow decline and eventual implosion of his marriage, when his wife had seemed to become his worst nightmare—granted, he'd turned into a nightmare of his former self, too—that was a welcome change. With a woman like Charlotte, maybe he could learn to trust again.

Was that asking too much?

Even the thought sent a shiver down his spine. Could he survive another rejection? Sure, she'd seen his leg and had acted as though she couldn't care less, and she'd accepted his dinner invitation, another good sign. But she was a nice woman who happened to be a pathologist and who'd probably seen it all in her job. Of course she wouldn't have let on if she'd felt disgust. He knew that much about her.

A memory of his wife finally telling him how much he repulsed her, even when he'd already known it, made his stomach burn.

He needed to make sure this date wasn't taken out of context. Yes, he wanted to get to know Charlotte more, see where it might lead, but there wasn't anything he could offer beyond that. He wasn't ready for anything else. Small steps. His policy was always honesty, so tonight he planned to put his cards on the table and see what she thought.

Keep things safe. Keep her at a distance. Protect himself.

He had to, otherwise he couldn't go through with the date.

Jackson picked up Charlotte at seven on the dot, fighting a swarm of jitters in his gut. Hell, he hadn't felt this nervous about a date since his high-school prom—and he'd taken his ex-wife as his date to that! *Man up, Hilstead. It's just dinner out. With a lady you can't seem to get out of your thoughts.*

He forced his best smile, even though he'd only made it to the security call box.

Once she let him through, he strode the rest of the way to her town house, wondering if he'd made a mistake in asking her out. Maybe it was still too soon to get back in the game. Damn the nerves—how was he supposed to eat with his stomach all tied up?

Then Charlotte opened the door and blew him away. She'd worn her hair down, which always messed with his head. It waved and tumbled to her shoulders, framing her face and highlighting her warm and inviting eyes. Plus she'd dressed to kill in a cream crocheted lace dress with a modest neckline and cap sleeves. Her light olive-toned skin blended well with the choice. The only color in her outfit was from her rainbow-dyed strapped wedge sandals and bright red and orange dangly earrings. As it was early summer, she'd fit right in for the restaurant he'd chosen.

She smiled and let him in and he pretended he wasn't the least bit anxious about this date. He just hoped she didn't catch on.

Her earth-toned, stucco-covered townhome was built into the side of a hill along with dozens of others. The place had a nice view of the Conejo Valley sprawl, and he was impressed with her taste in decor. No overstuffed and patterned couches or chairs, her taste was modern, clean and almost masculine. Several canvases covered in bright colors highlighted a few walls, and he recognized the style as similar to many he'd seen in the hospital foyer after it had been newly remodeled. He vaguely remembered hearing that one of the employees had painted them, and these looked very similar in style. Seeing the paintings on Charlotte's walls, adding vibrancy to her otherwise beige palate, he wholeheartedly agreed with her choices.

But what he noticed most of all, and constantly since stepping into her house, was her, and how fantastic she looked.

She'd grabbed her purse and was ready to leave, so he quit staring at the view from her living room—because the alternative was to keep staring at her, which he really wanted to do, but he didn't want to creep her out—then followed her out the door. He'd better think up some conversation or he'd be a total dud tonight. What was his plan? Oh, yeah, lay his cards on the table. Take control of the situation from the get-go. He could do it.

"Ever hear of a place called Boccaccio's?" he asked as they walked to his car in the building's lot.

"In Westlake? Yes. Wow, it's supposed to be really nice. Are you trying to impress me?"

"I should be asking the same question, seeing how great you look." She blushed and he not only liked how she looked, but the power her true response gave him. He could do this, have a date. "But don't get too impressed. Yes, the restaurant is right on a small lake and, yes, the view is great, but it's just a man-made lake in an otherwise landlocked city."

"Still sounds wonderful to me. I'll just pretend it's real. Can we sit outside?"

"I was planning on it."

She was tall and fit well next to his six feet two inches as they walked to his white sedan. So many things about her appealed to him, but he had to stand firm, let her know what he was and wasn't open to.

Keep that arm's length between them, though after seeing her all decked out tonight, the thought was becoming less appealing. After they'd uncorked a bottle of wine and shared a meal together, maybe she'd understand why he needed to do things his way. He hoped so anyway.

Once they'd arrived at the restaurant, having talked about work and Dr. Gordon the entire drive over, his unease had settled down somewhat. As it was a Tuesday night they didn't have long to wait to be seated outside. It was twilight, a gorgeous summer evening, and the small lake was tinted with a peach hue as the sun said good-bye for the day. There really was something special about Californian sunsets. Charlotte was impressed, he could tell by the bright expression on her face, and how she craned her neck to take in the view from every angle, and he thought it was cute. The choice of word struck him as odd for a woman who was so much more than cute, but something in the way she crinkled her nose with delight over her surroundings put it in his head.

"I've heard good things about this place. Now I understand why."

"The food is supposed to be as good as this view." So far his conversation had been stiff as hell. He ordered a bottle of a good sauvignon blanc with her approval, and they set about making their dinner choices. They ordered calamari, light and crispy, for starters to share. Next he ordered a salad and she lobster bisque. For the main, she chose baby salmon piccata, and he went for the Chilean sea bass. Then the waiter left and the sommelier poured their wine.

He sat back and relaxed in the comfortable woven wicker and wrought-iron chair, thought about stretching out his legs but realized he'd bump her with his prosthesis if he did, so he stayed sitting straight up. He glanced across the table at his date, who continued to enjoy the view of the small lake and the early evening lights around the shore.

Charlotte was his date. Wow, that was a new concept. She was pretty and so damn appealing, enough to shake him up all over again. She sipped her wine and he joined her. The sweet smile she offered him afterward warmed his insides far more than the wine. She could be dangerous. He took another drink.

"I should let you know that I haven't wanted to impress a woman this much in a long time." His honesty surprised even him.

She canted her head and gave a self-deprecating simper.

"But I've got to be honest, okay?" Build that wall.

Her intelligent eyes went serious.

"I've already told you I'm divorced, but you should also know it was a really bad one. So the thing is I'm looking for companionship, but I can't promise anything beyond that." *Oh, right, buddy, lay it on* her—*don't dare admit* you're *a coward.*

She didn't seem surprised by his opening statement, though he'd half expected her to be, and honestly, it did seem more like the opening remarks in a court of law rather than dinner with a great woman. "This is just our first date, so I'm on the same page."

Who was he kidding, trying to pull this off? What had happened to honesty? "I'm probably coming off like an ass, but I respect you too much to not be open." He leaned on the table, looked her in the eyes. "I'm not sure I ever want to get into a serious relationship again, not after what I've been through. I don't see myself ever marrying again, and I definitely don't want to be a father again."

She took another drink of her wine. "Hold on a second. Let's not get ahead of ourselves."

He had to laugh. He was jumping way ahead of a first date. "Yeah, I get that, but I think it's better to put it out there right up front." Wouldn't someone like her want the whole package, a career and a family?

"So now there are pre-dating rules, sort of like prenups? I guess I've been out of the loop awhile."

He laughed again, this time at how absurd he must have sounded. What a jerk he was being. Would she want to spend another second with him? He should have left well enough alone and never asked her out. But their kiss and the feelings she'd brought back to life for him had made him pursue her. Yeah, he still wanted that. He had to be honest with himself first.

Luckily the waiter delivered their starter and they spent the next minute or two distracted, sorting out sharing the appetizer. He took a bite and grinned over the taste of calamari done just right, surprised he could eat with the hard knot of nerves in his stomach. At least the food service was going well.

After she'd finished her part of the appetizer, she wiped her mouth and took another sip of wine. "I hear what you're saying, and that you're going out of your way to make sure I understand it. I get it. I know you've been there, done that, and you probably think I think my biological clock is telling me it's time to have babies." She swirled the half glass of wine round and round. "I'm thirty-four after all. So you figure you need to take the stars out of my eyes, not let me get any ideas. But I've also got reasons for not wanting kids. So don't worry about me getting any ideas about a long-term relationship. I'll be honest and say I like your company and I'd like to spend more time with you, but I don't plan to have children or, for that matter, get married either. Deal?"

Surprised she'd just released him from any future involvement, besides feeling relieved by her blunt answer, he wondered why a young and vibrant woman such as her would have ruled out marriage or having kids. Not with him necessarily, but with anyone. His laying his cards on the table had backfired, planting more questions in his mind than answers. "I wasn't suggesting we'd rush into anything."

"And I definitely don't want to rush into anything before I'm ready either."

If he had any question about what she'd been referring to before, he understood now. She'd like to date but not be intimate. At least, that was what he assumed her message had been. "I can understand that." Had he subconsciously been thinking about being intimate with her? Of course he had, but he'd already figured out he wasn't nearly ready for that. She'd probably read his mind and cut him a break. But, honestly, who in their right mind would want to get involved with him after all he'd just said?

Glancing at her in the evening light, with tiny decorative string lights in the background outlining her head like a sparkly crown, making her look even more beautiful, he wished he was ready to be with a woman again. Her.

"And just in case you're wondering, it has nothing to do with your leg." She interrupted his quickly shifting thoughts, and he was glad of it. She'd brought up his leg, or rather his missing leg, the elephant in the room. Good. "My hesitation comes from my side of things.

For personal reasons. Though I do want to hear how you lost your leg, and anything else you ever feel like talking about." She reached across the table and touched his hand. "I really want us to be friends."

"Friends?"

"Let's see where that leads, okay? No pressure on either side."

He could live with that, if it meant he got to spend more time with Charlotte. "Fair enough."

Salad and soup arrived and Jackson poured another glass of wine for both of them. Since he figured they'd already ironed things out, he relaxed and enjoyed the company of a woman who turned out to be as witty and warm as she was great looking. But he'd already known that, and that was what scared the daylights out of him.

The words from an Adele song popped into Charlotte's head. She'd once played it over and over after Derek had broken her heart. *This man would never let her or any woman close enough to hurt him again.* Jackson was proving to be a true wounded warrior, right to the core. Keep her at a distance. Keep things safe. Take control right from the start. Very military or surgeon-like. And she thought she had a stick up *her* back. Whew. Jackson was hurting hard. She finished the last of her wine—he was driving after all.

But she still liked him, and could totally relate to what he'd suggested. Admittedly, at first when he'd started his spiel she'd thought, *Step away from the walking wounded. This guy is not for you.* But after savoring dinner and getting past the rule book, she'd enjoyed the evening out. He'd even opened up and told her how an IED had blown off his leg while killing two of his medical team and injuring a dozen others in the midst of performing surgery in Afghanistan. Maybe they could be good for each other. Why not give this a try? If he wanted safety and distance, in her current insecure state she was more than down with that.

When they arrived back home and he walked her to the security gate, he surprised her by stealing a kiss. She liked his surprises, and slipped right into the mood. He was a good kisser, and she liked putting her arms around his neck, leaning into him. Really kissing him. Close like this, could he tell her chest was different than real breasts?

Damn. She'd ruined the moment.

She dropped away from their kiss, seeing a hunger in his eyes that, to be honest, frightened her. What happened to safety and distance? His rules.

"Thanks for a great dinner and a lovely evening."

His waning smile was tinted with chagrin. "Thanks for putting up with me."

"I like you, Jackson. You get that, right?"

"I do, and despite the mess I made of things earlier, I'm really glad you do." He dropped his forehead to hers, the intimacy of the act seeming out of the boundaries of his dating playbook. "I like you, too." She didn't pull away, just kept her arms resting on his solid shoulders, gazing at his eyes up close. "You want to catch dinner together at the hospital tomorrow before you go home?"

An odd offer, but…

"Or we could go out for a quick meal."

Had he read her mind?

"I've got surgeries up the wazoo on Thursday, need to buckle down and mentally go over the procedures, get loads of rest, you know the drill."

"That you're a doctor with a busy and demanding life? Yeah, I think I do."

They smiled wide at each other again, standing there forehead to forehead, his hands warm and resting on her hips. "So dinner tomorrow?"

"Yes. I'd like that."

He kissed her once again, a quick parting kiss, but it was enough to send a flutter through her stomach. "Great. See you tomorrow."

As he walked away and she let herself into the building compound, she dealt with the warm and fuzzy feeling in her veins. Somehow, him laying down the rules had freed her. It might be okay to tiptoe into something with him. Who knew what could happen?

Because it turned out that she really liked that wounded warrior, Jackson Ryland Hilstead the Third.

For the next couple of weeks they kept their word and enjoyed each other's company at work and after hours several times, even spending the entirety of the last two Sunday afternoons kicking around together. Who knew running errands could be such fun? But because of what Jackson had proposed with their dating, and what she'd said about not being ready, they didn't sleep together. Never even came close. The amazing thing was, Jackson still wanted to hang out with her.

People at work began to catch on, giving knowing glances or making little comments to Charlotte. "I see you and Jackson are getting along." And "Was that you I saw having lunch with Dr. Hilstead for the third time this week?"

"You want to tell me what's going on?" The last remark came from Antwan Dupree. "Because I'm warning you, Dr. Hilstead is only trying you out for fun. If I were you I'd be careful not to get hurt."

"It's none of your business what I do." Was he for

real? He'd come in here searching for a pathology report and had decided to lecture her on watching out for big bad wolves? He was the only wolf she knew. "Now, which specimen are you looking for a report on?"

He touched her arm, which in her book was a no-no, and she recoiled. "What I'm saying," he went on, unaware of how he'd turned her off already, "is that I'm for real." His cell phone went off and he took the call, having the nerve to carry out a brief conversation with "Baby," probably his current main squeeze, some OR nurse who didn't know any better. "I'll call you later, baby." He hung up, looked all earnestly at Charlotte and smiled.

The amazement on her face had nothing to do with his self-described—in her mind imaginary—charm. Check that. The appalled expression on her face. Did he have a clue about himself? She rolled her eyes in as big and overdone an arc as she could possibly manage to get her point across, in case Dr. Dense hadn't figured it out yet. "Mind your own business."

"I'm looking out for you, Charlotte. I'm just saying the guy's playing you. He'll drop you when he's done. Watch out."

"Your MO doesn't apply to every man, Antwan. Do me a favor and butt out of my personal life. It has nothing to do with you."

She gave him a quick report on the patient he was asking about and sent him on his way. But damn if her private insecurities about her body image hadn't flared up, letting the seed of doubt Antwan had planted about Jackson catch her off guard.

Yes, she did have continuing issues about believing any man would still want her once he discovered the truth. But Jackson seemed as reluctant as she was to take the next step. The truth was that over the last two weeks their make-out sessions had heated up and she wasn't sure how much longer it would be before she ripped off his clothes.

The attraction was definitely there for Jackson, too, if she judged rightly about certain body parts of his that had started becoming obvious in the last couple of kissing marathons. Wow. She longed to touch him, to feel the strength, the heat, but that would be playing with fire.

The man turned her on, often sending her home heated up and unfulfilled. How long could they keep this up?

She thought about him at night in bed, too, often imagining his sturdy body covering hers. Sometimes she'd touch her chest, running her palm across her scars, wondering what he'd think. Sometimes she'd fuel the fire of her imagination and let herself think about how it would be to feel him inside, bucking under him, or on top of him, taking him all in. How would he want to take her?

She was still a woman. Her breasts didn't define her. Her soul made her a woman. Would Jackson be able to get past her missing breasts and feel her soul if they ever made love?

She feared the answer, yet she imagined him panting on top of her; she dreamed about taking his weight and wrapping her legs around his hips so he could plant himself deeper inside.

Oh, yeah, she definitely wanted to rip off the man's clothes.

But the thought of the other half of that "ripping his clothes off" scenario—him seeing her completely naked—always sent her mind into a tailspin.

CHAPTER FIVE

JACKSON GRABBED THE pile of mail from his locked box at the condo building entrance and carried it into his apartment. It had been another long week, but spending a few evenings with Charlotte, plus looking forward to hanging out with her on Sunday afternoon, had made the grueling week completely tolerable. What more could he ask? He had a woman with a pretty face and an intelligent mind to look forward to being with soon. Actually, there was something more he'd like...

He shuffled through the mail, discovering an obvious—by the embossed gold foil envelope—wedding invitation from his cousin Kiefer. Aunt Maggie, his mother's sister, must be out-of-her-head happy. Then he thought of his own mother, who may have lost faith in him, and his mood shifted. He should call her more often.

The wedding was six weeks away in Savannah at Tybee Lighthouse. Hell, how many summers had he spent at the family beach house on Tybee? Too many to recall. Everyone had pretended not to mind the hot, sticky humidity while taking relief in the Atlantic Ocean. Mosquito-infested barbecues. Frantic capture-the-flag games after dark, which had inevitably turned into hide-and-seek scare fests. A smile crossed his lips

again, remembering his younger cousin looking up to
him like he was a god at fourteen. In fact, he sometimes
wondered if Kiefer may have gone into medicine because of him. He sighed. Yeah, he had fallen far from
that "god" title over the last couple of decades.

For one brief moment, a whimsical "what the hell"
thought about going to the wedding and inviting Charlotte to be his guest nearly had him filling out the RSVP.
Then reality forced him to think of the repercussions.
His ex-wife, being a lifelong friend with his extended
family, would most likely be invited. Having to face
Evaline after a year, her still angry and feeling self-
righteous. Facing his parents, Georgina and Jackson,
the man he was named after. What about his still alert
and oriented grandfather Jackson Ryland Hilstead the
First? He'd be there, and so would the rest of his family.

How would it be to see them all again after leaving
on such bad terms a year ago? It would be tough, for
sure. To be honest, he didn't know if he was ready to
handle it yet. Plus he didn't want his personal family
drama to take away from Kiefer and…he glanced at the
invitation to check the other name…Ashley's wedding.

His older son, Andrew, had sided with his mother.
How much poison had she filled Andrew's head with
concerning him? He understood—he hadn't been
around as much as he should have when Andrew had
been young. He'd failed him in that regard. But Andrew
had zero empathy about his father falling apart from
PTSD after his last army medical mission to Afghanistan, instead going along with his mother's opinion,
insisting the loss of his leg had been his own fault for
volunteering to go. Voluntary amputation, were they
serious? The thought still hurt and angered him.

Jackson understood he'd scared people when he'd

lost his grip on what was good and true and solid in life for those several months, but to blame him for losing a limb? He shook his head. At least he was making progress with Evan. Following him to Southern California had been the right move all around.

He set the invitation aside, not willing to say yes or no right away. Maybe he and Evan could make the trip together, and his son might act as Jackson's olive branch. He didn't want to write off all his relatives, but feared they may have already done the same to him.

Not wanting to slip into a funk over a simple wedding invitation, he thought about the gift of Charlotte. He'd practically blown any chance of getting to know her better on their first date, but she'd refused to be scared off by him. Hell, she'd even laid down a few rules of her own. He smiled at the memory. Spending time with a woman he liked and respected on so many levels had done wonders for his mental blues. She knew about his leg and it didn't seem to bother her in the least. Who'd have thought a pathologist would turn out to be warm and caring, not to mention easy on the eye? Now he grinned. She'd call him out in a heartbeat about painting all pathologists with such a broad brush. And that was what he liked about her, too. She didn't take his baloney.

Their make-out sessions had taken kissing to a new degree. Charlotte was responsive in every way, yet he sensed he couldn't cross an unspoken line, and so far he hadn't. As for him, he was definitely hot, bothered and ready for the next step. Sex! But Charlotte had been straight about taking their time the night he'd so brazenly laid out his terms for dating. *Don't dare think about marriage or kids.* As though he thought she'd been chomping at the bit to do just that. Maybe surgeons did have extra-big egos. So far she hadn't given any clear signals of change on the up close and personal level. He sensed something very private held her back, and he, of all people, needed to be understanding about that. But they'd been dating several weeks now and his dreams were growing more erotic by the night. Did taking things slow mean never?

There really was nothing worse than being forty-two, a father of two grown sons, an established surgeon, having a career that for the most part he could be proud of, still being well respected by his peers overall, and horny. Horny as hell.

He headed to the kitchen to grab a soda and digest the current state of his life. Wedding invitation. Possible trip back home. New woman. No sex. Yet. Maybe, if he remained patient, something about that last part might change.

Or was it time for him to take the lead?

Charlotte rushed to the skilled nursing facility where Dr. Gordon had been staying during his continued oncology care. She'd heard he'd be transferred off-site to another, smaller, extended care facility, which meant she wouldn't be able to pop in so easily anymore. They'd kept him far longer than usual in the hospital because the chemo barrage had wiped out his T-cell count, making him a sitting duck for infection and nearly killing him. He was stable now, staff member status granted, and they couldn't justify treating him as an inpatient any longer. She wanted to be there for him during this trying time, since his wife, Elly, had passed away and his son lived out of state.

When she arrived at his bedside, she found him smiling, which surprised her. Word was his treatment hadn't got the results the doctors had hoped for. Surely an intuitive and bright man like James Gordon knew the downward course of his prognosis?

"Hi." She tried her best to sound casual.

His milky eyes brightened at seeing her. "Hi, dear." Dr. Gordon had started calling her "dear" and the honor nearly tore her heart every time she heard it.

"So they're moving you to some swanky 'let's pretend this isn't a hospital' kind of place, I hear."

He chuckled. "Yeah, kind of like that place all the old actors go to die."

She flinched. "Please don't say that."

"Don't get your knickers in a twist, kiddo. I'm just being funny. You know my motto—life isn't about what might happen, it's about what's happening right here and now. Today I move. Personally, I fought with them, told them I can take care of myself. I don't see why I can't go home."

He was getting frailer by the day, and she'd heard he'd had a fall once and had almost fallen a second time but a staff member had caught him. If he were left on his own, he could wind up breaking something and making his situation worse.

"The bastards—pardon my French, but the medical insurance department ticks me off—say twenty-four-hour in-home care costs too much. I know they're lying. Hell, I'd even pay for it. I get I'm a risk to myself." He shrugged his bony shoulders. "So, I go, and I bid thee adieu." He touched his forehead as if lifting a cap.

She shook her head. "No. You can't say good-bye to me. I'm coming to see you at least twice a week."

"My dear Charlotte. The thing for you to know is I'm feeling good, no more fevers, and I continue to have high hopes of beating this blasted cancer. As crazy as it sounds, coming from a pathologist, I've decided to remain optimistic, to let my natural human spirit overtake the practical scientist inside. If they want to extend the treatment and move me to a smaller, cheaper medical facility, fine, I'll go. The only thing I resent is not having any say in the matter."

She wished she could take her mentor home with her—that she could request a leave of absence to care for him—but her job was to keep his department running and that, at least, could give him peace of mind. She held his hand and they sat quietly for a few moments until someone appeared at the door.

It was Jackson, and even now, after all the time they'd spent together, the sight of him made her pulse do a loop-de-loop.

"I wanted to come and say good-bye before they rushed you out of here. Damn hospital budget and all," he said.

"Yes," Dr. Gordon said. "You being a lowly staff surgeon wouldn't have an iota of clout, would you?"

They laughed together, Jackson being better at getting when a man was trying to be funny than she was. She could see past the thin facade of tough-guy banter, how Jackson cared for James, and the respect was mutual. The knowledge landed like a splat of thick, gooey warmth on her chest.

For the next several minutes they all sat around and chatted about anything and everything other than James's condition or his move. Which meant good old hospital gossip, the kind doctors enjoyed just as much as any other employees. Though Jackson did suggest there might be a good-looking nurse to ogle where he was going. That got a laugh, too. "I'm old but I'm not dead," he insisted. If there was such a nurse, he'd notice. He also wanted to know all about the pathology department, and had some suggestions for issues Charlotte had brought up before. She could tell he needed to feel useful, and she'd make sure he still knew how much he was needed as her mentor.

Two patient transfer attendants, a young man and woman, arrived in his room, and Charlotte and Jackson stepped aside as they packed up what little of James's personal effects were there, then got him on their gurney and carted him off to the waiting ambulance.

Charlotte and Jackson followed closely along until they were outside. She didn't care if it was inappropriate or not—she kissed James on the forehead and gave him a hearty hug before they could slide him inside. "I'll be in touch soon."

"I'll hold you to that." He patted her arm and she could tell he bit back a lot of emotion, so she stepped away to make it a little easier for him. And her. Soon the ambulance doors were closed and all she could see of her mentor was his chemo-ridden head with just a few remaining wisps of white hair through the small back windows. Her heart clutched and her eyes stung.

Once the ambulance had driven away, she let go of her tears. Jackson's warm grip on her shoulders gave her something to lean on. He turned her toward him and circled his arms around her. "You're a good friend to Jim."

"I think I've told you before he's my mentor, but in so many ways he's been a father to me these last few years."

"He's a good man."

"Yes. Just now he reminded me about something he says from time to time, and why I'd forgotten, I don't know. He said, 'Life shouldn't be about what might happen, it should be about what's happening right now.'"

The deep personal meaning of that statement, spoken the day she'd finally made her decision to have the radical surgery, plus the fact that James Gordon was the first and only doctor other than her personal surgeon to know, had made a deep impression on her. He'd told her that he didn't think she should spend her life worrying about getting the cancer that had killed her mother, and if the surgery could offer her peace of mind, then she should do it. Then he'd assured her she wasn't crazy for taking the matter into her own hands. Just now he'd admitted he wished he had more say in his own treatment, then just as quickly had told her he'd decided to remain optimistic about beating his cancer. His choice, and a good one.

"Sounds like a solid motto for a good life."

She nodded. "He blew me away, sounding so upbeat about his condition." She pulled back from his shoulder and looked up at him. "He said he's decided to be optimistic instead of thinking like a scientist. He intends to beat it from that angle."

Jackson squeezed her a tiny bit tighter. "Then let's do the same, be optimistic for him."

"Yes. That's good advice. My mother was hopeful until the very end. She was amazing." Oh, if she kept on with this line of thinking she'd be blue in no time.

"I've got an idea. What do you say we take a walk on the beach at Malibu? Then I'll take you to a funky but great little place Evan and I discovered a couple of weeks ago." Jackson must have read her mind about needing some serious distraction, and his suggestion sounded perfect.

"I'd love that, but isn't Friday your night with Evan?"

"He'll understand."

Before she could protest, Jackson had his cell phone

in hand and speed-dialed his son. Because she needed and wanted his company, she didn't try to stop him.

"Oh," he said, returning the cell phone to his pocket and pulling something else from the other one, "I almost forgot this." He handed her a candy bar. Her favorite, a Nutty-Buddy. "This should keep your blood sugar up until we eat dinner."

"How sweet of you!" This simple gesture proved his thoughtfulness and touched her more than she cared to admit. "Thanks. And the best part is I know I don't have to share it with you."

First dropping her car off back home in Thousand Oaks, they took the Las Tunas Canyon route through Agoura to the Pacific Coast Highway, and made it to the beach with plenty of daylight left. They parked and kicked off their shoes and walked a long stretch of sand, holding hands and listening to the waves crashing against the shore, while they inhaled the thick salty ocean air. They held each other as the huge-looking golden sun slipped bit by bit over the horizon, and Charlotte couldn't remember a sunset she'd ever enjoyed more. Because she was watching it with Jackson.

Then, as promised, he took her to a trendy though decidedly funky little hole-in-the-wall for a vegetarian meal complemented by organic pinot gris. Whatever they had done to the "green" wine, it tasted so good Charlotte decided to have a second glass. Why not? Jackson was driving.

Jackson wasn't being forward, but after dinner Charlotte seemed to have just begun to relax, so instead of taking her home, where she'd immediately start fussing about his needs, he decided to take her to his condo. Who was he kidding, calling it a condo? It was more like a glorified apartment, but it served his purpose, and since it was in Westlake, it cost a pretty penny for the privilege of living there. Why not show her how a new bachelor lived?

"So here's my place," he said, switching on the lights in the living room. The curtains remained drawn along the sliding glass doors, and the air felt heavy, especially after being at the beach. He strode to the wall and pulled back the drapes then opened the sliders for fresh air, suddenly aware how nervous he felt, having her here. It was another warm and inviting early summer evening, without a trace of humidity, which always amazed him, and the light breeze quickly chased out the stuffy air. He inhaled, forcing himself to relax.

"Make yourself comfortable," he said, heading to the kitchen to open a bottle of wine. He hadn't ordered any with dinner, though Charlotte had raved about the organic "green" wine. His thoughts had been that tonight she needed to let go a little, and if enjoying a glass or two of wine was the way, he'd make sure she got home safely. He picked up two wineglasses by the stems and carried everything to the other room.

Charlotte had made herself comfortable on the small but functional gray linen upholstered couch overrun with brightly patterned pillows, which she'd pushed aside. The pillows were only there because that was how it had been displayed in the catalog. What did he know about decorating? That had always been Evaline's job. When he showed up back at the sofa, her amused expression changed to a wide smile. Combined with the light blush of someone who'd been enjoying her wine with dinner, the look was more than appealing. "You've been reading my mind a lot tonight," she said.

"I try." He opened the bottle of chilled chardonnay

and poured them each half a glass. She sipped, and he joined her. "This is where I hang out when I'm not at the hospital." He wished he could read her mind a little more right now, but on the other hand, maybe he didn't want to know what had put that previously engaging gaze on her face. She was probably suppressing a laugh at his decorating skills, or lack thereof.

"Rented furniture?"

Okay. Maybe he had read her mind again. He dutifully nodded. Was it that obvious?

"Not bad, but it tells me you don't plan to stick around."

"I think I've told you that I came here to be near my son, and that was the extent of my plan. Oh, and then I found the job at St. Francis." He took another drink.

"And then you started showing up in my office." She quaffed more wine, looking self-assured. He liked it.

His eyes crinkled with another smile. The topic was starting to get good. Plus her attitude had taken a turn toward sassy. "That I did. There was a surprise beauty in that office."

He gave another half smile. She stared lightly at him. It made him think there was a lot going on inside her head right then.

"Did you have any idea how long I had a crush on you?"

So he'd been right about a lot going on behind that getting-more-relaxed-by-the-minute stare. "I thought *I* had a crush on *you*."

She sat sideways on the couch, one leg bent on the cushions, the other crossed over it. He faced her. With the tip of her now shoeless toe, she made contact with his knees. "I liked you from the first time I saw you, and I couldn't believe how interested you were in the slides."

"That's because I was interested in the person showing me the slides." He touched her, soon caressing her toes. She drank more wine, letting him have his way with her foot.

"I liked being in the dark with you, getting to test out whatever aftershave you threw on. You don't have a favorite, do you?"

He shook his head. Shrugged. He liked how she was opening up and he didn't want to stop her, so he kept quiet.

"I can remember the first time our knees touched. You inhaled and I thought it was so sexy. You realize how sexy you are, right?"

His brows shot up. This was really getting good. "Uh, I hadn't thought about that in a long time." Three years, to be exact. Since losing his leg.

"May I ask what happened to your marriage?"

Ah, damn, she'd pulled a quick one on him and changed the topic to something much less appealing, but Charlotte deserved to know the whole story. His version anyway. And, more importantly, he'd reached a point where he knew he could trust her with it. "Evaline was my high-school sweetheart, and she followed me to college. We got married sooner than I had planned. Actually, I wasn't even sure I was planning on it, but she, or rather we, got pregnant and, well, I did the right thing. We were parents at twenty-one, right when I started med school." He took a drink of wine, uncomfortable about reliving his past.

"Obviously, I wasn't around much, which didn't help things, but we muddled through. Two years later, she got pregnant again. I have to admit I was not happy. She'd stopped taking her birth control pills and didn't bother to tell me." He took another drink. "I'll be honest and say I kind of felt like she'd trapped me. Not very heroic of me, but I'm being honest with you."

"I can understand that. No judgment here."

"Thanks. She was the first woman I loved and I held on to that, and we just kind of kept moving forward. But when I signed on for the army reserve medical unit and was away from home a lot, I'd come home and feel distant. That's when I realized our marriage was in trouble. The thing was, she liked being a doctor's wife, and I liked being a surgeon, so at least we had that in common."

He tried to make light of it and even forced a laugh, but he glanced at Charlotte and saw understanding and empathy on her face, not sympathy. At least that was how he needed to interpret it. She reached across the couch and squeezed his forearm. *Keep going*, she seemed to say. "Fast-forward to my coming home from a second tour to the Middle East, this one voluntary, missing part of my leg and a total mental mess, and, well, I fell apart, and she fell apart, and so did our marriage."

An old lump of pain started radiating smack in the middle of his chest. He took a deep breath, feeling grateful to be here right now with Charlotte. He wondered about her, too. "And speaking of marriage, why isn't a fantastic woman like you married?"

Her brows lifted. She sipped from her glass, looking thoughtful. "I was engaged. I planned to have the American dream of a career, a husband, kids. We were all set for it, too. Then…" she slowly inhaled "…things changed." She stopped and looked at him. "Would you mind if we went back to talking about how much we like each other?"

So she didn't want to open up right now. Maybe it

still hurt too much, and if anyone in the world could understand that, he could. "I'll start. Knowing I'll see you at work at some point every day makes me happy to wake up. I haven't felt anything like that in, well, a long, long time."

A sly smile crossed her full and kissable lips. "My turn?" He nodded, eager to hear what she'd have to say. "Your blue eyes are killers, and there's something about your almost curly hair that drives me wild."

He hoped she planned to come on to him because the compliments were making him hot. He took a draw from his wine then put down his glass on the nearby coffee table. Something told him if she kept on with this line of conversation, he might soon want the use of both hands.

"And you've been the highlight of my day more times than I can count. Even when I first started at St. Francis. There you were, sitting in the dark." He moved closer, took a lock of her thick brown hair and played with it. "You always seemed calm, maybe a little reserved, but it was a welcome change from all the type A personalities in my department. I always looked forward to seeing you. Always." He leaned forward, and having moved her hair away from her ear, he lightly kissed the shell. "I thought you were sexy but you didn't seem to know it, which made you all the more appealing." He nipped her earlobe then watched the flesh on her neck prickle. "Now that I know you better, you're driving me crazy."

She took a quick last sip of her wine and set the glass down. He couldn't help but get his hopes up that tonight might be the night. Soon after their gazes met and melded, planting a solid yes in his mind. He kissed her, pulling her closer. She settled into his arms and kissed more hungrily than usual. They were getting pretty damn good at this part. Making out. He deep-ened his kiss and a tiny moan caught in her throat. His me-man-you-woman switch clicked on and his needy hands roamed her shoulders and arms and soon slid over her waist and up to her breast.

She stiffened so noticeably he stopped kissing in order to look at her. This wasn't the first time it had happened. "Am I doing something wrong?" He spoke quietly, his version of tender. "If there's anything I need to change, tell me so I can fix it."

She shook her head, switching from the relaxed sensual compliment-giver of a few moments before to a cautious woman with glistening brown eyes. She glanced over his shoulder rather than look straight at him. A sense of dread seemed to hover around her. "You've heard me talk about my mother."

He nodded, and he knew the stats about breast can-cer, too. Was that what held her back in life? The fear of getting cancer?

"On top of having the strong family history, I have the Ki-67 blood marker *and* the BRCA1 and 2 gene mu-tations, plus SNPs—single nucleotide polymorphisms."

So that was the rest of the story, and a tough one to accept for sure.

"Not good. Right?"

Still considering the stark reality of what she'd just said, he didn't answer right away, but he had to agree. The odds were against her. "Is that what stops you from getting closer?" Would she never let him, or anyone, into her life because of that?

She took a deep jittery breath, shifted her gaze to his hand, touching his fingers, playing with them. Every time she touched him he responded, and soon their fin-gers were laced together, his thumb rubbing along the outline of her palm. She worried her mouth. "So two years ago I had preemptive surgery, bilateral radical mastectomies without reconstruction." She may as well have blurted out there was a monster in the house—the sudden news felt as jolting.

He gripped her hand tighter as the realization of what she was telling him registered. This beautiful young woman had had her breasts removed to avoid being diagnosed with cancer in the future. As a surgeon, he knew exactly what she meant. He knew what unreconstructed mastectomy scars looked like. Hell, he'd given those scars to hundreds of women over the years. But most opted to have implants along with the surgery. From several of his own patients who'd taken Charlotte's route, he knew the sorrow the women went through afterward. Dealing with body image was always the toughest issue. Yet her surgery had been voluntary, and she'd made the choice not to have reconstruction.

It also became clear why her engagement had ended. The guy hadn't been able to take it.

So the natural curves on display in her clothes were thanks to that special bra he recommended to his own patients. It sure had fooled him. Now he understood why she always tensed up when he started exploring that part of her body.

He needed to make it clear that he wasn't that guy, the guy who couldn't take it.

He pulled her hand to his mouth and kissed it, kissed each finger and the inside of her wrist. He just wanted to love her, to ease her fears, to let her know that, though, yes, he was shocked, it didn't matter to him. His other hand caressed her neck. "If you're worried what I might think, I'm going to quote back to you what you told me

Dr. Gordon said. 'Life's got to be about what's happening right now, not about what might happen.' And right now I want more than anything to make love to you.'"

She leaned into his hand, and his thumb traced her jaw and earlobe. He pulled her to his mouth and kissed her again, a long warm and sensual message he hoped would get through to her. But he knew she needed to hear it from him, to make sure without a doubt he understood.

"You have no idea how much it meant to me when you didn't react over my leg. I didn't see the look of horror in your eyes that I've seen before. And, believe me, there's no hiding it if it's there. I've seen people try." He took both her hands in his and squeezed them. "Look at me." She complied and he gazed gently at her. "So, of all the people in the world, I know how it feels to be insecure about an imperfect body." He kissed her once more to prove his point, to hold her near, feel close to her again, hoping he was getting through. She seemed to welcome his kisses, as she always did. His hand slid to her shoulder and upper arm again, where he held her firmly.

"Charlotte, I've been fortunate enough to have lots of time to get to know you and you should know that I think you're a beautiful person both inside and out." A light ironic laugh puffed from his mouth. "Hell, I'm the perfect *imperfect* person to be with you tonight. But only if you want it." He could only hope his expression and invitation looked and sounded as sincere as he truly was.

Her hesitant, dark and worried eyes relaxed the slightest bit. Her hands moved to cup his cheeks as a look of deep gratitude crossed her face. Her fingers felt cold, nervous. But there was something more in that gaze, some kind of promise, or was it blatant desire, like he felt firing up again inside. She leaned forward and kissed him, lightly at first, then released all the passion she must have let build during his confession. Because that kiss soon morphed into a ravenous need to be close, to feel, to excite and take.

To make love with him.

CHAPTER SIX

JACKSON HOPPED OFF the couch and began searching through cabinets and drawers, leaving Charlotte confused. Had she turned him off? She'd thought she'd been giving him all she had, sending the strongest message possible—*I trust you. Take me, I'm yours!* She followed him into his small kitchen. He looked over his shoulder, apparently clutching some stuff in his arms.

"My mom sent out a bunch of things that I never thought I'd use in a hundred years, but guess what." He turned, showing her his armload of candles in various sizes and containers. "Tonight is the night."

She laughed with him, then reached out and relieved his overloaded arms of a few of the candles to help before he dropped something.

"What do you say we put these babies all around the bedroom and…" now that he had a free hand he pulled her close for a quick kiss "…light them up."

The fact he wanted to create some atmosphere for their first time being together made a powerful impact on her wavering mood. The gesture of using faint candlelight as a buffer hit her like the thud of a palm to the center of her chest. They were going to have sex tonight. He would see her naked. Rather than make a big deal out of it, and possibly make him self-conscious about his eagerness, she sniffed one of the candles, vanilla, then another, rose. "Things should smell pretty good, too." She gave her best shot at sounding anything but the way she really felt—nervous! "One more thing. I don't take birth control pills. I use a diaphragm, and I didn't bring it tonight."

He watched her for a second or two, understanding and tenderness like she'd never seen centered in his bright blue gaze. "I've got that covered." His sweet gesture calmed her jitters. "Follow me."

There was nothing quite like a man on a mission.

Once the candles were strategically placed around his surprisingly spacious bedroom, she took a quick trip to the bathroom while he circled the room, lighting each one. Just before she exited she looked into the mirror. "Are you ready for this?" she whispered, her pulse quickening from her jangling nerves, her fingers slightly trembling. Then she noticed a subtle reminder, the crutches leaning in the corner. Jackson would need them without his prosthetic to get in and out of the shower. His prosthetic. She'd made full disclosure just now in his living room. A man who wore a prosthetic partial leg would understand.

She refused to let Derek's memory ruin the chance for something new. Something better. Tonight she'd trust her gut—which seemed to have turned into a butterfly farm—trust Jackson, and maybe finally turn the corner to wholeness. She took a deep, shaky breath and opened the door.

Jackson stood in the center of his room, several feet from the foot of his bed, surrounded by soft candle glow, looking more handsome than she'd ever dreamed. While she'd been in the bathroom and he'd been lighting candles, she noticed he'd also found a condom or two, which were now sitting on the bedside table next to a tall, wide white candle. A man of his word.

He smiled at her, candlelight dappling the deep creases on either side of his mouth, looking sexy as hell, and she walked toward him. He took her into his arms and held her still for a few beats of her heart. She let go, melted into him, loving his welcoming warmth. He kissed her temple and ear and she inhaled the trace of his spicy aftershave along with the swirling candle scents, a mixture of vanilla and rose. And magnolia? Lifting her chin, she met his lips and soon didn't have to think, since their kisses always took on a life of their own.

Out of breath from his greedy kisses, her hands landed on his chest and slowly unbuttoned his shirt, mostly because she was nervous and her fingers weren't cooperating with her desire to get that thing off him! Pulling open the shirt, she reaped the benefit of her effort, being treated to the smooth skin of his muscled shoulders and his impressive chest dusted with brown hair. Her fingers traced over the tickly feel of him before she kissed him there and there and finally at the notch at the base of his throat.

He let her undress him, unselfconsciously needing to sit down when she'd pulled his jeans to the hard prosthesis with its silicone suspension sleeve. The layered muscles of his runner's thighs and his washboard tight abdominals distracting her from that detail. The thought of removing the prosthetic had never entered her mind.

"This one is different," she said, refusing to avoid the obvious, besides the fact they wanted each other.

"It's my everyday leg, complete with shoe." He smiled with understanding over her question. "The one you saw was my sports version."

"The blade?"

Now he grinned. "Yeah, I'm a blade runner."

She returned his smile, but wanted him to understand she was only being curious. "So how do I take this off for you?"

After a moment's hesitation, probably considering that he'd never been asked that question by a woman he was about to have sex with before, he showed her the button to click down toward the prosthetic ankle joint. She followed his instructions, and he guided her on how to slide down the bulkier and harder version of leg. As she studied it, he quickly removed the liner with the pin that clicked into the joint down by the ankle. And that was that.

She glanced at what remained of his leg beneath his knee, the flesh and bone part, then quickly back to the rest of him. Choosing to focus on everything about him, and not just the one area he might be self-conscious about, she ran her hands along the length of his thighs and looked into his darkening eyes. She perfectly understood how he'd feel if she stared at the part that was missing.

He pulled her to him, kissing her again, bringing things back on track—they wanted each other—with his hands roaming all over her. His fingers found the hem of her cotton pullover, his intense gaze seeking hers for the okay. Would she make this revealing moment one to dread or, just like him, a matter of fact? She pecked his lips in answer, so he gingerly lifted her top, giving her time to adjust to what he planned to do next. But when he reached for one of her bra straps, her hand flew to his.

"That look of horror you described earlier?" she whispered. "I know what it is."

His gaze narrowed with concern.

"I was engaged when I had the surgery. We were going to get married and go for the whole package—careers, kids, the works. He didn't want me to have the surgery, but I insisted it was what I needed to do. And afterward he couldn't accept me. He just couldn't. He tried, but I saw it. He was horrified. I disgusted him. He pitied me. I—"

Jackson stopped her from saying another word by lifting her chin with a finger and delivering a tender kiss. As their lips pressed together and their tongues found each other, he undid her special mastectomy bra and removed it, never breaking from her mouth, instead deepening their kiss. He lay back on the bed and pulled her with him on top until her nearly flat chest was flush with his. Being this close to him, skin to skin, excited her. His warm, large hands explored her back and moved downward to her jeans, pushing them lower once she'd unzipped them, then cupping her bottom. With his palms firmly attached to her backside, she remembered how much she'd missed being explored by a man, and how good it felt now, loving this moment.

He concentrated on every part of her, rather than putting her missing breasts at the center. Finally, when she was completely naked with him, the fingers of one of his hands crossed her chest as lightly as a butterfly. The surprise of how sensual it felt to have someone else besides herself touch her there sent a blast of chills across her skin. Soon, while he continued to devour her mouth, his palm rubbed where her breasts used to be, and though many nerves had been severed during the surgery, his touch warmed and excited her as if her breasts were still there.

"You're beautiful," he whispered over her ear, and for that instant she believed him.

As their bodies tangled and tightened together, clearly turned on—her aroused and longing for more, him noticeably hard between them—she forgot about what was missing from him, and he obviously hadn't been turned off by her surgery. Maybe, she hoped, he'd meant what he'd said about finding her beautiful inside and out. Hadn't he just told her so?

He rolled her onto her back, pushing her hands above her head and kissing her chest in several spots. She could swear, in her mind, the nipples that were physically no longer there responded. His kisses traveled onward to her stomach, igniting more thrills, and worked their way over her hips and down across her thighs until his mouth settled where her heat mounted, tightened and balled into raw need. As his tongue found her tender folds and circled the tip of her sex, setting off amazing sensations bordering on lightning and fireworks, every worry and insecurity about her body image left her mind, to be replaced by one thought. At her core she was a woman and nothing could take that away.

A few minutes later, when he sheathed and entered her, working her into another frenzy under the spell of his strength and persistence, and surrounded by flickering candlelight, she dared to look into his eyes. They were already locked on her face. Watching each other under the grip of bliss was more intimate than anything she could imagine. And like that she let go and shattered the boundaries she'd put on herself because of her wounds, and from his frantic reaction was fairly sure he'd done the same. She needed him and wanted to please him, bucking beneath him, and his near growling moan proved she was on the right track.

He cupped her hips, she tightened her legs around his waist, he steadily upped the tempo, and they soon ascended to that beautiful intensity she'd almost forgotten, where he suspended her with near agonizing magic. Faster and stronger, he took her there. Until she was so tightly wound and overloaded with sensations she lost it and came deep, long and forcefully. He soon followed her and they tumbled through that paradise together, and she felt more complete as a woman than she ever had in her life.

On Saturday morning her muscles ached from their making great use of the condoms and candlelight, until all had burned out. By then so had she, and falling into Jackson's arms, immediately going to sleep, seemed surreal. His rented bed was surprisingly comfortable, or maybe it was the man in bed with her? When she woke, she glanced up at him. He was already awake and watching her, lightly playing with her hair.

"Hi," she said.

"Good morning." His hand grazed her shoulder and arm. "You like eggs? I'm starving."

"I love eggs. You cooking?"

He sat up. "You bet I am. I intend to impress the hell out of you, too."

"I think you've already done that."

His slow smile and darkening blue eyes relit the lingering warmth right where they'd left off last night. He kissed her to help it along, and soon the thought of sleeping in on a Saturday morning seemed far more appealing than any old home-cooked breakfast.

Later, when they'd managed to make it out of bed, he loaned her a T-shirt to wear with her underwear while he planned to dazzle her with his culinary skills. Before putting it on, out of habit she reached for her fully formed bra, but he stopped her.

"You don't need that around me." He ran his hand across her chest, up her neck and across her jaw, then kissed her. "I like you exactly the way you are."

CHAPTER SEVEN

AFTER CHARLOTTE AND Jackson's first night together, some wild, wanton woman had been released, a part of her she'd never before explored. Complicating things, she never knew when Jackson would pop in her office, his mere presence reminding her how much she wanted him. Usually his visits were after a particularly stressful surgery. He would drop in, close the door, and dance her into the corner to kiss her hard and thoroughly then make no excuses for how much he craved her. And she loved it! Then, with her feeling all hot and flustered, they'd promise to spend the night together, and that would be that.

This time, late on a Friday afternoon, it was the night he routinely had dinner and a movie with his son. With that one earlier exception, they never planned to see each other on Friday nights, so they'd have to put their lust on hold. She'd worn a loose and flowing gypsy-style skirt to work, hoping he'd see it and compliment her. She loved his compliments.

When her lover came into her office and closed the door, he had a hungry look in his gaze. He took her hand and pulled her to him, kissing her, fingers digging into her hair, walking her backward to the wall, pressing her there. "Nice skirt," he said, playing with the fabric and just happening to find her hip and soon her bottom in the process.

In no time she had one thought on her mind and was totally grateful for her choice in skirts. Her leg lifted and attached to his hip, bringing his body flush with hers. Thanks to the thin fabric of his OR scrubs and her skirt, she felt nearly all of him as he stroked along her center. Wrapped up in the thrill of the moment, him igniting her and wreaking havoc with her good sense, she whispered, "Let's do it."

"You have no idea how much I want to." He kissed her roughly, slipped his hand between them and cupped her, moving up and down, fanning her fire nearly to the point of no return. He took a ragged inhalation to stop himself from going further. "But we could get fired, and I need this job," he reasoned. His hot breath tickled over her ear as she ignored his logical warning. "As much as I need you…"

"The department is practically empty," she interrupted. "Lock the door," she hissed, completely lost to him and the moment, and she meant it.

He gave her a questioning look and she nodded her undeniable consent. She saw the flash of heat in his eyes. He nipped her earlobe, then her lower lip. "I can't think straight around you."

With the oddest sensation, she'd have sworn she had nipples and they were tight and peaked with her longing to feel him inside her. "You do some pretty crazy things to me, too. Please," she begged, pushing her pelvis closer to him. "Lock the door."

It had never computed before how isolated her office was. Or the advantage of the other doctors routinely leaving early on Friday afternoons. She was at the end of a long row of offices in the basement of the pathology department. No-man's-land.

From having been with Jackson a dozen times before, she recognized the shift in his expression, his heavy-lidded stare. All resistance was gone. Her insides quivered, knowing what would happen next. "Just this once," he swore.

Lightning swift he locked the door and riffled through his wallet for a condom. They were back where they'd left off, his hand finding her secret places and working wonders, and when her powerful moment came she let him cover her mouth with his palm to stifle her response. The last thing they wanted to do was draw attention to what was going on in case anyone was within earshot. He loved watching her when she lost it. And just then, thanks to his skillful touch, she totally had.

Someone knocked on the door. "Charlotte, are you in there?" It was Antwan.

With Jackson's hand still over her mouth and tightening, her gaze shot toward the ceiling. *Really?* Of all the bad timing in the world.

Jackson removed his hand from her mouth and put one finger over his. *"Shh..."* She felt the sudden urge to laugh. This was ridiculous, and nothing she'd ever do! But her pulse hammered in her chest, more from what Jackson had just done to her than from Antwan's unwanted appearance. Though the risk of being caught having sex, well, partial sex, at work kept her heartbeat racing along.

"Has Dr. Johnson left for the day?" Dr. Dupree called down the hall.

"I don't think so," Latoya's distant voice answered from the reception area. "Dr. Hilstead came by. Maybe they went for coffee."

Antwan tried the door handle. The nerve!

They stared at each other, neither hardly breathing. She clutched Jackson's arms and squeezed tight, her mind flying in a thousand directions. What should they do? What would they say if they got caught? What would her mother think?

"Well, she's obviously gone." Finally, they heard footsteps going down the hall and Antwan's distant voice chatting up the young receptionist. "It sure feels dead around here."

Latoya gave the requisite laugh at his sorry attempt at a joke with the pathology reference.

"What are you still doing at work?" Antwan's attention had shifted. Good. They talked more, but Charlotte had quit listening.

Jackson gave her a stern look. "This can't ever happen again."

Feeling out of control and pumped up by the excitement, she grabbed his scrub top and pulled him near, then delivered a ragged kiss. "You're right—this has got to stop. But first it's your turn."

"We're crazy to risk it," he whispered over her ear, his hot breath melting her and dissolving into a cascade of chills down and over her breasts.

She got busy giving all of her attention to him, admiring how firm he'd stayed through the close call. He gave his rendition of a ragged kiss, far more intense than hers, taking her breath away. His weight pushed against her, her leg lifted again, and when he'd secured her to the wall, she lifted the other, clutching his hips.

"We really shouldn't," he murmured.

Farther down the hall, in the histology lab, the late shift technician stopped and listened, wondering where those muffled rhythmic thuds on the wall were coming from.

* * *

On a Monday, Charlotte had a phone message that Dr. Gordon was moving again. It was from his son Ely. He said he'd taken leave from work to be with his father and that Dr. Gordon wanted him to notify her.

She'd just got back from a quick but fun lunch with Jackson. No sex involved. Who knew how great hospital cafeteria food could taste when you were totally into someone? Now her lunch turned to a lump in her gut at the news.

Dr. Gordon had regained a lot of strength, and three days ago when she'd last visited he had been as feisty as ever. Maybe he'd figured out a way to beat the system. She wondered if Ely had volunteered to come or if Dr. Gordon had manipulated the visit. She wouldn't dare consider that his health circumstances had directed the move home. Had Ely implied he was there for hospice care?

Before she could form another thought her cell rang. It was Jackson.

"I just heard Jim Gordon left the extended care facility for home. Maybe we should go visit him this evening."

"I'm not sure if his family would want that, but I want to."

"I'll give a call, let you know."

"Thank you." She had a stack of slides fresh from histology to study from Saturday's surgeries, and though her heart and thoughts were with her mentor, out of respect for him she knew his department needed to carry on.

After work, Ely had given the okay for a visit, so Jackson drove as Charlotte let several scenarios play out in her thoughts, though she never expected the scene they found when they arrived.

Dr. Gordon was sitting in an obviously favorite chair, judging by the wear and tear on it, and how perfectly the man fit into it, too. He gave an ethereal smile, his skin ghostly white. "Hello, dear."

She bent to kiss him on the cheek, which felt warmer than he looked. "Did you have to pull some strings to move home?"

No longer a curmudgeon, his gaze more impish now, he smiled. "Ely and Sharon are staying with me for a while." He officially introduced Charlotte to his son and daughter-in-law. "The hospital decided I was in as good hands here as there. At much less cost to them!"

"That's wonderful."

Ely was a younger version of his dad with thinner eyebrows, though a bit taller with a friendlier face, and personality-wise, probably thanks to his mother's input, less off-putting. He hovered around his father, and Sharon seemed to sense her father-in-law's every need. Beyond giving him all the care and attention he'd require over the next few weeks, they radiated something that couldn't be faked—love for him.

Knowing her mentor would be surrounded by family and seeing how at peace he seemed, being back home, helped ease her worry about the significance of the move. No one mentioned the term "hospice care," and there wasn't a sign of medical equipment in the living room. Charlotte hoped for the best.

"I've asked Jerry Roth to take over as department head," he said. "There'll be a memo going out tomorrow."

So much for hope. Her heart ached at the news and what it might imply.

"He'll do a great job," she said, trying to sound upbeat. Jerry was the logical replacement—though she hated thinking that word—being the second most senior in Pathology at St. Francis of the Valley. Even with her foolish hope lagging, she wanted to reassure Dr. Gordon about his choice. "He's been steady as a rock while you've been in the hospital." Sitting nearby, Jackson subtly took her hand and squeezed his support.

"When I come back, it'll only be part-time."

The emotional teeter-totter had her sitting straighter. "You're coming back?" She couldn't suppress her surprise and happy relief, and for a man who didn't do impish, she could have sworn he savored playing her.

"I've been officially deemed in remission." As much as it went against his nature, her mentor beamed. "Don't know how long it will hold, but I'm feeling stronger every day, and hopefully, with Sharon's healthy cooking and the company of my son and friends like you, I'll be back in shape in no time at all."

"That's fantastic news, Jim." Jackson spoke up, a sincere smile on his face.

"Thanks. I'm just being realistic about not taking on too much when I come back."

"Wise of you," Jackson said.

Elated, and grinning to prove it, except probably sending a mixed message with the tears that had simultaneously cropped up, Charlotte clapped her hands. "I can't wait."

"To be honest, I can't either. I need a purpose besides being a pincushion and lab rat."

After a long drawn-out hug, and Charlotte realizing that the move and their visit may have taxed Dr. Gordon, she decided it was time to leave. But first, remembering all the things she'd wished she'd said to her mother during her ordeal, before it was too late, in case she never got the chance, she sat on the ottoman where Dr. Gordon's feet rested. Having him captive, she looked into his eyes.

"It's been hard, not having my mentor around these last few weeks. I want you to know how much you've taught me and how special you are to me. How much I still need you." She took his bony hand. "I've kind of put you on a pedestal, sometimes wishing you'd been my dad." She glanced up at Ely, noticing his approving smile. "I'm a better doctor because of you, and since I can't exactly go around saying this at work, I want you to know I love you."

He tightened his frail grip in hers. "Thank you. You're very special to me, too. Now quit worrying about me. You know my motto: life shouldn't be about what might happen, it's—"

Ely and Sharon joined in on the last part of the phrase, clueing Charlotte in that it really was a saying he lived by. "It's about what's happening right here and now."

She studied the man in his comfy chair, back in the home he'd made with his wife of fifty years before she'd died, his son and daughter-in-law like bookends on either side of him. Him being there "right here and now" looked pretty darned sweet, so she said good night and they left.

Moved by the warm and squishy moment that had just occurred inside Dr. Gordon's house, Jackson stopped Charlotte before they reached the car. "I've got a wedding to attend back home in Georgia next month, late August. Would you do me the honor of being my guest?"

Surprise registered in her eyes, and she didn't answer right away.

"I figure if Jim comes back on the job part-time, you

should be able to take a few days off." He opened the car door and let her slip inside, then walked around and got in, still waiting for her answer but not quite ready to hear it. "Before you make your decision, let me just say it's because we've got really close and I was hoping you'd come with me. The truth is, I'd feel better confronting the mess I left behind with you at my side."

"I'd love to go."

It was his turn to be surprised, especially because of the poor excuse he'd given for wanting her there with him. As backup? What had he been thinking? "You would? I didn't mean to imply you'd be a crutch or anything."

"I understand."

"Really?" Over the last few weeks he'd grown to know Charlotte's body as well as his own, and he marveled over that gift. Since they'd started dating, he knew her intelligence was both a source of challenge and comfort. They understood each other. Hell, he'd torn a page right out of Jim Gordon's rule book to help convince her to give him a chance: *Right here, right now. To hell with the future.* Her warm and loving attitude seemed a gift from heaven, yet she'd just dazzled him again by being so willing to step into his past without knowing how bad it could be.

"Yes. I'd love to go."

How much more proof did he need about how special she was? "Well, in that case, I think it's about time you met my son."

Charlotte snuggled into Jackson's arms in her bed after making love later that night. Being tall, it took a lot to make her feel petite, but his broad shoulders and long frame did just that. Now that her personal shock of having a double mastectomy had barely made waves for him, often, when they were just staying in and hanging out, she'd walk around in a T-shirt or sweater without strapping on her bra, her chest as flat as his. And it didn't faze him. He'd been the one to suggest it after the first time they'd been together. She considered that freedom a special gift from him. He really had proved to be the perfect *imperfect* man for her.

Just before she drifted off to sleep, one last thought crossed her mind: how life was looking up. Her mentor was in remission, the new guy in her life had just asked her to a wedding in his hometown, which proved he trusted her with a fragile part of his life. And now he wanted her to meet his son. She couldn't help but feel special. Yet he'd never come close to saying those three little words.

The big question was, was it safe to get her hopes up? Maybe he was just a guy like the rented furniture in his condo, temporary, useful for now, nothing to take for granted. He'd been very clear about never wanting to marry again or to have any more kids. Now that she knew the full story, she understood, too. He'd moved to California to be near his son, who would eventually graduate from college and move on. Why would Jackson stick around after that?

But right from the start, having laid down a few personal safety rules of her own for Jackson, like taking it slow before jumping into a physical relationship, she knew how easily a rule could be broken. Tonight that fact fed her hope.

Jackson was on his way out of the lunchtime surgical conference when he saw Dr. Dupree across the room. He'd had something on his mind and made a point to confront him.

"Dr. Hilstead. You need something?" Antwan was in the middle of sharing a recent conquest with a young resident.

"Yes, if you have a minute?"

The long-haired resident took the cue—in fact, looked relieved—and headed out of the auditorium with everyone else.

"I just wanted to let you know that Charlotte and I are a thing now, so you can step back."

"A thing?"

"Yeah, we're a thing."

"She knows this?"

"Most definitely. Anyway, you can step back now."

"Step back?"

"Yes, step back." Jackson emphasized the words for the guy who seemed to be playing dense.

"Sometimes ladies don't know what they're missing until they've tried it." His overconfident smile grated on Jackson's nerves. Was it a challenge? He also knew the jerk was referring to himself, Antwan, not Jackson, so he decided to spell it out for him.

"Trust me, she's tried it and liked it. I'm asking you nicely to leave her alone." Was he on the verge of flapping his arms and making monkey noises? *My territory. Leave!*

"If that's what she wants, fine."

Jackson stared at the dense doctor long and hard. But he didn't dare say the words that had just been planted front and center in his head. *She's mine.* That would make him feel a bit like he'd traveled back in time to a more dramatic stage, high school or college, when guys got all wrapped up in their women and proudly staked their claim. He was a mature adult now, in midlife, so-phisticated and above getting into the fray. Yet feeling the intense need to make his point perfectly clear with a womanizing bozo like Dupree couldn't be denied, and it shocked him.

Where had that come from? What had happened to the civilized forty-two-year-old surgeon? He bit back the long list of things he'd like to say, deciding to go for terse. "It's what she wants. We want." Like he had the right to speak for Charlotte, as Antwan had already insinuated. But it was. It was what *he* wanted. And he was pretty sure she wanted it, too.

He turned to leave, deciding to let Antwan figure out for himself what that meant, thinking the Southern gentleman-turned-caveman was a welcome change. He'd just publicly admitted he and Charlotte were "a thing," whatever the hell that meant.

The revelation of admitting he had intense feelings again on *any* level, and in this case for someone else— for his lovely *Charlotte*—made him grin. He left the meeting feeling taller than when he'd arrived, though admittedly he glanced over his shoulder for any evidence of a feminist posse hot on his trail for daring to be the tiniest bit chauvinistic. That didn't stop him from grinning, though.

That Friday night, Evan turned out to be tall, like his father, with piercing blue eyes, but much fairer and with lighter, straighter hair. From this Charlotte deduced that Jackson's ex was a blonde. She let her insecure imagination go wild and envisioned a stereotypical image of a pretty petite Southern belle, a Georgia peach, as she'd heard it called. The thought made her cringe and hurt all over. But she'd thought about all she and Jackson had shared over the last several weeks, and how close they'd got. Then on the spot she decided it was better to be the extreme opposite from an ex—tall, olive-toned skin, dark hair and eyes, big-boned—than a dead ringer. Wasn't it?

Occasionally during dinner the strained dynamics between Evan and Jackson were evident, but only on certain topics, like the wedding and whether or not Evan planned to go. They agreed that Evan should fly out a few days early to spend time with his mother and brother, and as an observer the decision lifted a weight from Charlotte's heart.

Didn't they know that they had the same laugh? A few times she had to double-check who had said what because they sounded so much alike, too. The kid was his son, there was no doubt, and they shared a lifetime together, well, Evan's lifetime, anyway. And she suspected the same would be true with the older son, the one who'd yet to offer Jackson a touch of grace. They shared genetic traits and familial similarities, and no matter how hard Andrew might try to ignore it, there was no way to forget it. Again, her heart ached for Jackson and his troubles.

As the evening moved on over tapas and beer at yet another trendy Westlake restaurant, Charlotte realized something important. When they talked about Evan's Bachelor of Arts major at Pepperdine, excitement radiated from the nineteen-year-old, and fatherly pride was obvious in Jackson's eyes, which were decidedly sexier and bluer than his son's. Then again, she was biased. She quickly figured how to keep the conversation focused on university and life dreams, and soon Evan seemed to see her as an ally instead of an adversary—the woman threatening to take his father away from him.

She made it clear how important she felt a well-rounded liberal arts degree was to send a person out into the world. Evan couldn't have agreed more. Jackson's endorsement may have come in delayed, but he finally chimed in.

After a couple of glasses of beer Charlotte let her truest thoughts slip out. "Thanks to science and extended longevity, what makes parents think their kids can know where their journey will lead at the ripe old age of nineteen?" Charlotte mused.

"Exactly!" Evan agreed. The look of appreciation she received from the young man nearly melted her heart. One day he'd have the world at his calling, but he needed to first figure out where he belonged. Pressuring him to make up his mind too soon would never help.

Then she glanced at Jackson, who didn't appear nearly as impressed with her statement as his son.

Evidently she'd hit a chord of contention between father and son, so she continued. "I mean, I know how I wanted to become a doctor at sixteen, and you, Jackson, probably had a similar experience, but not everyone knows for sure where they belong at such an early age. My sister tried going to college and discovered it wasn't for her. Now she's happy as a clam with three kids and running a family business."

She didn't want to imply that Evan should drop out, so she quickly added, "Getting a solid, well-rounded education seems like the best step forward for most. Right, Evan?"

Evan nodded.

"I want the best for my sons. If Evan is happy with his major, then I'm happy."

Charlotte believed Jackson, because of all the men she'd met in her life, he had proved to be honest and dependable, someone to trust, and these were three characteristics at the top of her "perfect man" list.

Before dinner was over Evan seemed to understand a little better where his father stood on his undergraduate degree choices, and Jackson had made extra points, proving he supported his son. Charlotte couldn't help but think maybe she'd had something to do with it.

Then, over dessert, the previously unspoken subject of Dad dating a new woman came up.

"So I guess you two are dating, right?" Evan said. "And you want my approval?"

Charlotte worked extra hard to not show her true reaction. *Yes, we're dating, but beyond that I don't know what's in store. Do we need your approval for that?*

Jackson glanced at Charlotte, she glanced back, and then he reached for her hand under the table. "Now that Mom and I are divorced, I hope you're okay with that."

"Hey, it's your life." Evan seemed to toss the answer a bit too quickly, maybe in an attempt to leave out the emotion behind it. Pain. "I mean, I know a lot's gone on with your war injury and PTSD and all, and things didn't work out between you and Mom, but, Dad, you're entitled to pick up your life and date again."

Jackson reached across the table and clutched his son's forearm. "You saying that means the world to me, Evan."

When they all said good night, Jackson gave Evan a bear hug, and Evan fully participated. The sight of the two of them hugging moved Charlotte nearly to tears, but she managed to keep her response in line, not wanting in any way to draw attention away from the big event of the night. Until, in true Southern charm fashion, Evan extended his hospitality to her and hugged her good night. As she hugged the bonier version of

Jackson, managing to feel his sincerity, she couldn't help the moisture that sneaked over her lids.

"It was so great to meet you." She said it over-enthusiastically, completely different from the response she'd intended to give. Cool. In control. Sophisticated. *Really fun to meet you.*

Evan smiled and nodded, as though he was also surprised about how well the night had gone.

On the drive home, overall Charlotte thought the meeting had gone well and that Evan seemed okay with his dad moving on. At least she hoped Evan was being honest. Though the question still remained—where exactly was Jackson moving on to?

"What did you think?" Jackson asked.

"I think you've got a great son on your hands."

While driving, he flashed her a grateful and reassured look. "I think you're right." Then, with his eyes back on the road, he added, "I'm really looking forward to the day Evan turns twenty-one and my job as parent will officially be over."

"Is that job ever 'officially' over?"

"The part about being completely responsible for them, yes. The being-a-parent part?" He grimaced. "Nope."

Now that the hurdle of meeting his son had come and gone, Charlotte focused on the next big event. Truth was, she'd interpreted the invitation to the wedding in Savannah as a turning point in their relationship. Though Jackson hadn't committed to the trip meaning anything beyond a few days together on his home turf. *With her as his backup.* Her thoughts, not his. She felt otherwise. He *needed* her there.

But if that was all he wanted, backup, she'd oblige. Because she knew exactly how she felt about him—this could be the start of something big! Old song or not, it was how she felt, yet she chose to hold her thoughts close to her heart rather than test the waters on Jackson. It was still too soon.

Two weeks before the big event she went shopping for a special dress. She whistled while she combed through the circular racks in the showroom, happily looking forward to visiting a state she'd never been to before. She loved it already since it was the place that had shaped Jackson into the wonderful, charming and sexy man she'd come to know and…and what? Was she there yet? Or was she stuck in the "start of something big" stage? Maybe she was waiting for him to catch up.

All the new and optimistic feelings ebbed when a wave of insecurity and anxiety took over and her stomach threatened to knot up and push out her lunch. She swallowed hard and forced herself to pull it together. Shocked by the emotional reaction the act of buying a special dress had caused—or was it thinking about feeling something more for Jackson than she'd ever expected?—she took pause.

Sure, Jackson had seen her and accepted her for who she was, but how would she measure up to the people back home? Wondering and fearing how she'd manage in a sea of people she didn't know, her only lifeline being Jackson, who would no doubt be dealing with a boatload of his own issues, she fretted. Suddenly depressed about her tall and sometimes clunky-feeling appearance—the hair that would probably frizz up in the summer Georgia humidity, not being able to buy a perfect dress right off the rack, not to mention a subtle competitive feeling toward his ex-wife, which annoyed her to no end—she passed off feeling out of sorts and generally unsettled on nerves about the upcoming event. Not the other way around—feeling profoundly sick to her stomach on a perfectly fine Saturday morning, and getting nervous about what it might mean.

Then she went back to hunting for that perfect dress that would make her feel like a knockout. A dress that would cause Jackson to see her in a different light.

As a woman he couldn't live without.

CHAPTER EIGHT

ONE WEEK LATER Charlotte sat in the laboratory with one of the histologists assisting while she examined, described and cut sections from yesterday afternoon's surgeries and clinic procedures. This morning there were no less than twenty-five bottles of varying sizes, each prefilled with fixative. An appendix, a gallbladder with gallstones, a cervical conization, a large, dark and oddly shaped mole, a wedge resection of lung—removed by Dr. Jackson Hilstead, she noticed on the requisition, which meant he'd probably pop by tomorrow to look at the slide with her. That put a secret smile on her face. She'd been doing that a lot lately, smiling for no reason.

In walked Dr. Dupree, looking like he had something on his mind, and he immediately wiped her smile away.

"Haven't seen you in a while," she said, opening the first bottle. Not that she'd wanted to see him or anything. Oh, man, she hoped he didn't read anything into her off-the-cuff, trying-to-play-nice greeting. The man was incorrigible.

"I've been told to step back."

Well, it was about time someone did. Who, though—hospital administration, the sexual harassment team? She kept her smirk to herself. "Step back?"

Not wanting to let him slow her down on the job at hand, she examined, then interrupted Dupree to describe and measure the dimensions of a piece of tissue, then used a scalpel to find the best possible section to represent the entire specimen for slides and put it into a cassette.

He waited impatiently for her to finish. "Jackson said you two were a thing and I should step back. It was a couple of weeks ago, so I'm just checking if that's still true."

Her line of vision on the specimen flipped upward, catching her assistant's gaze, whose eyebrows nearly met his hairline.

Jackson had staked a claim on her? Glad she was wearing a mask, she hoped her smile didn't reach her eyes, though the thought of irking Dupree even more was tempting. "Maybe in your world 'things' only last a week or two, but I'm sorry to burst your bubble. The official word is, yes, we are still 'a thing.'"

Did you hear that, world? Why did that put an entirely new spin on the right here and right now and make her feel amazing?

The histology technician pretended not to be listening to every word as he labeled the cassette then placed it in a large buffered formalin-filled container in preparation for the overnight process. The next day, after cutting ultra-thin sections of the paraffin-encased specimens, the histologists would deliver a set of pink, blue and purple stained slides neatly laid out in cardboard containers for the pathologists to read.

This was tedious but necessary work, which took at least twenty-four hours to complete from the time of receiving the specimen to stained slides. Charlotte took her duty seriously and focused her attention on the specimens. Not Dr. Dupree. Even though what he'd said, not his visit, was responsible for her mood being lifted to one of elation. "If you'll excuse me, as you can see, I've got a lot of work to do."

Undaunted, Antwan waited for her to look at him. "I'll check back in a couple more weeks." And off he went.

The nerve of that guy. She huffed and the assistant shook his head. Yeah, they were on the same page about Antwan Dupree's reputation around the hospital. But beyond agreeing the guy was an idiot, no one could possibly understand where she was, in the condition she might be in, at this exact moment. She was on her own with that.

The room had special ventilation to suck out the caustic fumes, and she wore a duck-billed mask as well as a clear face guard to protect from any formalin splash into the eyes. It was the same thing she did on any given day at work without any side effects. Yet today, during the cutting process, she felt decidedly nauseous.

Who was she kidding? It wasn't just today.

Dreading what a week of all-day queasiness might mean, she promised to take a test once she finished the morning's lab work. She couldn't push it out of her mind another second.

At noon Charlotte stole away to the hospital laboratory and had a trusted and super-skilled lab tech draw her blood, barely feeling the prick of the needle. Then all she could do was wait for the result with fingers tightly crossed it would be negative. She couldn't let her mind venture into the realm of what she'd do if the pregnancy test was positive.

Absurd. She couldn't possibly be...could she?

As a resident pathologist, she'd seen and examined

far more than her share of young women who'd wound up in the morgue, only to discover at the autopsy they'd died from blood clots related to their birth control pills. The clots may have lodged in their lungs or brain but, wherever they were, they'd wound up being the cause of death on the autopsy report. She'd stopped taking BC pills and, even knowing the odds of forming clots were extremely small, had chosen never to use them again.

So she'd been using a diaphragm with Jackson…except on that first night when he'd caught her by surprise and he'd used a condom. And that time in her office.

Later, with zero appetite, she forced herself to eat some lunch in her office when halfway through the intercom buzzer went off.

"Dr. Johnson? This is Sara from the lab. Um, your test is positive."

"Positive?" Had she heard right? Her heart tapped a quick erratic pace at those four little words. Her blood test was positive. She forgot to breathe.

"Dr. Johnson?"

"Yes, Sara, okay. Thanks." She'd done the worst job in the world of pretending she wasn't stunned. It seemed her little "thing" with Jackson, to use Dr. Dupree's term, had just turned into something much bigger. She was pregnant. No. No. *No.*

She hung up, reached for her trash can, bent over and lost the contents of her stomach into it. She was pregnant.

When she recovered, and was positive her voice wouldn't quiver, she picked up the phone and dialed Jerry Roth. "I'm not feeling well, just threw up. I'll need to take the afternoon off."

Since she was notoriously healthy and hardly ever

called in sick, he didn't hesitate to let her go. "Go. Take care. Feel better." If it were only that easy.

Once at her town house, having been suspended in a bubble of disbelief so she could drive home safely but now feeling numb, she got out of her clothes and into her pajamas. Why she decided it was the right thing to do she didn't know. But it was. Even though it was early afternoon and summer, she wanted—no, needed—to snuggle into her soft bathrobe, to hide out and hope to find comfort there. Then she made a cup of herbal tea, noticing a fine tremor in her hand as she dipped the bag into the steaming water.

One little blood test had, once again, turned her life upside down.

What was she going to do? She didn't dare tell Jackson until she'd made her decision. The man had been adamant about never wanting another child. He'd warned her on their first date, hadn't he, almost coming off as fanatical about it. *No more children.* If she hadn't already made up her mind about liking him by then, he would have chased her away with his proclamations. Even though the "no kids" rule had matched her own.

The night they'd first made love he'd opened up and admitted feeling trapped into marriage by his ex-wife. Not that she wanted to get married to him because she was pregnant. But right from the start he'd made it known he was off the market in the marriage department. She wouldn't do that to him. But the baby. What about the baby?

Out of nowhere a long-forgotten dream from before she'd learned about her genetic markers whooshed through her. Her once-upon-a-time hopes of having it all—marriage, a career, *children*. She'd loved her ro-

tation through pediatrics in medical school. Yes, she'd
wanted children. Little knockoffs of her and whoever
her husband turned out to be. Warm and lively little
bodies that hugged better than anyone else on earth.
The only munchkins in the world who would call her
Mommy.

She plopped onto her couch and hunkered down for
an afternoon of soul-searching with a potential life-
changing outcome. Who was she kidding? Her life had
already changed that first morning in the dress shop
with that odd sensation of illness that she'd brushed off
as anxiety. She just hadn't known it yet.

Was there a scientific way to handle the situation?
She'd already done the math and come to the conclusion
the risk for her getting cancer was too high, so she'd
had the operation. She also knew without a doubt she
never wanted to pass it on. Now, though, she couldn't
remember what the exact percentage was for a potential
"daughter" to inherit her markers and gene mutations.
A lot had to do with the father, didn't it?

She dropped her head into her hands, her thoughts
fogging up, and stared at the teacup on the table in front
of the couch. Besides being addled by nausea, her mind
was fuzzy around the edges with waxing and waning
emotions of fear and joy. She couldn't ignore the joy
part, keeping her thoroughly confused. What in the
world was she supposed to do?

She'd sworn since she'd discovered she had not only
the breast cancer blood marker but also the gene muta-
tion, hell, she'd been adamant about it, *never* to have a
baby. No baby. No how. Any baby. Ever.

She remembered the day she'd begged her sister,
Cynthia, to get tested and how she'd refused. Cynthia
had already had a child by then—a boy—so at least

that was one less concern for Charlotte. But when her sister had informed her that she and her husband were planning to try for another, Charlotte had stepped up her campaign. Finally Cynthia had relented and had tested negative. Charlotte had had to bite back her envy in shame. Of course she was happy for her sister, who'd gone on to have twins, one of whom was a girl, and she still worried about little Annie's future. Cynthia had the same parents yet didn't carry the markers. Where did that leave Charlotte, the bearer of the unlucky genes? Where would it leave her baby if it was a girl?

Though what she carried would only potentially affect a girl baby, for personal ethical reasons she could never take a chance, get pregnant and wait to find out the sex before making a decision. No way would she be a designer parent, picking and choosing the child's gender, so she'd accepted it would be better to never have children. At all.

So here she was.

She needed another cup of tea. Maybe a gallon of it.

Somewhere during the course of cup after cup of calming chamomile, her anxiety rose, and several visits to the bathroom later, cautious excitement tiptoed into the mix of out-of-control feelings.

What? How could she be excited about something she'd sworn she didn't want? A baby.

Well, because she'd never *actually* been pregnant before. And now that she was, it seemed like a quiet miracle. A gift she'd never expected but somewhere deep inside had still always wanted. A bubble of joy insisted on making itself known. For a few seconds Charlotte let herself feel it, float on it, dream with that joy. A baby. *I'm going to be a mother!* Say it out loud. Make it real. She whispered it. "I'm going to be a mother."

Oh, God, she needed to hug that toilet again.

A little later, groaning and lying flat on her back on the cold tile of the bathroom floor, she stared at the white ceiling and remembered Dr. Gordon's words— *Life shouldn't be about what* might *happen, but about what's happening* right now.

She'd been born with a genetic marker she'd had no clue about, had been a happy kid as far as she remembered, and a typical teenager, until her mother had got sick. Long afterward, she'd discovered her potential for cancer, something that could be measured and planned for, unlike most people who never knew or suspected anything until they got their diagnosis. She'd dealt with it in her own way, and now she had to search her soul to decide whether or not to allow that same chance for her baby because *life shouldn't be about what might happen.* The key word jumping out at her this time—life.

Right here and now a baby was taking form in her womb, and cells were dividing and multiplying at the speed of light. Amazing. A million things could change during the process of a pregnancy. The possibilities of "what might happen" were exponential. Extraordinary. But right this second it was a fact—she was pregnant. And it seemed amazing! But the scientific part of her brain sneaked back in. Yes, she was going to be a mother. Unless a long list of potentialities stopped the process. Most importantly, would she be able to live with the guilt if her baby turned out to be a girl and also carried the same genetic markers? Or the guilt of not letting her baby have a life at all?

Her head started spinning with overwhelming thoughts. Could a person overdose on chamomile?

She rolled onto her knees, stood and staggered to her room and her bed.

At this exact moment in time she, without a doubt, knew one thing and one thing alone—that she needed a nap.

The flaw with allowing herself to succumb to a long escapist nap—in this case several hours—in the late afternoon was having to lie awake with a gazillion thoughts winging through her head now, late at night. She couldn't get Jackson out of her mind. Of course. Every rule he'd laid down from the start. In spite of that, how wonderful and compassionate he'd turned out to be. What a great lover he was, how the thought of being with him always made her quiver inside. How he'd recently admitted to people other than her that they were "a thing," both at work with Dupree and his personal life with Evan. Hell, the whole hospital knew!

How he never wanted to get married again or have children.

Yeah, that part. Plus the fact his ex-wife had got pregnant and rushed him into marriage. There was that fear again—would he suspect her of trying to do the same thing?

She had to make sure he understood that wasn't her plan. Hell, she still had to wrap her brain around the pregnancy part. She was nowhere near ready to think about the concept of marriage.

Besides, he'd yet to tell her he loved her. A fact. Did she love him? If she ever married it would have to be for love, not because she'd felt forced into it. Nothing else would do.

What was she supposed to do about their relationship now that she was pregnant? Should she wait until after the wedding to tell him? Could she bear to be around him keeping such a life-altering secret, forcing a pretend face that communicated all was well, and, oh, hey, I'm having such fun, when in reality, since the wedding in Georgia was only a week away, she'd probably still be fighting morning sickness?

Would it be fair? To either of them?

She glanced at the clock. It was nearly midnight. Maybe he'd tried to call her this afternoon while she'd been passed out in a pregnant-lady stupor. She walked to the living room and found her purse. Sure enough, he'd called, not once but twice, and had left a message after each one.

"What's up? Where are you? I heard you left work sick. Can I bring you anything?"

And an hour later.

"So you must be feeling really crappy and you're sleeping, because I checked the hospital and you hadn't been admitted. Kidding, but not really. I'm kinda worried. Call me if you need me. Okay? I'm home."

The man deserved to know. Right here. Right now. She understood the bomb she was about to drop on him would probably— Who was she kidding about *probably*? It *undeniably* would jeopardize their relationship. Though the thought already broke her heart. She grabbed an already used tissue from the coffee table. He may only see what they had as a "thing," but for her he was the "start of something big" romance, the first man she'd trusted since Derek. For Charlotte trust was the step just before...

That didn't matter since it was probably all over now, and she owed him the truth. The man who couldn't wait for his youngest son to turn twenty-one so he'd be relieved of full-time parenting wouldn't want to start over again.

Making the call wouldn't be so scary if, in all the

times they'd made love, he'd just once whispered that he loved her. She'd been foolish enough to hope he would, even while knowing it was too early for a declaration like that. Now, since the probability of him breaking things off was huge, and she'd never get the chance to hear those words from him, she had to prepare for the worst. She used that tissue again, wiping her eyes and nose. Would she ever hear "I love you" again? From anyone? *Stop thinking about what may or may not happen, get on with right here and now.*

One thing she knew without a doubt: telling a man something as monumental as this needed to be done face-to-face. Too much could be hidden over the phone. With the news she was about to lay on him she needed to see his eyes, to see his sincere reaction. And he needed to see how important this change in life plan was for her.

Her insides quivered, and it had nothing to do with feeling nauseous.

With trepidation she speed-dialed his number, making a snap decision to do something completely out of character, to lead with her feelings. Tell him how she really felt about him. Could she admit she loved him, or would it feel forced right now? Then, definitely, she'd have to get around to the other part of the issue. Or maybe she should feel him out first, to see how he felt about *her.* Oh, hell, nope. It was her call. Her "situation," and she should be the one to be boldly honest. She might not be able to say "I love you" yet, but she sure as heck had other feelings about Jackson.

An unexpected sense of hope took hold as his phone rang. *I know what I'm going to say. But the instant I hang up I need to jump into the shower and clean up*

*because...man, oh, man...I'm a mess and he cannot see
me like this when I break the news.*

Jackson stirred from a restless sleep and looked at the
time. It was midnight. And Charlotte was calling. He
hoped she wasn't horribly sick. He'd left those messages, asking her to let him know if there was anything
he could do. He'd even considered stopping by on his
way home from work. But knowing how independent
she was, he'd opted to wait to be invited. On alert, he
sat up and answered the phone.

"Are you okay?"

"I'm crazy about you."

"What?"

"I've been meaning to tell you how crazy I am about
you for some time now."

Was she dialing drunk? She was the most practical lady he'd ever met. Why would she call and blurt
out such a thing unless...? Maybe she had a fever and
was delirious.

"Will you come over?"

She'd just told him she was crazy about him, was
probably a little tipsy, and now she'd asked him to come
over. With all the possibilities that proposition held,
how could he refuse?

"I'll be right there."

As he cleaned up and got dressed, an odd thought
about the midnight invitation to his lady's house made
him smile. Plus she'd said she was crazy about him,
which was totally out of character but made him feel
like a prince. Who'd have ever guessed when he'd first
noticed her all those months ago that the prim-looking
and earnest-as-hell pathologist would have turned out

to be a sexy drama queen? The funny thing was, he liked it. He *really* liked it.

Several other thoughts forced their way out of the recesses of his mind as he drove to her house. How Charlotte was healing him and how grateful he was for that. He'd been shedding layer after layer of protective defenses since he'd met her. Something about her had made him like her right off, but now that they'd got close—in fact, closer than he'd been to anyone other than his wife—it seemed he was becoming a new man. Because she'd made it okay. She accepted him. He felt things again. Life was something to look forward to, not simply to manage to get through day by day. And because of his changing, he thought about a future. Maybe right here in California.

Sometimes the way he and Charlotte got along made him wonder if he had ever really been close to his wife like that. Their hasty marriage hadn't felt like his idea. He hadn't felt nearly ready for it, or for becoming a father twice before he'd turned twenty-four. To everyone else, his family, hers, he'd been a young doctor with a bright future. They had been the perfect couple. So he'd learned to work that to his advantage. A wife and kids completed his package as a safe bet to hire into a respected surgical practice, to groom for bigger and better things, like taking on the role of department head of surgery at Savannah General. His stay-at-home wife had made it easy for him to shine, too. He was grateful for it. While he'd spent hours and hours working his way up, she'd raised the kids. Mostly alone. Especially after he'd signed on for the medical unit in the army reserves and had started volunteering for disaster missions. Had they ever been close?

Andrew and Evan had been the highlights of his

life, though—he couldn't dispute that, even when working sixty-hour weeks and going away one weekend a month. He smiled as he sat at a red light, remembering the heat he'd taken from his grandfather for not strapping Andrew with the name of Jackson Ryland Hilstead the Fourth. Evaline had stood by him on that decision. He sure hoped Drew appreciated it. So his ex-wife had given him his family and had stuck with him until he'd fallen apart. What more could a man have asked?

For better or worse? For both legs? For a wife who wasn't repulsed by him? Someone to stand by him through the toughest trials in his life, not just the successes?

His smile dissolved. Those wishes required a lot in return. He'd let their relationship grow empty. Truth was, he hadn't been there for her beyond providing a home and a lifestyle loaded with the perks of being the wife of a wealthy doctor. And that hadn't been enough. Because he hadn't been around. For most of their marriage that situation had been satisfactory for her. Until he'd changed for the worse after taking that second tour in the Middle East in the army reserves and had come home from Afghanistan.

Coming home a hot mess—to use his mother's favorite saying—broken and disfigured. Coupled with his PTSD and withdrawal, it hadn't been nearly enough for her anymore. He'd stopped being able to run a department. To do surgery! The one thing he'd come to think was the reason he'd been put on the planet.

Truth was, he hadn't been willing to fight for Evaline like he supposed he should have. He'd hit bottom so fast and hard his heart had splattered. He hadn't had anything left. It made him wonder if he'd ever really loved her. Or vice versa.

So now he was forty-two, driving after midnight to a new woman's town house because she'd dialed drunk, told him she was crazy about him and invited him over. Crazy, right? But he was excited about it. In fact, he hadn't felt excited about much in life since the war injury…until Charlotte. The woman who was helping him heal step by step. He was a better man because of her.

And if her calling meant she wanted to take him to bed, hell, yeah, he was all for it. Even if her virus or whatever it was that had made her leave work got him sick, it would still be worth it. Because there was something close and tender they shared beyond the crazy-hot sex. It was called total acceptance, and that special part, her accepting him as he was, and him doing the same with her, was bringing him back to life. He could only hope she felt the same.

Charlotte's heart fluttered when the security light came on from the entrance gate. She hit the entry button to allow Jackson to pass and park, her lungs forgetting to breathe on their own. With damp palms she finger-combed her hair and took a quick glance in the hallway mirror. Did it really matter how she looked? Something far greater than her appearance was at stake.

He knocked, and she nearly lost her nerve. Could she run to the bedroom and hide under her pillows?

Willing strength she wasn't sure she had, she bit her lower lip and opened the door. There stood Jackson in all his post-midnight glory. Hair dashingly disheveled, eyes bright and blue, huge questions in them. Late-night stubble. "You don't look sick to me. You look great." His expression was lusty and hopeful.

Her eyes closed as she inhaled before she could answer, picking up his fresh application of spiced aftershave and fighting a wave of nausea. "I'm not sick in the classic sense, though God knows I've been nauseous all day. Well, all week, actually."

He scrunched up his face, trying to follow her meandering explanation. With his high intelligence he was probably already putting the equation together. Or choosing to ignore it, in which case she'd have to hit him over the head with it.

"May I come in?"

Oh, God, she hadn't even let him inside. "Of course." She stepped back, but he reached for her arm and squeezed as he kissed her hello. She flinched, but for one instant the gesture, his warm lips pressing against hers, calmed her. What would he think? Then her roiling nerves took over again. "Have a seat."

His glance seemed to ask, *Why so formal? What if I want to stick around and keep kissing you?* Yet he dutifully went to her beige couch and sat. "I get the impression you have something important to say."

Her eyes lifted to the ceiling. "That's an understatement." She halted any further comment from him by using her hands to tap the air. "Let me figure out how to best say this. Okay?"

"How to say what?"

She paced and glanced at him, could read confusion or irritation in his expression, or maybe it was concern. She was being too obtuse, and needed to get to the point of why she'd called him out in the middle of the night. He might really think it was just to have sex. She stopped walking and faced him, then took a deep breath, deciding to go full speed ahead.

"Okay, let me start from the beginning." She had his total attention and the responsibility seemed more than she could bear, but she forced herself to pull it together. She had no choice, so she blurted, "It seems I'm pregnant."

The words had the expected effect of hitting him like a brick. He didn't smile or jump up to hug her with joy. No, that was the fantasy version of how this conversation would go. Instead, his eyes flashed wide and his head jerked back. Far too authentic for her to handle right now. Apparently she'd left him speechless. So, with her feet planted, she opted to continue her story. "I never expected to be pregnant. I'm not trying to trick you into marriage or anything." She assumed he'd gone right to the conclusion that history was repeating itself all these years later. "I swear. But since you're the father, I owe it to you to be honest and up front." She stopped to swallow and take a breath. "I'm choosing to keep my baby."

And there it was, the horrified look, the you-blew-every-great-thing-we-had expression. The tension around his brows reminded her how he'd laid out the rules right from the start. He didn't want to get married. He never wanted to be a father again. Her insides clutched.

"I know. You don't want to be a father ever again. You made it very clear. And yet here I am telling you I want this baby. After swearing I never wanted to pass my cancer genes on to a child of mine." Her chin quivered, but she refused to let the emotions gathering speed inside take over, so she bit down hard on her lip and counted to three. "I am afraid and filled with guilt about my decision, guilt for you and for the baby, but I can't say I'm sorry. I just can't."

Finally, she had the nerve to look into his face and eyes again. True, at first he'd looked horrified, or that was how she'd read it, but now his mien seemed perplexed, as though he was trying to solve a mathematical problem. A very big and complicated mathematical problem.

She remembered the words he'd repeated to her before the first time they'd been together, and the more that she was getting used to being pregnant and dealing with it, she bent those words from Dr. Gordon and decided to toss them back at him.

"You were the one who quoted the good doctor that 'life shouldn't be about what might happen,' otherwise we never would have made love in the first place, right?"

She suddenly had his undivided attention, the dumbfounded look nearly causing his mouth to drop open. She wanted to sit beside him and plead for him to understand, but she stayed right there, on the other side of the coffee table from him. "So that brings us back to what is happening right now. Yes, I'm pregnant."

"You're pregnant." Evidently he was still feeling stunned.

"Yes, and you made me that way." Her finger shot up. "No, that isn't exactly right. We got that way together. *We're* pregnant."

Still Jackson remained painfully silent. It cut like a blade through her center.

She'd just laid her fear, pride and guilt on the table and he wasn't rushing to save any of it. Her decision to stay pregnant seemed to be hanging in the balance of his grace. She couldn't allow him to have that control over her body and her baby. Could she stand to hear him tell her thanks but, no, thanks? Oh, God, no, it would hurt too much. Fear took over about what he might say, and as was her pattern of dealing with fear, she rushed into a response before he'd had time to digest her news and form the words for a reply. She simply couldn't take this agonizing pause. If he wasn't going to say anything right this instant, she needed to step in, take control, preempt the outcome. "Please, leave. Now."

"Charlotte." She heard pleading and frustration in the single word of her name.

She shook her head. "I promise not to upset your carefully planned-out life. I get it. You told me from the start. You've done the fatherhood thing and never want to do it again. You're counting down the days until Evan turns twenty-one." Her fear seemed to change to anger from one breath to the next and she couldn't bite her tongue to stop the next thought from coming out. "I know you never want to get married again. Hell, you can be an old lonely man for all I care. I'm having this baby." Damn the break in her voice, the surge of hurt childishness, the threatening tears welling in her eyes. Damn them all. And damn him, too.

She scanned the table for more used tissues.

"Wait a second," he said. "You're reading all kinds of things into this, and I don't deserve your insults. Can you understand that I might need to digest everything you've just told me? You owe me a little time to think, don't you?" He stood, imploringly, it seemed, taking a couple of steps toward her.

She moved back. "Sure." She sounded terse.

Had she hoped for and maybe even expected too much from her Southern gentleman? He didn't rush to her or make a single promise. He'd simply stood there looking all befuddled. *You're what?* What he asked for was time. And a reasonable person would grant him that. But she was anything but reasonable in her pregnant and scared sightless state.

The saying that actions spoke louder than words hit her like a full frontal head butt, knocking her fear aside and fueling her anger. He obviously didn't want any responsibility for this baby growing second by second inside her. If he didn't want to jump on board with the pregnancy, that said all she needed to know, and so she didn't have time for him. If she were a princess, she would have him banished, but she was a modern woman dealing with a life-changing event, and it hurt to have to go through it alone, to not get from him the support that she'd secretly prayed for. Her secret dream. But so be it.

"Go," she said, trying to cover up her true feelings. "Think all you want. Nothing is changing on this end. Go. Go!" Had she actually yelled at him?

Because he didn't budge, she grabbed his hand, pulled and led him to her front door, and only because he was still stunned and didn't seem to have the ability to resist her did he allow her to push him out. Or maybe he wanted her to, to let him off the hook. *She kicked me out!* he could claim later—which only made her angrier. She closed the door with a bang, nearly in his face.

She wanted to cry and scream and drop to her knees with disappointment, but the only thing she could do right that moment was respond to his muffled protests on the other side. "Charlotte. Charlotte. Come on. Don't be like this."

She searched for her voice and mustered all the nerve she had left. "Just to make it clear, I said nothing is changing on this end. Except whether or not I'll ever let you back."

CHAPTER NINE

JACKSON WASN'T EVEN sure how he'd made the drive home. His head swam with thoughts yet nothing seemed clear enough to grasp. Charlotte was pregnant, the one thing they'd both agreed from the start would never happen.

And she planned to keep the baby.

Where did that leave him? With an intense sense of déjà vu.

Think straight!

First, he needed to admit he loved her for helping him get his life back, and though he'd been on the verge of telling her—his midnight visit had seemed like the perfect time—the news that she was pregnant had knocked him completely off track. It had rocked the thoughts in his brain until they were so jumbled up he couldn't think.

The monumental revelation, that he loved something Charlotte had done for him, helping him heal and grow, deserved its own moment in time. He'd planned to indulge in the new thought for days to come, that he might be able to love again, to hold the concept in his hands and pass it back and forth, to get a feel for it, savoring the secret, and then and only then to find the nerve to say it out loud. To see how it sounded: *Charlotte, you've revived me, and I'm finally open to a complete relationship with you. Are you ready to see where this goes?*

It might sound awkward and clinical, but it was his true feeling, and she deserved to know.

But she'd just told him she was pregnant!

Now he'd have to jump ahead dozens of steps in the relationship to admit the big secret. The one he'd planned to carry around with him for days, taking his own sweet time to tease her with dumb grins, special touches, secret glances at work, all building to the big revelation. *I'm in love with you, can't you tell?* Now everything had changed. Because the pregnancy forced it. And long before he was ready he had to admit it. The truth shocked him, made his mouth go dry. This was never supposed to happen again.

She wasn't merely "a thing." She hadn't ever been.

He loved her. Damn it, he loved her. But there wasn't time or the luxury of basking in that knowledge because she was already making him a father. Again.

Part of him wanted to kick himself for getting into this position in the first place. Wasn't a man supposed to learn from his history? Why had he let himself think he could be normal, pick up his life, enjoy getting close with a woman again? He'd been playing with fire since he'd first asked her out. If only Charlotte hadn't made it so enticing and easy.

Sure, blame her. You wanted her long before she came around to the idea. His fingers flew to his brows and rubbed up and down, as if that might help clear his head.

He'd sat there just now at her house like a big dolt when she'd told him. His jaw had dropped open, mind numbed by the news, unable to respond. *This is all out of order. I need more time to get used to the first part! You're not just a thing to me. I think I love you.*

He'd seen her inconsolable reaction, as clear as her beautiful brown eyes. He'd hurt her to the marrow, ripped open her heart, left her bleeding, and she'd turned that hurt into anger and kicked him out. Could he blame her?

He paced his condo, unable to rest, wanting to call her but still not knowing what to say. *I love you but I'm not ready for more.*

A baby? He was forty-two, done with those things. They'd made a pact on their first date, hadn't they? She clearly hadn't keep her side of the bargain. But was that all they were to each other, a bargain? He stopped to breathe and felt the wall building itself around him, separating him from the living, keeping him safe from ever feeling again.

Was he done with Charlotte? Could he throw away that new love so easily? What kind of man walked away from a woman he'd finally and only just recently admitted he loved, because she was pregnant and he didn't want to be a father again?

An empty and damaged-for-life bastard, that was who. Write it down, put it in his packet—damaged goods. But was that who he really was? Now was the time to decide if he was still that other man. Or not.

He slid onto his couch, mind roiling, hands fisted, sweat beading on his upper lip. He wanted a stiff drink, the crutch he'd come to rely on years before. But he'd spent enough time on the dark side after the accident. He knew the path to hell backward and forward and never wanted to go there again. He'd traded in that prison cell for a new beginning in California. Which had opened him up…for Charlotte.

He called her. She didn't answer. He didn't leave a message.

He glanced at his watch—it was almost three a.m. His first surgery was scheduled for seven. He put on a pot of coffee, set the brew button for five a.m. then went to his bedroom, threw on his jogging shorts and exchanged his prosthetic for the running blade, then drove to Malibu for a long soul-searching run on the beach just before dawn. Maybe it would help clear his head.

Having a full surgical schedule would force him to compartmentalize. Charlotte deserved his undivided attention and so did his patients. He could only deal with one trauma at a time, and one hundred percent couldn't be divided during surgery. As much as it tore him up, since she hadn't answered earlier, he'd have to wait until that night to talk to Charlotte. Maybe he'd be more coherent by then.

In the meantime he worried what kind of a hard-hearted SOB she'd think he was. Because he cared. And because he was leaving her in limbo for a day, he deserved all of her negative thoughts about him. He could practically feel them with each step of his run. His pace was off, his muscles tight and tender, his breathing out of sync. Yeah, he deserved it for putting her through hell.

The problem with taking the "patients come first" approach in medicine was that when at the end of an unbelievably grueling day, when he hadn't had an hour's sleep the night before and had zero left to give, he wound up giving himself a pass on calling Charlotte. *I need to be well rested, to have my thoughts straight, to know exactly what I think and feel about the situation*, he rationalized. He hadn't had a moment to think about any of it that day, and with tomorrow's schedule he feared it would be no different then.

She'd probably be done with him by then. And he would deserve it. So he dialed her number again. She didn't pick up. Again.

He fell into bed, planning to call her once more in an hour, and amazingly slept through the night instead. But at five a.m. he was wide-awake, his head spinning with thoughts. It was too early to call her, so he dressed for another run. He needed to consider the consequences of his affair with the beautiful pathologist. The woman he loved. He was starting to get used to the phrase, the woman he loved. That was progress, wasn't it? Maybe by the time he had finished jogging, she'd be up. He'd call her. This time she might answer.

But what would he say? Could he make things right with her after this torturing delay?

It wasn't a good run—in fact, it was worse than the day before. Every step felt as sluggish as his brain. Anxious thoughts came to mind. How much he missed Charlotte. How he needed to talk to her, which left him edgy and stepping up his pace. One he could hardly keep up with. After the unheroic way he'd handled her news, why would she even want anything to do with him? She'd pushed him out of her house. Her life? Hell, maybe it was better to let things end as they had.

He wanted to kick himself for letting the negative and completely unacceptable thought slip in.

It was an old and sorry excuse, as familiar as a predictable movie. And totally unacceptable. Wasn't he a new man—a healing man, thanks to Charlotte—or had her news ripped off the new skin and left him back where he'd started three years ago with all of his old flaws alive and festering, dragging him down?

Was that really what he was made of? He hated to think of the answer. He was only forty-two, it had been over three years since everything had changed, and surely he was a better man now.

He stopped and called her. As predicted, it went directly to message. "Charlotte, we need to talk. When can I see you?"

He ran on, soon hearing a text message shoot through. Don't bother to call again.

Blast it all to hell. He really had blown it by letting the extra day go by!

Damn, he already missed her more than he had ever thought possible. His chest ached, fearing he'd lost her forever. She was pregnant with his baby. Their baby. He understood what an epic decision it had to be for her to have the baby. Her fears, her guilt of passing on imperfect genes. He wanted to be by her side every step of the way. Now all he had to do was convince her he wasn't the heel she must think he was.

Not an easy task.

He ran back to his car, remembering how important the role of being a father was, and how his wife had always complained he had never been there enough for the boys. If he was a new man, couldn't he be the kind of father for this baby that he hadn't been for his sons? Charlotte was giving him a chance to shine in life again. Together. Why would he want to crawl back to his "you call this living" cocoon?

Things could be completely different this time if she'd only give him a chance. Shouldn't she give him a break? Sure, he'd failed his first chance, when she'd told him the news. He could tell how hard her decision must have been—she'd looked like she'd been through the wringer. The fine skin beneath those beautiful eyes had looked bruised and tense. Her full, normally soft mouth bitten and tight. She'd left work early and had probably thought about her condition every second until she'd called him. She'd cautiously tiptoed her feelings out, testing him, and had blown him away with her words. "I'm crazy about you."

She'd put herself on the line and he could have been a robot for the lack of response he'd given her. Of course she'd be furious with him. In his defense, he'd been completely stunned. But he'd had time to recover, and all he'd chosen to do had been to let her down in the name of needing time to think things through and his demanding job. No wonder she never wanted to hear from him again.

He got into his car, wondering what good was a man who didn't risk it all for the woman he loved? Yeah, he'd had enough time to admit it and now he knew without a doubt that he *loved* her. Maybe he'd been forced to come to the conclusion, but the feeling had already been there, well hidden, of course, because even a breath of admitting he could love again had scared the hell out of him, let alone the thought of becoming a dad again. He knew he wouldn't feel the love so strongly now if it hadn't already been there, starting as a seed and growing every time they'd seen each other. Why else had everything felt so right whenever they'd been together?

He drove to her town house and pushed the security button.

"Go away." Her voice came through the speaker a few seconds later.

"I need to talk to you."

She clicked off and didn't open the gate for him. After a few minutes he revised his plan. Because now that he'd had an epiphany, he knew what needed to be done. If life was all about what was happening right then, not the past or what might be in the future, he wanted and needed with everything he had to be there for Charlotte *now*. And when the time came, he'd be a proper father for their kid, too. That was the beauty of new beginnings—he could start afresh, get it right this time.

He glanced at his watch. It was almost six on Thursday morning and he had another big surgery in less than two hours. Tomorrow, Friday, was the day they were supposed to leave for Georgia and his cousin's wedding. He'd bought the plane tickets and made reservations at the grand old hotel on the banks of the Savannah River. But forget about the wedding. He wouldn't go unless Charlotte was by his side. There was no way he'd go without her.

He'd been told all his life he was smart, but what this situation called for wasn't brains. It called for heart... plus a bit of resourcefulness. For a methodical surgeon, every once in a while he surprised himself with his creativity. A great idea popped into his mind. Sure, it was a risk, a huge risk, which made it all the more necessary. Charlotte had done the same with him the night before last, had laid it all out there. Now it was his turn. She deserved no less. The only question was, how would Charlotte respond to his over-the-top plan?

It was seven a.m. Jackson had performed the five-minute hand and arm scrub, and donned the first pair of his sterile double gloves. His surgical nurse had just helped him into his gown, his cap and mask were in place, and he used his elbow to push the plate on the automatic door opener on the wall. The important surgery required a frozen section. He'd seen Dr. Gordon's name on the list for the morning, so he'd called and, calling in a favor, had insisted that Dr. Johnson had to do it. It would be up to Jim Gordon, now that he was back part-time at work, to come up with a believable reason for Charlotte to step in. Knowing what a team player Jim was, Jackson trusted it would be a good one, too.

An hour later, after they'd cracked open the patient's chest and he'd biopsied the mass on the right lung, he put the fresh tissue into the waiting petri dish, which was sealed and labeled and quickly handed over to the OR runner. Pathology knew the specimen was coming. "Don't give it to anyone but Dr. Johnson."

"Yes, sir." The young summer volunteer, garbed in full OR regalia, took the specimen and fled like his life depended on the mission. Did he even know who Dr. Johnson was?

The entire surgical team waited for the report as the surgery was held in limbo and the patient constantly monitored.

While he waited, leaving the assistant surgeon in charge, he knew beyond a doubt what he had to do once he heard Charlotte's voice. He wanted to be a man Charlotte could trust and depend on and look to for support, for everything, and he didn't intend to waste another minute before he told her.

Within five minutes he heard Charlotte's voice on the OR intercom. There was a noticeably cool clip to it. "The lung biopsy is benign for cancer."

Great news for the patient, though it was imperative for pathology to figure out exactly what the mass was with further studies. He cleared his throat before Charlotte could disconnect. He couldn't let it matter that he'd be in front of the entire surgical team and anyone who was within earshot in the pathology department.

This was too important, and now was the time for desperate measures.

"Charlotte?"

A second, then two passed. "Yes?"

"This is Jackson, just to make it clear."

Another pause. "Yes."

He took a deep breath. "I never thought I'd have a shotgun wedding at forty-two, and I can't exactly get on bended knee here in surgery." The staff laughed and looked surprised, but when they realized he wasn't kidding around, everyone stopped to listen to what in the world he would say next. "But, Charlotte, will you marry me?"

"P-pardon me?" she stammered. "We're on the speakerphone, Jackson."

"I know. And I don't care. You won't take my calls and I figured if I came down there you wouldn't see me. So, with the OR staff as my witnesses, I'm asking, will you marry me?" Then, taking the biggest risk of his life, well, after proposing in front of almost a dozen people, he said, "I'll give you some time to think." Then he nodded for his surgical nurse to click off the intercom.

The instant she did, the operating-room team broke into applause.

He tried to ignore them, having a patient lying on the OR table and all, though he felt fantastic, like he'd just climbed Mount Everest, and smiled beneath his mask. He'd done it. Excellent. A wave of insecurity knocked him back a bit. His stunt didn't guarantee a "yes" from Charlotte, but at least he'd made his case loud and clear. With witnesses! He loved her. He wanted to marry her.

Now forcing his personal life to the back of his brain, he focused on the patient, who deserved to be front and center. When he'd finished resecting the rest of the mass and tying off all involved vessels, he asked the assistant surgeon to close for him. He knew and trusted the young woman's skill. Plus the team was completely on board with him needing to leave.

He disposed of his dirty gowns and gloves, washed his hands again, then strode to the doctors' lockers. He grabbed his work kit and headed to the bathroom to clean up and shave, to make himself as presentable as he could possibly be, before facing the woman he loved. Once he passed the mirror test, he gave himself a reassuring nod. "You've got this."

First off, he stopped to speak to the family of his lung surgery patient, sharing his good report, watching the tension vanish from their eyes and foreheads. Then, on his way to the elevator, while passing through the surgical ward, he noticed a patient getting discharged and there was a beautiful bouquet remaining at the bedside on the movable table. The staff rolled the table out of the room and into the hall in order to get the patient into the wheelchair in the tiny private room.

"You taking this?" he asked.

"No. I don't want to be reminded of this place," the young man said. "Flowers aren't my thing anyway."

"Mind if I borrow them?"

"Take 'em, they're yours."

Jackson removed the bright white daisies and yellow sunflowers from the glass vase and shook off the excess water. He grabbed some paper towels from the nearby dispenser to wrap around the stems. Pleased it was a proper enough bouquet, one fit for following up on a marriage proposal, he headed down to the basement and the pathology department. Since he didn't have a ring to offer her, these bright summer flowers would have to do.

* * *

Charlotte stood bewildered, staring at the OR intercom in the tiny room with the cryostat machine. Jackson had just asked her to marry him. The thought set off full body chills. The good kind. This after she'd spent the last two days trying to force him out of her life and heart. And had failed miserably. Was he serious? He wouldn't dare play a cruel joke on her, would he?

Of course not!

She'd laid a huge surprise on him the other night, then had gone ballistic when he'd been as stunned as she was right now. He'd needed time to think through the sudden life change rather than jump up and down with joy. Hell, *she* hadn't felt joyful when she'd got the news, yet she'd expected him to be. How unfair and unrealistic she'd been. But being frightened about her decision to become a mother, a decision as momentous as her double mastectomy surgery, she'd needed his instant support. Unreasonably so. And he'd been unable to give it to her right off. So she'd got mad.

It'd hurt, and sent her back to feeling like a needy teenager when her father had offered little support over the death of her mother. She'd freaked out and pushed Jackson out the door. Out of her life? She didn't know for sure because she couldn't think clearly at the time. All she knew was he hadn't met her unrealistic and unreasonable needs, so he'd become a villain.

Two miserable days later, deep down she knew without a doubt he was anything but.

He'd pleaded with her to understand, to give him time to think, to let him back in. Yet she'd said something hurtful and angry through the door about whether or not she'd ever let him back. How immature.

It hadn't been fair to him, not by a long shot. Most

guys would have just walked away and given up. *Her loss*, they could have rationalized. Yet Jackson had just pulled the craziest stunt she could ever imagine. He'd proposed over an OR intercom, with his entire surgical staff listening in. That proved he loved her, didn't it?

She smiled, tears welled in her eyes and she pushed them away. Except he had yet to say the words.

Now it was perfectly clear why Dr. Gordon had made that shabby excuse for not being able to do his scheduled assignment for the morning. She'd checked the surgery lineup and had seen Jackson's name and nearly lost her breakfast. They'd conspired against her.

Someone cleared their throat. She turned to see her mentor, who'd stepped around from being just on the other side of the laboratory wall. Though thinner than he used to be, the flash was back in his old eyes. "That was quite a scene," he said, unable to hide his pleasure.

"Did you know he was going to do that?"

"To propose? No. But he begged me to make you do the frozen section. What was a man to do?"

She shook her head, letting herself float on air just a little. What a stunt, asking a woman to marry him with an audience. Yet *not* hearing the most important part first, *I love you*, kept her tethered to the ground. He was going the traditional, honorable route. Girl gets pregnant, the guy marries her. It was probably a golden rule of the South. Was she supposed to clap her hands in joy? Was this what she truly wanted?

Dr. Gordon stepped closer and patted her back. Her mixed-up tears kept coming. It was great to have him at work again, even if only part-time, and for how long, no one could possibly guess. She was especially glad he'd been in on the most amazing proposal she could ever have dreamed of—minus a single phrase.

"I hope you have the good sense to tell him yes."

She went quiet, in all honesty not knowing for sure what her answer would be. "I'll let you know when I figure it out."

With that, they walked back to their respective offices, where piles of patient slides awaited their diagnoses.

She took her seat in front of the microscope, adjusting the head, resting her nose between the eyepieces, and, still feeling as light as a feather with hope and love, she focused on the slide in the tray holder. From time to time, though, she considered how she'd forced Jackson into the corner, and being the wonderful man he was, he couldn't stand to let her down. She worried she'd never know for sure if he loved her or was only doing his Southern gentleman duty. The honorable thing.

Would that be good enough?

Charlotte spent the next hour and a half in her darkened office with the shine of his big moment and proposal fading, reading slides, trying to put the man she loved out of her mind. A nearly impossible task. What would she tell him?

Her door flew open, the light was turned on, and in barged Jackson. She jumped. "I believe we left off at the part where I asked you to marry me." He pushed the flowers at her.

Enough time had passed for her to come off her cloud—in fact, with her growing doubt those clouds had turned a pale shade of gray. She didn't want to force him into doing something he didn't truly want. With a guarded heart she spoke. "You don't have to do me any favors, Jackson." She took the flowers anyway, laid them on her desk.

He looked puzzled, as if he couldn't believe that she still didn't get it.

* * *

Jackson had been so swept away with carrying out his risky task, he'd forgotten some very important words. He'd managed to mangle the proposal. What a mess. The whole thing had started with Charlotte feeling insecure about being pregnant and having to break the news to him, a guy who'd never wanted to get married or have kids again. He needed her to know something.

"Forgive me. I forgot to tell you something first—the most important part." Jackson approached Charlotte's chair and took her hands, bringing her to standing so he could look into those warm brown, though suddenly skeptical, eyes. He noticed her hands were shaking, and for a guy who'd just performed flawless surgery, his hands were, too. Why wouldn't they be? They were both about to embark on the biggest journey of their lives. This time together. If he could get Charlotte to cooperate, that was.

"I want to be there for our baby, Charlotte."

"And?"

"And? Oh, of course, and you! I want to be there for you."

"Because?" Now she looked downright impatient.

Because? Oh, for crying out loud, he really was sleep deprived and not thinking straight. "I love you. Didn't I say it?" In all honesty, the proposal in the OR, fueled by anxiety and adrenaline, was a blur.

"No."

Damn. He'd blown it big-time, but couldn't she read between the lines? "But I asked you to marry me. Surely that implies that? You know—"

She canted her head as if he'd been singing a beautiful aria and had just hit a sour note. He could fix that.

"I love you." He hoped the sincerity he felt down to

his bones was reflected in his eyes, because he needed her to understand how important this was to him. "I want to marry you, to be our baby's father, if you'll have me." She gazed at him, not as much as a whisper crossing her lips. He needed to step up his pitch. Maybe appeal to her practical side? "You'll need my help raising our kid because you have no clue what you're getting yourself into. Trust me, you need me. Our kid needs me." He would have missed her twitch of a smile if he'd blinked, because he was sweating through what had turned out to be a totally messed-up proposal. He hoped she needed him half as much as he needed her, now that he'd finally admitted it. He let go of her hands and framed her face then kissed her with everything he had, trying to communicate what he couldn't somehow manage to find the perfect words for. She kissed him back. A good sign. It occurred that she might need to hear him say it again. "I need you, because I love you. Marry me. Please."

She fell against him, and he held her tight.

"We've had a rocky patch," she said to his chest before she looked up at him. "It took a couple of days for you to come to your decision."

"You mean my senses."

"Yes." She smiled, but not joyfully, more of a sad or resigned kind of smile. Could his delay in figuring things out have taken that much life out of her? "Like you, I'd like to take some time to think over your proposal."

Had his hesitation and two days' lag time been enough to make her question what they had? He had no right to demand an answer right now, not after what he'd done, but it hurt to the center of his heart, realizing how he'd left her alone when she'd needed him most.

Now he could say he truly knew how she'd felt. All he could do was hope she'd come to her senses the way he had and say yes. Yes to their future. "I don't want to wait that long, but I have to understand after what I've put you through."

"It isn't payback, Jackson. I've got to think things over."

Suddenly feeling like a man walking a tightrope, he went still. "That's understandable." What would he do if she told him no? He didn't want to let her out of his sight but he had to finish his afternoon clinic and tie things up for the next few days away. "What about the wedding this weekend? Will you still go to Savannah with me?"

She kissed him lightly, then looked into his eyes. "Yes. I promised I'd go with you and I'll go."

That gave him time and the chance to make things right again. If he couldn't convince her that he loved her right now, maybe the beauty of his hometown would help her fall in love.

CHAPTER TEN

LATE ON FRIDAY night Charlotte stood at the window of her tenth-story hotel room in Savannah, watching a foreign container ship slowly pass by. The tall rusted ship loaded several stories high with colorful cargo crates almost reached her eye level. Definitely a working ship. With tons and tons of cargo, how could it possibly stay afloat?

"That thing's huge," she said loudly to Jackson, who was arranging clothes in the closet.

"Get used to it—this is one of the most traveled rivers for international shipping in the US."

"It's really fascinating. I kind of feel like the captain could be watching me with his binoculars."

"I wouldn't be surprised. Probably hoping to get a peep show."

That made her laugh. "Boy, would he be disappointed."

Out of nowhere Jackson was at her back, passing his arms around her waist and pulling her close and nuzzling her neck. "He wouldn't get the chance because I'd deck him if he tried spying on you."

She turned her head so they could kiss. "Thanks." She looked back at the ship, almost directly across from them. "Did you see that, Captain?" she called out.

Jackson chuckled along with her and hugged her closer.

It was the first time they'd gone away overnight and checked into a hotel room together, and the first time they'd cuddled today. He'd chosen a gorgeous and grand hotel and spa with a harbor view. Every detail about the place spoke of old wealth. For a San Fernando Valley girl who'd grown up in a lower middle class area, the obvious opulence, though beautiful and inviting, also made her a little uncomfortable. Even now, she'd never think to stay in such a place, but apparently the man with three names and a number was in his element.

Their spacious bedroom had plenty of room to sit on the love seat and enjoy the view. Like a grand lady wearing a shiny pearl necklace, the Savannah River looked extra pretty with the city lights from across the river.

"What's all that?" She pointed across the river to a long street still busy with activity at the late hour. Rather than deal with what was written on her heart, for now she'd stick to superficial talk. Which was pretty much what they'd done for the entire flight to Georgia.

"That's River Street. All those buildings used to be cotton warehouses. Now they've been converted into anything your heart desires."

"Wow."

She looked downward at the huge hotel pool accented with lights, then to the right where a white gazebo adorned in tiny café lights looked like a miniature toy in the center of a picture-perfect lawn. All the while, as she checked out the area, she enjoyed the warmth of Jackson's body against hers, his hands resting on her stomach. It made her think of their baby and how protected it was right this moment. "Looks like they have weddings here, too."

"They have weddings everywhere in Savannah. It's a very romantic city. I can't wait to show you the historic district tomorrow morning."

"In that case, I hate to be a party pooper, but since we've got a big day tomorrow I'd better get some sleep. I'm worn out from the flight and getting up so early." *And being pregnant and totally confused about your marriage proposal.* She glanced at her watch and realized that back home it was only eight o'clock. Was that what pregnancy did to a woman?

"I wanted to introduce you to an old college buddy of mine—we were roommates—but I can understand your needing more rest these days." Jackson had been completely accommodating the entire day, and now was no different. "You've got to take care of our baby, right?"

That was part of the problem. Since Jackson had come around and said he wanted to marry her and he loved her, she couldn't quite shake the feeling it was all about the baby. "I had no idea how exhausting being pregnant was."

He squeezed her a little tighter. "And I don't want to make you feel worse by pushing too hard. The point is for you to enjoy the wedding tomorrow evening. To enjoy Savannah." He kissed her cheek. "Would you mind if I met up with Jarod for drinks downstairs in the bar?"

"Of course not. Go right ahead."

"Okay, I won't be late. Just a drink and a little catching up on things."

Within ten minutes of Jackson leaving, Charlotte had done her nighttime routine and snuggled into the amazingly comfortable bed, choosing to leave the curtains open so she could continue to look outside before going to sleep. She may not have the energy to be out there, but she could still enjoy the hustle and bustle of River Street across the river. She was also rewarded with the grand entrance of another enormous cargo ship passing slowly through the waters. The sight put a smile on her face, making her feel oddly connected with the wide world while snug in her bed.

Unfortunately, she couldn't shut down her mind or stop her worries about Jackson. Honor was a large part of who he was, and she worried he was merely doing the right thing by asking her to marry him because she'd got pregnant. Just like he'd done with his ex-wife. Before the weekend was over she'd have to confront him about it. With her body dictating her needs, plus the fact she'd hardly slept last night from thinking nonstop about Jackson's true motives for proposing, within a few minutes she'd drifted off to sleep.

She heard voices and forced her eyes open. Glancing next to her in the bed, there was evidence that Jackson had slept there, and she remembered cuddling next to him at one point in the night, but he wasn't there now. Plus the sheets felt cold. How long had he been up? And who was he talking to? Should she hide under the blankets and play possum?

"Thank you," Jackson said, then closed the hotel-room door, before shortly appearing at her bedside with a full breakfast tray.

She sat up, mouth open. "Wow."

"Good morning, sunshine! Breakfast is served."

She had to hand it to him, he was really trying hard—the least she could do was be gracious.

She glanced at the digital clock on the bedside table. It was only seven-thirty in the morning. That would be four-thirty back home. "I feel like a princess. Thank you." She hoped the current wave of morning queasiness would pass so she could really enjoy the spread, rather than move things around her plate and hope he didn't notice. Especially after his obvious desire to treat her like royalty. She sipped some water. "Did you sleep much last night?" She threw back the covers, and in her sexy nightgown, which hung a little loosely around her chest, she stood.

Jackson came to her and hugged her good morning. They lingered in their embrace and she savored his solid warmth and the way he smelled fresh from the shower complete with yet a new aftershave, this one with a hint of sandalwood. Dared she dream about being his wife, secure in knowing it was her he wanted to marry, and not merely because of a ready-made family?

"Yeah, I was in before one. Had a good talk with my buddy. Got all caught up on a few things." It made her wonder if he'd talked about his current situation, having a pregnant girlfriend and having to get married *again*, but she didn't ask. It was too early for drama. "Let's eat. We've got a big day ahead of us."

"I'll do my best," she said, smiling up at him, hoping she'd make it through the day with such a heavy heart.

"There are twenty-two squares to share with you."

She popped her eyes wide open. "Twenty-two?"

"I drive fast, but we'll only have time for a few today, my favorites like Lafayette Square, Chippewa Square, Monterey Square and I'll tell you all about the Mercer house then. Oh, then we'll stop by Ellis Square so we can hit City Market. I've got a favorite restaurant there where we can have lunch. Then tomorrow we can spend a little more time checking out more squares. How's that sound?"

It sounded wonderful, but it surprised her that he

hadn't marked out time for his family or for introducing her. Could he feel ashamed of the fact that, if she said yes, he'd be having another "shotgun wedding," as he'd called it in the OR? But she didn't want to spoil his enthusiasm first thing in the morning, so she kept her uncomfortable thoughts to herself.

"Great!" She glanced at the tray of breakfast food and thought about the wedding that evening. "But that sounds like a lot of eating."

He laughed. "Can you tell I'm really excited to have you here?" He sat and slathered a piece of toast with Georgia peach jam.

Maybe she should try to believe him. He wanted to share his world with her, and that knowledge set off a warm feeling tumbling through her body. Her queasiness vanished and she was suddenly more than ready to dive into the scrambled eggs and O'Brien potatoes. And, mmm, the fresh fruit and pancakes looked good, too!

Charlotte had never seen such a picturesque area as the historic district in Savannah. While they drove, she felt like she'd gone back in time with the beautifully preserved buildings and famous blocked-off squares, each with its own charm and individual appeal. Spanish moss draped every tree, and there were hundreds of oak trees throughout the area, as well as palmettos and magnolias.

"Lucky for you you're here in summer to see the crepe myrtles bloom."

The heat made her feel sticky, and she wasn't convinced she should feel lucky to be here in the heart of summer, but she completely agreed that the crepe myrtles were gorgeous. She was also glad he'd put on the air conditioner for the drive. "They certainly are beautiful. But with all the trees everywhere, everything looks beautiful here."

Jackson lucked out and found a parking spot. "We've actually got a nickname as the forest city because of that." He helped her out of the car and a wave of hot humidity hit her like a wet sauna towel. "But with heat like this, our ancestors had to plant trees just for the shade to survive. It was a practical idea that's brought all kinds of benefits."

She fanned herself as she felt a fine sheen of perspiration cover her face, wondering how crazy it would make her hair. Yeah, lucky her for being in Georgia in August. As a San Fernando Valley girl, she certainly knew about heat, but the humidity here brought "hot" to a new level. As they walked, she wondered how the bride would survive wearing a wedding dress in weather like this. She knew the wedding was out toward the beach at a lighthouse, which would probably help.

Holding hands and strolling to the heart of Ellis Square, they watched the children and a few adults playing in the big fountain, which was obviously meant for water play. The sight of little kids squealing with joy as the dancing water shot up made her think of her baby. She looked at the man she'd been positive she loved a few short days ago.

He pointed to the busy market and shop area. "Ever had shrimp and grits?"

"Had shrimp. Never grits."

"I'm going to take you for the gourmet supreme version of that dish. Follow me."

During lunch, she ventured to bring up one major portion of her worries. "Jackson, what if this baby is a girl?"

"Is that what's been on your mind?"

She nodded. "In part. Yes."

"You've got to quit thinking of yourself as poison for a girl baby."

"But if I pass on my genes…"

"You can't let yourself obsess about that. We could have a boy. Or a girl who'll be perfectly fine. If you want to have her tested, I'll stand behind you, but worrying and feeling guilty isn't going to help anything. Who knows where breast cancer research will be in twenty years? Please, stop doubting yourself. Think about the wonder of having a baby. Period. Not a single child born is guaranteed to come problem free."

Moved by his sentiment, she reached across the table and touched his arm. This was part of what she loved about him. "Are you really okay with me being pregnant?"

"Once I got used to the idea, I have to say I'm excited. It'll give me a chance to be the kind of father I should have been with my sons. I promise to be there for you, to help you raise our kid."

She believed him and burst into tears to prove it, but what he'd just vowed had sounded more like a dutiful co-parent than a loving husband. If she could only believe he felt as strongly for her.

After a huge lunch, and visiting a couple more beautifully impressive town squares, Jackson was considerate about Charlotte needing to rest before they got ready for the wedding. So he delivered her back to the hotel room so she could take a power nap and he headed out to the gym and then the pool. She definitely wanted to look her best for the wedding that night, for meeting his family, too, but most especially for him. She needed to see the love in his eyes before she made up her mind about his marriage proposal.

"Wow!" was all that came out of Jackson's mouth. Charlotte stood before him in a pale peach-colored dress that flowed in tiers to her ankles with a snug and wide fitted waist and a halter-style top embellished with a beaded and jeweled collar.

"The color is called blush." She looked anxiously down at her dress toward her toes. "I chose it because it works with my complexion. Plus I thought it would be complementary no matter what the bride's colors are."

As far as he was concerned, she didn't need to explain anything. Indeed, her light olive skin and dark hair glowed in contrast to the pastel shade. "You were meant for that dress, or I should probably say that dress was meant for you."

She smiled shyly and turned a slow circle, causing the skirt to flare out the slightest bit. The cut of the back of the dress was high, she hadn't gone for sexy other than a slit opening beneath the halter collar, yet she still looked like the sexiest woman on the earth to him.

"Thank you. Too bad I'll only get to wear it once."

The ironic statement made him grin. Not if his plans played out as expected. "After the bride, you'll be the most beautiful woman there." Because heaven help any woman who tried to show up the bride!

She shook her head, like she couldn't believe him. Anyone seeing her would never have a clue she'd had bilateral mastectomies. He hoped that didn't still make her feel self-conscious. How many times had he proved she was all he ever wanted or needed? He saw her as the woman he loved, a completely beautiful person, sexy and appealing, and though she had scars, they were part of her. Part of who he loved and wanted to spend the rest of his life with. Like the missing part of his leg was part of who he was now. The guy he'd finally accepted, with the help of Charlotte.

"Those sandals are a knockout, too." She wore strappy beaded silver sandals and had had a flashy pedicure. Though he'd memorized her body with all the times they'd made love, he'd never realized how sexy her feet were. Wow. "I may have to get a special permit to take you out in public. You might cause accidents and general chaos."

She smiled demurely and blushed, and he took a mental picture of that perfect moment in time to cherish and keep in his heart forever. Until she said yes to his marriage proposal, he couldn't let down his guard. He really wanted this. A life with her. Without a doubt. Now he had to convince her.

It wasn't until they got into his rented car that a tight coil started knotting in his stomach. He was ready to see his parents, had talked extensively to them about his plans for this trip back home. That wasn't the problem. He and Evan had worked things out, but Andrew was still avoiding him, and that hurt. Otherwise, if Andrew had been open to it, he would have spent time with him earlier today. The one break he'd caught had been Evaline deciding not to attend the wedding. That had taken a huge weight off his mind.

From what he'd heard, talking to his parents, well, mostly from his mother, Kiefer's future wife, Ashley, was a councilwoman from the tough town of Southriver and the wedding would be attended by the locals and act as a big thanks to her for helping revitalize her home front. She and his cousin Kiefer had met when he'd become the director of the new neighbor-hood clinic. People would be attending from all walks of life from blue collar up to high society. It should be an interesting mix. Knowing his community activist aunt Maggie, she was probably thrilled by Kiefer's choice of a wife. Since he and Kiefer had always kept in touch, especially as they were both doctors, Jackson knew he'd be welcomed.

Due to summer traffic it took Jackson almost twice as long as it normally should to reach Tybee Island Lighthouse Station. But what perfect timing for Mother Nature, at just about sunset. Once they'd parked, they headed toward a huge white tent set up on rich green grass next to the famous lighthouse, black with one wide white stripe in the center. It sat in the middle of five historic support buildings, a perfect little community. It had been made into a museum compound in 1961 and people lined up to have their weddings here. In the backdrop the sun quickly made plans to set in the west. To the east, the Atlantic Ocean made itself known with a light breeze scented with salty sea air. It lifted Charlotte's hair, which looked fuller and wavier since they'd got out of the car.

What could he say but she was the most beautiful woman in the world. His peaceful, loving observation quickly got jostled by his mother's strident voice.

"Jackson, yoo-hoo!"

He turned. "Hi, Mom." Her hair may be going silver and white, but there was no mistaking his mother's sharp blue eyes hadn't lost a hint of their passion for life.

She grabbed him and hugged him as if he were still a kid. "Look at you—you look so handsome!" He fought a grimace. "And this must be Charlotte. Aren't you lovely. Hi, I'm Georgina, Jackie's mom."

She greeted Charlotte in the same exuberant way, making her almost lose her balance. "It's great to meet you."

"You'll have to sit at our table later so we can get to know each other, okay?"

"That'd be great."

Did they have a choice? But Charlotte was being a wonderful sport, and he loved her even more for it. Off in the distance he noticed Evan, who waved to him, then shortly brought Andrew over. The fact that Drew smiled, and it seemed sincere, when they said hello meant the world to Jackson. Maybe all was not lost between him and his elder son, and maybe mending his relationship with Evan had helped. He'd make a point to talk to Andrew tonight, and to invite him out for a visit to California. Fingers crossed Drew would be open to that.

Music started to play as the sunset was imminent, and the open seating quickly filled up. Jackson guided Charlotte to the closest available seats. By the look of the large crowd, Ashley and Kiefer had a lot of friends in their community.

Handsome as always, tall, with brown hair and having Aunt Maggie's green eyes, Kiefer stood with the lighthouse as a backdrop in a dark suit, waiting for his bride. Ashley soon appeared in a classic white dress but with a light green sash, dark shoulder-length hair and eyes that reminded him of Charlotte's. She looked pretty and proud. She held her head high and smiled with all her heart at her friends and family as she walked down the aisle, but most of all she smiled for his cousin.

Jackson felt it in his gut—these two were meant for each other. Then he glanced at Charlotte, eyes bright with excitement over the wedding, the setting, the couple, and that same gut reaction helped him know he'd made the right decision in asking her to marry him. Now, if she'd only realize they were meant for each other and say yes.

The reception was a bit chaotic, thanks to the standing-room-only crowd and the low-key wedding plans, but everyone still managed to get fed. A local group played typical wedding reception songs, and Jackson even convinced Charlotte to dance with him a few times. He'd never get tired of the feel of her in his arms.

He didn't want to push the point, but she hadn't given him an answer yet. He was kind of hoping she'd get all swept away with the wedding tonight and tell him yes. The music was romantic, they were dancing, and it was time to prod things along. "You know I love you, right?"

Hope showed in her gaze. She rested her forehead on his cheek. "I know I love *you*."

He squeezed her tighter. "So let's get married." The song ended. No answer. He didn't want to let go of her, so he stood holding her close until the makeshift dance floor had cleared. She took a breath. He waited for her to say something.

"When are you going to come visit me?" the familiar voice of his grandfather called out from the edge of the dance floor.

Jackson led Charlotte to where he sat. "Gramps, this is Charlotte Johnson."

"Miss Johnson, it's my pleasure to meet you." His wiry, silver-eyed and white-haired granddaddy looked enchanted, and had obviously partaken of the champagne punch. She sat beside him and let him continue to hold her hand. They chatted briefly about the weather, where she'd grown up and a few other superficial topics. Then Gramps jumped right to the heart of things. "I've been around over eighty years, and I think I can judge when a man is smitten with a woman. It seems Jackson the Third here is sportin' the look of a man in love. So I must ask you, are you the one who put it there?"

Her hand flew to her chest as her cheeks blushed. Jackson could tell she didn't know whether to take his granddad seriously or not.

"I don't want to speak for Charlotte, Gramps, but I can answer that question easy enough. Yes."

Her gaze flashed to his and he didn't waver. If there was ever a time for her to know how he felt, it was now. Any man willing to get called out by his grandfather for being in love deserved an answer to his proposal. But he sensed she still wasn't ready, and he didn't want to force the point, so he let the moment pass.

"There you are!" Kiefer said. "I finally tracked you down."

Jackson greeted his cousin and made the proper introductions between the bride and groom and Charlotte. He almost spewed his champagne when out of the blue Ashley asked if another wedding was planned for the near future. Was she a mind reader?

Charlotte smiled graciously and blushed again, but still didn't venture to answer. He couldn't let that make him feel daunted. If there was ever a time to go out on a limb for the woman he loved, it was now.

As things were winding down, and he'd said his final good-bye to Kiefer and Ashley and, of course, his parents and grandfather, he escorted Charlotte back to the car. He'd left his mother with some flabbergasting—to use her word—instructions, but she'd agreed to carry them out to the T, had even cried a little about it.

He also banked on Charlotte needing another good night's rest so he could finish planning.

Making his job easy, Charlotte was nearly asleep on her feet by the time they got back to the hotel. "Looks like you're ready to turn in."

"Sorry I'm such a drag!"

"No, you're not. You're carrying my baby. It zaps the energy out of a person."

"So you understand?"

"Believe me, I do. Plus Drew and Evan are going to meet me in the bar for a quick drink. I've almost got Drew convinced to come visit before summer is over."

"That's wonderful."

"Since I met you luck has been on my side and my life has taken a turn for better. You know that, right?" He hugged and kissed her long and hard, hoping his message had sunk in, then said good night. Before his sons arrived he needed to talk to the hotel staff to help him make those special arrangements for Sunday evening.

He'd asked Charlotte to marry him, she'd yet to say yes, but he still intended to tie the knot right in his own backyard. Hopefully before tomorrow was over, she'd come round.

He'd often heard that a wedding in Savannah was destined to last as long as the city's ancient oaks. That sounded about right to him. Good thing he'd shopped for her ring online at the best jeweler's in his hometown, in case she still needed proof about how he felt. He had it in his jacket pocket. Jarod had dropped it off last night, along with some expedited official paperwork.

Walking down the hotel hall toward the elevator, Jackson couldn't help but think he was wearing down Charlotte's resistance, so he grinned.

Charlotte had a great night's sleep filled with dreams of celebrations and dancing and happy faces. It made her miss her family, what was left of it. Her brother, Don, had made a career in the service and was rarely in California. Her sister, Cynthia, her husband and their three adorable kids, her nephews and niece, her baby's cousins. She missed them all.

It occurred to her it was time to phone both of them and break the news. She promised herself she'd do it as soon as she was back in LA. Maybe by then she'd have made up her mind what to do about Jackson and his proposal. She could imagine their jaws dropping when she announced, *I'm pregnant*.

Jackson was already up and whistling away in the bathroom while she was still yawning and trying to open her eyes. Where Jackson got all his energy Charlotte didn't have a clue. Usually dealing with estranged families drained a person, but he seemed focused and happy, and she hoped she had something to do with his good state of mind.

He popped his head around the corner from the bathroom. "I got tickets for us to tour the Mercer house this morning. I pointed it out to you yesterday when we were at Monterey Square, the place with the huge statue of General Pulaski?"

She knew exactly which square he meant, it had been her favorite, and she considered it the prettiest of the ones he'd taken her to. "Yes. The *Midnight in the Garden of Good and Evil* house?"

"Yes, that one, the Jim Williams story."

"Neat. I'd love to peek inside." Last night, when he'd said "So let's get married" she had been on the verge of saying yes. Every second they'd been together she'd felt her love for him growing stronger and stronger. Did it really matter that he wanted to marry her *because* she was pregnant?

"You feel like walking today? We can take the water taxi across the river and walk from there."

"After all the eating I've been doing, that sounds like a great plan." Fortunately, she'd worn comfortable shoes for the plane ride. When she'd finished with her morning routine Jackson was dressed and waiting for her.

"I'll make sure you're back in time for a nap this afternoon, too."

"Since our plane doesn't leave until midnight, that's probably a good idea. I'll have plenty of time to pack tonight before we leave."

"But I've made some special plans for dining tonight. Maybe you can pack this afternoon after that nap. I want you to be rested to enjoy our evening."

"Sounds romantic." And he'd probably want his answer then, too.

He took her hand. "If all goes as planned it will be," he said, guiding her out of the hotel room. "Oh, one more thing—you know how you said it was too bad you'd only get to wear that knockout dress once?"

"Yes?"

"Wear it again tonight, okay?"

What did Jackson have planned? "Sure, if that's what you want." She didn't know why but chills rose the fine hair on her arms over his request.

Once downstairs they went out the waterside exit, passing the pool on the left and the pretty grassy area on the right. "Oh, it looks like they're setting up for a small wedding today," she said on the way to the water taxi.

"Well, they are famous for their wedding packages here."

"Looks charming." Only a handful of round tables were set up with white tablecloths, making a half circle around the small gazebo at the center. Someone had already draped cream-colored organza fabric at the entrance, and another employee was in the process of hanging crystal prisms on varying lengths of string, catching the light and casting rainbows everywhere. Maybe she should take notes and add them to all the mental notes she'd taken last night at Kiefer and Ashley's wedding.

Jackson was right, Savannah was a truly romantic city, and her old dream of having it all kept sneaking back into her heart.

A man of his word, Jackson made sure Charlotte was back at the hotel by mid-afternoon to pack and rest up before their special dinner plans. Later, as promised to make the man she loved happy, she put on the dress from yesterday's wedding, feeling just as elegant today.

She thought back to the day she'd bought it, the first time she'd noticed something different had been going on with her body, and the one purpose she'd had in mind while she'd searched for the perfect dress—to make herself a woman Jackson couldn't live without. Had she been successful? Maybe over dinner tonight she'd give him her answer.

Jackson had also put on the dressy suit he'd worn to the wedding yesterday, looking handsome as always, and very Southern. She'd noticed his speech had changed a little since coming back to his home state, sounding a little slower and warmer, and she really loved the Georgia accent.

She studied him. His brown wavy hair had got curlier in Savannah, just like hers had, and the light tan he'd picked up over the past two days made his bright blue eyes stand out even more. She wondered if their baby would get his classic nose or her own nondescript one.

Or his shocking blue eyes. For no reason he smiled at her like he had a big secret, and the grooves on both sides of his cheeks highlighted that grin. Damn, he was sexy, and she suddenly had the need to tell him exactly what she was thinking.

"You are *so* good-looking."

He grinned. "And you, my lady, are a goddess." His eyes seemed to sparkle when he said the last word.

Well, that did it. They didn't have to leave the room, as far as she was concerned, because she'd been acutely aware that since they'd arrived in Georgia they hadn't made love. She might be pregnant and a little more tired than usual, but all he had to do was look into her eyes with those killer blues and touch her just so and, well, right about now she'd pretty much sign up for anything he had in mind. If he happened to whisper he loved her, she'd definitely give him her answer.

"So you want to get together?" she offered playfully and hopefully.

He took her into his arms and kissed her thoroughly, the kind of kiss that would require a reapplication of lipstick once they were done, and she started thinking they were definitely on the same page. But then he stopped kissing her. "Call me old-fashioned, but I'd kind of like to wait until after you decide if you want to marry me or not."

Was he blackmailing her by withholding sex? "Seriously?"

"A man's got to stand his ground for honor's sake." He winked.

Again, there was that secret worry that his proposal had been more about honor and not enough about love.

A minute later, with one last fluff of her hair and

that reapplication of peach-colored lipstick, they left the hotel room just as the horn of another container ship blared its arrival and floated by their window.

"I'm gonna miss it here," she said.

"We'll make a point to come visit often, then."

She tossed him a look and got chills. He obviously wasn't backing down on his offer to marry her, making all these future plans and all. Maybe the guy really did love her for herself and not just because she was pregnant.

When they caught the elevator and ended up at the main floor, instead of heading for the five-star hotel restaurant, as she'd expected, he escorted her outside. She immediately remembered the small private setup on the golf-course-green grass near the gazebo and watched for it.

"Oh, look, isn't that just beautiful?" she said, wondering what the occasion was. Obviously it was a small and private affair.

"It sure is." He put his hand at the small of her back and guided her toward it.

She resisted him. "We can't crash someone else's party."

"Of course we can. Do you see anyone around? Let's just go and have a look."

Only because she was dying to see everything up close, especially now, since small clear glass vases of bright summer-colored gerberas had been placed at each perfectly set table, she agreed. "But isn't this taking nosy to a new level, at the expense of someone else's private affair?"

"I don't see it that way." Once they got close enough for her to see the fine hotel china and silverware, Jackson cleared his throat and raised his hand. "Can we get some help over here, please?" he said to a nearby waiter.

Her heart palpitated and her face flushed. "What are you doing?"

"Hold on, don't freak out."

The silver-haired server, wearing a white waistcoat, immediately snapped to attention. "Yes, Dr. Hilstead. Are we ready?"

"Just give me two minutes first, please."

Charlotte's heart went still as Jackson dropped to one knee and took her hand. With the other hand, he fished inside his jacket for the pocket and something small.

"I love you. I've been trying to prove it all weekend, and I hope you've caught on. Because I mean it. I'm a better man because of you, and I want to spend the rest of my life with you. I love you with all my heart, and I want us to be a family. Charlotte, since I met you I've discovered I'm full of love. There's room for my sons, and our sons or daughters, but most especially for you. Right at the center. Forever. Do you believe me yet?"

Her face crumpled. How had she not known his proposal had been sincere from the very start? He was a man of his word, but also a man of the heart. If he said he loved her, he meant it. "Yes. I believe you."

"Then will you marry me?"

"Yes."

Jackson's expression of joy promised to plant itself in her heart for life. "Thank God." He stood and kissed her, then flashed a beautiful ring as he gave some high sign. She could have sworn she heard muted applause.

"We'll hold the record for the world's shortest engagement." He slid the ring on her finger and she took a moment to admire the pure solitaire diamond's beauty.

With Jackson's affirmation and a snap of the head waiter's fingers, soft classical string music began to play the Pachelbel concerto, and a group of people came out from what seemed nowhere.

Now her heart thundered in her ears. She recognized Jackson's parents and grandfather—how could she ever forget him?—and both of Jackson's sons, plus a few other people she remembered to be relatives of his, one being his aunt Maggie. Nearly dizzy with wonder, she couldn't speak, even though her mouth was open.

A husky man around Jackson's age came toward them and Jackson introduced him to her. "This is my old college roommate, Jarod. Or Judge Campbell these days. He's a county judge, and he's managed to pull a few strings for us, and since we were here for a wedding, I thought why not make it two? Jarod's going to perform the ceremony. Are you ready?"

Her chest clamped down so hard she didn't think she could draw her next breath. Of course she wanted to marry Jackson, but right this moment? Right here? It was all his family and friends, and she didn't have anyone to represent her. She didn't want to spend one second ruining this moment with sadness, but the emptiness flicked her hard.

"He's going to marry us now?"

Jackson gave the most confident nod she'd ever seen. "Remember our saying? Life is all about what's happening right now. So what do you say? Let's get married."

"But I don't have anyone here, Jackson."

"We can get married again in California and you can invite the whole hospital if you want, but I can't wait another second to be your husband." His swoon-worthy words sank in and they seemed to be accompanied by the scent of magnolias. She was sure she'd never forget this singular moment when the man she loved asked her to be his wife. In front of a crowd!

"Actually," he said, "you do have someone here for you, and he's the perfect person to walk you down the aisle. All we have left to do is say *I do*. So if you'll excuse me, I'll just go stand up there..." he pointed to the decorated gazebo "...and wait for you." He smiled so reassuringly she couldn't think of a single reason to refuse tonight as the night to take her vows.

Doing as instructed, Charlotte turned to see Dr. Gordon standing at the back of the lawn, a sweet smile on his face, wearing a white summer tuxedo jacket and black slacks, and holding a small bouquet, which was apparently meant for her to carry. The head of the waitstaff walked her to him, and Jim Gordon proudly held out his elbow for her to clamp her arm onto. And, boy, did she need something to hold on to right now because Jackson had just knocked her for a loop! It seemed a lifetime of stored-up feelings had been unleashed as she took her place beside her mentor, and she'd never felt more alive in her life.

Her chin quivered and her eyes welled, and Jim gave her a fatherly, encouraging look. "Don't worry, I'll get you there, dear. It's time for your happily-ever-after. Now, on the count of three, follow me."

With that, she took his advice and dived into the moment, the what-was-happening-right-now part, and quickly remembered the special bridal walk from all the movies she'd watched growing up. *Step, together, step, together.* She thought about her mother and knew this would have made her ecstatic. And on wobbly legs, in front of a new family she couldn't wait to get to know better, she made her way to the gazebo, with the help of her mentor and stand-in father. There, the handsomest groom in the world, and the most perfect *imperfect* man she could never have dared to dream of, waited for her to say *I do*.

EPILOGUE

CHARLOTTE LOOKED UP at Jackson, holding her hand while she lay on the examination table. He smiled reassuringly and squeezed her hand.

"So at twenty weeks we do the official ultrasound. Are you ready?" the magenta-haired sonography tech said.

Charlotte studied the young woman's brow piercing while she considered the question. Was she ready? Now that she was married and she and Jackson were a team, any potential outcome of what they might find out about their baby seemed far less scary. "Yes," she said.

Jackson grabbed her hand again as the tech squeezed cold gel onto her stomach and began moving the transducer around her growing abdomen. Soon a pie-shaped section appeared on the screen and shortly after that a profile shot of their baby's head appeared. They gasped together in wonder. Charlotte's other hand flew to her mouth. Her baby looked perfectly formed with a cute upturned nose and a really big-looking head. Was there a thumb in the mouth?

"I'll snap that picture for you, if you'd like. Or maybe you'd rather wait in case we can identify the sex."

Charlotte's gaze jumped to Jackson's and he nodded,

indicating, like they'd previously discussed, it was up to her. "I'd like *that* picture, please."

"Done." As the technician moved on, she described every part of the fetus's anatomy that came into view. "Depending on whether or not you want to know the sex, you may want to look away during this next portion." She held steady at the point she'd left off, waiting for Charlotte's reply.

Charlotte smiled contentedly, knowing without a doubt since she'd married Jackson that no matter what the sex of their baby, their love for each other and their future child would see them through any and all the challenges in life. Whether it involved DNA or not.

Right here and now she saw for herself that her baby was perfect in every way, growing as it should be. Jackson had been okay either way about knowing or not, so he kept quiet, just gazing benignly at Charlotte as she finally made up her mind.

He bent and kissed her forehead as she closed her eyes. Did she want to know the sex today? Would knowing add or detract from the wonder of her pregnancy? Since passing through the first trimester, she'd loved being pregnant. Feeling her body change and knowing something she and Jackson had created together grew inside her had put her in an incredibly happy place.

If there was ever a time to think of Dr. Gordon's recipe for living it was now. *Life wasn't about what might happen, it was about right here and now.* She had proof of a perfectly forming baby on the computer screen. Sonography didn't lie. Then she thought of her mother, because since the wedding she'd been doing that a lot. Her mom had once told her all about the day she'd been born. Back in the day they chose two names for every pregnancy. One for a boy and one for a girl. People gave generic gifts at showers, and the parents had the joy of discovering the baby's sex at birth. She'd loved hearing the story about the day she'd been born and how happy her mother had been that she'd had a girl.

Because she'd started to show, the women at work all seemed to want to share their own birthing stories, and one lab technician's stuck out in her mind. The ultrasound had indicated the baby was a girl, and they had only got girls' baby clothes and items at her shower. The problem was, she'd wound up delivering a boy! Her mother-in-law had had to return all the baby items and buy new ones, adding stress to the shock. They'd been expecting a girl and now had to adjust to having a boy. The ultrasound wasn't always one hundred per-cent accurate.

Charlotte turned to Jackson, his brows lifting as he waited for her decision.

"Let's do it the old-fashioned way and wait to find out when I deliver."

He laughed and clapped. "That's a great idea."

"Then look away," the technician said as she con-tinued the test.

"You're peeking!" Charlotte teased Jackson, both of them giddy with excitement for their future as they stared at each other for the next few moments rather than watch the monitor.

"I'm not, I swear. You know I'll be happy with what-ever we have…" he bent and kissed her, and she re-membered why she hadn't doubted for one second how much he loved her since his amazing proposal in Savannah "…because whether it's a she or a he, our kid will make us a family."

Charlotte had lost the heart of her family way too early when her mother had died. Things had never been the same and when she searched her heart she realized that for years and years she'd longed for a family of her own. Until she'd met Jackson, she'd never dared to dream it could actually happen. "I like the sound of that."

"Our family?"

"Yes, *our* family."

* * * * *

LET'S TALK
Romance

For exclusive extracts, competitions
and special offers, find us online:

MILLS & BOON
True Love

Romance from the Heart

Celebrate true love with tender stories of heartfelt romance, from the rush of falling in love to the joy a new baby can bring, and a focus on the emotional heart of a relationship.

CS